PRAISE FOR
THE COACHMAN

As authentic as they come with an eye on the past and future of historical fiction. You're immediately and irrevocably thrust into pre-war Philadelphia. Switching back and forth between perspectives, in the tradition of Faulkner, you'll find yourself grasping for the next page to find out what might befall our characters. Impressively, Smith continues to teach an old genre new tricks.

—**Matthew Di Paoli, author of** *Holliday*, **winner of the Wilbur and Niso Smith Adventure Writing Prize**

Roger A. Smith's *The Coachman* is historical fiction at its finest. In Book Two of the monumental nine book series, protagonist Rian Krieger continues her thoughtful, thrilling, and consequential journey. With an informative Author's Notes, this is the perfect series for history buffs, plot aficionados, and character-driven literature fans alike.

—**Kate Dike Blair, author of the historical novel**
The Hawthorne Inheritance

Roger A. Smith writes with authority and exquisite attention to detail, vividly capturing not only the social and political conflict of the era but also the warring desires and goals of his characters in this well-wrought historical novel.

—**Ginny Fite, award-winning author of** *The Physics of Things*

Historical fiction requires not only a rich imagination, it must come from a firm foundation of understanding the past. I was impressed by the well-rounded characters, moving plot, and vivid descriptions of early Nineteenth Century life in Philadelphia. I would put this book on a par with some of Horatio Alger's novels of mid-nineteenth century New York. Another series that came to mind as I worked my way through *The Coachman* is Jack Finney's time travel novels.

—**Mark Carlson, CL, ACS, Historical Novels Society,
Military Writers Society of America**

In Roger A. Smith's captivating novel *The Coachman*, echoes of the tumultuous landscape of the 1830s reverberate across a panoply of characters. As the Underground Railroad whispers tales of courage and survival, the Krieger family's industrial empire faces challenges that threaten its foundations. Amid personal struggles and societal upheaval, young Rian Krieger defies convention to navigate a world of gender expectations, embarking on an astonishing journey to Russia.

—**Maryka Biaggio, award-winning author of** *Parlor Games,*
Eden Waits, The Point of Vanishing, **and** *The Model Spy*

With a colorful cast of characters, Roger Smith creates an exciting adventure story in the vibrant and growing Philadelphia of 1837, a center of industry and a crossroads in the fight for emancipation. Jules, a free Black man, struggles to maintain his new business and his freedom, Seamus, a young Irish American man, fights for a place at the table, and Rian, a bright young woman, seeks to move beyond the prescribed role for women to make her own life.

—**Nancy Kilgore, author of** *Bitter Magic,*
Wild Mountain, **and** *Sea Level*

THE COACHMAN

BOOK 2 OF RIAN KRIEGER'S JOURNEY

ROGER A. SMITH

MILFORD HOUSE

an imprint of Sunbury Press, Inc.
Mechanicsburg, PA USA

MILFORD
HOUSE

an imprint of Sunbury Press, Inc.
Mechanicsburg, PA USA

For information about special discounts for bulk purchases, please contact Sunbury Press Orders Dept. at (855) 338-8359 or orders@sunburypress.com.

To request one of our authors for speaking engagements or book signings, please contact Sunbury Press Publicity Dept. at publicity@sunburypress.com.

FIRST MILFORD HOUSE PRESS EDITION: October 2023

Set in Adobe Garamond Pro | Interior design by Crystal Devine | Cover by Ashley Nichole Walkowiak | Edited by Maresa Whitehead.

Publisher's Cataloging-in-Publication Data
Names: Smith, Roger A., author.
Title: The coachman : book 2 of Rian Krieger's Journey / Roger A. Smith.
Description: First trade paperback edition. | Mechanicsburg, PA : Milford House Press, 2023.
Summary: Philadelphia, 1837. 13-year-old tomboy Rian Krieger dreams of some day running her father's locomotive factory. When he learns she is a conductor on the Underground Railroad, he plans to send her to a Swiss finishing school. This is a fate Rian cannot abide, as it means she would have to wear a dress all the time.
Identifiers: ISBN : 979-8-88819-139-2 (softcover) | ISBN : 979-8-88819-140-8 (ePub).
Subjects: FICTION / Historical / General | FICTION / LGBTQ+ / Transgender | FICTION / African American & Black / Historical.

Product of the United States of America
0 1 1 2 3 5 8 13 21 34 55

Continue the Enlightenment!

For Clyde McGeary

Who gave me the courage to declare myself an artist.

CHARACTERS

Rian	Krieger – twelve-year-old tomboy
Otto	Krieger – Rian's father, owner of Krieger Coach. Rian calls him Vater, which is German for father
Adrian	Krieger – Rian's uncle, owner of Krieger Locomotive
Mila	Krieger – Adrian's wife
Kurt	Krieger – Rian's youngest uncle, ship's carpenter
Levi	Howes – Rian's uncle, Captain of the Baltimore Clipper *Bridger*
Jabez	Howes – Levi's son, Rian's cousin
Conor	McGuire – Rian's best friend, an orphan who sometimes lives with the Kriegers
Jules	Freeman – foreman at Krieger Coach, owner of Freeman Hydraulics, formerly enslaved, self-emancipated
Maddie	Freeman – Jules's wife, a founding member of the Philadelphia Female Anti-Slavery Society
Martha	Freeman – Jules and Maddie's oldest daughter
Rufus	Freeman – Jules and Maddie's oldest son
Hercules	Angell – Maddie's father, caterer
Seamus	Gallagher – Rian's cousin, Production Designer at the Krieger factories, president of the United No Name Fire Brigade
Logan	Gallagher – Seamus's little brother
Lucretia	Mott – outspoken Quaker abolitionist, Otto and Rian's next-door neighbor. With Maddie Freeman, a founding member of the Philadelphia Female Anti-Slavery Society
James	Mott – Lucretia's husband, businessman, abolitionist
Hugh	Callaghan – president of the Moyamensing Hose Company, Seamus's nemesis
Siobhan	Callaghan – Hugh's daughter, Seamus's girlfriend
Randolph	Tucker – slaveholder who summers in Philadelphia
Penelope	Tucker – Randolph's wife
Olivia	Tucker – their daughter, Rian's friend

Nicholas   Biddle – President of the United States Bank of Pennsylvania, which had been known as the Second Bank of the United States before Biddle's "Bank War" with Andrew Jackson

George   Shippen – Chairman of the Board of the Bank of Industry, railroad entrepreneur, Olivia Tucker's uncle

Ida   Shippen – George's wife

Trey   Shippen – George's son

Edward   Schiffler – President of the Bank of Industry

Billy   Schiffler – Edward's son

Austin T.   Slatter – slave catcher

Hans   Schmidt – former Krieger Coach employee now working with Slatter

Harold   Foote – reporter for the Philadelphia Independent

Aaron   Bassinger – bookkeeper for the Krieger factories and president of Krieger Rail

Ernst   Winther – employee at Krieger Coach

Harry   Vogel – foreman at Krieger Locomotive

Bennie   Holt – employee at Krieger Locomotive

Joheim   Fischer – employee at Krieger Locomotive

Heinrich   Aldridge – steam engine designer at Krieger Locomotive

Robert   Purvis – wealthy Philadelphia landowner who finances numerous abolitionist and Underground Railroad initiatives

James   Forten – probably the wealthiest Black man in North America, Robert Purvis's father-in-law

Thomas   Forten – James Forten's son.

John   Ellsworth – Captain of the *Elizabeth*

Braden   McSweeney – owner of McSweeney's Saloon

Dylan   – member of the United No Name Fire Brigade

Peach   – self-emancipator

In the court of Magistrate Hyram P. Stone

Jonah   Arbuckle – slaveholder

Alton   Davis – attorney who represents slaveholders

Jonathan   Simmons – attorney who represents self-emancipators

Pluto   – self-emancipator

Joseph   Bride – slaveholder

The Tarbell family – in jail as suspected fugitive slaves

In Russia

Vladimir   Sheremetev (Count) – tasked by Tsar Nicholas to purchase locomotives for Russia's unbuilt railroads

Alexander   Malkovich (Colonel) – Sheremetev's partner

Mikhail   Stepanov (Captain) – Head of the Tsar's Imperial Horse Guards

Lev   – serf, woodcutter

Pyotr   Volkonsky (Prince) – Minister to the Imperial Court, the Tsar's gatekeeper

George   Dallas – American Ambassador to Russia

Nicholas   Romanov – Tsar of All the Russias

Henry   Sommes – manservant to Adrian and Seamus

Detail from "Bird's Eye View of Philadelphia, drawn from nature and on stone" by John Bachman. Image courtesy of the Library Company of Philadelphia.

1837

1887

FRIDAY, MARCH 3

· PEACH ·

Ten days: That's all the Good Lord had given me. Ten days when the air smelled sweeter, the cold of winter lost its chill, and the food—food offered by strangers—tasted better. Better than even the cornbread hash that Big Ginny threw together when she could slip leftover meat off the plates that came down from Master's table.

And those strangers—well, Preacher weren't no stranger, but he's the one who listened to my longing to bolt and told me he knew a way. "But it'll be dangerous for a young woman like you," he said. "A girl has to be special careful." We waited for a night when the full moon was going to rise long after the slaves was asleep. I didn't doze a bit, of course, but pretended like it until all the usuals was snoring, then I snuck out and headed for the privy like we planned. Three steps outside the cabins, the spring peepers down at the pond drowned out the snores. I'd heard them every year since I was a sprout, telling me that new beginnings was just about here, but now they was telling me they was something different. They was the sound of freedom.

Preacher stepped out of the trees and into the moonlight. I felt scared as I've ever been—but happy, because I was actually doing this. For three hours, Preacher and I hustled hard to the Chesapeake, where a waterman was waiting.

"The dogs'll follow you this far," Preacher said when he helped me into the boat, "but this is where your trail will end." Then he shoved the boat away from the shore, gave me a wave, and was gone so's he could get back to Twenty Willows before anyone saw I weren't in my bed.

The waterman and I sailed all night with naught but the moon to show the way. As the sun came up, he steered his boat with his foot and started shucking oysters for me, and I slurped 'em down as fast as he could shuck, which amused him. I'd only eaten oysters on Christmas Day when the slaves was given a day of rest. The waterman said he'd bought his freedom ten years ago but never forgot where he came from and helped folks like me run when folks like Preacher found him.

The second night we passed a marsh to our left, and those old peepers was peeping away. I said to the waterman, "They're my friends. They're reminding me I'm free," and he said, "Well then, you're in luck, because I figure spring travels north about twenty miles a day, so they're gonna be singing your song your whole trip." That thought made me smile. But then he said, "Twenty miles, every day. That's just about what you gotta do to stay ahead of the broadsides."

"What's a broadside?" I said, and he said, "It's a poster telling the slave catchers that you are on the run. The devils read it and start looking for you."

The waterman handed me off to a Quakerman, and he planted me amongst bags of grain in the back of his wagon. Now and then, when he said no one was about, I stuck my head out and looked at the countryside. The last time he said, "You can look now," I saw a city for the very first time. This weren't no wide spot in the road like some of the other towns we'd passed through those days. This was Philadelphia, the second largest city in America, the Quakerman told me. The buildings was big and made of brick. Every single one spouted a chimney, sometimes two, and each one was busy as Little Ginny's hearth, spewing out so much smoke that sometimes when the wind blew it down at us, it took its time rising and stung my eyes. The streets was straight as rows of tobacco back at Twenty Willows. The wagon clattered on the cobblestones, more cobblestones than I'd ever seen.

The Quakerman took me to the backside of a house and said, "This is your next station." I didn't know what a station was, but I got out of the wagon. A man opened the back door, waved to the Quakerman, and shook my hand as he pulled me into the warmth of his kitchen. He said, "Welcome to my home," but he didn't tell me his name. He was Black, for sure, but lighter-skinned than his woman, though she weren't as dark as me. They had six kids, some as dark as her, some lighter, like him. The house had a wooden floor and two stories, like the Big House back home, but not as big. I couldn't imagine a Black man being so rich that he could live in a house like this. They set up a cot in the girls' bedroom so's I could sleep but showed me a secret hidey-hole if the slave catchers caught up, which they said weren't likely. They fed me for three days, meat at most every meal, and gave me a coat and a dress.

Jules and his woman Maddie—they never told me their names, but I could hear them talking right through the floor when I was upstairs and they was downstairs—came up to the bedroom and asked me, "How old are you?" and I said seventeen. They asked me about where I come from and why I wanted to bolt. I told them Calvert County, Maryland, and that Master had been eyeing me ever since I turned womanly.

Then Jules asked me something curious. He said, "Have you ever heard of a woman by the name of Hattie Taney?" I said, "I got sick when I was a sprout. Big Ginny sent over to the next farm for a woman named Hattie Taney. She was good with herbs and potions. My momma always told me I wouldn't be walking this good earth if it weren't for Hattie Taney. Why? Who's Hattie Taney to you?" He said, "She's my mother. I was sold away from her when I was twelve. Do you think she's still at that farm?" and I said, "I know for a fact she's not, 'cause that entire family moved South, and they took Hattie with them."

Jules said, "I've asked about my mother to every runaway who has passed through this house—hundreds of people—and you are the first one who has known anything. I am in your debt. I miss my mother to this day, and someday I am going to set her free, but I've got to find her first." My first thought was, so here's a free Black man with more luck than any slave I'd ever known and even he's got troubles. My next thought was, so this is what freedom does for a person. It makes him so powerful he can dream that what ain't likely to happen will come to pass if you work at it.

Jules and Maddie got into a fix lining up the next leg of my trip, and that's what allowed the broadsides to catch up with me. Jules brought one of them home and read it. A Black man who can read, imagine that. But then I learned that Maddie and all their kids could read as well. Maddie took her turn, and she read out loud so's I could hear it. "You've got a $250 price on your head," she said. "Your enslaver really wants you back." Then she read, "Must be returned unharmed," which Maddie said she'd never heard of before, but those words scared me like the dickens because that meant Master had special plans for me, just like he'd had for some of the other comely slave girls.

And then Maddie said, "We'll have to give you a new name and forge some papers of emancipation." I never heard of emancipation before, but figured out what it was for myself.

Maddie asked me what I wanted my new name to be, and right away I thought of the sweetest thing I'd ever eaten, and I said, "Peach." So from then on, I was Peach.

After three long days, this white young'un showed up behind the house driving a pair and a freight wagon filled with wooden boxes. I could hear Jules and him talking when I was in the girls' bedroom and looking out the window. Jules called him Rian, a name I'd never heard before. He said, "REE-in, thanks for doing this."

There was a place in the wagon for me to stretch out right behind the driver's bench so's we could talk, but Rian said, "When I say so, pull this tarp over you because I don't want anyone to see you." We started talking as we was heading to some man's farm that was twenty miles away.

I said, "I've got a new name, and I'm never going back to my slave name again."

Rian asked me, "What did your slave name used to be?"

I told him, but I said, "You're the last person I'll ever tell. I ain't never going to tell anybody what it was ever again. That's part of my slave past, and I ain't no slave anymore."

Rian told me, "I'm twelve years old, but my next birthday's coming up in about three weeks."

I told him, "Peepers sing the song of freedom, even though they ain't singing at this very moment, 'cause they only sing in the evening."

He told me, "I haven't heard the spring peepers here in Philadelphia yet, but they should be out any day now."

I asked him, "Why's that man's house called a station?" I didn't let on that I knew his name was Jules.

He said, "That's because you're on the Underground Railroad. If we do our jobs right, it's like you just got on a train and disappeared. His house is a station. He and his wife are stationmasters. I'm a conductor." Then he said, "You're the sixth runaway that I've conducted to freedom."

Well, I'd heard tell of trains, but I never saw one, so I just had to take his word for it. I told Rian, "My brother got sold South when I was eleven, and that's when I decided I was going to bolt as soon as I got the chance."

We was quite a ways out of town when I asked, "Is it usual for boys your age to drive a pair a great distance like you are right now?" That's when Rian tells me, "Well, two things: my daddy's away on business, so he don't know I'm doing this. And second, even though I dress like a boy and like it when strangers think I'm a boy, I'm really a girl."

I had a hard time putting that all into its proper place and thought this is a very strange land that I'm passing through.

The farm that Rian took me to was as fine as Twenty Willows, except the buildings was built in a manner that was unfamiliar. Lo and behold, Rian told me a Black man owned the farm, but she wouldn't tell me his name because she said that Rule Number 1 in helping slaves escape to freedom is if you don't need to know something, you don't get told.

But there was two men at the farm when we arrived, which surprised Rian because she wasn't expecting no one but the caretaker. Rian got out of the wagon and walked over to the gentlemen. I could overhear them but pretended to be out of earshot. The caretaker was as black as me. The other—Rian hugged him and said, "I didn't know you were going to be here."

"Just leaving," he said. "Going back to Philadelphia."

Then the caretaker said, "Travel safely, Mr. Purvis." This Purvis fellow looks over in my direction to see if I was listening, but I pretended to be admiring his fine house. Well, Mr. Purvis was about as white as Master, yet Rian said he was a Black man. I could never imagine a person who could pass as white telling the world he was a Black man, but there it was.

I had only been free for eight days, but I was seeing and learning by the bucket-load. This indeed was a strange land I was passing through.

Rian left, which made me sad because we both had secrets about ourselves that we shared. A Black man showed up at the farm to guide me on the next leg. He said he's never done this alone before. He was so nervous he said, "Nice to meet you. My name's Willis," but then he said, "Dang it. I'm not supposed to do that." We laughed about it at the time.

Willis and I walked at night. We arrived at a farm just as the sun was rising, and we rested the whole day in a barn. There was food there, so I figured the farmer knew what was going on.

The next day was when my ten days of freedom came to an end.

We walked all that night, same as the night before, and just as the sun was rising again, we got to a bridge that crossed the Delaware River at a city called Trenton. Trenton weren't nearly as big as the city of Philadelphia, at least as far as I could see from across the river. Willis asked me, "Do you want to hole up for another day or take your chances crossing the bridge right now at first light?" Well, I didn't cotton much to crossing a bridge like that at night, now that the moon had narrowed down to a sliver. I feared that I would misstep and fall into the drink. "Besides," I said, "I have to stay ahead of the broadsides."

We were halfway across the bridge when this big old devil comes striding toward us with the rising sun right at his back. I shaded my eyes to give me a better look at him and spied a set of shackles draped over his shoulder. Willis turned to me and said, "Peach, that's Austin T. Slatter, the meanest devil there is. It's time to start running back the way we came. Split up when we get off this bridge. He can't catch us both."

Well, the devil came after me and knocked me down after chasing me for about fifteen minutes. He picked me up rough 'cause he was all out of breath. I thought he was going to belt me, but he didn't. He held me by the back of my dress and called me by my slave name. I said, "I ain't a slave. My name's Peach, and I've got a paper to prove it." The devil said, "Lemme see your paper," and I showed him. I was shaking so hard I almost peed myself right there.

Then the devil said, "What was the name of your master?" and I said, "Jonas Brock." I remembered that name because Jonas Brock was the man who owned the general store in St. Leonard, and Maddie told me when she was writing my paper that the name had to be one I could remember right away if someone questioned me, just like the devil was doing now. Then he asked me, "What county were you set free in?" and I couldn't remember the name because the only county I'd ever lived in was Calvert, and even though Maddie said I needed to remember it, I was so scared

I forgot. I started crying. The devil took me back to the bridge, boosted me into the bench of a buckboard wagon, and chained my hands to the seat with his shackles.

Once he got me chained up, he turned all talkative. I was too scared to remember much of it, but one thing I'll never forget as long as I live: "I've been waiting for someone like you for a year now. I'm going to take you back to Twenty Willows. Your owner is going to give me $250, and then I'm going to tell him I'm in no hurry to go home. He can do whatever he wants with you, but when he's done, I'll give him half of that $250 back if I get to spend a little more time with you. By the time I'm done with you, you're gonna tell me everything you know about all the people who helped you get to that bridge. Then I'm going to hunt each one of them down. There's people who want them put out of business, and they're willing to pay a lot more than a measly $250 for me to do it."

The next afternoon, we passed a pond, and I listened for the peepers. They was quiet as the slave quarters after one of us gets a licking from Strawboss. I figured that was it. My days of freedom are over. I think that may have been the saddest moment of my life.

Miles down the road, evening closed over the devil, me, and the buckboard like a blanket. I could barely see the road, but I could hear things. The night birds calling, sometimes the lap of the river to our left when we got close.

And then I heard just one little lone peeper singing to me. We passed him by, and his song faded. I figured that was it, but later we passed through a wet spot where the devil had to encourage the horse to slop his way through the muck, and a handful of my peeper friends was singing to me, but we left them behind as well. But the next time . . . the next time, a chorus of my freedom friends was singing to me louder than they had ever sung before, telling me not to lose heart.

SATURDAY, MARCH 4

· RIAN ·

For six months, twelve-year-old Rian Krieger tried to be the first person to arrive at Krieger Coach in the morning. She wanted to be well into the day's bookkeeping by the time her father got there. *Because I wanted Vater to find me at my desk when he arrived. I wanted him to notice how hard I work and how important the Krieger companies are to me.*

Now? Now it had become her habit. Arrive at the factory before anyone. Open the shop six days a week. *And Vater has never commented about it. Not once in six months.*

This morning, Rian kept to her usual get-up-and-get-out routine, even though her father was still away on business. She dressed in boy's pants and a shirt by the light of her oil lamp.

When anyone asked her why she didn't wear dresses in the shop, she said it was because a dress would get too dirty and it might get caught in the machinery. That shut most everybody up, but it wasn't the real answer. She told the real stuff only to Conor. He knew she hated dresses, hated the way they felt on her, and most of all, she hated the way strangers talked to her when she dressed like a girl. *Even people who know I'm a girl treat me better when I wear boy's clothing. They're all a bunch of gumps.*

What she wouldn't say even to Conor was that she would rather look like a boy—a boy who was so unremarkable that he was almost invisible—than a silly-looking girl. And a silly-looking girl was what Rian saw every time she wore a dress and looked in a mirror—a girl in a garment that might as well have been a court jester's outfit.

Before she left her bedroom that morning, Rian practiced smiling in front of the mirror, trying for the thousandth time to grin without revealing the huge gap between her two front teeth. This Krieger family trait—the source of incessant teasing—was shared with every descendant of her Grandfather Krieger. *Ugh, Eena, the one thing that makes sure you're not invisible.*

Rian's cousin Jabez Howes started calling her *Eena* when they were both toddlers because that was as close as he could come to saying *REE-in*. He never quit calling her Eena, even when they got older. The only other person who called her Eena was her mother. But Dierdre died when she was eight, the same month Jabez was whisked off to sea by his father. That left only Rian to say Eena, and it was only in her thoughts.

Rian tucked her long brown hair into her flat cap with practiced efficiency, and her costume was complete. She turned sideways. Her chest was flat as one of the teak boards in the shop, which was fine with her. *Good enough, Eena*, she said to herself. The look she had constructed for herself was the best of a bad deal.

Downstairs, she shrugged into her heavy frock coat and called, "Conor, it's time to wake up! I'm leaving!" Without waiting for her best friend to give a groggy reply, she left the house and shut the front door behind her. She bounded down the five steps from the porch and leaned into the cold of a March that had not yet yielded to spring. It was still dark.

Walking the ten blocks to the three Krieger factories would take her fifteen minutes. *All three factories—Krieger Coach, Krieger Locomotive, and Krieger Rail—are busy. We should be hiring more men. Every time Vater goes away on business, he comes back with more orders.*

Rian acknowledged the bakery man on his delivery wagon with a slight wave. The only other person within sight on Broad Street, his horse's hooves made a lonely *clop-clop-clop* on the cobblestones. *Vater doesn't much approve of me being out in the shops, but he's not here that often these days.*

The frost on the brick sidewalks glistened when she approached the light of a gas lamppost, then disappeared until she neared the next one. *I keep the books in the mornings. Afternoons, I'm out in the shops. Jules wishes I would spend my shop time at Krieger Coach because he taught me everything I know about woodworking, and he loves the shop.*

A stray black cat skulked across Broad Street, stopped momentarily to assess any threat from Rian, then slowed its pace to a mosey. *But my dream? My dream is across the alley in Uncle Adrian's factory, Krieger Locomotive. That's the shop I'm going to run someday.*

Leaving the light of the last lamppost, she crossed James Street and approached the block that contained the family businesses. *I don't like it when my Underground Railroad work takes me away from the shop, but it needs to be done.*

Rian unlocked the door to her father's factory and, even in the dark, could sense its cavernous size as her footsteps echoed back to her. She lit gas lamps along the wall as she strode the length of the building toward the office. They hissed a muted, one-note chorus that comforted her as she walked. *The sound of my day starting, just the way I like it. Soon enough, the shop will be deafening.* She passed table saws, band saws, planers, shapers, and lathes and could smell the aromas of woods they had been milling in recent days. The sweet smell of local woods like walnut and pine wafted up to her, as did exotic woods like mahogany from Honduras and teak from Siam.

Near the office, she opened the door to the firebox of the steam engine that drove all the machines in the building. She peered in. *Perfect. The coals from yesterday are still glowing.* She pulled some wood ends from the scrap box, threw them onto the coals, and noted with satisfaction that they started a slow burn. She tossed two shovels of coal on top and closed the door. She checked the water gauge to assure herself that there was plenty of water in the boiler. *It'll be boiling by the time the workers arrive.*

She entered the office and shut the door, and for the first time she thought about how the rest of her day would go.

Skipping out of work on Wednesday to take Peach to Robert's farm got me behind in my bookkeeping. I should be able to get caught up for all three Krieger factories in a couple of hours.

Then I'll walk across the alley to Krieger Locomotive and find something to do there.

* * * * *

Harry Vogel, the foreman across the alley at Krieger Locomotive, disliked Rian's presence in the shop as much as her father did. "Girls don't belong in a locomotive factory," she had heard him say more than once. Harry never said anything about her age. Hundreds of children her age worked in the cotton mills along the Schuylkill, both boys and girls. But here? Here she was learning manly skills that girls had no business learning. *But since Uncle Adrian owns the factory, there isn't much you can do about it, is there, Harry?*

The men? Well, the men were pretty much split down the middle. Those who liked her treated her like their pet. They used to give her errands to run, but now that she was almost thirteen, that didn't happen so much anymore. They let her help them. They taught her how to operate, maintain, and fix the machines, read a set of plans, make models and molds for castings, assemble all the parts to build a steam engine—any task that temporarily needed another pair of hands.

Those that didn't like her? The Germans called her "little bogtrotter" behind her back. The Irish called her "little *ispini*."[1] That's because she was half-Irish and half-German. *It's all right. Mostly those men ignore me. At worst, they shoo me away. I can handle that because somebody else always needs some help.*

Although most of the men took the noon hour break to walk home and eat, a growing number chose to bring their dinner and eat in the room set aside for meetings and treating injuries. Today, Rian chose to join them. Harry stuck his head in the room, frowned at Rian's presence, and announced to no one in particular, "Tell the others when they get back that I expect *Number 7* to be in the Finish Room by the end of the day."

Even though Harry didn't want Rian in the locomotive shop, she didn't hate him. He wasn't as good a foreman as Jules, who oversaw the Coach factory, but he had his strengths. Harry didn't tell the men what to do; he told them what he wanted done and let them figure out how to do it.

Reflecting how strong business was at Krieger Locomotive, *Number 7* was one of two locomotives that were supposed to be shipped the following week. Given how quickly the shop and its competitors were innovating, *Number 7* looked dramatically different from *Number 6*. It would be called *Number 7*—the seventh locomotive the factory had produced since it fired up nine months ago—for a few more days. When it emerged from the Finish Room painted a brilliant forest green with complementary yellow highlights, it would become *The Spirit of Schenectady*, with its name emblazoned on both sides of the engine driver's compartment.

Harry's directive got the men talking even though they were off the clock. There was much to do before *Number 7* was ready for the Finish Room. Install the valves and gauges above the firebox. Test fit the piston rod to the drive wheel. Fabricate the smokestack and bolt it to the boiler.

With no forethought, Rian blurted, "The sheet metal for *Number 7*'s smokestack is already cut to size. I can rivet the pieces together, and I'll also bolt the smokestack to its flange. I'll have it ready before the end of the day."

The men started laughing, even those who taught her things.

"No, I'm serious," she protested. "I can do both those things, and that will free you and the others to do the other stuff." She hadn't planned this, but she warmed to the idea. *This is my chance. This can be the day I prove to everybody I belong in the shop.*

---

1. Irish for sausage

Well, that got the men all yammery, and the lines started to form between *I think she can do it* and *only a skilled worker could do those things by the end of the day*. Before she knew it, the betting was on. When the rest of the workers filtered back from dinner, they started buzzing about it, too, and surprisingly, some of the men who didn't much like Rian lined up on the *I think she can do it* side.

Everyone agreed that no matter what, they had to keep Harry away. He would blow his stack if he learned that Rian was involved because there was no way a twelve-year-old girl could make a smokestack that adhered to Krieger standards. Two men volunteered to keep their eyes peeled for the foreman and distract him if he wandered out of the office. All agreed that muscling around that eight-foot piece of sheet metal was too big a job for any one person, so Benny Holt, one of the newest and greenest workers, would assist Rian. The betting intensified.

Three hours later, the sound in the shop was deafening—the mammoth steam engine that drove all the machines *choosh . . . choosh . . . chooshed*. Two rows of heavy machinery banged and clanged. Men yelled back and forth to one another.

Three hours to go. You're going to do this, Eena. Although one of the men had previously sliced the sheet metal to size, it had not been run through the crimping rollers to give it the desired cylindrical shape, and the holes for the rivets had not been drilled. Rian did all that and joined the pieces together with the steam riveter.

She stole a moment to admire her work. *Damn, I've built a smokestack, and it sure as hell will meet Harry's standards.*

Then the trouble started. There were no three-eighths-inch bolts anywhere in the fooking shop to bolt the flange onto the bottom of the smokestack.

Rian waved over Joheim Fischer, who was hovering nearby because he was in charge of the betting. Jo didn't much like her, but he surveyed her work so far and gave her a begrudging shrug of admiration. "Whataya want?"

"There's no bolts for the flange."

"Too bad," Jo yelled over the din. "Make them yourself."

Damnit, Rian muttered. She pulled a three-eighths-inch bar out of the bin and headed to the threading machine, now assuming she was likely to lose.

Benny Holt grabbed her by the collar and yelled good and loud so she could hear him. "Rian, there's a new threading machine at the end of row two. Use that. The job'll go a lot faster. You can still beat the deadline."

"A new machine? Since when?"

Bennie gave Rian a look like he knew some secret that he wasn't letting on, then started walking toward the new machine. "Three days ago," he yelled. "The day you pulled one of your disappearing acts."

Rian caught up to Bennie, curious because she had no idea the men took notice when she wasn't in the shop.

"Everyone talks about you. Both shops." Bennie didn't have to yell as loud the farther they got from the steam engine. "Even the men who don't much like you."

Uh-oh. "What do you mean?"

Bennie hooked his arm around her neck to pull her close and talk into her ear. "You do bookkeeping for all three factories with Aaron in the morning. Then you spend the afternoons working in either Krieger Coach or Krieger Locomotive, but never Krieger Rail. Everyone knows that even though Jules Freeman loves having you over on his side of the alley and Harry hates it, you usually try to weasel your way into something going on over here."

This isn't good. "My father doesn't pay me to work in the afternoons, so I can do whatever I want."

"That's not my point. Rian, every once in a while, you disappear from both factories. And it only happens when your daddy's on a business trip."

Bennie's last comment almost made Rian stop walking, but she recovered. "I was probably running errands for Jules."

"Then why didn't you tell anyone what you were doing?"

Rian didn't respond but resolved that she would return with a credible story the next time she had to disappear from the factory.

A half-hour later, Rian had fabricated six of the twelve bolts necessary to connect the flange to the smokestack. Just like every other machine in the factory, the new threading machine drew its power from a rotating shaft high above that was driven by the steam engine. A five-inch-wide continuous belt transferred power from the shaft to the machine. *I can still win the bet, but it's going to be a squeaker. It would have been a lot easier if Harry had stayed on top of inventory so there were enough bolts. Maybe he's not as good a foreman as I thought.*

She tightened the chuck around the three-eighths-inch bar and muscled the thread cutter into place. Then a tug on her shirt broke her concentration. She turned around to bark at Bennie, but it wasn't Bennie; it was Jules.

"Come with me. I need you," Jules yelled over the machines.

Rian turned from her machine. "Jules, I can't. I've got to finish six more bolts, and then I've got to connect the smokestack to its flange, and I've got to do it by 5:00."

Jules shook his head and shouted. "No, I need you now!"

No, not now. Please, not now. "Jules, I told the men I could do this. It's my chance to finally prove I belong here."

"Get someone to finish your job. We've got to leave."

This wasn't how Jules usually spoke to her, even when she factored in all the noise surrounding them. "What's so important?"

"I'll tell you outside. Railroad business," Jules responded. "Get someone else to finish your job. Make it quick."

If anyone could have heard their exchange over the din of the shop, *railroad business* would have sounded innocuous in a locomotive factory. Rian knew that, in this case, Jules meant the Underground Railroad. *The reason I disappear from the shop. That's why I can't tell anyone here what I'm doing. And I can only do it when Vater is away because he would pop his cork if he ever found out what I was doing.*

Rian found Bennie Holt speaking with Joheim Fischer. "I've got to go. Jules needs me to run an errand."

Bennie looked at Rian with consternation. "Rian, you can't leave now. Half the men have money riding on you. Leave now, and you won't have a friend left in this shop."

"Jules's errand is important. Tell the men who bet on me that I'm sorry."

Bennie threw up his hands. "See? This is exactly what I was talking about. This is what you do."

Jo smirked briefly, then turned and started announcing the news of Rian's departure as if he were a town crier.

Rian shifted the belt of the threading machine to its idler pulley and put the six completed bolts in a metal dish where her replacement could find them. As she walked back along the long row of machines, she heard whoops and cries above the clank and clatter of the machines. *Word of your desertion is spreading faster than you can walk.* Harry Vogel stuck his head out the office door to see what the commotion was about. *That's the last time anyone in this shop will give me the time of day. Shit, Jules. Shit. Shit. Shit.*

Rian put on her coat, exited into the alley between Krieger Locomotive and Krieger Coach, and stepped over a clump of snow that had fallen off the factory roof. Jules was waiting for her.

"Where are we going?" she asked.

Jules ignored her question. "Your father's not supposed to be home until tomorrow afternoon, right?"

"Right. He's still in Harrisburg."

"Are you and Conor eating at the Motts' tonight?"

"No, that was last night."

"Good, because you'll probably be gone all night. We need to get to the stable."

Gone all night? Rian's anger at being pulled from her job shifted to apprehension. She followed Jules to Kent's Livery Stable across Broad Street.

Rian often picked up horses at Kent's when she and other workers delivered finished carriages to ships berthed along the Delaware. These days, Krieger Coach, which expanded into the railroad business last year, built railroad cars of all descriptions for railroads around the country. When it came time for delivery, workers hoisted the cars onto a hulking transport wagon using four sets of block and tackle and four of Jimmy Kent's horses.

Jimmy was among the few non-Black, non-Quaker people with an abolitionist sentiment in Philadelphia. Jimmy and Jules worked out a system the first time Rian had conducted a self-emancipator to Robert Purvis's farm. All Rian had to do was say, "I'm running an errand for Jules," and Jules would pay for the horse rental later. Every time Rian had said those words, Jimmy had walked over to her, said, "Be careful," and then handed her a quarter dollar. "Here, take this. You'll probably need to buy something for yourselves along the way."

Jules and Rian saddled two horses. "Rian's running an errand for me," Jules told Jimmy as they led the horses out of the stable. "Let me get Rian on her way, then I'd like to come back to talk to you."

Rian and Jules left the stable directly onto cold, wind-whipped Broad Street. "Where am I going?" she asked as she mounted Bonnie, a horse she knew well.

"South. Austin T. Slatter caught Peach on the bridge to Trenton yesterday morning. We're going to get her back."

The scar on Rian's back tingled, a souvenir from her last encounter with Slatter. "Peach? Oh shit, this is a disaster."

Jules ignored Rian's comment. He handed her the reins to the second horse. "Don't gallop while you're leading another horse because you'll attract attention, but don't go slow, either. Ride to my house. Pick up Rufus. My son knows you're coming. I want you two to meet us on the other side of Gray's Ferry Bridge. There's a tavern about a quarter mile down on the right."

"Who's *us*?"

"Robert Purvis and as many men as he and I can gather. Mount up. There's no time to lose. I'm going back inside and see if I can talk Jimmy into going with us."

Rian gave the reins a slight tug to the right and squeezed her legs. Bonnie responded and broke into a trot. The second horse obediently followed. Rian tried to stuff down a feeling of dread. *You screwed up, Eena. Screwed up bad. Rule Number 1 in the Underground Railroad is that if somebody doesn't need to know something, you don't tell them. You spent five hours in the wagon with Peach. You told Peach a bunch of things that you shouldn't have. You violated Rule Number 1, and it has come back to bite you. Shit. Shit. Shit.*

* * * * *

· JULES ·

Jules's brain buzzed as he and Jimmy Kent cantered south on Broad Street.

As a self-emancipator who had escaped bondage seventeen years ago, he was used to weekly—sometimes daily—threats to his freedom. Occasionally, he wished he had kept moving in 1820 to New York State or Canada. But if he had, he wouldn't be living the life he had now, with a loving wife and a beautiful family. He had a good job at Krieger Coach. He'd started his own business. He had status among his Black brethren. All his many blessings made every problem bearable.

But the main problem, Jules said to himself, *is Philadelphia itself.*

Philadelphia was located mere miles from Maryland and Delaware, two slave states. Its economy relied on commerce with the South. Northern bankers, insurance agents, cotton brokers, mill owners, and shipping companies welcomed Southern planters into their offices with camaraderie and a sense of shared purpose: making money. The rest of the city tacitly supported their endeavors by buying slavery-tainted products because they were cheaper.

Southerners, especially from the Carolinas, spent their summers in the City of Brotherly Love to escape the heat and yellow fever. Their arrival in June marked the beginning of the social season, and that was when the real business of the summer got underway. Eligible young men and women from both societies courted during a ten-week string of balls, teas, horse races, regattas, and ice cream socials. The eventual marital unions further cemented the bonds between Philadelphia and the South.

Thus, Philadelphia was a Southern city in a Northern state. Abolitionist sentiment was almost nonexistent, as was any love among the white citizens for the free Blacks who constituted ten percent of Philadelphia's population.

Slave catchers openly roamed the streets. Though fugitive slaves were their primary target, it was not unusual for them to kidnap free Blacks and ship them South. Jules always kept a forged certificate of emancipation in his pocket. The paper had deterred dozens of slave catchers, not to mention ferry captains, steamship ticket takers, and train conductors, who took it upon themselves to enforce the letter of the Fugitive Slave Act of 1793. The document was so well crafted that the chances of him ever being returned to his former enslaver were small. However, Jules was still breaking the law because he declared himself a free man seventeen years ago.

"Okay, Jules," said Jimmy Kent, riding next to him. "I know you're in a stew, but it's time you told me what I've signed up for. I've never joined you for an excursion like this. I just supply the horses and wagons."

Jules pulled a broadside out of his coat pocket and held it out to Jimmy. "Austin T. Slatter recaptured a self-emancipator that Rian and I helped a few days ago. Her new name is Peach."

Jimmy grabbed the broadside and started reading as they rode. "Slatter. The gump who beat you up in my stable last year?"

"Yeah, that's the one. He and I have been playing cat-and-mouse for a couple of years now. We don't much like each other."

Jimmy handed the broadside back to Jules. "Trouble with cat-and-mouse is that the mouse can only lose once."

"That's why I asked you to come along. Now that he has Peach, Slatter can end the game for good. I could go to jail for abetting a fugitive slave." *Or,* Jules thought, *my life could fall apart. I could be returned to slavery.* "Peach spent three nights in my house. They could get my wife, too." *And the waterman, the Quaker, Rian Krieger, Willis, Robert Purvis, and his caretaker.*

Jimmy waited until they passed a man on a horse who had stopped in the middle of the street to talk to two ladies in a carriage. Once they could no longer be overheard, he said, "By law, Slatter's gotta take her to a magistrate first. Prove that she's the fugitive named in the broadside. That could take days. Why the rush?"

"The conductor taking Peach to Trenton tailed them to see which magistrate he took her to. Slatter blew past the nearest magistrate's office and continued south toward Philadelphia. The conductor didn't panic. He borrowed a horse from a farmer who he knew was sympathetic and rode hard to one of the stations he and Peach had stopped at." *Robert Purvis's farm.* "The caretaker from the station rode to Philadelphia and alerted his boss. The boss threw a plan together on the fly. I was his first recruit."

"Jules, I'm okay to be a part of this, but I can't stay all night. If Slatter doesn't show up by midnight, I've got to get home. You're welcome to hang on to the horses, though."

"Jimmy, we're thankful for whatever help we get."

And maybe it's better if you aren't around if we get Peach back. Purvis's plan is good, but it doesn't go far enough. The chances of capturing Slatter and freeing Peach are slim at best. But if I am successful, I will end this game of cat-and-mouse once and for all. If it is within my power, I will kill Austin T. Slatter before dawn tomorrow.

* * * * *

· RIAN ·

Rian kept Bonnie at a steady canter with one hand on the reins and the other leading the second horse. *Slatter. If it's Slatter, we're fooked. He's big, strong, smart, and mean. He'll squeeze every bit of information out of Peach and roll up Jules's string of stationmasters and conductors from Maryland to New Jersey.*

It took ten minutes to travel the sixteen blocks to Jules and Maddie's house in Moyamensing. Jules's son Rufus dashed from the porch to the street and mounted the other horse. His mother, Maddie, exited the house, stood at the door with arms folded, then belatedly waved. Rian and Rufus wheeled their horses around and backtracked half a block to turn left on Shippen.

The two not-yet-thirteen-year-olds rode side by side. *I wonder how much longer we'll be able to do this,* thought Rian. *A white kid and a Black kid can ride side by side, and nobody in this town pays attention. But put a Black man and a white man side by side in a wagon, and it's like they're committing a crime.* "Your father said you'd fill me in."

"All I know is that Pop-Pop says he and Robert Purvis don't have enough people. That's why he recruited us. Slatter didn't take Peach to a magistrate like he was supposed to. He's taking her back to Maryland directly."

Rian and Rufus rode west on Shippen Street, then turned southwest on Gray's Ferry Road. They passed the U.S. Naval Asylum, with its Greek Revival pillars. Then half a mile later, they rode by the U.S. Arsenal. At 4:00, they reached the Schuylkill River and Gray's Ferry Bridge.

The bridge was a thousand-foot "floater"—two strings of wood-decked log rafts chained end-to-end and connected by a drawbridge. The rafts were anchored to the riverbed, making it possible to raise the drawbridge for river traffic. Horses didn't like the bridge because it was so tippy. The rafts lurched unpredictably when traffic from opposite shores met. Encountering pedestrians wasn't bad, other horses were irritating, and wagons were downright challenging. Rian usually walked her horse across the bridge to keep her calm.

The draw was up when Rian and Rufus arrived. The river was bloated with spring melt. Slushy snow and chunks of ice floated downstream. So much ice was piling up against the rafts that the bridgetenders took advantage of the open draw to guide the ice chunks to the opening with long pikes.

Rian looked downstream. An oyster boat and a shallop were approaching, and it would probably be ten minutes before the bridgetenders lowered the draw and traffic resumed across the Schuylkill. Robert Purvis arrived on a horse and lined up behind them. Two wagons, one with three Negroes,[2] the other with two whites, pulled up behind Robert. No one acknowledged one another, although Rian suspected they were all recruits for the mission.

When the bridgetenders lowered the draw back into place, Rian and Rufus started to lead their horses across the rafts. *Not a good day to take a swim*, Rian said to herself. They were halfway across the bridge when a freight wagon entered the bridge from the other shore. It was so heavy that it sank each raft a few inches below the water's surface. With no desire to get their feet wet, Rian and Rufus mounted their horses and continued to ride across the bridge. *Sorry, Bonnie. It's a good thing you're a steady one.*

They rode the quarter mile to the tavern and stopped to water their horses. Robert Purvis, who waited for the freight wagon to cross the river before he started, arrived considerably later, as did the two wagons that were in line behind Robert.

Jules was waiting for them with half a dozen men, including Jimmy Kent. "Okay, we don't know what Slatter's plans are. There are four likely routes back to Maryland, two by water and two by land. We're responsible for the land routes, and we'll be at it until dawn. If we haven't got Peach back by then, she's as good as lost. We're going to break up into two groups. Half of you will take Creek Road, and the other half will stay close to the river."

Jules handed his son a sheet of paper. "Rufus, you're going with Robert and five men. They'll establish a choke point on Creek Road about five miles from here to intercept Slatter if he goes that way, but you are going to continue on. Follow these directions. There's a barber farther down the road who's president of another Vigilant Committee. Tell him what's happening and ask him to send his men out. Rian, you stick with us for the moment."

Rian was a little disappointed not to be going with Rufus.

---

2. A note to readers: With the wish to keep this narrative as historically appropriate as I can, I have injected into the narrative three terms that African Americans used in the 1830s to describe themselves. In order to justify the use of terms that have since gone out of fashion or even become offensive, I cite African American civil rights icons who used those terms with dignity. James Forten identified himself as colored; W. E. B. Du Bois called himself a Negro. Martin Luther King used that term as well and also called himself black. In recent years, the term *black* has been capitalized to *Black*. I have chosen to use that more modern form throughout Rian Krieger's Journey.

Jules turned to the group. "Gentlemen, it's time to go. I want to remind you that from now on, we do not use one another's names. Keep your neckerchiefs handy so you can disguise yourselves if necessary."

After a mile, Jules slowed his horse so he could ride next to Rian. "Sorry to drag you into this, Rian, but you can see we're a little shorthanded. This is the first time we've done anything like this. I'm afraid you're not going to get much sleep tonight."

"What do you want me to do?"

"I want you to keep out of harm's way. Just like Rufus, your job is to alert one of the Vigilant Committees to the south of us. This one's outside of Chester."

"Jules, what's a Vigilant Committee? You said this is railroad business."

Jules sighed. "Until a few months ago, when a slave catcher recaptured a self-emancipator, he returned the poor wretch to his enslaver, and we were helpless. We formed the Vigilant Committee to do something about it."

"Who's *we*?"

"Robert and me. A dozen others, but we're the only ones you need to know about."

"Rule Number 1?"

Jules nodded.

Rian eyed Jimmy Kent and the other riders up front, then turned in her saddle to count noses in the two wagons behind them. "There are five Blacks and four whites, including you and me."

"Most committee members are Black, but we do have some white support. Wish it were more. We're happy for any help we can get to disrupt the slave catchers."

"How have you done?"

"The slave catchers are winning, mostly. By law, they're required to take any self-emancipator they capture to jail, prove they've got the right person, and get the court's permission to return them to their enslavers. In those instances, we try to intervene. We force them to go before a magistrate. We supply a lawyer and funds for the self-emancipator's defense."

"But Slatter didn't take Peach to a magistrate."

"Yeah, and that makes this foray different, but we anticipate there will be more like this. We hope to rescue captured self-emancipators."

The thought of rescuing Peach exhilarated Rian, but confronting Slatter scared her to the point that her scar tingled again. "Jaysus, Jules, this isn't Underground Railroad business. It's something new."

"You're right, but you won't be part of it."

It was getting close to sunset. To their left lay a marsh that looked boggy and impassable. Beyond that, the Delaware River threatened to overflow its banks with spring melt. To the right, a bank rose steeply away from the road. Jules whistled for the riders ahead to halt. "This is a good spot," he announced.

Without needing any more instruction, one of the men in the wagon pulled out an axe and started chopping at the base of a maple tree. It wasn't very big—only four or five inches in diameter—but when it fell, it blocked all but a few feet of the road.

If I first occupy constricted ground, I must block the passes and await the enemy, Rian thought to herself, quoting Sun Tzu.[3] *I think the great general would be pleased with this spot.*

Jules handed Rian a sheet of paper. "Here, read these instructions. I want you to ride to Chester. There's a shopkeeper who lives above his shop just this side of town. Tell him what's happened and that he needs to muster his men. The rest of us will stay here and jump Slatter if he comes this way."

*****

Rian had found the shopkeeper in Chester without a problem. The man thanked her for alerting him but then went about his business without giving her any further instructions. She mounted Bonnie and headed back the way she came, now with the Delaware on her right.

If Rian hadn't been on a mission to rescue Peach, and if Jules hadn't yanked her out of the locomotive shop and ruined her chances to be accepted by the men, the trip in the dead of night would have been quite enjoyable. It was well past midnight. The temperature had stayed above freezing. There was no hint of a breeze. Hundreds of stars had made the trip almost magical. Now, the waning crescent moon, a mere sliver, rose in the east, and its light reflected off the river and danced through the trees.

On two occasions, travelers on horseback approached her coming the other way. One, holding a torch, gave her a polite wave. The other, barely visible in the moonlight, reined his horse to a halt.

"Careful up ahead," he said. "Some folks about a quarter mile yonder. They're up to no good, I suspect."

"What are they doing?"

---

3. Readers of Rian Krieger's Journey were introduced to the work of the Chinese philosopher and general Sun Tzu in Book 1. *The Art of War*, written 500 years before the time of Christ, laid out strategies to overcome opponents—often avoiding combat altogether—using tactics such as alliances, deception, and delay. In 1837, *The Art of War* had not yet been translated into English, but copies did exist in French.

"Dunno. Didn't bother me none. They're lookin' for someone, that's for sure."

Rian proceeded to the Vigilant Committee's blockade. Hundreds of peepers—the first Rian had heard this season—chanted their high-pitched peeps from the marsh near the river. Two men smoking cigarettes sat on the back of a wagon. She steered Bonnie by them and found Jules standing at the felled tree.

Rian dismounted and gave her report to Jules. Then . . . "Where's Jimmy?"

"He and most of the others left. They all had obligations. We're down to three. We'll be all right. Chances are Slatter's chosen some other route anyway."

All this for nothing, Rian thought. *I could have finished the job at the shop. Those men who bet I could finish in time probably hate me now. No one at Krieger Locomotive will ever give me the time of day.*

It had been a long time since she had spent six hours in a saddle, and she had another two to go before she delivered Bonnie back to the stable. Normally, she would have been asleep for five hours by this time. "Do you want me to stay and help, Jules?" she asked, hoping he would say no.

"No, you've done your job, Rian," said Jules. "Thank you. You should head home. You might even get half a night's sleep."

Rian led Bonnie around the felled tree and mounted. She urged the mare forward with a squeeze of her legs and a kissing sound. Rian sensed rather than saw that the road was still relatively narrow, the perfect spot for an ambush. *What if Slatter and Peach are on horses? If Slatter smells trouble, he could just turn the horses around and escape. Sun Tzu would have positioned the other men right here to bottle him up. Those guys shouldn't be smoking cigarettes, either. If Slatter smells the cigarettes, he'll know there's people up ahead. Jules shouldn't have allowed them to take a break at the same time.*

Two hundred yards down the road, as Rian rode away from the peeping chorus, she heard the light thrum of a wheeled vehicle and the *clop-clop* of a single horse. She reined Bonnie to a halt and detected motion in the faint moonlight.

The wagon stopped next to her. The driver remained mute. Rian could see a form—a bulk, but no features. "Good evening, stranger," Rian said, trying to make her voice sound as low as possible.

"Anything up ahead I need to worry about?"

Rian recognized Slatter's voice. She summoned up all the composure she could muster. "There's a tree down across the road. Maybe a couple hundred yards. You'll have to walk your horse around it, but there's room on the left. Be careful, because there's a bog right there that you'll want to avoid." Rian winced at her words because they probably sounded unnecessarily informative.

"You sound like a youngster. Kind of early for someone your age to be out."

Uh . . . "My pappy's sick. I'm going to fetch the doc."

Slatter slapped the reins without saying another word and his wagon jolted forward. *Four wheels. Probably a buckboard. I've got to help Jules.*

Rian dismounted, led Bonnie up a slight rise away from the river, and tied her reins to a branch. She felt and stumbled her way back to the road and matched her pace to that of the wagon. The thrum of the wagon wheels obscured the sound of her footsteps. Then, closer to the marsh, the chanting peepers drowned out even the wagon wheels.

The wagon came to a halt in total darkness, shaded from the light of the crescent moon by the trees along the river. Rian continued to walk forward, confident that the peepers would mask the sound of her footsteps on the gravel. Second thoughts crept in. *You shouldn't be doing this, Eena. Jules said he didn't want you in harm's way.*

She heard Slatter mutter something, then get out of the wagon. *You can't see, but you can listen. Concentrate.* Rian heard the distinctive click of a pistol being cocked. A second click. *Jaysus, he's got two pistols.* Cautious footsteps moved away from her.

For a moment, Rian thought she heard the beat of a drum, separate from the chorus of peepers, more distant. Then she realized it was her heart, beating so hard that it thumped in her ears. *What are you doing here?*

She crept up to the back of the wagon and felt into the bed from the rear. *Nothing.*

The horse stirred a bit and took a step forward, pulling the wagon ahead a foot or two. The sound of Slatter's footsteps diminished as he approached the fallen tree.

Rian smelled cigarette smoke. *Those idiots. Slatter can smell it, too.* She felt her way around to the left side of the wagon, probing the bed again with her hands. *Nothing.*

Then a movement. Just a slight stirring from the wagon seat. Rian felt her way to the front of the buckboard. A figure sat barely visible in the darkness.

"Peach," Rian whispered.

The figure stirred. "Rian?"

"Come on. Let's get you out of there."

"I can't. My wrists are chained to the seat."

"Oh, Jaysus."

Slatter yelled, "Eat this!" and fired his first pistol. A bright flash shot out toward the felled tree. The horse stirred.

"Peach, can you reach the reins?"

A clank of chains. "No, I think he wrapped them around the brake. It's on your side."

Rian felt her way to the brake lever, released it, and unwrapped the reins. She gathered them in until she reached the horse's muzzle, grabbed his halter, and started to circle him around the narrow road to head the other way.

You did too good a job, Jules. You picked the perfect ambush site. It's almost impossible to turn a wagon around here.

Two shots. Streaks from Jules's position. The bullets whistled overhead.

Bang! *Slatter's second shot.*

Rian stepped into water up to her ankles. Skittish, the horse reluctantly followed. The two right wheels of the wagon rolled into the ditch. The wagon tilted precariously, then halted. "No-o-o!" Peach cried.

Rapid footsteps approached, with two men running in pursuit.

"Heeya!" yelled Rian, pulling hard on the horse's halter, encouraging him forward.

Rian let go of the halter and pulled on the reins instead. "Come on!" she yelled to the horse as she ran through the muck. The horse surged. Rian stumbled but recovered. She found firmer footing back on the road and ran away from the melee.

But the melee caught up to her. Slatter grabbed the reins and yanked them hard, pulling Rian toward him. Before she even thought of letting go, he smacked her hard on the cheek with his gun butt. She spun around and fell heavily to the road.

Then, sounds of a struggle. Slatter screaming. Slatter being pinned to the ground by two men. Slatter being pummeled.

* * * * *

· JULES ·

Jules knew that someone had tried to rescue Peach in the darkness. Scared that it was Rian and she had been shot or injured, he knelt next to the figure lying a few feet from Austin T. Slatter. "Are you hurt?"

"No, I . . ."

Rian. Jules clapped his meaty hand over Rian's mouth, fearing that she would blurt out something incriminating. As a result of her presence, his plan to kill Slatter was falling apart. *I can't kill him in front of her.* He hauled Rian to her feet.

Hanging on to Rian's coat with one hand to keep her steady, his other hand still over her mouth, Jules led her toward the fallen tree. "You shouldn't have come back. Now there's going to be hell to pay." He turned her around and forced her to sit on the tree. "Okay, we're in a bit of a fix here. Whatever you do, don't call anyone by name."

"What are you going to do with Slatter?"

Jules turned and started walking away from Rian. "I don't know. I haven't decided yet." *Kill him, but not until you're out of earshot.*

Sunrise was more than an hour away, but the crescent moon had risen higher in the sky and provided a glimmer of light. Two men with pistols guarded Slatter, who knelt in the middle of the road.

That'll do for a few minutes, Jules thought to himself, *but I need him restrained for at least an hour, and these men have work to do.* Without uttering a word, he leaned over Slatter and roughly fished through his pockets until he found a key.

Jules walked to the buckboard and unlocked Peach's shackles. "Let's get you out of this wagon, Peach. We need you to help us out."

Jules led the horse and buckboard across the ditch and onto the boggy stretch between the road and the river. Rian and Peach unhooked the horse from the wagon and removed his harness. Jules walked back to the guards and directed them to stand Slatter up, muscle him to the buckboard, and force him to sit with his back to the rear wagon wheel.

Jules handed Peach the irons. "Lock these around his wrists good and tight. Make sure you run the chain through the wheel spokes so he can't escape."

Peach did as Jules told her, taking her time to be thorough about it. "What are you going to do with him?"

Jules didn't answer as he knelt beside Slatter on the wet, soft ground. He confirmed by feel that Peach had woven the chains back and forth through the spokes. *Good job, girl.* When he rose, the knees of his pants were soaking wet.

As they walked back toward the road, Rian grabbed Jules's shirt. "What are you going to do with him? Just set him free? Sun Tzu wouldn't do that."

Jules summoned up as convincing a tone of certitude as he could. "Sun Tzu served a powerful emperor. Our only power is to disrupt the slavers without scaring people to the point that they unite against us. Killing Slatter would be a bad decision." *Even though that's precisely what I will do as soon as you and Peach can't hear the gunshot.*

He grabbed Peach by the arm and pulled her close. "Do you know how to ride a horse?"

"Of course I do," said Peach.

"Bareback?"

"Never rode with a saddle."

"Okay, I want you to ride Slatter's horse back to Philadelphia. The sun will be up soon, so don't ride together. Peach, you follow Rian at a distance but keep her in sight. She knows where to go. When you get close to town, dismount and let the horse go. I don't want any connection between Slatter and you. Rian, you'll have to slow down when Peach starts walking."

"That devil's got my emancipation paper. I want it back. I've got a new name now. A name I chose for myself. I ain't never going to change it again."

I like this girl, Jules said to himself. He returned to Slatter, who was sitting in the almost-freezing muck.

"I'm going to kill you when I get out of this," Slatter muttered as Jules fished through his pockets.

Jules didn't respond. He found the paper and returned it to Peach. He could just make out her face in the dawning light.

Peach put the paper in her coat pocket. "Thanks for coming to get me. The peepers started peeping to me again."

"The peepers?" asked Jules.

"Yup. They been keeping me company this whole trip, singing their song of freedom. Then that devil caught me, so I stopped believing. Then, just before we got here, they started in again. I didn't believe them for a while, but you all came to get me. They didn't lie." Peach turned to Rian. "That man caught you real good with his gun butt."

Rian put her fingers to her cheekbone. The left side of her face was already swollen. "I'll have to make up some lie to tell my father."

"Your daddy still don't know you're out here?" asked Peach.

"No, he doesn't. He's been away for the better part of a week."

Jules looked toward the growing light over the east bank of the Delaware. "We'll have to make up a story. You always have to get your stories straight."

I guess that should be Rule Number 2 of the Underground Railroad business.

* * * * *

Jules watched the two riders until they were out of sight, then approached the two remaining vigilantes. "We've got a lot of work to do before the first morning travelers come down this road. There's a shovel in the wagon. Find a boggy spot near the river and start digging. Make the hole at least three feet deep. I'll drag the harness to the river, and then I'll pull the tree off the road. As soon as the youngsters are out of earshot, I'm going to shoot Slatter and we'll bury his body. When we push the buckboard into the river, no one will know we were ever here. Slatter will have disappeared, and Peach will be back on her way north."

The Delaware River was a hundred yards away, and the footing to get there was cold and mushy. With the harness tossed into the river, Jules turned to walk back to the road.

"He's getting away!"

Jules looked up to see the two gravediggers running toward the road. He ran through the slush and mush toward the wagon. When he arrived, the entire rear wheel was gone. His men were running south on the road. In the dim light, he saw Slatter, still shackled to the wagon wheel, running on the road. *He can't outrun them with that wheel on his back. His only hope is to get to the river.*

Jules doubled back to the river and started running south, hoping to intercept Slatter when he made his cut to the river. He tripped on a root and fell, picked himself up, and continued to run. Then, in the distance, he saw Slatter, the wheel still on his back, run into the icy river at full speed and continue to plod toward deeper water until he lost his footing and fell forward. He didn't surface. The Delaware's current caught the wagon wheel and floated it away faster than Jules could run. Slatter was nowhere to be seen.

He'll either drown or freeze to death. Either way, he's gone. Burn in hell, Slatter.

* * * * *

Martin Van Buren Inaugurated as Eighth President
Vows to Continue Policies of His Predecessor
President Jackson Recognizes Republic of Texas on Last Day in Office
Exclusive to the *Philadelphia Independent*
by Harold Foote

March 4, 1837. Today Martin Van Buren of New York was sworn in as the eighth president of the United States in a ceremony held at the Capitol Building. Chief Justice Roger B. Taney administered the oath of office.

Mr. Van Buren rode to the Capitol Building with outgoing President Andrew Jackson in a phaeton built from the wood of the *U.S.S. Constitution*. In his inaugural address given from the Capitol's East Portico, the new president vowed to strictly adhere to "the letter and spirit of the Constitution as it was designed by those who framed it, looking back to it as a sacred instrument carefully and not easily framed, remembering that it was throughout a work of concession and compromise, viewing it as limited in national endeavors, regarding it as leaving to the people and the States all power not explicitly parted with."

Thus, despite his Northern roots, virtually all Washington insiders assume Mr. Van Buren will not meddle with states' prerogatives to determine property rights. Just as under the Jackson administration, the institution of slavery will not be challenged at the federal level. Almost all of President Jackson's cabinet is expected to be retained by the new president . . .

SUNDAY, MARCH 5

· SEAMUS ·

After early mass, Seamus Gallagher left St. Philip de Neri Catholic Church with his ma and two sisters. Seamus had found a new motivation to once again become a regular at church: Siobhan Callaghan. The black-haired, black-eyed eighteen-year-old beauty was three years younger than him, fiery, feisty, volatile, and the daughter of Hugh Callaghan.

That last item presented a wee bit of a problem. Hugh was the president of the Moyamensing Hose Company, and Seamus ran the upstart United No Name Fire Brigade. Their fire companies were rivals in putting out fires in Moya and pilfering cargo along the Delaware wharves.

Moya referenced Moyamensing, the poorest political district in Philadelphia, and Hugh's fire company. In Moya-the-district, Irish and Blacks lived cheek to jowl in a hodgepodge of neighborhoods, making Moya a powder keg of distrust and animosity. On the other hand, Moya-the-hose-company was proudly all Irish—equal parts a social club, a gang that dominated crime along the waterfront, and firefighters who often engaged in extortion.

This morning, talking with Siobhan wasn't Seamus's priority. *The truce between Moya and No Name is falling apart, and Hugh isn't doing his bit to hold it together. The problem is that I don't know if he wants to let the truce die or if he's asleep at the switch. No matter what, the man is half crazy.*

Callaghan strutted out of St. Philip's like a rooster with his hen and three chicks, donned his beaver hat, surveyed the after-mass crowd, and scowled at Seamus. Seamus gave Hugh a polite wave and nodded, indicating he wanted to talk. The two ambled to a meeting point midway between their families.

Hugh exhibited more interest in appraising the crowd than talking to Seamus. He pulled a toothpick from his pocket and placed it in his mouth. "Whataya want, Seamus?"

Just take your time, Boyo. Don't seem too anxious. "I hear you've been blowing in me brother's ear about joining Moya. I want you to cut it out."

"Not sure you're in a position to make such a demand. Your little brother takes his drinks at Clancy's, not with your tribe at McSweeney's. I think he finds our company more compatible. I just take the opportunity to discuss the advantages of becoming a Moya member."

"You use my brother to run errands and act as a lookout when your boys are pilfering stuff off the docks. Same as you did with me before I was old enough to join."

"Well, you can relax in that regard, Seamus. My understanding is that Logan is only seventeen. He's got a year or so before he's voted in. But I'll tell you right now, me lads like the boy. Unlike you, he doesn't demonstrate any affection for the Africans. But I'll make you a deal: You stop seeing me daughter and I'll lay off your brother."

Seamus shook his head. "You and I both know that I'll stop asking your daughter out for a stroll only when she tells me to stop. I guess I'll have to figure out how to save me brother some other way."

The toothpick protruded slightly from the side of Hugh's mouth. "Yeah, he told me you've hired him at your uncle's factory. He didn't sound very enthusiastic about taking orders from Jules Freeman."

"His first day of work is tomorrow. We'll see how it goes."

Hugh turned toward his family. "If that's all you've got, I'll get on with me day."

Don't lose him, Boyo. "Uh, not quite. I've got a bit of information that may interest you. A ship called the *Bridger* entered Delaware Bay yesterday. The captain alerted the authorities from Cape May that they had a sick crewman aboard. They were pretty sure it's yellow fever."

Hugh leaned back a bit as if Seamus were the one with the disease. "Little early in the season for yellow fever, isn't it?"

"Not in Havana, which was their last port. The captain voluntarily put into Lazaretto.[4] They took the man off, inspected the ship, and told the captain he was free to set sail after first light. The *Bridger* should arrive later this morning."

Hugh surveyed the after-mass crowd, giving little indication that he gave a shit about the good ship *Bridger.* "So, why are you telling me this, Seamus?"

Just give him a little information at a time, Boyo. Make him want it. "Well, usually the *Bridger* puts in at the Imlay & Potts Pier, which we agreed seven

---

4. A yellow fever epidemic killed almost ten percent of Philadelphia's residents in 1793. In response, the city opened the Lazaretto Quarantine Station ten miles downriver to inspect all inbound passenger vessels. Passengers deemed unfit for entry were quarantined on the station's ten-acre campus. Those who died were buried there.

months ago is No Name's territory, but Mr. Imlay wasn't interested in chancing yellow fever, so now the *Bridger*'s going to be berthed at Clapier & Cuthbert, which is Moya's turf. I just want you to know that if your boys are going to make their usual mischief, they better be careful."

Hugh looked hard at Seamus for the first time. "I guess the risk depends on the potential reward. What's on the ship?"

Nice and easy, Boyo. You've got his attention. "Coffee, sugar, and molasses."

"The coffee might have been worth an evening expedition, but given your yellow fever story, I think we'll stay away. How'd you come by this information?"

Almost there. Almost there. "Turns out, a couple of ways. I've got a source in one of the telegraph towers."[5]

"Who's your source?"

Seamus smiled, enjoying this game. "Nobody you need to know about." *It's Rian's friend Conor McGuire. And he doesn't work in one of the towers; he runs messages from the Merchants' Exchange Building. He figured out a way to read the messages before he delivers them.*

"That sort of information can be valuable to people in our line of work."

Time to change the subject. Make him come back to this. "Now get this. Me sister Nora empties bedpans at the Quarantine Station. She overheard a couple of men talking after they inspected the ship. They'd been down in the hold. There's platforms with four levels down there. There's rings for shackles bolted to the shelves. The *Bridger*'s a slave ship."

Hugh frowned. "The captain'll lose his ship if the Navy catches him smuggling those people. It's pretty brazen of him to sail up here with the hold still looking like that." He sucked on his toothpick for a few moments and then said, "You know, Seamus, I'm not sure I approve of the *Bridger* bringing those Africans over to this side of the Atlantic."

Seamus smiled. "I've already brought your daughter over to the light. You thinking of becoming an abolitionist, Hugh?" *Come on, Hugh, I'm not here to talk about abolition. Take the bait . . .*

Hugh shook his head, indicating no interest in the anti-slavery movement. "That's not it at all. The way I see it, some percentage of them is gonna escape every year, and where do they end up? Right here in the City of Brotherly Love.

---

5. A consortium of businessmen had operated the "optical telegraph" between Cape May, New Jersey, and the Merchants' Exchange Building in Philadelphia since 1809. Coded messages traveled a hundred miles in less than an hour via a string of towers equipped with large mechanical arms. Consortium members derived a significant competitive advantage by receiving information about incoming shipping on the Delaware at least a day before the ships arrived at the Philadelphia wharves.

I've told you a thousand times, Seamus—the Irish are at war with the Africans. The more we drive out of Moya, the better. But now that you've got me thinking about it, a better solution would be to leave the Africans in Africa."

Seamus made eye contact with Siobhan, who stared back at him, her arms folded. *Patience, darlin'. I'm almost done here.* He returned his attention to Hugh. "Interesting that the captain is willing to enslave Black people yet has scruples about bringing yellow fever into town."

Hugh didn't want to talk about scruples. "Your contact at the telegraph towers interests me . . ."

Bingo!

"Any chance you'd be willing to share some of his information?"

"Now that depends. Your boys have been nibbling at the edges of the truce, and you're letting it happen. They're lifting stuff from the piers in No Name's territory. They fooked with our pump at that fire on Catherine Street last week. If you get the lads back in line, I might start sending some information in your direction." *C'mon, Hugh.*

"I'm willing to consider it."

Okay, Boyo, seal the deal. "Commit, and I'll give you another piece of information right now."

"You give me a taste, and I'll tell you if it's worth it."

Seamus took a sheet of paper out of his pocket. "The price of firewood is sky-high right now. It's five dollars a cord. Two ships—the *James Cropper* and the *Peddler*—entered the bay around three o'clock yesterday. They're filled with nothing but seasoned oak and locust. By this time tomorrow, the price of firewood is going to drop. My best guess is to two dollars a cord. If you can't do something with that information, Hugh, you aren't much of a businessman."

Hugh sucked on his toothpick for a long moment, then held out his hand. "Not bad, Seamus. You've got yourself a deal. I'll keep me boys in line."

Seamus shook Hugh's hand. With his mission accomplished, he turned his attention to Siobhan and smiled. She gave him a stern look and stomped her foot.

"I guess that's it for the moment, Hugh. Gotta go. Your daughter's getting impatient, and you, of all people, should know what it's like when she's not happy. See you at the next fire."

The two rivals parted.

Siobhan brightened and sashayed over to Seamus. He noted more frowns than smiles amongst the other mass-goers who watched her. His romance with Siobhan was well reported among the gossips of Moya. Not many people thought highly of the United No Name Fire Brigade and its willingness to put out fires in Black residents' homes.

Siobhan gave Seamus's ma an affectionate peck on the cheek and took Seamus's arm. "You promised me a memorable afternoon. I hope it involves food."

Seamus smiled. "It's been a good couple of weeks. I'm taking you for dinner at the United States Hotel." He gave Siobhan an admiring look. "Your Sunday best should be perfect for the occasion."

Siobhan released his hand and backed up a step. "Seamus, are you fooking daft? That hotel doesn't serve women."

"Not in the main dining room. But I've reserved a private room for us."

"But we're Irish. We'll never get past the maître d'. Me da says he guards the dining room like a hawk."

"Well, that one's a bit tricky. For the afternoon, I'm going to be Adrian Krieger."

"Your uncle? He goes to the hotel every day."

"No, that's me Uncle Otto. Uncle Adrian never leaves the shop during the day. I don't know that he's ever set foot inside the hotel. Once they see the color of me money, they'll serve us same as if we were the Shippens."

Siobhan snorted at the name of the prosperous banker and railroad entrepreneur, then smiled and hooked her arm into his again. "Seamus Gallagher, you're a dreamer and a schemer. I've got to give you that. Two years ago you were a ditchdigger. Now you're taking your best girl out for Sunday dinner at the finest hotel in Philadelphia."

"Not me best girl. Me only girl."

* * * * *

· RIAN ·

Rian sat at her kitchen table with a chunk of crusty snow pressed against her cheek.

Her best friend Conor McGuire handed her a towel. "Put this around the ice or you'll give yourself frostbite. Your da's going to kill you when he sees your cheek."

"No, I'll be okay. *Vater* doesn't pay much attention to me in that way."

Conor shook his head. "He is away a lot, but when he comes back this afternoon, he's going to notice. Now I'm glad I'm running messages in the afternoons. If I'd been with you, your da would blame me for aiding and abetting when he finds out. He's bound to kick me out of the house when he starts raging."

The orphaned Conor lived on and off with Rian and her father, depending on his three older brothers' circumstances. Sometimes his brothers had room for him in whatever cramped quarters they had secured. Then, after they were evicted, he would return to the Krieger house at 134 North Ninth Street. This latest stay was approaching five months.

Rian felt the irritation well up. "Conor, I'm telling you, he's not going to find out. Jules and I made up a story together. Besides, he'd never kick you out. He's got too much of a sweet spot for you. You're the son he's always wanted." *We've been joking for months about how Vater dotes on Conor. That part is funny. The sad thing is, I know in my heart that if I were a boy and doing the things in the shop that I do, the buttons on Vater's vest would be popping.*

Conor shrugged off the *son he's always wanted* comment. "If he loved me so much, how come he never extended me hours to work in the afternoon? I'm paid to work half a day, just like you."

"He's probably never thought about it. You should ask him for more hours. *Vater* doesn't think much about such things. He likes to design new rolling stock and sell for all three of our companies. He complains about everything else and pushes it off as much as possible." Rian put down the icy towel to give her jaw a break. "Does the dispatcher at the Merchants' Exchange suspect we broke his code?"

"Not that I can tell. I delivered seventeen messages yesterday."

"Anything interesting?"

"Eight ships entered Delaware Bay yesterday morning—mostly standard stuff. Your da might be interested in a load of mahogany that's coming in from Honduras on the *Righteous*. They're going to dock at the Bickley Wharf. There's two loads of firewood coming in. Oh, and there's a ship called the *Bridger* that had a crewman who came down with yellow fever. The captain agreed to put in at the Lazaretto Quarantine Station before he docks in Philadelphia. I passed those last two bits of intelligence on to Seamus."

Then Conor picked up the towel-covered snow for Rian to hold it to her face again. "What did Olivia say in her letter?"

The mention of Olivia Tucker sparked a trace of a thrill—a feeling so slight that Rian left it unacknowledged. Rian hadn't heard from Olivia, the daughter of slaveholders from Charleston, South Carolina, since she sailed home at the end of last summer's social season. Seven months ago, Rian, Olivia, and Conor had spirited Olivia's Mammy-Rose, the woman who had raised her, out of the Tuckers' summer house on Spruce Street and set her on her way to freedom.

"What letter?"

"It came in the mail yesterday while you were out saving Peach. I put it on the window sill next to the stairs."

Rian got up from the table, dashed to the parlor, retrieved the letter, and returned to the kitchen table. She broke the wax seal and started reading aloud.

February 28, 1837

Dear Rian (and Conor, if you are living at the Kriegers)

Our summer plans are now in place and I wanted you to be the first to know. We're coming early this year! Even before the Social Season begins!

My Grandma James died last October. You never met her. She lived in a big old mansion near the wharves on the Delaware and refused to leave even when the neighborhood turned a little dodgy. Mother and I are sailing to Philadelphia early to go through her possessions with Aunt Ida before they sell the house.

We're already booked to arrive in Philadelphia on the Carolina Princess on May 13. Isn't that exciting?

When we got home last August and news spread amongst the slaves that Mammy-Rose had run away, there were all sorts of celebrations, of course none that Mother or Papa were aware of and even I wasn't supposed to know about them. Now that Rose is gone, I don't have anyone I can talk to who trusts me, so my life has changed quite a bit.

Mother and Papa are both distraught that Rose self-emancipated last summer. Papa is taking extra special care that whatever slaves we bring this year will have family back at Long Pond, so they will be sure not to bolt. Papa has made it known he will whip anyone they ever loved if they try to escape. Mother and Papa know I hate it all. We argue about it a lot. I wish I could move into the Krieger home and have Conor's bedroom. (Sorry, Conor, if you are reading this. I know you need it more than I do.) So maybe I could move in with Uncle George and Aunt Ida (a distant second choice, because sympathies at Shippen House, including Cousin Trey, aren't much different from here).

Rian, I have missed you terribly. There is a schoolhouse nearby, but Mother won't let me go. Instead, I get tutored every day along with three other girls from the next farm over. They are all stupid and don't share my interests.

I miss you and hope we have more adventures when I get to Philadelphia, although maybe not as exciting as last year (or the year before).

~~With love,~~
Your friend,
Olivia Tucker

Conor chuckled when Rian finished reading the letter, including the cross-out. "Is that how girls write to each other?"

Rian shrugged. "How should I know? I don't have any girl friends."

"You don't have any boy friends either, except for me."

"That's not so. Trey Shippen is kind of a friend. And Tom Mott."

"You haven't spent time with Trey in months. He consorts with Billy Schiffler, who you hate. Tom Mott is your next-door neighbor, so he doesn't count. The problem with you is that you never want to play rounders[6] anymore, and you only want to work at the locomotive shop. Plus, you're bossy . . . So why do you think Olivia crossed out the *with love* part?"

"I don't know. I think she should have just left it in. It doesn't mean anything."

"Olivia loves you."

"No, she doesn't. She can't. Girls can't love girls. Everybody knows that."

* * * * *

· SEAMUS ·

James the maître d' held his slate before him as if he were Moses wielding the sacred tablets. "May I help you?" he asked Seamus and Siobhan, his practiced disdain just a hairbreadth under the surface.

Seamus squared his shoulders and smiled. "Ah, yes, me good man. Me name is Adrian Krieger. I have reserved your private room for me wife and me for a two o'clock dinner."

James consulted his slate and stole a glance at Siobhan's ringless fingers. "I'm sorry, I don't have a reservation in your name, Mr . . . uh, Krieger. I'm afraid we will not be able to accommodate you."

Uh-oh, thought Seamus, *I might have misjudged the situation here.* "I left a note at the front desk yesterday. Included a fifty-cent piece."

"Ah, so that explains it. There was a fifty-cent piece at my desk this morning, but no note. Here you go. Please accept the return of your money with my apologies. We are not able to accommodate you."

Seamus was embarrassed that his plan was collapsing in front of Siobhan. "But I sent the note . . ."

"And through an apparent miscommunication on our part, we will not be able to accommodate you."

---

6. Rounders was a ball and bat game that both kids and adults had played in Philadelphia since the days of William Penn. Historians consider it a precursor to baseball.

"I demand that me wife and I be seated." *You officious little guinea cock.*

The maître d' stiffened. "Apparently, you will not take this circumstance gracefully. The United States Hotel will not be able to accommodate you. You couldn't possibly be Herr Otto Krieger's brother Adrian because you are Irish. The United States Hotel does not serve Irish. In fact, we do not employ Irish. I am sure there are lesser establishments in the city that do, but I'm afraid that I don't know of any. Good day to you."

Humiliated, Seamus turned to go, but Siobhan wasn't having any of it. "You'll be sorry for this, you self-important little prick!"

The maître d' turned his attention back to his slate, then muttered, "And your outburst is exactly why your kind is not admitted to this dining room."

Seamus pulled the sputtering Siobhan out of the dining room's entry alcove, through the lobby, and then out of the hotel. Once back on the street, Siobhan, still hopping mad, said to Seamus, "What's the next best restaurant in the city?"

"I don't know. The Continental Hotel?"

"We're going there."

Jaysus, I screwed up. I should just cut me losses. "Siobhan, this didn't go the way I planned. I'm sorry. Let's just go back to Moya and find a grog shop. The food'll be passable."

"I did *not* stay in my Sunday best to go to a fooking grog shop." She turned on her heel and marched west on Chestnut. After five paces, she turned again. "Are you coming or not?"

Seamus reluctantly followed. *Sooner or later, her anger is going to find its way to me for putting us through this.*

"And let me do the talking," Siobhan said when he caught up to her.

The Continental Hotel's maître d' stood guard at his podium and greeted Siobhan as Seamus lingered five feet behind. "May I help you?"

"I hope so," said Siobhan with a flirtatious smile. "Our train on the *Philadelphia & Columbia* has been delayed," she said in perfectly accented King's English, "so my husband and I have two unexpected hours on our hands before we can board. We were hoping to take a leisurely meal to while the time. Might you have a private room available?"

The maître d' looked Siobhan up and down and brightened. "Well, we do have a room . . ." He consulted the ledger on his podium, then looked up at Siobhan with a smile. ". . . that is free until five, so we would be happy to accommodate you." He snapped his fingers and a waiter appeared. "David, please escort this couple to the Independence Room."

David led Siobhan and Seamus through the dining room, past men who paused to admire Siobhan, into a private room that could have seated ten, and held Siobhan's chair for her.

Seamus seated himself across the table and waited for David to leave. "Well, this is more like it. This is what I was hoping for. Now I'm glad we didn't get into that other place."

"Don't be all smiley yet, Seamus. I'm not letting you off the hook that easy. We were both humiliated back there. That was not the kind of memorable event you promised."

Here it comes, Seamus thought. He tried to stall the onslaught. "You told me a long time ago that you could speak the King's English if the situation called for it. I'm impressed. And you say your da can do the same thing?"

Siobhan refused to be distracted. "The problem with you, Seamus, is that you don't know who you are. You're an Irishman, pure and simple. That should be enough. But you've turned your back on your own kind. You work for the *ispinis.* You put out fires for the coloreds. You try to pretend to be something you're not to get into places you don't belong."

That got Seamus's dander up. "First of all, that's not how I look at it. I don't think there's any place I don't belong. Andy Jackson was president of the United States for eight years. He was just as poor as we were when he was little."

"Jackson's kin was Scots-Irish. They're Presbyterians. Just because they lived in Ulster for a few generations, it doesn't make them Irish. We're Irish through and through. There's a world of difference."

"Look, two years ago, I was a ditchdigger. Then Uncle Otto hired me to work in his shop because he knew he was going to grow his new business and the Irish were becoming such a force. He hired me *because* I was Irish, for Chrissakes." *If I can't get Siobhan to come over to my side on this, I'm gonna lose her.*

Siobhan leaned back in her chair. She played idly with her fork. "That was before I met you."

"Aye, and I wasn't there very long before I proved me worth in other ways. Jules Freeman and I were the only two in the whole fooking organization who could figure out how to put a modern factory together. Three factories, actually—Krieger Coach, Krieger Locomotive, and Krieger Rail. They made a special position for me: their production designer. I met regularly with William Strickland, the finest architect in Philadelphia, maybe even America. I made the factories hum."

"Yeah, you were a cocky one. Even then I wondered if you knew who you were."

Keep at it, Boyo. Maybe you can save the afternoon. "Now, most mornings, while Jules is starting up his own new business, I sit in for him as the Coach foreman. I can do all that, yet an officious little guinea cock won't let me eat in his fooking hotel? That makes me more than a little perturbed."

Siobhan stared at him for a few seconds. She leaned forward, put down her fork, and folded her hands in front of her. "I don't agree with my father about much, but I do agree with him on this. Aye, you've got a good job. You've got enough money in your pocket to take me out for a splendid meal. But you want to go out to places where we're not welcome. I'm not sure I want to be married to a man who pretends he's something he's not."

Shyte, Boyo, you're losing her. "I made a mistake. I figured me money would make me welcome."

"This is Philadelphia, the so-called City of Brotherly Love," Siobhan snorted. "Money's part of it, but so's who your father and grandfathers were. All of them, and you, were born in County Clare. No matter what you make of yourself, you'll still be bog Irish in that maître d's eyes. You'll never be welcome in the United States Hotel."

"Well, then maybe I should live someplace where I would be welcome. Where me Irish accent isn't held against me."

"And where the hell would that be?"

Siobhan's question caught Seamus up short. "I dunno, Siobhan. I dunno."

MONDAY, MARCH 6

· ADRIAN ·

Adrian Krieger stood with his hands in his pockets, watching his niece Rian and two other workers polish up *Number 6*, Krieger Locomotive's next delivery.

Number 6 was shaped like a giant cigar box with a boiler in the middle. Two stout pistons jutted upward at acute angles to directly power the drive wheels, thus making the big machine look like an ungainly mechanical grasshopper. For two years or so, major locomotive manufacturers in Philadelphia had cranked out "hoppers" and sold them all over the world.

Dressed in her shop clothes, Rian looked like what her neighbor Lucretia Mott called a ragamuffin. This morning, that description was reinforced by a swollen cheek, which Rian claimed came from a kicking horse.

Adrian had asked Rian to clean up *Number 6* before it was shipped. He had assigned Seamus's two new hires to work with her.

Harry Vogel saw what was going on and got all huffy. "That girl shouldn't be working in this factory. No female of any age should."

Adrian brushed Harry's ire aside. "Aw, let her have some fun. She put a lot of work into that locomotive."

"A lot of men worked on it. They should be up there," Harry fussed.

"The other men were busy. They didn't seem interested in working with Rian, so I put the new guys on it."

"I'm the foreman. I should be making those decisions."

"You weren't here, so I made the decision. And I should remind you that I own the shop."

Harry stomped off. Adrian chuckled to himself at this teapot's worth of tempest. He knew Harry disliked having Rian in his shop. On the contrary, Adrian loved her enthusiasm and dedication to improving her skills. *And it's also fun to tweak Harry's tail every once in a while . . . Where's my brother? He should be here by now.*

For the past year, it had been the custom for one brother or the other to "walk across the alley" to celebrate every completion. At Krieger Coach, that meant a fine horse-drawn carriage or a railroad car. At Krieger Locomotive, it was always the latest iteration of one of the finest steam engines in the world.

As if Adrian's silent question had summoned him, Otto Krieger appeared at Adrian's side, but he showed no sign of the good spirits that the occasion warranted.

Adrian gave his brother an affectionate pat on the back in greeting. "Welcome home. How was your trip?"

Otto barely looked at Adrian. "*Produktiv. Ich werde Ihnen später mehr darüber erzählen* [Productive. I can tell you more about it later]."

Adrian knew that Otto reverted to his native German when he was either among his own kind or too preoccupied to speak in English. He suspected it was the latter. Out of deference to his older brother's mood, he continued the conversation in German. "*Ich bin froh, dass du zurück bist* [I'm glad you're back]. I'm sure Rian is, too."

Otto grunted, giving no indication whether he agreed or disagreed. He jutted his chin toward the locomotive. "*Das ist also der letzte dieser Reihe* [So, this is the last of this line]?"

"Yes, we thought the hoppers would make us a bundle. Instead, we only made three of them."

Otto shook his head. "*Ich fand sie immer hässlich* [I always thought they were ugly]."

Adrian chuckled. "Yes, they're not beauties. Things changed."

Otto shrugged.

Something is wrong, Adrian thought to himself. *He is never this uninterested.* He persisted. "Every order seems to have different priorities. Faster for passengers. Heavier for freight. We got an inquiry yesterday for an engine that can make it around tight turns outside a mine. At this rate, we'll never be able to produce big numbers of the same low-cost engines we originally envisioned. Innovations and special demands come too quickly."

"Why do you care as long as you keep making a lot of money?"

"Otto, are you sure your trip went okay?"

"My trip went fine." He held out a letter to Adrian. "This was in the morning mail."

Adrian looked at the letter. The return address said *Frau Gilberts Schule für Junge Frauen. Lucerne, Schweiz* [Mrs. Gilbert's School for Young Women, Lucerne, Switzerland]. "So she got back to you. Will she take Rian now that she's old enough?"

"Read the last paragraph."

Adrian scanned down to the bottom of the letter and read aloud. "I am a little confused. My school never stopped taking eleven-year-olds. We have never placed advertisements in any Philadelphia newspapers. We have never had to advertise anywhere. I wrote two letters to that effect to you over a year ago. Someone is giving you false information."

Adrian handed the letter back to Otto. "I don't get it. What's going on?"

"I think my daughter pulled the wool over my eyes. I think she placed fake advertisements in the pennies that stated the wrong ages, assuming that I would read them and not send her away. I suspect she also intercepted Frau Gilbert's letters."

Adrian laughed, almost relishing his older brother's discomfort. "If she did that, it worked. Otto, it's no secret; Rian doesn't want to go to Switzerland. She wants to work in the Krieger factories. She should be running one of them someday. If you don't want her at Coach, I'll take her at Locomotive." *It is so much fun to yank my brother's chain. And so easy. But honestly, I would take Rian over here in a heartbeat. It's too bad you can't envision that sort of future for your daughter in your own shop, Brother.*

"You know that is not the life I want for her. She has developed too many bad habits. Yesterday, I learned that someone or some animal hit her in the face. She claims she got clipped by a horse, but I don't believe her. I think she got into another fight with one of the boys who tease her about the gap in her front teeth and she made up the story about the horse."

"Did you check with Jules? One of the men told me she was working on *Number 7* on Saturday, but then she dropped everything and left with him."

As if on cue, Jules Freeman joined them and lined up next to Otto. "Welcome back, Otto. I can't find Rian on our side of the alley. Is she over here?"

Otto jutted his chin toward the hopper just as Rian pointed to a spot that needed attention. "*Da oben* [Up there]. Giving orders to someone twice her age." He tsked and shook his head in disapproval. "Do you know anything about that bruise on her face?"

Jules responded in German. "Yeah, I'm sorry about that. It's partially my fault. I needed Rufus to ride to Trenton to get a part for a machine for Freeman Hydraulics. I asked Rian to go with him. It's a tad risky for a Black kid to be on the road alone. One of the horses kicked her. I think she's lucky it wasn't worse."

Otto pulled his pipe from his coat pocket, knocked it against a post, and tamped some new tobacco into the pipe. "This is actually good news. I am happy to hear this story from you since I am learning that I cannot trust my daughter. This is still a bit of a surprise, though. She knows her way around horses. She should never have allowed that to happen."

"I don't know about the particulars. Like I said, I wasn't there."

Otto took a loco-foco[7] out of its tin and struck it on a small piece of sandpaper. It sparked and sputtered into a flame. Otto held it to his pipe and took a few puffs. "Jules, I was just telling my brother that I have started corresponding again with that finishing school in Lucerne. This time I will not relent. Hopefully, a few years in Europe will smooth off some of her rough edges."

Jules assumed the same posture as the brothers, also putting his hands into his pockets. "Did you talk to her about it yet?"

"No, it's a fight I'm not looking forward to."

"Can I put in my two cents?"

Without taking his eyes off the activity on the new locomotive, Otto responded, "When have you ever not given me your two cents?"

"Don't send her off to Lucerne. Keep her here. Doing just what she's been doing for the past two years."

"She has developed bad habits in the two years she has worked in the factories. She needs an education, Jules. Some refinement."

"She's getting a better education working in the Krieger shops than she'll ever get in Europe."

"Not the kind of education she needs. Look at her. She's covered in tallow. She's bossy. She engages in fistfights. She lies. She swears like a sailor." Just then, Rian jumped four feet from the deck of *Number 6* to the floor. "She's impulsive."

And there goes my brother, the pot calling the kettle black, Adrian thought. "Impulsive. Where do you think she learned that? You are the most impulsive man I know." *Admittedly, Rian is a handful, but a finishing school in Switzerland will kill everything that makes Rian Rian. Otto, don't do this.* "Heinrich had her working on the formulas for piston length and diameter on a new freight engine."

"It's very kind of Heinrich Aldrich to assist in my daughter's education," Otto said with no enthusiasm.

"That wasn't my point. Rian found an error in Heinrich's calculations. She's not yet thirteen years old, and she found an error made by a man who virtually invented the modern steam locomotive. She was born to do this work."

---

7. Since 1834, friction matches called loco-focos had been manufactured in America.

"She's a girl. This isn't the life she should be leading."

My brother is so dense sometimes. He wished Dierdre had given him a boy, but he got a girl. Well, why not make the best of it? Accept Rian for who she is, not for what he thinks she should be. Oh, Dierdre, you could have talked sense into him. We miss you so much. Adrian pointed to *Number 7*, twenty yards away. "That locomotive down the way is going to be the first one ever built—by anyone in the world—in which the engineer will be in an enclosed cab. Whose idea do you think that was?"

Otto shrugged.

"Three months ago, I was meeting with the president of the *Utica & Schenectady Railroad*. We took a break to eat but kept on talking in the meeting room. He told me that the Erie Canal folks have bribed so many legislators that the New York State Assembly has passed laws restricting how his railway can operate. The only time he'll be able to make a profit is during the winter, when the canal is frozen over. Rian sat with us and listened to the conversation. She piped in . . ."

"My daughter had no business interjecting herself into your meeting."

Adrian held up his hands defensively. "Well, that may be true, but she suggested we build a compartment so the engineer doesn't freeze to death. The president loved the idea. He put down cash money before he left to nail down his place in the queue."

Jules jumped back in. "Otto, the reason I wanted Rian is because she's the most accomplished wheelwright we have. I need her to work on some spokes with me so we can stay on schedule."

"Jules, she is your best wheelwright because you've shifted our best men to other tasks. Besides, that is for carriages—yesterday's skill."

Jules was undeterred. "Carriages are still thirty percent of our business. And you're only partially right. We've got a labor shortage, at least skilled labor. But Rian's a hard worker. She has a fine eye for detail. And not just on the shop floor. It's the same for bookkeeping. Aaron Bassinger was laughing when he told me yesterday that if he dies, Rian should take his place keeping the books. She amazes him. She already understands how the money flows. She should be the one running Krieger Coach when you decide to give it up."

"First of all, I'm never going to give this up. Second, these days she seems to gravitate over to this side of the alley."

A sense of gratification for that last comment filled Adrian. *Otto, if you don't embrace her, I will.*

His brother wasn't finished. "Third, how could a woman survive in this world? It would never work."

Both Jules and Adrian hooted in derision.

"I'm a Black man," Jules said, stating the obvious. "I'm your foreman. I'm in charge of 25 whites. Both Irish and German. I'm one of a very few Black men in the city who has white men working under him."

"That's because you saved my life 17 years ago. You didn't start as my foreman. You joined me when I opened up my carriage shop. When I hired my first laborer, I just put you in charge of him. You had the brains to learn German when we hired the next man."

"But we've proved that a Black man can be in charge of whites and make it work."

Adrian picked up the thread. "And for the past year, we've added some of Seamus's Irish to our Germans. People said that wasn't going to work either. So why not Rian when she's old enough?"

The three men watched Rian direct the other two workers as they cleaned up around their worksite. Otto shook his head. "Those are both Seamus's new hires. They don't know the ropes yet."

Jules and Adrian both turned and stared at Otto. Their unspoken statement: *She's a twelve-year-old giving orders to two men, and they're doing what she's telling them to do.*

"No," Otto responded. "It's Switzerland. In four or five years, she'll come home, and we can marry her off to the son of some old Philadelphia money, and they will become a force in Philadelphia society."

Adrian wasn't particularly surprised by his brother's aspirations, but he was surprised to hear Otto blurt them out. He didn't share Otto's yearning to enter Philadelphia society's upper echelons. "I think there will be a lot of water under the bridge before that time comes, Brother."

Otto looked down the length of the factory. "Adrian, how many engines do you have in the queue?"

Ah, Otto, changing the subject because you know you've overexposed your ambitions. "Three in production right now. Contracts are out to be signed for another eight. Negotiations for maybe a dozen more."

"Jules, how about railway carriages?"

"Dozens. We can't make them fast enough."

Otto took a drag on his pipe. "Aaron says the same about steel rails. I think it's time we bought the property across the street. We're bursting at the seams."

"Are you sure that's a good idea, Brother? Remember what Nicholas Biddle said? The Specie Circular[8] is going to suck all the sound money out West. He says we should be building our cash reserves."

"That was six months ago. There's no sign that our business is slowing down. Arkansas joined the Union last year. Michigan just joined. As long as the U.S. keeps adding states, America will build railroads. Every week I get a letter of interest from South America or the Caribbean. I say it's time to take the risk. Jules, if you need Rian, now is the time to grab her. It looks like she is done giving orders to Seamus's Irish." Otto clapped Adrian on the back. "Congratulations on this new locomotive." Then he turned and strode toward the door to the alley between the two factories.

"Where are you going?" asked Adrian.

"To the Bank of Industry. I want to talk to Shippen about a loan for the property across the street."

Otto was through the door before Adrian had a chance to react. *My beloved brother. There's never been an impulsive decision that he didn't like. Gotta admit that some of them are worthy. But some of them were real stinkers. No telling which way this one's going to go.*

* * * * *

· JULES ·

Jules and Rian said not a word as they left the din of the locomotive factory, walked across the alley, and entered the slightly less noisy coach shop. He had to admit he was much more comfortable here. *Over there, it's all clang and clatter. Metal striking metal. The smell of the tallow that lubricates every moving part. Here? The machines cut wood, plane it, and shape it. Here I smell freshly cut walnut or pine or mahogany, each of which I can identify by smell alone as soon as I make my first cut.*

He was a bit disappointed that after spending so much time teaching Rian so many woodworking skills, she now gravitated to Krieger Locomotive. *At least*

---

8. In the preceding three decades, millions of acres of land had been stolen from Native American tribes by states along the American frontier. These states were anxious to sell the land to derive revenue. Most of the buyers were speculators, individuals with enough money to sit on their purchase for a few years before selling at a tidy profit.

Andrew Jackson didn't want people buying land with cheap money to build fortunes. In 1836, he issued the Specie Circular in an attempt to curb this land speculation. The Specie Circular declared that Western lands could be purchased only with specie (hard money) fully backed by either gold or silver. Nicholas Biddle, former head of the defunct Second Bank of the United States, denounced the Specie Circular and predicted that it would precipitate a depression.

I have the wisdom to accept it. Jesus, Otto, when will you wake up and appreciate your daughter for who she is?

Five minutes later, Jules and Rian sat shoulder to shoulder, each straddling a shaving horse. Jules used his feet to clamp down the end of an oak blank an inch square and eighteen inches long. He pulled his drawknife toward him along the blank, shaping the block of wood into what would shortly become a wagon wheel spoke. The stroke produced a ribbon of oak—*ah, that distinctive smell*—but he considered the drawknife somewhat of a gross instrument, designed to tear off a lot of material very quickly. Soon he would switch to a spokeshave to finish the work.

Jules had taught Rian how to shape spokes when she was ten years old, and now she was better at it than only a handful of workers at Krieger Coach. Although Jules had produced ten spokes in the time that Rian had produced eight, she made no attempt to race him. He kept track of her work and noted that her spokes rivaled his in quality and consistency.

Rian, normally talkative during these sessions, was quiet.

"How's your face?" he asked.

"It hurts. It was the first thing *Vater* asked me about when he got home yesterday."

"What did you tell him?"

"What we planned I should say. That Bonnie kicked me when Rufus and I went to Trenton to pick up a part for Freeman Hydraulics."

"Good. You should know that your daddy's talking about sending you off to that finishing school in Switzerland again."

"He can't make me go to Switzerland. I'll run away first." Rian said nothing more for perhaps a dozen strokes with her drawknife. "Jules, what did you do with Slatter?"

Jules shook his head. "He got away. The last I saw him, he was floating in the Delaware with an entire wagon wheel on his back. My best guess is that he died in the river."

Jules finished a spoke to his satisfaction and clamped down a new blank. *Rian insinuated herself into Railroad business seven months ago and got away with it. I should have stopped it right there. Instead, I used her as a conductor. Then, because of me, she was a hair away from witnessing a murder. That was my fault. I was in a jam and made a desperate decision. As it is, if Otto ever finds out that she's been conducting, there'll be hell to pay.* "I think it's time you took a break from Railroad business."

"Were we breaking the law or not?"

She isn't going to put this down. "We were breaking the law to interrupt someone who was also breaking the law. Like you, Conor, and Olivia broke the law seven months ago when you helped Rose escape from the Tucker house."

"Yeah, but there weren't guns involved. We were sneaky."

"Two nights ago, we didn't have the time to be sneaky."

"What happened to Peach?"

"Peach spent the whole day yesterday at our house. Maddie helped her memorize her fake emancipation papers again. I'll invoke Rule Number 1 for the rest of the story, but it's okay for you to know she is safely out of town." *A friend snuck her into the hold of a steamer to New Bedford this morning. The accommodations weren't much, but she'll only be down in the hold for two days. There's a stationmaster in New Bedford who will take care of her.* "Rian, just so we're clear, I want you to take a break from conducting."

Rian rubbed her cheek. "Did I make a mistake coming back to try to save Peach?"

"You put yourself in danger—more danger than a twelve-year-old should be in. You did the best you could with limited information and no time to think about it. Can I give you some advice?"

"Sure."

"Next time you're in a tough situation, don't rush into a decision. Follow Sun Tzu's advice. Surveil the enemy. Make a plan. Hatch the plan. You'll do fine."

"Can we talk about something else?"

"Happy to." Jules was relieved to change the subject. "So, did you read the pennies today?" For two years, since she had started working in the shops, Otto had demanded that she read four newspapers each day, two in English and two in German. He had asked Jules and others to quiz Rian about the day's events, and she readily went along with it.

"Yup. Mr. Foote wrote an article from Washington. About our new president."

"What did you think?"

"I don't think Mr. Van Buren will help us much. Not like Mr. Harrison would have."

"Why not?"

"Mr. Harrison wanted federal money for internal improvements, like canals and railroads. That would help us out. Mr. Van Buren doesn't seem to be in favor. I wish Mr. Harrison had won for another reason."

"What's that?"

"That carriage that Mr. Van Buren rode in. One of Mr. Van Buren's supporters made it. *Vater* says that if Mr. Harrison had won, Krieger Coach could have made his carriage. He says making a carriage out of wood from Old Ironsides was a stroke of genius. It would have guaranteed sales of our carriages for years. But he says we backed the wrong horse."

As had been so for the past two years, Jules was impressed by the sophistication of Rian's thinking. "Ah, we've already got more business than we can handle. What else did you read?"

"Mr. Jackson recognized Texas as an independent republic. I think that's going to vex Mexico more than a bit."

"I imagine you're correct, but tell me why you think so," *Otto asked me to engage in these sessions to teach her how to formulate opinions. No worries there. She has no shortage of opinions.*

"Texas used to belong to Mexico. Mexico abolished slavery in 1827. Now Americans are moving into Texas in droves, and they're bringing their slaves with them."

Jules sensed that Rian was happy they were no longer discussing the confrontation with Slatter. He shaved his spoke in silence.

"Lucretia says Mr. Van Buren will wait until the dust dies down and then ask Texas to become a state. That will mean another slave state."

Lucretia Mott was Rian's next-door neighbor. Much to the consternation of most people in Philadelphia, she spoke about the evils of slavery to "promiscuous" audiences—men and women sitting together—in Quaker meeting houses and abolitionist societies around Pennsylvania and as far away as Boston.

"What do you think?" Jules asked.

"Now that Michigan is a state, there's the same number of slave states as free states. I understand why the senators might want a balance, but I think the fewer slave states there are, the better."

"Good answer. What did you read in the German papers today?"

Rian released her spoke from the grip of the shaving horse and held it next to the first spoke she had shaped. Satisfied, she used her pocket knife to take a series of chips off the end of the mortise so excess glue would have a place to ooze. After clamping down a new blank, she pulled a good 15 times with the drawknife before she answered. "I stopped reading them. They don't even come close to telling the truth. Even when it's a paper that favors Mr. Harrison, they make the stuff up. It's all a pile of *scheisse.*"

Jules no longer chastised Rian when she used unladylike words. She had spent far too much time with the men on the shop floor and could swear effectively in

English and German. "Your father wants you to read the German papers so you can keep up with the language. There must have been something of interest."

Rian put down the drawknife, picked up the spokeshave, and worked on her spoke for at least a minute—so long that Jules wondered if she had heard him. Finally, she said, "Do you remember Halley's Comet?"

"Sure, but that was a year and a half ago."

"Well, *Das Philadelphische Patriot* had an article about it. A lot of people say that a comet is a bad omen—a sign that bad things are about to happen. Well, they figured a year and a half was long enough. Nothing really bad has happened."

"So, do you think comets can predict the future?"

Rian took four more strokes, and the wood ribbons fell into a growing pile on the floor. "I think it was a stupid article. The world is a big place. Bad stuff happens somewhere every day. I reckon those people who died in that earthquake in Galilee would say it was a bad omen, but we're doing pretty good right now, so it wasn't a bad omen for us. So no, I don't think anything can predict the future."

Jules smiled. "Phew, I guess that's one thing we don't have to worry about. What else did the *Patriot* have to say?"

Rian took a full minute to respond. "You don't want to know."

"What's up?"

"There was an article that mentioned the Krieger factories."

The news hit Jules with a dull sense of dread. "I hope it said nice things about us."

"It said that the Negroes and the Irish in Philadelphia are taking good jobs from deserving German workers."

Jules shook his head. "Seems to me that free Blacks and Irish are both clinging to the bottom rung of the ladder. I don't think we're much of a threat to the krautbreath workers." As soon as he used the pejorative for Germans, he regretted it, but Rian showed no offense.

"Yeah, well, the article named the three Krieger companies as a prime example. It didn't name you, but it said Blacks are in charge of whites at Krieger Coach, and that shouldn't be allowed. And all three companies are hiring Irish, too."

This time it was Jules who was silent.

"What's wrong?"

Jules finished one spoke and secured a new blank into the jaws of the shaving horse. "Aw, you know, just the old me, afraid we might be out on a limb.

Whenever the Black community in Philadelphia gets a little ahead of how the whites think we ought to be, somebody smacks us down."

"But you didn't let that feeling stop you from starting a new business."

"Well, it's barely started," he said. "But I suppose that will give the *Patriot* something else to write about." *Yeah, my business—Freeman Hydraulics, the first manufacturer of steam-driven fire pumps in Philadelphia. A Black-owned business that hires Blacks and sells fire pumps primarily to white fire companies. My business, where I can bring my children to work and they can have the same opportunities to learn and grow as this amazing young woman. This amazing young woman who, two days ago, I dragged into a situation that no twelve-year-old should have been involved in. If Otto ever finds out about this, he's going to kill me.*

* * * * *

· SEAMUS ·

Seamus Gallagher was standing at his shop desk in the Krieger Coach factory when his younger brother Logan ambled in. Seamus put down his pencil and contemplated the seventeen-year-old. "You're late for your first day of work."

Logan smiled shyly. "Late night at Clancy's."

"You told me you wanted this job, Logan. You said you were tired of digging ditches."

Logan squared his shoulders and looked Seamus in the eye. "Well, that's not entirely true, is it? You never worried about me digging ditches until you heard Hugh Callaghan asked me to be a lookout when the Ratters were doing a job. You're just jealous that they blackballed you but want me."

This might be a little harder than I thought. "No, I don't want you joining Moya because it's the wrong path. They beat up the coloreds. If business is slow, they start a fire so they can get paid to put it out. They control all the crime on the docks below Walnut Street."

"No Name swipes stuff off the docks from Walnut Street up. What's the difference?"

You overplayed your hand there, Boyo. "Okay, that part's true. I'll concede you that."

"Which makes you the most money? Working here, running No Name Fire Brigade, or swiping stuff off the docks?"

Seamus tried to stuff down his irritation. *He never really knuckles under. He just changes the subject.* "It depends. This work's steady. Uncle Otto pays me well. The Delaware was frozen solid for two months, so there wasn't anything on the docks to shake loose. The fire business can be lucrative if we're the first to get our hoses on a fire, but there haven't been many fires lately. So I guess you'd have to say this job is why you haven't woken up to a freezing-cold apartment all winter."

"Hugh Callaghan says I can make better money working for Moya."

"Look, right now you work sunup to sundown in a ditch. You don't know how to read. I convinced Uncle Otto to give you this job so you could leave that behind. If you're going to do that, you have to stop thinking like a ditchdigger. You can't just decide that you don't feel like working and not show up for work. From now on, it's ten hours a day, six days a week, same as I've been doing for the past two years. Make a choice, Logan. It's this, or turn around and walk out the door."

Logan looked around the cavernous shop. "So you designed all this?"

"Jules and I did."

"Jules. Your African friend."

Seamus stuffed down the impulse to smack his brother in the side of the head. "Who you will be taking orders from when he gets here."

"So he gets to come to work late?"

"Jules is starting up a new business of his own. Freeman Hydraulics. They make steam-powered fire pumps. He starts his day there, then comes here. There's lots of people rooting against him because he's a Black man."

"He'll probably fail."

Seamus ignored a second flash of irritation. *I feel like I'm playing rounders. We'll be here all day if I swing at every bad ball he bowls at me. Come on, Boyo, keep your eye on the ball.* "Jules and I didn't design the building. An architect named William Strickland did that."

"What about the steam engine that drives all the machinery?"

"Nope, not that. A man named Heinrich Aldrich did that."

"So, what did you design?"

"Everything else," Seamus said with more than a bit of pride. He pointed high above to a shaft close to the ceiling. "That shaft that runs overhead. The pulleys and belts. Half of the machines. I had a hand in all of it."

Logan kept his hands in his pockets and didn't comment.

"Before Uncle Otto hired me, Jules Freeman was the only non-German at Krieger Coach. Some of the Germans aren't enthusiastic about taking orders from a Black foreman, but Otto's a good boss, so they let it go. Otto takes heat from other business owners, too. He doesn't knuckle under to the pressure. Jules was with him when Krieger Coach was a two-man operation. When new men were hired—all Germans—Jules became their boss."

Seamus hooked his thumb toward himself. "I was the experiment. Otto wanted to see if Germans and Irish could mix."

"Did you have any trouble?"

"Oh, a tad. Nothing I couldn't handle. Otto knew that when Krieger Coach moved into the railroad rolling stock business, he would have to hire more workers, specifically Irish workers." *I think you're pulling him in, Boyo.*

"Where's your puppy dog?"

"What do you mean?"

"Your cousin Rian."

There he goes again, changing the subject. "She's your cousin, too. I haven't seen her today."

"So why don't you know where she is?"

"She kind of floats—looks for something that needs to be done, then does it. She could be somewhere here, or she could be across the alley in Krieger Locomotive."

"How does she get away with that? When we're digging ditches, the straw-boss barely gives us time to take a leak."

"Well, she's only paid for the bookkeeping. She doesn't get paid for her time on the shop floor, no matter what she's doing. I've never seen her take a break."

"You sound like you really like that little *ispini*."

Seamus let the *sausage* insult slide. "She's half Irish. You should give her some slack."

"Does she speak *Gaeilge*?"[9]

"Not to my knowledge."

"Does she speak German?"

"Yes."

"Then she's an *ispini*."

Seamus stopped and turned to Logan. "Look, maybe this isn't going to work out. I shouldn't have to convince you to take this job. But look at it this way: Two years ago, I was a ditchdigger, just like you are now. I worked sun-to-sun, and we went to bed hungry half the days. Now, Ma doesn't have to work in that filthy cotton mill. We've got a roof over our heads, meat for dinner most nights, and enough coal to keep the stove running all day. That could be your life, too, but only if you want it."

"So you run the shop while the African's away in the morning?"

Seamus smacked his brother hard on the back of the head. "One more time, and I'll kick you out of here meself. His name is Jules. He deserves to

---

9. Gaelic

be called Mr. Freeman but he doesn't demand it. But to answer your question, Jules is gone half the day getting his new business off the ground. That leaves me in charge, and lately, I've even been ordering new materials. Pretty remarkable, since two years ago I could barely add. It's time to decide. Are you going to take the job or not?"

"I'm not sure I feel good about taking orders from that . . . from Jules."

Why does this have to be so hard? Seamus grabbed his brother by the sleeve and started walking. "Come with me."

"Where are we going?"

"There's something across the alley I want you to see."

Still hanging onto Logan by the sleeve, Seamus led him out of Krieger Coach, across the alley, and into Krieger Locomotive. They walked through the cavernous, cacophonous building until they came upon a queue of three locomotives in various stages of completion. "I don't work this side of the alley much, but Uncle Adrian and I talk. Look at these locomotives. What do you see?"

Logan looked at the machines. "They're all different," he said without much enthusiasm.

"Exactly. A year ago, Adrian was sure he could keep costs down by mass-producing locomotives like *Number 6* right in front of you. He had a design he liked. He created patterns to produce the same model scores of times. Well, those patterns didn't do him much good because the other manufactories in Philadelphia kept improving their machines, just like we do. *Number 4*, the first hopper, was ahead of its time. Two companies, Baldwin and Eastwick & Harrison, had already built better machines before he started *Number 5*."

"So why are you showing me this?"

"This locomotive will be useful for a long time. The line is reliable and cheap to operate. But if Adrian made another one, no one would buy it."

"Why?"

"Because his competitors are already making better ones—bigger, faster, more reliable."

"So what is he going to do?"

Seamus looked at Logan, a smile on his face. "Innovate or die—with every machine. This is the business we're in, Logan. It's exciting to come to work every morning. We're part of an industry that is going to change America. It used to take five weeks to get to St. Louis. Because of the locomotives, railroad cars, and rails made right here in Philadelphia, you can now get there in three weeks. In another ten years, it will take a couple of days, and that's because of us. Don't you want to be a part of that?"

"So to be a part of this, I've got to take orders from . . . from a Black man?"

"Yes or no? I've wasted enough time on you already."

"Yes."

* * * * *

· OTTO ·

The clerk ushered Otto into George Shippen's office without an appointment. Shippen—a scion of old Philadelphia money—had increased his already considerable wealth by investing heavily in the banking and railroad industries. He conducted all his business from the same office, acting as Chairman of the Board of the four-year-old Bank of Industry and as the motivating force and significant stockholder in the *Mauch Chunk & Lehigh Railway* and the numerous corporate entities that made up the *Philadelphia, Wilmington & Baltimore Railroad Company*.

Shippen rose from his desk and greeted Otto with a firm handshake. "Krieger, it's been a while. I trust things are going well at the Krieger factories."

"Yes, exceedingly well, thank you. So well that I want to purchase the block of land across the street."

"Marvelous. Your timing is impeccable. I just received a new infusion of funds from the federal government. Treasury Secretary Woodbury seems to think there is more than enough activity in the region to justify having three Pet Banks in Philadelphia." Shippen leaned forward in a conspiratorial fashion. "It certainly doesn't hurt that all our board members are Democrats. Please, sit."

Otto took a seat in front of Shippen's desk. "I thought you did not like the term *Pet Bank*. President Jackson's detractors used it so viciously."

"Oh, I would never use the term publicly, but amongst my intimates, it is a bit of nomenclature we can all have a little chuckle over."

"I appreciate being described as part of your club, George. I do not know how you do it. You lined up with Andrew Jackson regarding monetary policy, yet you seem to be so well connected in Harrisburg when it comes to your railroads."

"Never let politics interfere with business, Krieger. Washington and Harrisburg both know that a man has to make a buck. For that matter, so do legislators in Dover and Annapolis. If I can make some of them rich along the way, all the better. Before we get down to business, how is your little experiment with your daughter going? Are you still educating her in your shop?"

"I would say there have been mixed results. Rian has demonstrated a wide range of abilities. She helps to keep the books for all three companies. She even grasps how the money flows. She spends afternoons in either the coach or the locomotive factory. She is adept at finding tasks that help the workers. I believe they appreciate her help."

"Sounds rather masculine to me. Are you sure all that thinking and hard labor are good for her over the long haul?"

"That is the other side of the coin. She is developing some bad habits. I intend to send her to the finishing school in Switzerland that your daughter attended."

"A wise decision. You will not be disappointed. Get her properly educated to become a helpmate to the right man, and the two of them will dominate Philadelphia society."

"You and I are in agreement on that, George. That is what I hope for." *Strange that I can admit this to Shippen, but when I blurted it out to my brother this morning, he scoffed at me.*

"Good. Now that all that is settled, let me call Schiffler in and we can talk turkey."

Shippen lifted a handbell off his desk and gave it a brief tinkle. His secretary entered the room seconds later.

"Johnny, please tell Mr. Schiffler that Mr. Krieger and I are ready for him."

"Certainly, sir," said Johnny. He turned and left the room, shutting the door behind him.

"Johnny is the son of Representative Bell of Chester County. It helps to have even the honest legislators indebted to you."

Moments later, Edward Schiffler, President of the Bank of Industry, entered the office carrying a ledger book. Otto didn't like him much because of his antipathy toward Negroes. And Irish. And poor people. Sadly, he was a necessary evil, as he made day-to-day decisions at the bank and recommendations to the board that they usually followed.

Schiffler greeted Otto with little enthusiasm.

Shippen leaned back in his chair and opened his arms to turn the floor over to Otto. "So, tell me about this land you've got your eye on."

"It has been just over a year since our move to the new factories. Krieger Coach and Krieger Locomotive are already bursting at the seams. It seems we got Krieger Rail right when we built it. They have no need to expand. I want to purchase the parcel across Buttonwood Street. It's smaller than the block we are on now, but I figure Krieger Coach could take the entire block and Krieger Locomotive could expand into the old Coach factory."

"A bold move," responded Shippen. "A move I applaud. I'm sure the board will not hesitate to loan you the money to purchase the parcel and build a new building."

Schiffler, who had been making a show of tamping tobacco into his pipe, finished his task. "I believe it is appropriate to demand additional collateral in this circumstance."

Otto turned to Schiffler. "What would that be?"

Schiffler crossed his legs to accommodate the ledger book, which he opened and ran his finger down a column. "I believe you own your house free and clear, Herr Krieger. You made your last payment on that a few months ago. Offering that up as security would assure me that you are confident in this expansion."

"My understanding about the value of owning a corporation is that it is supposed to protect me from this sort of personal risk."

Schiffler gave Otto a condescending smile. "Normally, that would be true, but in this case, you are expanding your business before your original loan is even remotely paid down. This additional collateral will be necessary, but I could do something here. I could recommend a lower interest rate to the loan committee if you fired that African foreman of yours. They have never much cottoned to your employment practices."

Otto's warrior nature prepared him for battle, but he restrained himself. "Krieger Coach is in the position it is today because of Jules Freeman. However, he works at Krieger Coach for only half of each day now. He has started his own business."

Schiffler smirked. "Oh, I heard about that. He's undercapitalized, from what I understand. I doubt he'll even last a year."

Shippen leaned forward. "We've discussed this before, Krieger. Your hiring practices are quite . . . progressive."

"Too progressive for my taste," interjected Schiffler. "I say fire the African even though you have a soft spot for him. Hire a good German whose loyalty isn't divided between his enterprise and yours. Someone who knows how to put in an honest day of labor. Do that, and I can almost guarantee the board will grant you a lower interest rate."

"And if I don't?"

Shippen stood, signaling an end to the meeting. "Krieger, you are one of our most valuable clients. I am sure you will get the loan, but I believe Schiffler is right. With an unreliable worker in a key position, the board will be unwilling to assume this greater risk without an increase in interest."

Schiffler also rose. "And you will have to use your house as collateral no matter what."

Otto reluctantly stood. "Then I will just have to eat the extra interest. Jules stays."

* * * * *

· RIAN ·

Rian and Jules had been working in comfortable silence for 20 minutes when Jules spotted Conor ambling through the shop and called him over. "Rian's got me back on schedule with the spokes." He handed Conor his draw-knife. "Here, you can finish my job. There's only two more to go." Then he left the two youngsters.

Conor readily settled onto the shaving horse. "Your da talked to me when we walked to work this morning. He didn't believe your story about getting kicked by the horse. He asked me what I knew, but I played dumb."

Rian barely paid attention to Conor. The impact of Jules's news about the finishing school started to sink in. "Yeah, well, my Switzerland problem just came back."

Conor took a couple of pulls with his spokeshave. "You knew you'd only delayed being sent there with that scheme of yours."

"But I figured that would give me enough time to prove my worth. I've done that. It's just that *Vater* doesn't see it."

"Or want to see it." Conor looked up from his work and saw a tall, gaunt man wearing a top hat stroll through the shop. "Who's that guy?"

"Oh my goodness, that's my Uncle Levi Howes."

"He doesn't look Irish."

"He's not. He's English. He was married to my Aunt Monika, *Vater*'s sister. I haven't seen him in a couple of years. As soon as I finish these last spokes, I'm gonna go find him. My cousin's probably with him."

"I thought all your cousins were on your mom's side."

"No. Aunt Monika came to America with my father and my two uncles."

"Where's she now?"

"She died when Jabez was born. He's two weeks older than me. Uncle Levi was away at sea and didn't know she had passed until his ship sailed back into Philadelphia weeks later. He asked Uncle Adrian and Aunt Mila to raise my cousin because he was a ship's officer."

"But now your cousin is with your uncle?"

"Yeah, 1832 was a bad year. Jabez and I were eight. We were best friends; we'd grown up together. We looked a lot alike, so we used to play tricks on my mother. We would switch clothes and see how long it took her to notice. Then Uncle Levi showed up. He'd just become captain of a new ship called the *Albatross*. He said Jabez was old enough to go off to sea with him. Uncle Adrian and Aunt Mila argued with him. They wanted Jabez to stay with them, but Uncle Levi took him anyway. Aunt Mila has never had any children of her own."

"Jaysus," said Conor.

"Then the cholera epidemic swept through Philadelphia and took my mother."

"And took me ma and me da."

"Like I said, it was a bad year."

Fifteen minutes later, Rian and Conor had finished all the wagon wheel spokes. "I'll see you later," said Rian. "I'm going to find Uncle Levi."

* * * * *

· ADRIAN ·

As the contractor closed the office door on his way out, Adrian threw his steel-tipped pen across the office. He instantly regretted it for fear of damaging the nib, but rather than rise and retrieve the pen, he sat and stewed.

He knows he's got me over a barrel. Krieger Locomotive was doing so well that Adrian and Mila had decided to add a library and parlor to their house. They had made a generous down payment to another contractor who started the project, opened their home to the elements, then fled from town with the down payment and another man's wife.

This new man had looked at the wreckage and quoted an outrageous price that Adrian knew he had to pay to make the problem disappear. *I hate being taken advantage of. Skilled artisans are scarce as hens' teeth. Everyone already has more work than they can handle.*

Adrian was still stewing when his brother-in-law Levi Howes knocked deferentially at his door and entered. A tall, gaunt individual of stern demeanor, Levi invariably dressed in a black frock coat and vest. He looked more like a fire-and-brimstone preacher than a lifelong seafarer, but any sailor who mistook Howes's aspect for weakness quickly found out differently. Levi's iron will was buttressed by his faith in God and a ruthless temperament.

Adrian put aside his personal construction problems to greet his rarely seen brother-in-law. "Levi, I didn't know the *Albatross* was in port. How is Jabez? Is he with you?"

"I am no longer the captain of the *Albatross*. I have a new ship now. Another Baltimore Clipper, faster than the *Albatross*. It is called the *Bridger*."

"And do you still make the run to China?"

Howes either didn't hear Adrian's question or didn't want to answer it. "I wonder if we could talk about Jabez."

Adrian waved toward a chair across from his desk. "You have my full attention, Levi. Please sit down and tell me what's on your mind."

"When Monika died, you and Mila were kind enough to take Jabez into your home until he was old enough to join me at sea."

You bastard, Adrian thought to himself. *That's not the way it was at all. You never told us you intended to take Jabez off to sea someday. We thought he was ours forever.* Adrian stuffed down this spasm of long-simmering ire and smiled. "We loved our eight years with Jabez. He is a wonderful boy." Sensing the reason for Levi's visit, he added, "We told you when you reclaimed Jabez that we would be happy to take him back if things didn't work out. That offer still stands, Levi."

Howes nodded only slightly. "It is not working out."

Adrian sat back in his chair, tented his fingers, and said nothing. *Mila is going to be overjoyed.*

Levi looked down at his hat. "Something has changed him. He used to be enthusiastic about his life at sea, our lives together. Everything. It didn't matter. He happily absorbed anything I could teach him: navigation, mathematics, history, the creatures of the sea. He was trustworthy. He ran errands for me on the ship and in port. He learned Spanish and Portuguese well enough to get on with crew members and ask directions in whatever port we were in. He loved climbing in the rigging. Perhaps loved being aloft best of all.

"Then, seemingly overnight, that changed. In the past few months, I feel I have lost him. And, truth be told, I've boxed myself into a corner. Now my last resort is the lash, and I have decided that I will not do that to my son, and I cannot countenance other crew observing me with a different set of standards for him. I am here to see if you will take him back."

I can't imagine he's changed so much. He will thrive in our household. "Mila and I will treat him just as we did before, as our son."

Levi nodded slightly, still looking at his hat. "I hoped you would say that."

At that moment, Rian entered the office. Levi demonstrated little warmth toward his niece.

He barely acknowledged her. He's so . . . cold, Adrian noted. "So, where is Jabez? When can we see him?"

"I'm not sure."

"What do you mean?"

"My son did not report to morning muster. I believe he has jumped ship."

* * * * *

· RIAN ·

Sparks Shot Tower, Philadelphia, Courtesy of Alamy.

Uncle Levi left to return to the Bridger at the Clapier & Cuthbert Pier, hoping that Jabez would be at the ship when he arrived.

Uncle Adrian left the shop to tell Aunt Mila the news. "Maybe Jabez headed to our house," he said as he put on his coat. *He looked pretty excited,* Rian thought.

Without Uncle Adrian to overrule him, Harry Vogel chased Rian out of the shop. She left, followed by derisive hoots from those who shared his sentiments.

Rian returned to the Krieger Coach office and told Jules about Jabez. "I'm going to go look for him."

"Plenty of work for you here," Jules ventured.

Rian ignored the offer, put on her coat, and headed for the door.

Jules called after her. "Be careful if you are heading to the waterfront."

Rian turned around and gave Jules a look. *Two days ago, you dragged me into a situation that got me smacked by a devil.* "Don't worry. You and I are always so careful."

As Jules had guessed, she headed straight for the waterfront. She walked the length of Water Street from Pine to Willow, stopping strangers to ask them if they'd seen a thirteen-year-old boy who looked like her with light brown hair, a gap between his two front teeth—just like her own—and about her height. No luck. She reversed her direction and worked her way south, poking her nose into every grog shop, barbershop, cigar store, fish house, warehouse, temperance house, and whorehouse for sixteen blocks. Still no luck.

The eight-year-old Jabez that Rian remembered was funny, adventurous, and full of mischief. *We did everything together. I hope I find him. I'm glad he's going to move back in with Uncle Adrian and Aunt Mila. Conor is going to love him. He never stops smiling.*

At Cedar Street, she turned toward the river to find the Clapier & Cuthbert Pier. Cedar dead-ended at the river, and just to her left, the raked lines of the *Bridger* drew her gaze. Baltimore Clippers were built for speed, with narrow hulls and massive sails. The *Bridger's* sails were furled, but the height of her two masts and breadth of her yards hinted at the amount of canvas she could put out. A crane raised a pallet loaded with burlap bags out of the hold. A crew of men on the pier pushed a wagon toward a warehouse. A sailor stood guard at the bottom of the gangway.

"I'm looking for Captain Howes," Rian announced.

The guard regarded Rian for many seconds before responding. "Captain's busy."

There's no way I'm getting past this guard. "Has Jabez Howes returned to the ship?"

"Not that I know of. Thought you was him for a minute. Would have got me a five-dollar gold piece."

Rian saw no reason to waste any more time. "Please let the captain know I'm looking for Jabez and haven't found him."

"And who might you be?"

"I'm Rian Krieger," she said over her shoulder.

She continued walking south along the wharves, almost to the Navy Yard. Looking to her right, she spied the tall shaft of the Sparks Shot Tower[10] over on John Street. Timmy Sparks's uncle owned the tower, the tallest structure in Philadelphia.

Jabez once climbed to the top of the tower with Timmy. He told me that he loved the view of the harbor from the top. He said he wanted to buy the tower and live up there when he grew up. Rian looked back up the length of Water Street. *I imagine Jabez could see the tower from the Bridger's pier.*

Rian turned right, away from the river. She had never walked through this section of town. Pleasing odors assaulted her. After passing a cigar factory, she smelled roasting coffee beans, raw hemp soon to be twisted into rope, and the rich, oily pungency of a saddlery.

One- and two-story industrial buildings that Rian assumed were used to finish and store the shot sat at the base of the tower. She found an unlocked door and entered.

A man wearing a leather apron turned from his task at the sound of Rian's entry. "I told you, I'm not hiring."

The man's statement took Rian aback a bit, but she forged ahead. "I'm not looking for a job. I'm looking for my cousin. I thought he might have stopped in here."

The man stared at her for a bit longer than the situation warranted. "We get all sorts of youngsters through here. Mostly runaways. They never last, though, once they get a taste of the stairs."

"This one would have arrived last night or perhaps this morning."

Then from behind him, Rian heard, "Hi, Eena."

---

10. Until the 1780s, spherical bullets, called *shot*, were cast in molds and frequently flawed. Then an Englishman named William Watts discovered that when molten lead was run through a copper sieve and dropped from a great height, by the time it hit a vat of cold water it had formed a perfect sphere. Watts built the world's first shot tower in England in 1782.

In 1808, responding to a scarcity of lead shot due to the American Embargo Act of 1807, Thomas Sparks and a Quaker named John Bishop borrowed heavily on Watt's ingenuity to build the first shot tower in America near the Philadelphia Navy Yard. The 150-foot tower was 3 feet in diameter at its base and 15 feet at its top. In the early years, the partners sold shot to hunters, but during the War of 1812 the tower supplied millions of musket balls to the American military. Bishop, uncomfortable that his factory was now used to support war, sold his share to Sparks. Thomas Sparks became rich.

Rian turned. Standing before her was an older Jabez, but Jabez for sure. Dressed in his "shore clothes"—a woolen suit complete with vest, collared shirt, and cravat—he looked like the son of a prosperous merchant. Had there been any doubt about his identity, when Jabez smiled, he revealed the gap between his front teeth, the trait shared by so many members of the Krieger family. *The same smile that I practice in the mirror every morning.*

And that fleeting smile brought her to her next thought: *My God, he still looks just like me. That is, when my face isn't so swollen.*

Rian moved in to give Jabez a hug. He accepted but he didn't hug her back. He just stood there, wooden, with his arms at his sides. Rian released him, stepped back, and looked at him again. That fleeting smile was long gone, with no hint that it would ever return.

* * * * *

Rian and Jabez stood outside the tower office. Rian pointed north toward the Clapier & Cuthbert Pier. "We should go. Your father's worried about you."

Jabez put his hands in his pockets, pivoted, and looked up at the tower. "Maybe. Not yet. I want to climb up there first. No one's working there today. The key's in the same hiding place as it was before. I already checked."

* * * * *

They climbed the circular stairs toward the top, their way occasionally punctuated by a patch of light from a window. Rian looked over the railing to peer into the dark abyss in the tower's center. "Hello . . . !" Her voice echoed off the brick walls and disappeared into the depths.

"Keep your voice down," barked Jabez. "Somebody might hear you." Then he changed his tone. "Wait 'til you see the view. We only snuck in here once before Captain took me off to sea."

He calls his father Captain. Sweating from climbing more than one hundred steps, Rian took off her frock coat.

The stairs ended at a room about fifteen feet in diameter and lit by four windows. A brick smelter dominated the rest of the floor. Various tongs and ladles hung on the walls.

Rian leaned over a railing surrounding a hole in the center of the room and peered back down into the tower's interior. Jabez started climbing a ladder to a hatch in the roof. "Don't even bother looking out the window. The view's better from outside."

Rian followed, shinnied herself onto the roof, and stood. The sunlight of a late-winter afternoon momentarily blinded her. The roof sloped gently, causing her to work her way cautiously to the rail at the edge. The city of Philadelphia, blanketed in a layer of haze, stretched out below. Smoke from thousands of chimneys rose straight up. Then, through some trick of the weather, the smoke diffused and reformed into a gauzy layer that Rian looked down upon. "Whoa," she said as her eyes adjusted to the light. It was much colder at this height than on the ground 150 feet below. She put her coat back on.

Rian had never observed anything from such a height before. She looked east across the Delaware River toward New Jersey. "You can see Camden from here!" Always with one hand on the rail, she walked around the roof. Less than a mile to the north lay the center of the city. Two miles to the west, she could make out the lazy Schuylkill River with its gritty coal docks. *And a few miles beyond where the Schuylkill meets the Delaware is where we freed Peach.* Just to the south stretched the Philadelphia Navy Yard with its massive ship houses, warehouses, and dry docks.

Jabez sat down, facing north. He dangled his legs over the roof's edge and draped his arms atop the horizontal board that would have been at knee height had he been standing. Rian sat down next to him and mimicked his posture. Before them lay three miles of wharves and piers that defined Philadelphia along the Delaware. The masts of hundreds of ships looked like a thinly forested hedgerow. Rian spotted the *Bridger* less than half a mile away.

"I'm never going back there," Jabez said.

"Where?"

"To the *Bridger*. Ever."

Rian pulled her gaze away from the magnificence of the Philadelphia waterfront and looked at Jabez. "Why?"

"I can't tell you."

"Why?"

Jabez started carving his initials into the lower railing with his pocket knife. "I don't want to talk about it."

"Now or never ever?"

"Never ever."

Rian fished out her pocket knife, unfolded it, and started carving her initials into the wood. "So if you aren't going back to the ship, what will you do? You can't live up here like you wanted to when you were eight."

Jabez brushed some wood slivers away from his newly carved initials. "Dunno. Maybe figure out how to get to St. Louis. Maybe New Orleans. Any place but on a ship."

"Uncle Adrian and Aunt Mila want you back. You should live with them for a while before you head out West."

"What do they want me for?"

Rian ran her fingers over her carved *R*. "You lived with them for eight years. They love you. They want you back. Your father already asked Uncle Adrian to take you back, and he said yes."

"He did? What would I do if I lived with them?"

"I don't know. Go to school, I guess. Or you could work at one of the Krieger factories like I do."

"I don't think I want to work in a factory."

Rian and Jabez talked, carved, and watched the traffic along the docks for half an hour before she convinced him to walk with her to Adrian and Mila's house. On the way there, they dropped a note with the guard at the Clapier & Cuthbert Pier telling Captain Howes what they were doing.

* * * * *

· OTTO ·

Levi Howes had been holding court at Otto's dinner table for half an hour. *He has not stopped talking since he entered my home,* Otto thought to himself. *Adrian described Levi as subdued and somber. That is not at all how I would describe him.*

As Adrian and Mila's house was in shambles from the botched construction project, Otto had volunteered to host a dinner celebrating both Jabez's return and his thirteenth birthday tomorrow. There were seven of them at the table: Otto, Rian, and Conor; his brother Adrian and sister-in-law Mila; and his brother-in-law Levi and his son Jabez.

Levi had barely taken a bite of his meal, even though the others were already half finished. "So I convinced my business partners that even though the *Albatross* had been built to ply the Atlantic coast between New York and Buenos Aires, she was perfectly designed to make a bigger profit by sailing to China."

Otto didn't much like his brother-in-law. He was too pious for Otto's liking. He was very filled with himself and considered life at sea to be man's greatest adventure. Still . . . *Levi is a sea captain at the peak of his profession. A captain's share of the profits from the China trade is astronomical. I am surprised that he's been nattering on for half an hour and has not yet mentioned his new ship.*

Levi continued his monologue. "The problem with the China trade is the pirates in the South China Sea. The British respond to the problem by arming their ships with cannons, which necessitates ships with a broader beam, which means they are incredibly slow. I said to my partners, 'We already own one of the fastest ships in the world. I'll outrun the pirates.' She's sleek as a thoroughbred."

Otto surveyed the table. *Rian is in a huff, although that is probably because I insisted that she wear a dress to dinner. She repeatedly touches her cheek and probes the swelling. I'm sorry I doubted her story. Jules confirmed that a horse kicked her, but it is not like her to allow that to happen. She's been around horses since she could walk.*

Levi filled the silence at the table for lack of competitors for the floor. "There was another problem, actually. There wasn't much that we produced that the Chinese wanted. Then we found out that they value a plant called ginseng because they think it can make them live longer. Well, it turns out the largest supply of ginseng outside of China is in the Appalachian Mountains, right in western Pennsylvania. I sold my first load of ginseng in Guangzhou for 250 times its weight in silver."

Adrian is nervous, Otto thought to himself. *Levi has not yet ceded responsibility for his son. Adrian is ready to assume it but marking time until Levi leaves in two days. Mila is overjoyed at the child's return, but she is still trying to figure out who this youngster has become during his five years at sea.*

"America's appetite for things the Chinese produce seems insatiable," Levi continued. "I buy tea, fireworks, silk, kites, fans, and porcelain. I saw a man of an obvious lower class when I walked here wearing trousers made of nankeen. I wouldn't be surprised if it were from a shipment I brought here two years ago."

And, of course, here is Jabez, the guest of honor. He is different from the eight-year-old that I remember. This one is subdued, and his eyes never meet mine. Otto had a difficult time taking his eyes off his nephew. Jabez and Rian were born three weeks apart; Rian was the daughter of a German/Irish union; Jabez was German from Otto's sister Monika and English from Levi. But they both took on the physical characteristics of the Krieger side of the family, most notably the gap between their front teeth. But the resemblance went further than that. Both had green eyes and light brown hair. Otto noted that the square jaw, high cheekbones, and slightly olive skin that didn't work well on his daughter made Jabez handsome. *Or at least he will be handsome someday. I'm afraid that is not my daughter's fate.*

"On my second and third trips to China, we shifted the *Albatross* to the opium trade. We purchased Turkish opium and smuggled it into Guangzhou. Even with bribes to the local officials, the profit is astronomical."

And there was something else. Something I am not proud of, but it is there. Of course I am happy for Adrian and Mila. They will do exactly what they told Levi they would do: care for Jabez like he was their own. But I must admit that sitting across the table, next to my daughter, is the son I always wanted.

Bang! Bang! Bang! Someone pounded hard on the front door.

Otto threw his napkin on the table and picked up one of the table's candelabras. "Please excuse me," he said to his dinner guests. "I will see who is intruding on our joyous occasion."

Otto opened the front door and stepped into the cold. He shut the door behind him and held the candelabra up high to find the slave catcher Austin T. Slatter. Otto disliked Slatter because of his profession and because he had made a point of harassing Jules.

"Get off my porch," growled Otto. "If you have business with me, make an appointment at the factory."

"I don't have business with you. I've got business with your African-loving daughter. I want to see her before the swelling goes down."

A sense of dread instantly replaced Otto's ire at Slatter for interrupting his evening. "What do you mean?"

"At three o'clock in the morning yesterday, I was accosted on the Chester Pike by four people. I suspect that three of them were Africans, and I know the other one was a kid. Your kid. They stole a slave that I was returning to her owner. While I was fighting off the Africans, your little brat tried to steal my horse and wagon and the slave girl. I slugged her in the face with the butt of my gun. Caught her good."

Panicked at the ramifications of all this information, Otto tried to parry Slatter's accusations. "There was barely any moon out the other night. You couldn't have seen a thing. Why do you think it was my daughter?"

"By the time they turned my horse loose and shackled me to my wagon, it was almost dawn. The three men were Africans. The kid was white. Your daughter's about the only white kid in Philadelphia who fraternizes with Africans. That's your doing, by the way."

"What do you want from me?"

"I want you to drag your brat out here. I won't touch her. Figure she and I are about even. But I want to confirm it was her by seeing the swelling on her face and I want her to tell me who she was with. Suspect I already know, but I want to hear it from her lips."

"Wait down on the walk. If you come back up on my porch, I'll throttle you."

* * * * *

Otto was reeling. The swelling on Rian's cheek proved that Slatter was telling the truth. *Or at least enough of the truth to put Rian on the Chester Pike in the early hours of Sunday morning.* Otto shook his head in astonishment and growing outrage. *Rian was with Jules when she was hurt. It happened while I was still in Harrisburg. Slatter's suspicions will be confirmed if I take Rian out on the porch. That is unacceptable.*

He returned to the dining room. Rian, Conor, and Jabez were missing. Adrian, Mila, and Levi looked up at him expectantly.

"Trouble?" asked Adrian.

"A bit. Where is Rian?"

"She peeked out the window, saw you were talking to someone, then she grabbed Jabez and Conor, and they ran upstairs."

Otto walked to the bottom of the stairs. "Rian, come down here right now."

No answer.

"Rian!"

Still no answer.

Candelabra in hand, Otto took the stairs two at a time, strode to Rian's bedroom door, and entered without knocking. Rian stared back at him in the candlelight, still in her dress, her swollen cheek now proof of her deception. She held the cap that she usually wore at the shop. Jabez, his cravat, vest, and shirt on the floor, was buttoning up the blouse Rian had worn to the shop today. Conor, who had been holding Jabez's jacket, let it drop to the floor.

Rian held her cap out to Jabez, and he put it on. Jabez, looking every bit like Otto's shop-daughter, turned to him with a tentative smile.

Otto felt like someone had punched him in the gut. The guilt on Rian's face confirmed his worst suspicions, but standing before him was a temporary way out of his immediate dilemma. He pointed to Rian. "Do not leave this room." He grabbed Jabez by the arm. "Do not say a word when we go outside."

Otto and Jabez descended the stairs, exited the front door, and stepped out onto the porch. Slatter waited on the walkway below.

Otto led Jabez to the top of the porch steps. "Stay right there." He descended two steps with the candelabra. "Which side of the face did you cuff the child on?"

"Left," said Slatter.

Otto illuminated the left side of Jabez's face with the candelabra. "Look, not a blemish."

Slatter stood on the walkway, his hands in his pockets, indicating no physical threat. "I was so sure," he stammered.

"Come closer. Take a closer look. Make sure you have no doubts. I never want to hear any of this nonsense about my daughter again." Otto tried to build as much indignation into his voice as he could, even though his world was collapsing as he spoke.

Slatter stepped forward. He examined both sides of Jabez's face. "I was so sure . . ." he repeated.

"Do you see anything? Even the smallest bruise?"

Slatter looked, then took a step back and shook his head.

Otto raised the candelabra so it cast more light on Slatter. "An apology is in order, sir."

Slatter stared back at Otto but said nothing. His mission thwarted, he turned to walk toward the street.

"Be gone now. And never try anything like this again."

Slatter stopped and slowly turned back toward Otto. "Really. Accuse your innocent daughter of doing something improper? I think you should examine her back. I'll bet there's a pretty good scar there somewhere. Ask her how she got that."

Otto turned and ushered Jabez Howes, a perfect shop-daughter impostor, back through the front door.

TUESDAY, MARCH 7

· JULES ·

Freeman Hydraulics occupied the buildings that had been Krieger Coach and Krieger Forge before the Krieger brothers transitioned to the railroad business and built much larger factories 12 blocks to the north. At 5:30 a.m., Jules was standing at his shop desk when Otto entered with Rian in tow.

"Hello, Boss. What brings you back to your old stomping ground?"

"This is not a social call. I assume we can speak in private in the old office."

"Sure. I might have to shoo some of my kids out, but yes, we can talk there."

Anticipating the storm about to descend, Jules led Otto and Rian to the office and opened the door for them. He had occasionally fantasized that Otto's first visit to Freeman Hydraulics would be a moment of personal triumph. *Otto, I would like you to meet my senior staff. You know Maddie, of course. She is teaching our daughter Martha how to keep Freeman Hydraulics's books, such as they are. This is Grace. She is fifteen. I have her researching every fire company in every city in the Northeast so that we can send them advertisements for our steam-driven pumps. Rufus is around here someplace. He should be assisting Grace, but I assume he has snuck off to work in the shop, which seems to be his preference. My children are here because you inspired me by bringing Rian into your shop when she was kicked out of school . . .*

"Martha, Grace," said Otto, interrupting Jules's fantasy, "it is good to see you again, but I have important business to discuss with your father. Could you please give us some privacy?"

Both girls looked at Jules for guidance. He gave them a nod. They got up from their desks and left the office, closing the door behind them.

Otto folded his arms in front of him. "Last night, I was confronted outside my home by Austin Slatter, who claimed that the bruise on my daughter's face was his doing—the result of an altercation on the Chester Pike before dawn on Sunday morning. That means that you and Rian have lied to me. I pressed Rian for more information. She refused to talk until you and she were together, but she promised to tell the truth. I want to know what you have to say for yourself."

Jules leaned into his desk. *Slatter's not dead*, Jules said to himself. *This moment is my fault.* "Otto, I didn't tell you because the fewer people who know about our activities, the better."

"Our? You include my twelve-year-old daughter in your 'activities,' which are apparently quite dangerous, not to mention illegal, and you choose not to tell me about it?"

"By *our*, I meant Maddie and me. We are stationmasters in the Underground Railroad."

"And apparently, you recruited Rian to help you in this pursuit."

Rian stepped forward. "That's not true. I figured out on my own that Jules and Maddie were harboring fugitive slaves. Then Olivia Tucker's mammy—her real name is Rose—she told Olivia she wanted to run away when the Tuckers brought her up North last summer. Olivia and I promised to help her, but we didn't know how, so we went to Jules."

Otto turned his attention—and his ire—to Rian. "So this was not a situation of helping a slave who had already run away. You instigated the act?"

Rian momentarily looked at her shoes, then returned her regard to her father. "Well, it was Rose's idea. Olivia and I helped."

"You were involved in that incident, Jules? The bully boys turned Moyamensing upside down looking for her. They ransacked your house along with half the Black houses in Moya."

Jules nodded. *Just let the storm come. You deserve it.*

Otto plowed on. "Rian, last night you showed me that scar on your back from Slatter's belt buckle. How did that happen?"

"Slatter was on guard at the Tucker house. The Tuckers knew Rose was planning to run away but didn't know when. They were fixing to catch anyone who tried to help her. I threw some horse manure at Slatter and he chased me. He had me trapped on the upper deck of an omnibus and caught me good with the belt buckle before I jumped to another omnibus."

"So, from the beginning of your involvement with Jules's Underground Railroad, you engaged in dangerous behavior. You taunted a violent man. You jumped from one omnibus to another. You broke the law by helping to steal another man's property."

"Otto," interjected Jules, "you have said yourself that you believe all slaves should be freed right now and their enslavers should not be compensated."

"What I believe and the law are two different things." Otto returned his attention to Rian. "So you distracted Slatter while Rose ran away. Who did she run away to?"

Rian hung her head. "*Vater*, Rule Number 1 in the Underground Railroad business is that if someone doesn't need to know something, you don't tell them."

"Tell me, Rian, and tell me now."

Rian sighed. "Conor was driving the transport wagon. We were bringing that beat-up old locomotive tender from Camden."

"Conor doesn't know how to drive a team of horses."

"Right. I was driving, but we had to make our plan up as we went along. He only had to make one turn and drive a couple of blocks. Conor, Olivia, and I had to hurry up the escape because Olivia's mother threw a fit when she heard Rose was planning to escape. She was going to take her back to Charleston the next day."

"So Conor drove a team of horses for the first time to aid in the escape? I know that you didn't take her to Jules's house. Where did you take her?"

"I can't say."

"Can't or won't?"

Jules interjected. "Otto, people who harbor self-emancipators do so at great risk. Their anonymity has to be protected. The fewer people who know their identities, the better."

"Yet somehow, you felt it was appropriate to let a twelve-year-old know these closely guarded secrets. How many times has Rian helped you spirit fugitives out of Philadelphia?"

"Six." Jules paused as the enormity of the number sunk in. "Boss, I'm sorry for involving Rian in my activities. I should never have gone along with it. I told her that I was stopping her activity after this last incident."

"*Vater*, this isn't fair," interjected Rian. "Jules didn't ask me to do anything I didn't want to do. Everyone I helped was escaping to freedom. I did what I did because it was the right thing."

Otto turned to Rian. "You are twelve years old . . ."

"I'll be thirteen in a couple of weeks . . ." Rian interrupted.

Jules winced. *That didn't help, Rian.*

"You have no idea what the right thing to do is!" Otto stormed. "And as for you, Jules, you persisted. On six occasions, you recruited her to escort fugitive slaves to some location outside of Philadelphia that you refuse to identify. Then three days ago you involved her in an action that turned violent. This

I cannot abide. Jules, as of this moment, you are no longer the foreman of Krieger Coach. I forbid you to have any further contact with my daughter. Rian, it is time for us to go."

* * * * *

· OTTO ·

That afternoon, Otto walked next door and knocked on Lucretia Mott's front door. He and the Motts had been neighbors for years, and he respected the Quakers' perspective on many things. Lucretia ushered him into the kitchen. "Otto, thee looks distressed. What can I do for thee?"

Otto sat down heavily at the kitchen table. "I need your advice, Lucretia. My daughter is out of control. Jules has cast a spell over her that I cannot abide."

Lucretia brought a teapot from the stove to the table and set a cup and saucer in front of Otto. "I had a PFASS[11] meeting with Maddie this afternoon. She told me a bit about your visit to Freeman Hydraulics."

Otto nodded, somewhat surprised that Lucretia was close enough to Maddie that Rian's Rule Number 1 didn't apply. "This morning, I learned that Jules and Maddie have harbored fugitive slaves for years. On top of that, Jules and his confederates have started to disrupt slave catchers that are returning escapees to their enslavers."

Lucretia took a sip of her tea, swallowed, and looked Otto in the eye. "Jules and Maddie are part of a network of people who help transport escapees to the North. Many pass through Philadelphia, but very few stay here. It is too close to home, and there are very real fears that they could be snatched off the streets and returned to their enslavers."

"You speak as if you know intimately about the Underground Railroad. Until today, for me it was a laudable pursuit, to be sure, but nothing that affected me personally. Now I find that my twelve-year-old daughter calls herself a conductor, and my former factory foreman and trusted friend is a stationmaster."

"Maddie told me you fired Jules."

Otto nodded. "He betrayed me. I fired Conor as soon as I got to my shop. That boy has lived with us on and off since he was eight years old. He showed no loyalty, no gratitude, for any kindness I have shown him."

"Otto, thee is in great distress. Please understand that the Underground Railroad is a very secretive business. The first rule in this grand conspiracy of

---

11. Philadelphia Female Anti-Slavery Society

ours is that if a man doesn't need to know something, he is not told. Thee wasn't told, not because thee wasn't trusted, but because if thee was asked questions, thee could tell with sincerity that thee knew nothing."

"You said 'this conspiracy of ours.' Did you know about Rian's actions?"

"Only the escape of the house slave, a woman named Rose. I sheltered her here in my house while the bully boys were looking for her in Moyamensing. Rian and Conor brought her here because they had no place else to go."

"You knew my daughter was involved in the Underground Railroad?"

"Just that one incident, Otto, but yes."

"And you didn't tell me."

"No, Otto."

"I think it is time for me to take my leave."

WEDNESDAY, MARCH 8

· SEAMUS ·

The day after Otto fired Jules, Seamus left the din of the shop floor and entered Otto's office. He found Otto sitting at his desk, writing a letter. "Rian said you wanted to see me. Jules never showed up yesterday. Otto, what's going on? People say he quit."

Otto looked up from his desk. "Yes, he quit. He wants to devote all his time to Freeman Hydraulics. You have been running the shop in the mornings. I would like you to become a full-time foreman."

Seamus sat down heavily in the chair at Rian's bookkeeping desk. "Now that's a bit of a surprise. Two weeks ago, Jules told me he was happy to have this job because things were slow to take off at Freeman Hydraulics."

Otto went back to writing his letter. "I guess things have changed. I want you to take his place."

Something's wrong here. If he's giving me Jules's old job, he should be all smiley about it. "So, your Black foreman leaves, and you replace him with your Irish nephew. Think that's going to go over very well with your Germans?"

Otto continued writing. He didn't look up at Seamus. "You have established yourself with the men. You understand how the work flows. You identify little problems before they become big problems. I believe you are up to the task."

"Oh, I'm not worried about me, but I anticipate some problems with the men."

"Then you will just have to figure out how to handle it, the same way that Jules did."

What am I not getting here? "Uncle, why did Jules really leave?"

Otto put down his pen and pinched the bridge of his nose. "He involved Rian in dangerous illegal activities. Activities that he chose not to tell me about."

"Hmm, I believe it was Rian who initiated that little escapade. She swiped Rose without anyone's help and then dragged Jules into it."

Otto looked up at Seamus for the first time. "You knew about that?"

Uh-oh. "Not beforehand. I just put together the last piece to get Rose out of town."

"And you didn't see fit to tell me that my impressionable daughter had committed a crime?"

"Well, no, not when you put it like that. But it didn't seem to be something smart to talk about. It was already over and done with. Are you saying that Rian continued with this Underground Railroad stuff?"

Otto rose from his desk. "Seamus, I just fired my most trusted employee and oldest friend in America because he dragged Rian into dangerous activities and lied to me about it. Now I find you knew about these activities and chose not to tell me. Two minutes ago, I told you I wanted to promote you to foreman. Now I'm telling you that you are fired. Good day."

Oh my God, Siobhan is either going to kill me or laugh at me. "Otto, who will run the shop if Jules and I aren't doing it?"

"Ernst Winther can handle it."

"Uncle, Ernst is a good guy, but he can't even run the carriage side of the business without running out of materials he should have ordered a month ago. He doesn't get along so good with the Irish. They will be gone in a week."

"Then so be it. And we will declare my little experiment to have Irish working with Germans a failure."

"Otto, I understand you're angry, but now you're making decisions that will kill your business. Don't do this."

"Good day, Seamus. I'm sorry this didn't work out."

Thursday, April 20

· SEAMUS ·

Seamus sat down next to Conor at their usual table in the back of McSweeney's Saloon and placed two mugs of coffee between them. They had met there every afternoon since Otto fired them both from Krieger Coach six weeks ago. "Good afternoon, Partner. Whataya got for me?"

Conor sifted through a stack of messages from the Merchants' Exchange Building. "Not much. Only three ships entered Delaware Bay this morning. Dispatcher sent me out with the list to all the consortium members."

"Anything interesting?"

"The brig *Charlotte* is coming in from Mexico. She's loaded with silver."

Seamus pulled out the morning edition of the *Philadelphia Independent*. He consulted the Harbor List—*which always contains news of arrivals from the day before, a day after Conor and I learn about them.* "The *Charlotte* generally ties up down in Hugh's territory. We'll pass that information on to him, even though it won't do him any good. Too many guards on the silver ships. What else?"

Conor shifted to the next paper. "A load of spermaceti oil on the *Cincinnatus* out of New Bedford. Harbormaster hasn't decided where she's gonna tie up yet."

"That might be interesting—the price of whale oil is sky-high right now. I've been holding onto a few casks I stole a couple of months ago. I'll unload it tomorrow morning before the price drops."

Conor reacted to Seamus's wheeling and dealing with a faint smile. "The brig *Commerce* has a bunch of stuff from Ireland, mostly linen."

Seamus took a sip of his coffee. "The impatient class will love that. The only way our people will see fine Irish linen is when they wash it behind the richies' houses."

"So the only thing I pass on to Hugh is about the silver?"

"Yes. Just tell him that's all the information I gave you. He doesn't suspect you're the source of all this intelligence you've been passing off to him?"

Conor stuffed the sheets of paper back in his pocket. "Nope, he thinks I'm just your delivery boy. Every once in a while, he asks me where you get your information, but I tell him I have no idea. Any luck with a new job yet?"

"Nope, nothing. How about you?"

"I'm scraping by okay. I help out Jules at Freeman Hydraulics most mornings because he lets me sleep in his office. I run messages in the afternoons. Then I come here to work in the kitchen. Braden makes me something to eat most evenings."

"You're a resourceful one, Conor. I never had any doubt you would land on your feet."

"I'd rather be working at Krieger Coach. Do you think Otto will ever take us back?"

"I figured he'd take us back as soon as he cooled off. Guess he's not as forgiving as I thought."

"Seamus, the dispatcher says he wants to give me more work, but not running messages from the telegraph towers. These are just messages from the Merchants' Exchange to businessmen all over town. It'd be in the mornings. Do you think I should take it?"

"If Otto hasn't taken us back by this time, I don't think he's gonna. Yeah, I think you should take it."

MONDAY, MAY 15

· RIAN ·

Rian closed the accounts book and got up from her desk. "Father, I'm going to take the afternoon off."

She pointedly didn't use the term *Vater*. *Vater* would have been too endearing, a sign of affection she had withheld from Otto since he fired Jules, Seamus, and Conor. *For ten weeks, I've finished my bookkeeping as soon as possible so I don't have to talk to him in the office. I spend most of the day in one of the shops, mainly across the alley at Krieger Locomotive. I play violin with him only in the evenings when he asks me, and even then, sometimes I say no.*

By this time, her father was used to her smoldering "business only" demeanor. He took off his reading glasses and looked at her. "I do not pay you for your afternoon work, so you may do as you please. How did your bookkeeping session with Jabez go this morning?"

"Cousin Jabez never showed." *He's supposed to put in a full day of work at Krieger Locomotive but rarely comes in on time. He doesn't give a shit about bookkeeping. I have to go over the same things again and again. He's sloppy.*

"Maybe he was out in the locomotive shop."

"He hates Krieger Locomotive more than bookkeeping."

"Perhaps I should spend some time with him. Maybe he would prefer things over on this side of the alley."

"Maybe." *Good luck with that. Jabez has been a problem since he moved back in with Uncle Adrian and Aunt Mila. Aaron Bassinger refused to hold bookkeeping tutoring sessions after the third time he didn't show up for a lesson. That's how he got kicked down to me. Uncle Adrian has already thrown up his hands because he has found him smoking out in the alley so many times. And worse yet, he often has talked another worker into going out there with him. If he's smoking cigarettes at age thirteen, what will he be doing when he's seventeen?*

"Since you are leaving early, may I ask what you are doing?"

"Olivia Tucker arrived from Charleston yesterday. We haven't seen each other since we helped her mammy escape." *Since you know about that now, and you've fired everyone who knew it before you did, I might as well throw it in your face.* "She and Conor and I are probably going to walk around the reservoir, or maybe we'll cross the bridge and watch the workers install new Krieger rail at the Belmont Incline."[12]

"I have lost track of what is happening at Krieger Rail these days. Tell me about the new rail."

Rian allowed a bubble of ire to break to the surface, and it manifested in her icy response. "Aaron showed a sample of his steel T-rail to the president of the *Philadelphia & Columbia Railroad* a couple of months ago. The *P&C* bought enough rail to replace all the strap-iron track up to the top of the Incline. If it performs well, they'll replace the remaining 79 miles of track." *How can you not know about this? The letter K for Krieger is stamped on every rail that goes out the door.*

"I am surprised I did not know about this."

"You've been away a lot." *You were in Ohio, and you made a huge sale of rolling stock, but I'm not going to say that out loud because I don't want to give you one fooking bit of praise. Ever.*

"I should go over and congratulate Aaron."

"I doubt you'll find him in the office. He's been across the river overseeing the installation for the past week until he's satisfied the *P&C* crews know what they are doing."

* * * * *

· MADDIE ·

Maddie returned to the Freeman Hydraulics factory after walking payments to their suppliers to save money on postage. As she passed through the shop, she glanced into an ash can and saw *Das Philadelphische Patriot*, the notoriously anti-Black, anti-Catholic, and anti-Irish German language penny newspaper. *Who in the shop is reading that rag? The only person here who knows German is Jules.*

She fished the paper out of the ash can. Scanning down the front of the paper, amidst the German gobbledygook, she saw the words *Jules Freeman* and *Freeman Hydraulics.*

---

12. On the west side of the Schuylkill River, the *Philadelphia & Columbia Railroad* tracks climbed the problematic Belmont Incline, a rise of 187 feet in just half a mile. Too steep for most steam locomotives of the era, trains were connected to a cable and hauled to the top by a sixty-horsepower steam engine installed on the plateau above.

Those bastards, she said to herself. Then, farther down the column, she spotted her father's name: Hercules Angell. *Oh sweet Jesus,* Maddie said to herself. She entered the office on the fly. "What's this ridiculous . . . ?" but then looked over at Jules's desk. Her husband was leaning back in his chair with his head facing the office ceiling, mouth agape, sound asleep and snoring.

Jules had to make a conductor-run to Robert Purvis's farm the previous night. *He returned home as dawn broke, ate his breakfast, and came straight to work. The man is running himself ragged*, Maddie said to herself. As she often did, she looked at her husband, and a flood of memories washed over her.

* * * * *

She was twenty years old. Her father, one of the most prominent caterers in Philadelphia, rarely had bookings on Mondays, so the Angells generally ate their Sunday dinners a day later. Maddie brought three bowls to the dinner table, placed them before her father, and sat at her usual spot. "Mother says to help ourselves to bread. We'll say grace when she joins us."

Hercules Angell cut a slice of the steaming hot bread for himself, placed it on his bread plate, and handed the small cutting board to his daughter. "How was your morning at the Aid Society today, Maddie?"

"Slow. I had only one customer."

"Interesting?"

"Different. A runaway from Calvert County."

Hercules picked up his table knife, shaved a ribbon of butter from a small crock, and buttered his bread. "Doesn't sound very different to me. Fugitive slaves are no rarity in Philadelphia. I hope you encouraged him to keep on running."

The clunk of a ladle against a tureen suggested that Maddie's mother was wrapping up in the kitchen and dinner was about to be served. *Mama doesn't need any more help.* "No, this one doesn't seem inclined to run any farther. He already has a skill. He was sold from his original circumstance to a new enslaver when he was twelve. That man trained him to be a carpenter. Not just a nail banger. Finish work. Fine craftsmanship. His enslaver's wife taught him how to read and write and do his figures."

"Doesn't sound like your typical field hand, I'll grant you that."

"He kept spouting Ashanti proverbs that his mother used to impart before he was sold. This man is one generation away from Africa. He's proud of his blackness, although he's lighter than we are. Reminds me of you, actually."

"So, he's good-looking?"

Maddie was a bit flustered by her father's humor. "No. Well, yes, he is, but that's not what I'm talking about. I would describe him as wise."

"Interesting term. Do you mean confident?"

"No, on the contrary, he's quite skittish. But he's wise because he knows the magnitude of what he doesn't know."

"How old is he?"

"He doesn't know. Probably a little older than me."

"How long has he been in Philadelphia?"

"Less than a month, I think. Already has a job. A place to stay."

"So why did he come to the Aid Society?"

"That's just it. He came to volunteer. He wanted to help teach our brethren to read and write."

Her father frowned as he pondered this. "What did you tell him?"

"I said yes, of course. But then the conversation changed a bit. He noted that I spoke the King's English. He said he wants to learn to speak that way, too."

"And what did you say to that?"

"Well, I said yes. I was delighted, really."

"Watch out, Maddie. I don't want you falling for some fast-talking flim-flammer who thinks he can improve his life by marrying into our family."

"Don't worry about me, Father. I'm not interested in him that way. He's pretty rough around the edges."

"What's his name?"

"Jules. Jules Taney, but he's thinking of changing his slave name."

"To what?"

"To Freeman."

Her father took a sip of coffee, then placed his cup back in its saucer. "A bit trite, isn't it? Couldn't he pick something a little more original? There must be a hundred Freemans in this city."

"Well, I didn't come right out and say that, but I implied it when we were talking about it. He said, 'Don't light a fire when you are hiding.' That was one of his mother's proverbs. He doesn't want to attract much attention to himself. I guess being one of a hundred Freemans has its appeal."

"I don't know about this guy, Maddie. Asking you to tutor him to speak well? Are you sure he's not just interested in getting under your skirt?"

Maddie's mother entered the dining room just in time to overhear her husband's comment. "Hercules, do not talk like that at the dinner table." She placed the tureen of beef stew in front of her husband.

Maddie gave her mother a slight bow of appreciation. "As I said, Father, I am not interested in him in that way."

"And what do you think he thinks?"

Maddie reached into the pocket of her dress and took out a folded piece of paper. "Oh, he might disagree. He quoted another one of his mother's Ashanti proverbs. I wrote it down." She held the paper up to the candlelight. "If you understand the beginning well, the end will not trouble you."

"What is that supposed to mean?"

"I think it means that if you start something well, it will end well."

Maddie's mother sat down opposite her husband. "And what is it that this Jules Taney, soon to be Jules Freeman, is starting?"

"At the time, I thought it was our English lessons. Now that I hear myself explain it all to you two, I'm not so sure." Maddie felt the blood rush to her cheeks.

* * * * *

Jules's snoring became so loud that he woke himself up. He sat foggily in his chair.

Maddie, at her desk, gave him a few moments before she said, "Husband, I can run things here for a few hours. Why don't you go back home and get some proper sleep?"

"No . . . Maybe . . . We'll see . . . You were working on a projection when I dozed off. What did you figure out?"

"You've been asleep for a while. I figured some things out and then delivered three payments to our noisiest creditors. We'll make payroll this week. We'll be good for a few more weeks when we receive the final payment for the pump we sold to the hose company in Syracuse. Herr Busch said he would be happy to sell us a steam riveter, but then he found out we are a Black-owned business. Now he will do it only with cash up front."

Maddie held the newspaper up so Jules could see it. "I wondered why the color of our skin suddenly became so important to him, but then I saw this in the ash can. What does it say?"

Jules waved his hand as if the article should be of no concern to Maddie. "We knew that would come sooner or later. It's an article about Black-owned businesses in Philadelphia. It names Freeman Hydraulics as an example of an outfit that will probably go out of business."

"Not if I have anything to say about it."

"If we do, it will be because we started on a shoestring. He implies that I'm mismanaging things."

"And my father, why is his name in the paper?"

"A Black man who is offering a service to whites. Good white people should hire white caterers."

"Not if they want the best. Ugh. It makes me want to strangle someone."

"What are the kids doing?"

"Martha took the other half of my payments and is delivering them around town. Rufus is working on a new design and worrying that his father's business might go under. Jules, your daughter is seventeen and your son is thirteen. Is this what we wanted for them when we started this business?"

"The problem-solving? The creativity? The skills? Yes. The pressure? Not at all. You don't want to fold, do you?"

"No. I don't want to give the editor of *Das Philadelphische Patriot* that pleasure. But I worry about you and the children. When we started Freeman Hydraulics, you went down to part-time at Krieger Coach, but Otto still paid you very well. Now, without that income, every month is a squeaker. Plus, we put up self-emancipators at a moment's notice, and then you leave at the drop of a hat because we can't find a conductor. It's becoming overwhelming."

"My mother used to say, 'a worthy cause is worth pursuing to the end.' My business, my family, and the Underground Railroad. All worthy pursuits. We can get through this."

Maddie shook her head. "We have been married for 18 years, and you still spout Ashanti proverbs that I've never heard. How do you remember them all?"

Jules smiled. "I don't know. They just come to me. My mother's greatest gift to me. You know, I can barely remember what she looks like?" Jules stared at his desk for a long moment. "What are the problems that need to be solved immediately?"

"Immediately? We need that steam-riveting machine. We need that payment from Syracuse. I need to strangle someone at this ridiculous newspaper."

Jules chuckled. "Let's see what we can do about the first two."

* * * * *

· RIAN ·

Rian stopped by her house to spruce herself up for her meeting with Olivia. She sponged off using the washbowl in her bedroom, changed into clean pants and a shirt she never wore to the shop, and enhanced her costume slightly with a vest. Mid-May weather was still unpredictable, so she shrugged into a lightweight double-breasted frock coat she had bought at a used clothing store. She folded her long brown hair into her flat cap as she descended the stairs.

It took her 15 minutes to walk to Spruce Street. She knocked on the front door of the Tucker summer home, a mansion that the Tuckers had made considerably larger after they bought it two years ago.

Rian admitted to herself that she was nervous. *Mrs. Tucker doesn't like me because of the way I dress. And my best friend is Irish. And trouble seems to find the three of us when we're together. Okay, that's a lot of things.*

A woman opened the door, which Rian should have known was going to happen but was unprepared for. *A slave. I am standing on the porch of a white man who owns Black people. As a white, I don't have to smile at this woman. I don't have to say thank you because she has no option but to do what she is told. No wonder Olivia hates her father.* Rian smiled at the woman. "My name is Rian Krieger. I am here to see Olivia."

The woman looked Rian right in the eye and made just the slightest of bows. "Please come in. I will get Miss Olivia directly."

"Thank you," said Rian, making her own protest to the slave system that was embodied in this one person whose name Rian didn't know and maybe would never know. *But maybe you do have some choices. You left me standing here in the vestibule rather than showing me to a parlor. I'm only thirteen, but I know that's a sign of disrespect.*

Rian eyed the vestibule. It was two stories tall. Two curved staircases ascended along the far walls. A statue—*Ceres, perhaps?*—stood directly opposite her.

Rather than Olivia, her mother appeared. *Ah, now I understand why I've been left in the vestibule.*

Penelope Tucker greeted Rian with a forced smile. "Miss Krieger, it's been a while," she said in a Philadelphia accent flavored by years of living in South Carolina. "I see your taste in clothing hasn't changed."

That didn't take long. Rian chose not to take the bait. "Good morning, Mrs. Tucker. Yes, since last August. I hope your voyage was smooth."

"It was, thank you. Usually I would expect Olivia's cousin Trey to accompany her around town, but of course he is in school. I am surprised you aren't as well."

You know darn well that I got kicked out of my old school. "No, ma'am, I'm getting a pretty good education in my father's shop."

"I can only imagine," Mrs. Tucker said, her voice dripping with disdain. "I would have expected your father to have found a tutor for you by now rather than having you ensconced in the trades."

"I am being tutored. Three times a week in French, Latin, and Greek. Is that a statue of Ceres, by the way? It's very beautiful."

Mrs. Tucker looked a bit surprised at Rian's question. "Yes, it is. Mr. Tucker and I purchased her in Rome when we were there three years ago. She inspired the look of this vestibule when we bought the house and decided to remodel. So, you are tutored in French and the classics. Nothing else?"

You're doing your best to make me uncomfortable, but I won't let that happen. "The rest of the time, my responsibilities at my father's factories keep me pretty busy."

"Your responsibilities?"

"Yes, I keep the books for all three factories."

"But how old are you?"

"I turned thirteen in March, the same as Olivia. I learned bookkeeping from a brilliant teacher named Aaron Bassinger two years ago, but now his job as president of Krieger Rail has kept him so busy that I do most of the work."

"I am surprised that your father and his partners are willing to put so much responsibility into the hands of one so young."

Rian shrugged. "People say I've always acted a lot older than I am. Most afternoons I work in one of the shops. I've learned a lot there, as well."

"So young to be working amongst all that machinery . . ."

"Eight-year-olds are working in the mines of Mauch Chunk. Same in the mills along the Schuylkill. I think I'm pretty lucky to be doing something I love."

Mrs. Tucker folded her arms in front of her. She said nothing for a moment.

That's because none of your barbs have hit home.

"Olivia tells me that you are going to go for a walk around the reservoir."

"Yes, ma'am." *Or go watch the rail installation. Since Olivia didn't mention that to you, I'll keep it under my hat.*

"And will anyone else be joining you?"

She's really asking, "Will your Irish friend Conor McGuire be joining you?" Yes. He's waiting for us in Washington Square because he knows he isn't welcome here. "No ma'am, just us."

"And what will you do about lunch? Would you care to eat with us before you go?"

"We call the noontime meal *dinner* here in Philadelphia. We'll probably buy a meat pie from a cart vendor." *I know you were born and raised in Philadelphia, and you remember we call it dinner, not lunch. I want to remind you that two can play your game.*

"Cart food. Cart food can make you sick."

"I've bought from them ever since I can remember. Haven't gotten sick yet. We'll be fine."

Just then, Olivia descended the stairs, wearing a below-the-knee dress with a scooped neck. It was an older girl's dress, not yet an adult's, but not like the young girl's dresses she had worn last summer. Just like Rian, Olivia's body was still all straight lines, but the dress's bodice implied curves to come. Olivia's auburn hair hung in ringlets to her shoulders, shorter than last year but fashionable like the wealthy Philadelphia women who shopped on High Street. Olivia smiled at Rian. Rian smiled back. *And I'd forgotten about those iridescent blue eyes . . .*

"Miss Krieger?" Olivia's mother repeated.

Rian's attention shifted back to Mrs. Tucker. "Excuse me, what?"

"I said this is Olivia's first time out in the city in almost a year. Please do not take her to any place that is unsafe."

Rian continued to admire Olivia as she arrived at the bottom step. "No, ma'am."

Olivia approached Rian with her arms wide open and hugged her. Rian was surprised by the demonstration but returned the gesture.

"Olivia, dear," Mrs. Tucker said even before they finished hugging. "I don't want you buying any street food. Here's enough money for the two of you to have a light dinner at Parkinson's. And here's a little extra for ice cream."

"Yes, Mother," said Olivia. She gave her mother a peck on the cheek and then threw on a short cape appropriate for springtime. "Mother, don't worry about us. We'll be fine. Rian knows the city like the back of her hand. She'll have me home before supper."

Olivia hooked her arm into Rian's even before they reached the sidewalk. "I am so happy to see you. I've missed you so much. My God, it's been a year! Mother is driving me crazy. Is Conor going to join us? Has anyone heard from Mammy? What are we going to do this afternoon? You've grown at least two inches since last year. I'm so happy your father didn't send you to that finishing school in Switzerland . . ."

Rian didn't know what to make of all the questions, but assumed that Olivia was nervous. *Still, this could be a long afternoon.*

Conor was waiting for them at the fountain in Washington Square. Olivia hugged Conor in the same manner that she had greeted Rian. By this time, she seemed to have settled down a bit.

Olivia decided that she wasn't much interested in eating at Parkinson's. "Mother gave me enough money for two of us, but not three. We can buy meat pies from the cart woman and still have money for ice cream."

They ate and chatted as they walked. Olivia reported that she was teaching some of her father's slaves to read without her parents' knowledge.

Rian told Olivia that her father had fired Jules, Conor, and Seamus when he found out about Rian's involvement with the Underground Railroad.

Conor talked about delivering messages for the Merchants' Exchange. He didn't divulge that he and Rian had broken the merchants' code and he was passing the information on to Seamus.

Olivia reported that her mother had brought five slaves along this year, each with loved ones back home. Therefore, there was no way she could help anyone else escape.

The trio decided to go to the Belmont Incline to watch the track construction. On the way, they strolled along the stalls on High Street. Olivia spied a top hat at a booth that sold all sorts of used items, from tools to kitchen utensils to a baby carriage. The hat could have been separated from its owner by a gust of wind, or it could have been stolen. Olivia decided that Rian's flat cap didn't go well with her frock coat and that a top hat would be more fashionable. She insisted that Rian try it on. Rian had difficulty tucking all her hair inside the hat.

Rian looked into a mirror. "Okay, I like the way I look, but it's too much trouble to fold all my hair up into it, and it would make me stand out in a crowd too much. I prefer to go unnoticed."

"I'll buy it for you. Please? You bought the meat pies. I have more than enough money."

Rian was tempted but said no. "If I saw someone my age wearing this, it would be a perfect target for a snowball."

Unable to convince Rian to buy the hat, Olivia shifted her attention to Conor. "I'm so sorry you aren't living with Rian and her father anymore. Are you living with your brothers?"

"I was there for a while, but then we all got kicked out of our place when we couldn't make rent. Now I'm sleeping in Jules's shop. I help out at Freeman Hydraulics however I can. I deliver messages for the Merchants' Exchange mornings and afternoons. I work in the kitchen at Braden McSweeney's after I've delivered me messages."

"So Rian's father fired you and kicked you out of the house at the same time?"

"That's about the size of it."

"You don't seem very angry about it."

Conor shrugged. "We Irish are a resilient bunch. I'm getting by. The funny thing is that Rian and I used to joke that I was the son that her father always wanted. We thought he liked it when I lived with them. He often paid more attention to me than her, although he had no luck teaching me the violin. Well, I guess I was his favorite until I ired him. Then I got the old heave-ho."

Rian nudged Conor playfully, validating his words. "Conor may not be bitter about it, but I am. I still haven't forgiven my father."

Olivia joined the teasing. "So, with Conor gone, you still haven't moved up to become the son he's always wanted?"

Rian shook her head. "My father thinks that my future is to get married and become the helpmate to my husband. Maybe the man I marry will one day run one of the Krieger factories. Then my father will have the son he has always wanted."

They walked to the Vine Street Station and the double-tracked platform of the *Philadelphia & Columbia Railroad*. One set of strap-iron tracks had already been replaced with new Krieger rail. Rian pointed out that the rail was shaped like an inverted *T*, and the letter *K* for *Krieger* had been stamped on the side. The new rails could accommodate the heavier engines that all the locomotive shops in Philadelphia were building these days. They made the remaining old track—strap-iron bolted vertically to wooden boards—look primitive.

They followed the double track as it took an arcing turn from Broadway onto Hamilton and when it veered off to parallel the river past the reservoir. With its shaded walking paths, the reservoir was Rian and Olivia's alleged destination. They passed it without a glance. After another half mile, they walked through the covered Schuylkill River Bridge and emerged onto the narrow, flat plain across the river.

All the reasons why Rian had liked Olivia were now coming back to her. She was hardy, adventurous, generous, funny, and very willing to disobey her mother. Rian didn't know any other girls like her.

Beyond the plain rose the imposing Belmont Incline, a 187-foot rise in a mere half mile. The old westbound track had been torn up to the top of the incline, the strap-iron rails and outmoded granite supports cast aside. The track layers were working industriously but hadn't yet reached the Incline. A work train had been backed onto the new rails—the locomotive and its tender; a flatcar carrying tools and spikes; a flatcar carrying railroad ties; and closest to the work, a flatcar carrying rails. Rian pointed with pride to the locomotive—Krieger Locomotive *Number 2*, which had never been given another name because the *P&C* purchased it as a lowly utility engine.

"We hadn't established our reputation for quality locomotives yet, so *P&C* wanted to see if our machines were any good. They've ordered more since then."

The trio found a fallen beech tree that was the perfect height to sit and watch the construction crew.

Rian looked for Aaron Bassinger but couldn't find him among an army of workers who milled about like ants moving their eggs from a nest to a new location.

Teams of two beefy men muscled the new railroad ties from the flatcar and walked them to their approximate resting place on a thick layer of ballast stone. A man peering through a transit used hand signals to communicate with a man who carried a level. Level-man told another set of workers to either dig down a bit or build up a bit under each new tie. When those men had properly placed five ties, another team of six workers, each man armed with a set of large tongs, clamped onto a 16-foot rail and hauled it to the newly positioned railroad ties.

They set the rail down, always following level-man's instructions. He then leaned his level against a toolbox and picked up a wheelbarrow-like contraption with two flanged steel wheels. *Level-man becomes wheelbarrow-man*, Rian thought.

"Those wheels on that wheelbarrow are four feet, eight and a half inches apart," Rian told Olivia. "One of the men at Krieger Rail invented it. All that guy has to do is run the wheelbarrow along the rails, and he can automatically tell if they are the right distance apart. Plus, it carries a load of spikes."

With the rails properly placed, the men dropped their tongs, grabbed sledgehammers, and secured the rails by pounding spikes into the ties.

"Have you seen them do this before?" asked Olivia. "You seem to know a lot about it."

Rian nodded. "All the railroads are replacing their strap-iron tracks with T-stock because it is more durable. While they're at it, they're taking out the granite blocks that supported the old rails. Granite turned out to be too rigid, so they're being replaced with wooden ties. I watched them do it last fall on the *Philadelphia & Reading* to the north. Mr. Shippen's *Philadelphia & Wilmington* is under construction to the south and is going straight to the modern rails and ties. Aaron took me there a few times when he was overseeing the installation until their guys got their systems down."

"But you never want to run Krieger Rail?"

"Nope, I like building locomotives. The funny thing is, I think Uncle Adrian likes having me in his shop."

"Yeah, as opposed to your da," interjected Conor. "He thinks you don't belong out in the Coach factory."

"My father doesn't think I belong on any factory floor. He isn't my favorite person right now."

With a new pair of rails laid, transit-man yelled that it was time to move the work train. He signaled to the engine driver, who inched the train backward onto the recently laid rails, gradually revealing a group of people standing on the other side of the track. Aaron Bassinger was talking with a man with a set of drawings unrolled on a table. And there, pointing toward the newly positioned work crew, was Rian's father.

Otto Krieger's arm was resting on the shoulder of Rian's cousin Jabez Howes.

Olivia followed Rian's gaze. "Who's that with your father?"

"That's Jabez Howes," said Conor. "He's Rian's cousin. His father's a ship captain but couldn't handle him, so now Jabez lives with Rian's Uncle Adrian and Aunt Mila. But right now? Right now, it looks like he's my replacement. The new son that Otto Krieger always wanted."

What had been a funny joke when Conor received more than his share of attention from her father was no longer funny. "Fook you, Conor," said Rian as she stood to leave. But Conor had merely said out loud what Rian was thinking.

Rian kicked at an errant ballast stone. *The son he's always wanted . . . Jabez Howes, who never comes to work on time. Who refuses to learn bookkeeping. Who smokes cigarettes with the workers. Who is sloppy in everything that he does. Who I guess is going to run one of the Krieger factories someday because he's got a penis. Shit. Shit. Shit.*

THURSDAY, MAY 18

· RIAN ·

Rian found what she sought in the *Paid Bills* file box, sighed, and walked two bank invoices to Otto's desk. "Father, I don't understand this. I think the bank made a mistake."

Her father didn't bother to look up from the design of a new passenger coach he was drafting. "The bank rarely makes mistakes, *Liebling*. What have you found?"

Rian noted he still called her *Liebling. He always calls me that, as if using the term will make things okay between us. Never.* She placed the two invoices on Otto's desk—on top of his sketch. "These invoices don't match up. Our payment for the bank loan for the land across the street for this month is less than it was for the first two months. Should we notify them they've made a mistake?"

"No, that is not necessary. It is not a mistake."

"How come the amount is lower?"

Otto kept at his drafting. "I assume because they lowered the interest rate."

"Why would they do that?"

"I have no idea. Sometimes banks find themselves in a position to give a break to their favored customers. That must have been it."

Rian placed a sheet of paper on top of the invoices. "Then why was this letter included in the invoice that came in today's mail?"

Otto finally stopped drawing, looked up briefly at Rian, and picked up the paper. Rian watched him read the letter, which she knew by heart.

May 17, 1837

Krieger,

As anticipated, the Board of Directors of the Bank of Industry looked favorably upon your decision to address your employment issue. Please note that this month's invoice reflects the new interest rate we discussed.

Your humble servant,

Edward Schiffler
President
Bank of Industry

"What was the employment issue that you discussed with Mr. Schiffler?"

Her father shifted uncomfortably in his seat and looked up at his daughter again. "It is nothing that concerns you, *Liebling*. I followed some of their advice, and they gave me a lower rate."

Rian noted her father's discomfort, which confirmed her suspicions. "What was their advice?"

"Don't worry about it. Please continue with your filing."

"What did you agree to?"

Otto rose from his chair, put his hands into his pockets, and started pacing. "I agreed to nothing. Edward Schiffler did not like that I had a Negro in charge of whites. He said that if I let Jules go, the bank would give me a lower interest rate. I refused, of course. But when I fired Jules for involving you in his activities, I returned to the bank and told Schiffler that Jules was no longer employed by Krieger Coach."

Despite her current anger at her father, she had always believed he was an honorable man. She felt like someone had punched her in the stomach. "You fired Jules to get a better interest rate?"

"No, of course not. I fired him because he involved you in the Underground Railroad."

"But when you did that, you went back to the bank and told them you followed their advice."

Rian's father kept pacing, hands in his pockets, eyes on the floor. "No, I did not tell them why I had done it; I just told them it was done."

"But you let Schiffler believe you did it because of him."

"Schiffler can believe what he chooses to believe. I have no control over that."

"Unless you told him that you fired Jules for a reason other than just because he's Black."

Otto stopped, pulled his hands out of his pockets, and turned to Rian. "If I had done that, he would have wanted to know why. I could have told him about Jules involving you in his evening activities. Would you have preferred that?"

"No, I just don't like that Mr. Schiffler thinks he can get Negroes fired just because he's an important banker. What about the Irish?"

"What about the Irish?" Otto responded.

"Mr. Schiffler doesn't like the Irish. Did you get a better rate for firing Seamus and Conor?"

"I could have received a better rate if I had fired all the Irish unless they were sweeping floors. As you know, I only fired my nephew and your best friend."

"Two Irish have quit since then. There are only two left, Dylan and Logan. If they leave, will you go back to the bank and ask for a lower interest rate?"

"I would be a poor businessman if I did not do so."

"So you have no intention of hiring an Irishman to replace the two who left?"

"We aren't hiring at all at the moment. Business has slowed."

* * * * *

· SEAMUS ·

It had been ten weeks since Seamus was fired from Krieger Coach. He did nothing for a week, waiting for Otto to cool off and hire him back. When that didn't happen, he applied for a foreman's position at two other factories that built railroad cars.

Then manufacturers of horse-drawn carriages.

Then locomotives.

Then any factory needing a man with experience in making things run efficiently.

Then any factory needing someone to maintain and fix their machines.

He got the same answer in every instance: *We don't hire Irish.*

A month ago, he started getting a different answer: *We're not hiring right now.*

Then last week: *We're laying off workers.*

In the good weeks, he made ends meet when the United No Name Fire Brigade put out a fire or he shook something loose on the docks. In the bad weeks, the pile of dollars and coins under his mattress got smaller.

Conor McGuire regularly slipped Seamus valuable intelligence that he'd intercepted from the optical telegraph. Twice it had led to a big payoff, but mostly Seamus used the information to grease the skids for other deals he had in the works. Conor passed on enough information to Hugh to keep the truce between Moya and No Name.

Unwilling to go back to ditchdigging, Seamus started showing up at the docks before 6:00, hoping to be chosen as a stevedore for the day. Eventually, the strawboss at the Imlay & Potts Pier started picking him regularly.

Stevedore work pays a fraction of what I earned at Krieger Coach, but at least it's a ten-hour day. That gives me time to clean meself up after work and take Siobhan for a stroll. Plus, I note everything that's being loaded and unloaded. If there's something of interest, I just might make a midnight visit.

"All right, gather 'round!" the strawboss said to the men who had shown up hoping for work. He held the slate with the names of the men he intended to pick.

Seamus and about 20 other men crowded closer. He tried to peek at the slate, but not to see if his name was on the list—*the strawboss always picks me.* Every morning, he guessed how many men the strawboss would pick. He looked at the ship, knowing it was carrying rice from Charleston. *The strawboss is going to pick 15 men, and he's gonna put me in charge of the men in the hold.*

The strawboss didn't begin reading off the names of workers. "There's new rules starting today. Today, you're working until sunset. Starting tomorrow, you're working sun-to-sun, so if you want work, show up before dawn."

"For the same pay?" one of the men asked, his voice not even remotely concealing his ire.

The strawboss looked up from his slate. "Yeah, whataya think? For the same pay."

There was noticeable grumbling amongst the men. "Come on, lads," one of the men said, "let's try down the way."

The strawboss looked at his slate. "Suit yourselves. Word is that all the dockmasters have talked. Everyone's offering their day workers the same deal—sun-to-sun."

"But the sun rises before five o'clock," the same man said. "This time of year, that's a 14-hour day."

"Yeah, and it'll be worse in a month. That's the deal. Take it or leave it. That is, if I pick you. Today I need 11 men. Gallagher, you're going to be running things in the hold . . ."

Seamus knew there was no use trying his luck at another wharf. Traffic was down the entire length of the Philadelphia waterfront. *Jaysus, I'm right back where I was two years ago, working sun-to-sun for the strawboss.* And Siobhan was going to be more than a little irritated that he stood her up for their evening stroll. *And I've got no way to tell her I won't be able to make it.*

TUESDAY, JUNE 20

The Panic Arrives in Philadelphia
New York City Banks Suspend Specie Payments,
Spark Trouble Throughout the Nation
Exclusive to the *Philadelphia Independent*
An Editorial by Harold Foote

Where is the Second Bank of the United States now when we need it? Murdered by Andy Jackson when he refused to renew its charter in 1836. Reviled as a high-handed tool of the merchant class, the Bank imposed a discipline on the country's financial industry that has been cast aside. With it gone, the number of state-chartered banks doubled in three years, and each had the prerogative of issuing its own currency. Many were lax about keeping minimal reserves of gold and silver to back their notes.

On May 10 of this year, with depositors clamoring to redeem their paper money for gold and silver, New York City banks announced they would no longer redeem their notes at full value. This act was the first acknowledgment by any financial institution or government agency that the economy of our great nation was in trouble. The Panic was on. Banks all over the country have since followed the lead of the New Yorkers.

In our modern era, the American economy has become a complex machine. Southern cotton is woven into cloth in Northern factories. Eastern banks lend money to Western farmers. Western grain flows down the great Mississippi to feed the people of the South. Disrupt any cog in the machine, and the engine can grind to a halt.

Make no mistake about it. If this Panic gets worse, and there is no reason to believe it won't, the fault lies not at the feet of the current president, but at those of his predecessor. Andy Jackson killed the Second National Bank. He distributed federal funds to undisciplined Pet Banks around the country. Then he issued the Specie Circular—sand in the cogs of the American economy.

In Philadelphia, the effects of the growing Panic are being seen daily. Banks are closing, workers are being laid off, and factories are shuttering. On May 15, the largest crowd in Pennsylvania's history gathered outside the State House to protest banking as a system of fraud and oppression. Those workers who have not been laid off have been forced to return to the 12-hour day they fought so valiantly to kill just two years ago. The demeanor of people on the street, which used to be described as confident and jaunty, is now sullen and angry.

* * * * *

· JULES ·

Jules left Freeman Hydraulics to walk 12 blocks north to Krieger Locomotive. As he entered the factory, he felt a tinge of apprehension. He hadn't spoken to Adrian Krieger in three months and had no idea what sort of reception he would get.

He entered the factory, noting as he walked the length of the long building that the machines were idle. The mammoth steam engine at the far end was not even fired up. He saw only two locomotives in the production queue. Workers who usually would have been busy creating a mechanical marvel were instead transferring metal scraps from bins to a wagon, washing windows, and sweeping floors. He knocked lightly at the office door, which was ajar, and pushed it farther open to reveal Adrian seated at his desk.

The president of Krieger Locomotive put down his pencil and rose to shake hands with Jules. "Hello, stranger. This is a pleasant surprise. I miss not having you across the alley to talk to. What brings you here?"

Adrian's friendly greeting emboldened Jules to ask the obvious question. "Adrian, what's going on? It's pretty quiet out there."

Adrian chuckled. "Yeah, it is a bit unusual, but not as dire as it appears. We're hosting a meeting at Krieger Coach today. Otto wants to give everyone a tour of the factories before the meeting starts. That gave us an excuse to clean the place up a bit."

"It looks like more than a bit to me. And lose an entire day of production? When's the last time the steam engine wasn't fired up during a work day?"

"Never. Jules, business is down in all three Krieger factories. It's not just us. We're hearing from all over the city that business is off. We've invited some of our most important suppliers, customers, a few bankers, and even our competitors to a meeting to discuss the downturn."

"So when's this shindy going to take place?"

"Late this afternoon. I'm surprised you didn't know about it. Your father-in-law is the caterer. We've given Hercules the Finish Room in Krieger Coach for the day. He's probably setting up over there right now."

"Nice to know you're going with the best caterer in town. How many people?"

"Fifty. We plan on touring the men around before the meeting. Hard to believe how trashed up they've become in just a year. Actually, Otto admitted the other day how much messier Krieger Coach has become since you and Seamus left."

"You mean since he fired us."

"Well, yeah, that." Adrian pointed to the door. "Come on. I might as well show you the place while it's looking good. How are things at Freeman Hydraulics?"

Jules followed Adrian out into the cavernous production floor. "Helluva time to be starting a business. I have a new appreciation for you and Otto. There's a world of difference between being a foreman and owning a business. I never stop thinking about it. Failure is one bad decision away."

"Any thaw between you and my brother?"

Jules shook his head. "I stopped trying a couple of months ago."

"Otto told me about your evening activities. I think it's laudable. I even understand why you didn't tell us about it. The fewer people who know what you are doing, the better, as far as I'm concerned. Hopefully, at some point, Otto will understand this."

Jules acknowledged various men as they toured the factory. Some nodded and waved in a friendly manner. Others emanated no warmth at all. "But I put Rian in danger."

"Yeah, his forgiveness for that may take a little more time. Is that why you're here? To talk about Otto?"

Jules shook his head. "I never paid much attention to what you folks do on the Krieger Locomotive side of the alley. Woodworking has always been my forte, not metal. When I first cooked up the idea for Freeman Hydraulics, you and I made a deal that Krieger Locomotive would make the boilers and engines for my fire pumps."

"For six months, until you can get all your pieces into place."

"Well, that's a bit of a problem. Starting up is taking more money than I thought it would. I can't go back to Robert Purvis for more, and the banks won't lend to a Black man, so I can't buy the metal fabricating machines I need. They are all demanding cash up front because I'm Black. I wonder if you would be willing to extend our deal indefinitely."

Adrian hesitated for a few moments. "If you had asked me this a month ago, I would have been forced to say no. We had a queue of orders a mile long. Things have changed."

"So, you'll do it?" *If you say yes, I won't have to buy a steam riveter and five other machines.*

Adrian nodded. "If this trend continues, we'll be grateful for any business. Here, let me show you our latest locomotive. It's a dandy, but we have no solid orders after this one. From now on, we'll build anything at cost if it means I can keep the men working and the gas lamps on."

* * * * *

· RIAN ·

Rian had been looking forward to the gathering of business leaders since she heard about it. She loved to listen to adults in conversation as she lurked in the periphery. This occasion would be perfect for that. *I'll watch how they interact with one another. What they talk about and how they say it. Who talks with who and who doesn't talk with who.*

That afternoon, her father had told her to drive the junk wagon filled with metal castoffs from the Krieger factories to a scrap dealer in Northern Liberties. Harnessing a team of four horses and hooking it up to the junk wagon took a while, as did returning the horses. Mission finally accomplished, she skipped across the street from Kent Livery and reentered the uncharacteristically quiet Krieger Coach. She looked over her shoulder at the large mechanical clock above the door. *Rats, it's 6:30. That errand took longer than I thought. I've got to catch up with the tour.*

A hundred paces into the factory, she noticed Jabez Howes standing at the massive sliding door that separated the Finish Room from the rest of the shop. He was dressed in his shore clothes, the same outfit he had been wearing when she found him at the Shot Tower.

"How come you're all dressed up?" she asked.

"Uncle Otto asked me to. I had to go home to change. He wanted me to greet any late-arriving guests while he's leading the tour. Once the meeting's going, he wants me to stand guard so I can open the door if guests arrive late."

A stab of jealousy shot directly into Rian's heart. "He asked you?"

"Yeah, I think this is stupid. It's hotter than blazes, and this wool suit makes it even hotter. Emmanuel and Trey asked me to go swimming. Now I can't go."

Rian heard the door to the alley open. Her father entered, using his lumber-estimating rule as a pointer and leading the group to the end of their tour. The sound of many animated male voices echoed around the shop.

Once all fifty men had entered, Otto turned to the group. "This brings the tour of the Krieger factories to an end, gentlemen. Please join us in the Krieger Coach Finish Room, temporarily transformed into our dining area. Our caterer this evening is Hercules Angell."

A smattering of applause rippled around the group, but not as much as Rian would have expected. *Jaysus, Das Patriot's stupid article had an effect.* Disappointed, Rian watched as the businessmen filed into the Finish Room. Her father, one of the last to pass by, was in a lively conversation with George Shippen.

Rian stepped into his path. "*Vater,* may I watch the meeting?"

Otto Krieger stopped his conversation with Shippen. If he noticed that Rian called him *Vater* for the first time in three months, he showed no sign. "I'm sorry, *Liebling,* but you are not dressed appropriately for the occasion."

A wave of desperation washed over Rian. "What if I go home and change?"

"This isn't an event that a young woman should attend." Her father watched as the last stragglers entered the room, then turned his attention to Jabez. "I think that's everyone, Jabez. It is cooler in the Finish Room than in the rest of the factory. Please shut the door so the heat doesn't seep in."

Reluctantly, Jabez leaned hard into the handle of the sliding door to pull it closed. He made eye contact with Rian the entire time. As the opening diminished, he mouthed the word *sorry.* The door closed with a soft *thunk.*

* * * * *

Rian ran home and changed into the outfit she wore during her outing with Olivia and Conor. She returned to the factory in time to see Jabez leaving the building.

"The meeting was boring," he announced. "I'm going swimming."

Rian slipped into the Finish Room. Hercules Angell's crew had set up chairs to populate nine circular tables, and the guests were finishing their supper. She inhaled the fading aromas of beef stew and baked bread.

After a few minutes, the dinner smells gave way to cigar smoke. George Shippen rose to speak and identified himself as Chairman of the Board of the Bank of Industry and President of the *Philadelphia, Wilmington & Baltimore Railroad.*

Good, thought Rian, *I haven't missed anything.*

The sun was setting. Light from the cupola windows dimmed. Rian took it upon herself to circumnavigate the room and turn on all the gas lamps—*Otto will certainly see me*—then returned to the back so she could listen to the speakers. Rather than *Vater*, she had been calling him *Father* for the past three months. If she noted it was now *Otto*, it made little impression on her. *Let's see how he reacts to his precious favorite son now. He's gone swimming.*

"The problem is," declared George Shippen, "that people have lost confidence in the banks. They are pulling out their savings for no reason except fear. If they leave their savings with us, there will be no problems."

"Which one are you?" asked a baritone voice from behind Rian.

Rian turned to see Hercules Angell, Jules's father-in-law, whom she had heard stories about but had never met. "What do you mean?"

"You are either Otto Krieger's daughter Rian or his nephew, whose name I can't remember."

A man interrupted Mr. Shippen by standing and addressing the group. "The more fundamental problem is that Pet Banks like yours, Shippen, have been printing money willy-nilly without regard to the long-term consequences. Now all the sound money—currency backed by an appropriate amount of gold or silver—has gravitated to the West to pay for land the states are selling, leaving us here in the East with a lot of worthless paper."

Rian ignored Angell's question. "That speaker, do you know who he is?"

"That's Nicholas Biddle. President of the United States Bank of Pennsylvania, the bank that used to be the Second Bank of the United States before Andy Jackson withdrew all the federal funds and spread them around to his Pet Banks."

"How do you know him?"

Angell looked at Rian with a wry smile. "I'm a caterer. Sooner or later, I meet everyone in this town. So, given what I have heard from Jules, I'll bet a bowl of beef stew that you are Rian Krieger."

Rian smiled but continued to observe the two speakers. "Your beef stew is safe. I wouldn't eat anyway. I want to listen to what the men are saying."

"Me too."

Rian turned and looked Angell in the eye. "You do? Why?"

"Same reason as you, I suspect. I might learn something."

Mr. Shippen stole the floor back from Mr. Biddle. "I am confident that the American economy will emerge from this little storm in a few short months."

"So the one at the door was your cousin," Angell stated, his eyes still on the speakers.

Rian nodded. "His name is Jabez. He went swimming; I wanted to be here. I'll do whatever he was supposed to do."

Mr. Shippen stood up on a chair and held out his arms. "My confidence is so great that I am extending an invitation to everyone in this room. As you know, I wear two hats. I am a banker and a railroad man. In less than three weeks, the *Philadelphia, Wilmington & Baltimore* will have completed two of its three sections, from Baltimore to Wilmington, with the two tied together by the ferry at Havre de Grace."

"Your father didn't want you to be here?" asked Angell.

Rian shook her head but continued watching Biddle and Shippen's interaction. "He told me it wasn't the kind of event a girl should attend."

Angell surveyed the crowd. "Nor a Black man, apparently, unless you're the caterer."

Mr. Shippen continued. "I have made provisions for the steamboat *Telegraph* to transport everyone in this room plus their families to Wilmington on Sunday, July 9, at which point we will all transfer to a train to carry us to Havre de Grace. We will board a second ferry, steam to the middle of the Susquehanna River, and anchor to witness the biggest fireworks display you have ever seen."

The crowd erupted with enthusiastic whoops and applause.

Angell elbowed Rian. "Well, there's one thing I learned. Maybe I can line up a catering job on July 9."

Mr. Biddle tried to regain the crowd's attention amid the continued applause. "Anyone who believes that our coming economic troubles are a little storm is a fool. We are about to experience a hurricane that will last years."

No one's paying attention to him, thought Rian. *They've been swayed by a boat ride and some fireworks.*

Angell put the cover on a chafing dish, a signal that it was time to stop listening and start cleaning up. "If your father sees you, I suspect he'll be upset."

"He probably already knows. I turned on all the gas lights. I figure if he hadn't noticed me before, he did then. But, you know what?

"What?"

"I don't care."

* * * * *

At the end of the meeting, Rian helped the catering crew return the Finish Room to its workday state. She found herself tearing down tables with Hercules Angell.

"Well, did you learn anything?" Angell asked.

Rian helped Angell turn one of the large circular tables on edge. "Yeah, a lot. Business is down, so employers are laying off workers or making them work longer for the same pay. A couple of banks have closed, and they've taken people's savings with them. It's not just in Philadelphia. It's all over the country. What about you? What did you learn?"

Although the next logical task would have been to roll the table to the sliding door and pass it off to other workers, Angell stopped. "You are something, just like Jules described. He misses you, you know."

"I miss him, too. Something awful. I hope he knows that when I'm older, I'm going to get back to doing the thing we got in trouble for."

Angell handed the table off to one of his crew members and kept his attention on Rian. "Jules knows that."

"He said that to you?"

Angell nodded. "My daughter married a good man. Seventeen years ago, she saw things in him that I was too busy to notice. He, in turn, knows a person of character when he sees one, and he's known you since you were born."

"Rian!"

Angell and Rian both looked toward the door of the Finish Room. Otto Krieger was beckoning her with a wave of his hand.

"Good luck with your father," said Angell. "I hope you're not in too much trouble."

Oh, I'm in a lot of trouble, but what can he do to me? Rian said to herself. Rather than give in immediately to her father's summons, she tipped another table on edge. "But what did you learn tonight?"

Angell's eyes widened, indicating incredulity at her blatant defiance. "Too much to relate now, but in a nutshell, the Black man can't rely on white businessmen to solve his problems. We're going to have to do this ourselves."

"My father agrees with you, but he says white people have to get out of your way."

"Your daddy is a good man. I hope you aren't being too hard on him."

Rian started folding the legs of the table. "He fired Jules. He fired my cousin Seamus. He fired my best friend Conor. He pays my other cousin Jabez to do work I do for free."

Angell picked up a heap of tablecloths piled on the last round table still standing. "That's a long list. Did he tell you that he was getting heat for hiring me because I'm Black?"

"No, he didn't. Because of that article in *Das Philadelphische Patriot* last month?"

Angell nodded. "So then you should know this: Your father asked me to pass on whatever information I learned back to Jules. He may be angry at my son-in-law, but he's not vindictive."

Rian looked toward her father. *Jaysus, this is getting hard.* Although Otto was saying goodbye to one of the guests, he occasionally looked in her direction. "I've gotta go. It was nice to meet you."

Rian wended her way to the door, dodging members of Angell's crew as they carried serving pieces out to a wagon. "Sorry, Father."

Otto finished shaking Nicholas Biddle's hand and turned to her. "I do not believe that you are sorry in the least bit. I want you to walk home with me. Do not leave without me."

Rian knew she was about to catch it. She busied herself with the catering crew. It took her father another half hour to usher out straggling guests and pay Hercules Angell. Father and daughter extinguished gas lamps as they walked down opposite sides of the factory. Otto locked the shop, and they turned south onto Broad Street.

"Rian, I want to talk to you about something."

Rian braced herself but said nothing.

"I have resumed correspondence with *Frau Gilberts Schule für Junge Frauen* in Switzerland. I know that two years ago you placed fake advertisements in at least two newspapers. They led me to believe Frau Gilbert was not accepting students your age. I assume you also intercepted numerous letters between the school and me."

Rian stopped dead in her tracks. There was no need for her father to say anything more. She knew exactly where this conversation was heading. "No. I'm not going."

"You will be with other young women your age. Your stature. Your abilities."

"There is no way you can make me go."

"Rian, of course I can make you go. But I would rather you go willingly because you see how beneficial it will be. This past year you have run wild and deliberately deceived me on many occasions. You broke the law numerous times. You engaged in dangerous behavior. And tonight, you openly defied me."

"Father, all I wanted to do was listen to the meeting. I turned on the gas lamps when the sun went down. I helped Mr. Angell clean up. What part of that meeting was not suitable for a girl?"

"Since I can no longer control your actions, I have decided to send you to Frau Gilbert's School."

"If you make me get on a boat, I'll jump off before it clears the Navy Yard."

"*Mein Liebling*, that will be difficult. You will be sailing out of New York."
After eating a cold dinner alone, Rian went to her room and fumed.

* * * * *

· JULES ·

Jules sat at the kitchen table and only half-listened as Maddie greeted someone at the front door. Instead, he contemplated the list before him, congratulated himself on his modest accomplishments, and mulled over the remaining items.

~~Talk to Adrian about making boilers~~
~~Cancel order for steam riveter~~
~~Figure out how to trim more expenses~~
Sell more fire pumps
Do something about newspaper articles?
Find Mama?

It had been a long and rewarding workday. Adrian Krieger had committed to continue making boilers for Jules's fire pumps, so he didn't need to buy new machine tools. A contract and bank's draft for a new steam-powered fire pump had arrived in the afternoon mail, thus temporarily alleviating the need to cut expenses further.

Jules didn't know why he even bothered to write down the last two items. He could not prevent *Das Philadelphische Patriot* from writing more anti-Black articles. And find his mother? Every list that he had ever made had included that task. He didn't know how to go about it except quiz every self-emancipator who passed through his door. That girl Peach was the only person who had ever heard of her, and her news placed his mother even farther away.

His musings ended when Maddie escorted Robert Purvis into the kitchen. Jules rose to shake his visitor's hand. "Robert, this is a pleasant surprise. What brings you here?"

Purvis and Maddie both joined Jules at the kitchen table. "Jules, I apologize for interrupting your evening. I feel the need to spread the word about a disturbing development. As you know, the Constitutional Convention has been meeting in Harrisburg since May. Under the current state constitution, men who do not pay a certain threshold of taxes may not vote."

Jules knew of the convention but had not followed day-to-day doings in the pennies. *Whatever changes are made to Pennsylvania's constitution won't affect me*. As a longtime taxpayer, he had voted in numerous city, state, and national elections. Although he had experienced simmering anti-Black hostility every time, his personal experience with voting had never escalated into violence.

Purvis continued. "The stated purpose of the convention was to amend the document so that voting rights would be granted to poorer members of the Commonwealth."

"Yes, this is a good thing," commented Jules. "I applaud this."

"Well, this afternoon I received a visit from Phineas Jenks. He is a Whig from Bucks County. An old friend." Purvis pulled a folded piece of paper from his coat pocket. "Jenks told me that two days ago a delegate named John Sterigere from Montgomery County moved to insert a clause into the new constitution"—Purvis's hands shook as he read the paper—"restricting the right to vote only to 'free white male citizens who have paid a state, county, road, or poor tax.' That still restricts poor people from voting *and* removes our right to vote. He cites similar provisions in 18 other state constitutions. This is a disaster. Free Blacks in Pennsylvania have had the right to vote since 1790."

Maddie slumped back in her chair. "And here I was fantasizing about maybe women gaining the right to vote in this constitution."

"Just the opposite, I'm afraid. We cannot allow this Sterigere amendment to pass. Jenks has moved to alter the motion. He wants to strike the word 'white.' I'm sorry, Maddie. Your fantasy will never be possible when we find ourselves fighting a rearguard battle trying to preserve our rights as stated in the current constitution."

For over an hour, Purvis and Jules discussed measures to fight Sterigere's amendment. When Purvis left, Jules again looked at his list of things to do. He inserted *Fight Sterigere amendment* above *Find Mama*.

* * * * *

· SEAMUS ·

Seamus stuffed down his nervousness as he walked into Clancy's Saloon. Clancy's was the unofficial headquarters of the Moyamensing Hose Company, and Seamus used to be a regular here. This evening was the first time he had entered enemy territory since he was blackballed from Moya last year.

Clancy looked up from his usual spot behind the bar and started pouring Seamus a glass of whiskey. "Long time no see, Boyo. Is this business or pleasure?"

Seamus relaxed a bit because of Clancy's reception. "Little bit of both. Is Hugh here?"

Clancy hooked his thumb toward the back room. "Holding court, as usual."

Seamus nodded to table after table of Moya boys, who Hugh Callaghan had kept in check since Seamus had proposed the optical telegraph deal. There was no love lost between the two fire companies, but since Moya was so much larger than No Name, Seamus assumed the rivalry was a bigger deal for him than it was for these guys.

As Seamus entered the back room, he saw Hugh playing cards with five other men. *No surprise there,* thought Seamus. A raucous cheer erupted, but it wasn't in response to his arrival. A man sitting opposite Hugh raked in a hefty pot of money as Hugh steamed, a toothpick sticking out of his mouth.

Callaghan looked up and noticed Seamus. "Jaysus, me day's complete. What're you doing here, kid?"

"Came to see you. Can we talk?"

Hugh looked at the table to see that another hand was already being dealt. "If you can wait a bit. We're playing a new game called poker. I don't quite have the hang of it yet. I need to win some of me money back first."

Poker was just becoming known in the saloons and grog shops of Philadelphia. Seamus had played a few times and liked it. It wasn't a good sign that Hugh was making him cool his heels. *The longer he makes me wait, the less respect he has for me. Hopefully, it'll be one hand, just to put me in me place.* He sipped his whiskey and watched the game.

Three hands later, Hugh declared, "I'm out." He stood up, scooped up some bills, grabbed his jacket, and marched to the door. "I wanted to talk to you anyway, kid," he announced as he passed by Seamus. "Walk with me."

The two exited Clancy's into the cool June air. They had to step over a newly dug ditch running along Plum Street. *I used to be a ditchdigger,* Seamus thought to himself. *I'm one bad day at the docks from going back to that.*

"This better not be about Siobhan," Hugh said as he turned toward the Delaware River and started walking at a rapid clip.

Seamus's heart sank as he hurried to catch up. "That's just it. It is about Siobhan. I want to ask her to marry me."

"You're too late, Boyo. Mikey McGuire just asked me. I told him to go ahead."

This is bad. This is really bad. "Mikey? He's going nowhere. Wasn't he the one who stole the printing press off the docks? Who the hell's gonna buy a stolen printing press?"

"Well, in fairness, the printing press was boxed up at the time. He didn't know what it was. He just knew it was heavy."

Seamus didn't feel the need to press the point.

"Besides," Hugh continued. "There's another reason I'm saying no. I'm calling a halt to the truce."

Surprisingly, Seamus felt himself relax a tad. *Ah, now I get it. This is a negotiation.*

Seamus took off his cap and rubbed his hand through his hair. "But the truce was for a year." *You could have done this differently, you old windbag, but you always have to throw your weight around.*

"And I'm changing it."

"Why are you doing this?" *I know exactly why you're doing this. I didn't know this would be the time or the place, but I'm a step ahead of you, just like I was the last time.*

"Me boys are restless. They don't like all the help you're giving the Africans."

"Why do you care? You never put out the fires of the Black houses anyway."

At an intersection, Callaghan pointed to direct them across the street. "I guess you'd have to call it a matter of principle. I've told you before. This is a war between us Irish and the Africans. You've turned your back on your own kind."

"Not at all. I just don't believe in us Irish getting ahead over the backs of somebody else."

"Me boys don't see it that way."

"You want to go back to the way it was before? Stealing our fire pump? Ambushing each other? Starting fires in the homes of innocent people just to get the reward for putting out the fires?"

Hugh smiled. "It has its allure."

"Hugh, I really don't want to go down this road. Is there any way we can extend the truce indefinitely?"

Hugh sucked on his toothpick for a few seconds. "Your man at the telegraph towers. I want access to all his information."

Finally! Jaysus, Hugh, it took you long enough. "Hugh, that will never happen. I don't even get everything."

"Do you want to extend the truce or not?"

Seamus feigned indecision. He looked at his feet. He looked up at Hugh. "So, if I get you all me guy's information, we extend the truce?" *You could have made this so much easier, but I knew you wanted to squeeze me. I've still got to get your blessing to ask Siobhan to marry me, so I'll just let you think we're playing it your way.*

"That's about the size of it. *Quid pro quo.*"

Seamus nodded in agreement. "Okay." Then, "What about Siobhan?"

"I told you. Mikey McGuire already asked me. I said yes."

"You think Siobhan's the first girl who's ever had two men after her? C'mon, Hugh, give me a shot."

"Let's see how Mikey fares first." Hugh led them to Water Street. He seemed more interested in casing out the warehouses than continuing his conversation with Seamus. He turned right onto the Almond Street Wharf and halted. "We've paid the watchmen to look the other way for an hour this evening. There's two boats here. Which one would you pick?"

Seamus was reeling. Deep down, he figured Hugh would say yes to him marrying Siobhan. *Don't throw in the towel yet, Boyo. You can still dazzle him.* "What're me choices?"

Hugh took the toothpick out of his mouth and used it to point. "This ship over here is the *Republic*. She's heading to South America. Stops in Montevideo to drop off a steam engine we've got our eye on."

"A stationary steam engine, not a locomotive? How big is it?"

"Not that big. Apparently they're going to use it for an irrigation project down there. This ship over here is the *Palma de Mallorca*. She loaded up ten whiskey barrels this afternoon and is headed to the Mediterranean."

"You've done your research. Despite what I said earlier about Mikey McGuire and the printing press, I'd swipe the engine."

"A bold answer. Tell me why."

"Well, admittedly, I'd have an easier time getting rid of the whiskey than a steam engine. Hell, Clancy would probably buy half of it. But I wouldn't steal the engine in hopes of selling it."

Hugh put his toothpick back in his mouth. "Keep talking."

"The key here is that both items are already on the boats, not in that warehouse over there. Once cargo is loaded onto a ship, it's automatically insured. The engine is worth a lot more than the whiskey. The insurance company would rather pay me a small but significant fee to get the engine back than pay the manufacturer for the whole thing."

Hugh continued to gaze at the two ships. "*Cliste* [Clever]."

"Plus, the *Republic* ties up here regularly. I suspect she's registered and insured right out of our fair city. That means all me negotiations would be local. The insurance company would be interested in paying me immediately to get that engine on the next boat to South America. Maybe even back on this one if I can cut a deal fast enough."

"Not bad, kid."

Seamus wasn't finished. "Plus, if I dominated these docks the way you do, down the road I would cut an additional deal with the same insurance company. If they'd give me a cut of everything they insure going in or out of these docks, I'd agree not to steal it."

Hugh pivoted to look at the *Republic* as if considering Seamus's thoughts. "I can't believe you're not working for me," he muttered. "If your sensibilities were a bit different, you'd be in line to lead Moya someday."

"Ah, Hugh, we both know that wouldn'ta worked out very well. We woulda got on each other's nerves pretty quick."

"Well, in any case, there's still no way you're going to marry me daughter."

SUNDAY, JULY 9

· RIAN ·

Rian and Olivia were strolling aboard the promenade deck of the side-paddlewheeler *Telegraph*. The boat was steaming toward Wilmington on the Delaware River with two hundred of George Shippen's guests.

Rian was wearing a dress and not happy about it. "Ugh. This is how I'll have to dress in Switzerland for the next five years."

Olivia pulled Rian in close by the crook of her arm. "It's okay. I don't care how you are dressed. I just enjoy being with you."

Rian fumed. "But it's torture."

Olivia adjusted her pace to match Rian's. "You have to admit, this is a pretty fancy event. Uncle George rented the *Telegraph* to make a special run to Wilmington with all his business associates. If that's not a special occasion, I don't know what is."

"Otto made me wear this. I look like . . . like a clown."

At that moment, a pack of boys ran by them, their third lap around the boat—Trey Shippen, Billy Schiffler, Jabez Howes, and some others Rian didn't recognize. "You look stupid in that dress, Barn Door," Billy yelled over his shoulder after he ran by. "I can't believe you were even invited."

Rian's temper immediately reached its boiling point, and she started disengaging herself from Olivia to run after Billy.

Olivia clamped down hard on her arm to prevent it. "Don't even think about it. I know you want to wail the tar out of him, but that's what you did when you were eleven. You're thirteen years old now. He's not worth it. Plus, now he's a lot bigger than you are. Come on, let's look at the scenery."

Rian put aside her ire, at least for the moment. "You don't want to go play with the boys?"

Olivia stopped and pivoted toward the starboard side. "Goodness no. They're all too rammy for me. Except for your cousin Jabez, but he's always in such a brood."

A spasm of jealousy shot through Rian. "When have you talked to Jabez?"

"When Mother and I visit Aunt Ida at Shippen House. Trey is there, of course, and so is Billy Schiffler because they're so thick, but sometimes Jabez stops by. If Trey and Billy ignore Jabez, he comes to find me."

Rian put both elbows on the railing and watched the Pennsylvania country-side go by. "What do you talk about?"

"Not much. I don't think his father taught him the art of conversation. He sits there. I ask questions. He gives me one-word answers and doesn't ask me questions back. I pick up my book. He asks me a silly question. I put down my book and answer him and ask a new question. He gives me a one-word answer. I pick up my book. The best conversation we've had was while we were waiting to board the *Telegraph* this afternoon. He thinks your Uncle Adrian and Aunt Mila have a lot of rules. He didn't like school. Now he doesn't like working at the Krieger factories during the summer. He'd rather ram around with Trey and Billy."

Rian spit into the Delaware and watched the ripple disappear in the turbu-lence of the side paddlewheel. "It's funny he doesn't like Krieger Coach. Otto treats him like he's the son he's always wanted. Conor and I think Otto wants him to move into Conor's old bedroom."

Olivia elbowed Rian. "Jabez thinks there would be more rules in your house. Your father may want him for a son, but that's not what he wants."

"What's he want?"

"He wants to spend the summer swimming, not working. Plus, he says your Uncle Adrian likes you more than him."

Rian stood up and faced Olivia. "He said that?"

"Yes. He heard your uncle tell the foreman there to let you help the work-ers even though the foreman doesn't like you. Your uncle said you are a good worker."

"Uncle Adrian would lighten up on Jabez if he worked like he was supposed to. So Otto hates it when I go out and work in Krieger Coach because I'm a girl, but Uncle Adrian likes it when I work at Krieger Locomotive."

"Yup, and Jabez hates both. How are you and your father doing these days?"

Rian returned her gaze to the passing Pennsylvania shoreline. "Terrible. I almost never call him *Vater* anymore. He tried to exclude me from that meeting in the Finish Room. I say no when he tries to get me to play violin with him. He makes me wear this clown dress."

"It's not a clown dress. You'd look fine if you weren't all stiff."

Somewhere along here is the place where we rescued Peach, Rian thought to herself. *But I've learned my lesson. I can't tell Olivia about it.* "Otto says I'll have to get used to it because I'll always wear a dress in Switzerland. I'm going to run away instead."

Olivia also put her elbows on the railing and watched the passing river shore. "Where are you going to run away to?"

"I don't know for sure. Probably stow away aboard Uncle Kurt's ship. I can become a cabin boy. Sail the seas."

"You'd pretend you were a boy?"

"Sure. People who don't know me think I'm a boy anyway."

"I think that's a dumb idea. I might never see you again."

"Uncle Kurt puts into Charleston sometimes. I could come and see you."

Olivia looked down at the water. "You'll never do that. You would hate Long Pond. I can barely stand it myself. My parents are going to send me to a boarding school in Columbia in a few years anyway. Maybe I can get them to send me to Switzerland instead. We could be there together."

Rian briefly considered the thought of attending school with Olivia. It sounded appealing, just not appealing enough. She shook her head, then surveyed the *Telegraph*'s promenade deck and all the guests strolling and chatting. "Your Uncle George spent a bundle on this little expedition."

"Mother's angry at him. Well, Aunt Ida's angry, and mother's angry for her. Mother says Uncle George is whistling in the dark. He thinks all this talk of the Panic is scaring his investors, and he thinks a big event like this will assure them everything's okay, but it's really not."

"Work is down at all three Krieger factories."

"Mother says Uncle George's bank almost had to close because so many people were pulling their money out. He's hanging on by his cuticles. And Papa says the price of cotton in New Orleans dropped like a stone in the last month. Of course, that doesn't affect us because we grow rice at Long Pond."

"I'm not so sure it won't affect your father's business. A couple of weeks ago, Mr. Biddle said we're all in this together, no matter what section of the country we live in. Mr. Biddle says we're all going to catch it, and we're gonna catch it good."

MONDAY, JULY 17

· OTTO ·

I should have listened to Biddle, Otto thought to himself.

One month had passed since Krieger Coach hosted the meeting of Philadelphia's business leaders. Otto and Aaron Bassinger stood on the shop floor and looked at the finest, most opulent landau that Krieger Coach had ever built, and it was a testament to the truly international nature the Kriegers' businesses. Mahogany from Central America. Teak from the East Indies. Leather from Argentina. The hinges and latches, manufactured by Krieger Locomotive, had just returned from a shop in London that had plated them with gold. The factory's most skilled finish workers had applied extra coats of varnish and had buffed the entire landau to a high gloss.

And now, the prince who had commissioned the carriage, Friedrich of Hohenzollern-Hechingen, had backed out of the deal. The Panic of 1837, which up until this day Otto had assumed was a purely American problem, had reached Europe.

A year ago, Nicholas Biddle, the most brilliant financial mind in America since Alexander Hamilton, advised Otto to maintain his cash reserves and avoid becoming overextended. In March, Otto had ignored Biddle's advice and taken out the loan to purchase the land across Butternut Street from the three Krieger factories.

When Otto somewhat sheepishly divulged the purchase to Biddle over lunch one afternoon, Biddle clucked and congratulated him on what would probably prove to be a sound investment in the long run. But in the short run, Biddle thought it was a bad move. "Otto, I hope my prediction is wrong, for all our sakes."

* * * * *

Aaron Bassinger, who wore two hats as the bookkeeper for all three Krieger factories and president of Krieger Rail, ran his hand over the graceful curves of the landau. "What are you going to do?"

"I don't know. No one is in the market for such an expensive carriage anymore. No one is buying anything—not carriages, not railcars, not even a cart. I guess we'll park it over in the corner until someone walks in the door. How long can this downturn last?"

"Otto, you have to make a decision."

"Just because other companies are forcing their workers back to a 12-hour day does not mean Krieger Coach should do it. Besides, we don't have the work. What would we have them do?"

"I'm not talking about cutting pay; I'm talking about firing workers. You're bleeding money. You have to cut expenses somehow."

"I'll sell some of my railroad stock."

"That will help, but only for a few weeks."

Otto fished in his pocket for his pipe. "Look, they are launching the *U.S.S. Pennsylvania* down at the Navy Yard tomorrow. A few men have asked me if they can have the day off to watch it. What if we close the shop for the day and give everyone the day off?"

"Without pay?"

Otto started to lose patience with Aaron's relentless assault. "Can we exhibit a little compassion here?"

"Otto, you are a brilliant designer and a gifted salesman, but you are a terrible businessman. I can tell you where this is all going to lead. After your railroad stock is gone, you won't be able to pay your bills. Your creditors will scream, but there won't be much they can do about it save whisper about you during lunches at the United States Hotel. The last bill that will go unpaid will be your monthly mortgage remittance to the Bank of Industry. Unlike the rest of your creditors, they will not hesitate to foreclose on this factory. So you will have lost your business out of loyalty to a few workers who will lose their jobs anyway when you shutter your doors."

Otto hung his head. "All right. We close our doors for the day tomorrow. The workers go without pay. I will tell the workers about tomorrow."

Although the task of telling the workers was undoubtedly going to be unpleasant, that was not his most troubling thought. *When I took out the loan to buy the land across the street four months ago, I added our home as additional collateral. If I default on the loan, I lose everything.*

* * * * *

· LOGAN ·

Logan Gallagher entered Freeman Hydraulics, more than a little uncomfortable. He was the only white person in the building. *If this were reversed, a lone colored would probably get the shit kicked out of him.* Instead of stares and glares, the few men and boys in the shop paid little attention to him. When he knocked at the open doorway to the office, a pretty young woman smiled at him, rose from her desk, and walked around to greet him.

"May I help you?"

Her gaze was direct, her bearing confident. She appeared to be about his age. Unlike most of the girls Logan knew, she stood up straight. She looked him right in the eye. Her skin was lighter than most Negroes he'd seen, although she couldn't have passed as white. The fact that this was a Black-owned enterprise that only hired Black people was proof enough of her Negro heritage. *But still, if I weren't with me boys and she walked by me on the street, I'd sure give her a whistle.*

"I'm looking for Jules Freeman," he stammered. "I've got a message for him from Adrian Krieger."

"He's not here at the moment. I am Miss Freeman, Mr. Freeman's daughter. What's the message?"

Logan had tried to read Adrian's note when he was walking from Krieger Locomotive to Freeman Hydraulics, but even block letters were challenging, and Adrian had written the note in script. "I don't know. Something about the boilers."

The girl held out her hand. "Then do you have something in writing?"

Logan handed her the note, chastising himself for not doing so in the first place.

Miss Freeman unfolded the sheet of paper and read. Logan watched her eyes shift rapidly side-to-side down the page, reading words with ease that had been a mystery to him. *She doesn't even move her lips.*

Miss Freeman looked up from the paper. "Please tell Mr. Krieger that my father will send a crew tomorrow to pick up the boiler and the pump. Or would you prefer that I write a note to that effect?"

Logan was desperate to reclaim a bit of dignity, even though this young woman was likely unaware that she had made him feel small. "No, I can deliver the message, but tomorrow won't work. They're closing all the shops so the men can watch the *Pennsylvania* get launched."

"Of course. Now that you mention it, my father has made the same decision. Are you going to watch?"

"I'll be down by the Navy Yard, but I'll be working with some friends. Mr. Krieger is going to want to know who I spoke to. I know Jules has a number of daughters."

The young woman smiled, and her gaze again met Logan directly. "I'm Martha. Maybe I'll see you at the Navy Yard tomorrow."

"Not likely," Logan responded. He regretted his words immediately because he saw a mask descend over this pretty young woman's face. He tried to recover. "There's supposed to be a hundred thousand people there tomorrow. The chances of us running into one another are pretty slim."

But it was too late. The mask remained.

"Please tell Herr Krieger my father will send a crew to pick up the boiler on Wednesday."

* * * * *

Shyte, Logan said to himself as he left Freeman Hydraulics. *I didn't mean it to come out the way it sounded.* If he noticed that he was chastising himself for inadvertently hurting a Black girl's feelings, the thought was fleeting and forgotten before he reached Broad Street.

* * * * *

· RIAN ·

Rian was sitting on the front steps of her house when she looked south on Ninth Street. A man walked toward her with the distinctive rolling gait of a sailor just off his ship. He was big, beefy, and tanned by the sun. Even from two blocks away, she knew it was her Uncle Kurt.

Kurt Krieger had fled Wurttemberg with Rian's father, Uncle Adrian, and their sister Monika in 1820. The allure of the sea had captured him before they landed in America. While his brothers started to establish themselves in Philadelphia, he haunted the wharves until he signed onto his first ship. Since then, he hadn't settled anywhere. These days he worked as a ship's carpenter on whatever coastal schooners sailed up and down the Atlantic Seaboard. Whenever his ship docked in Philadelphia, he headed to 134 North Ninth Street to bunk with Otto and Rian. Rian had come to expect him to visit every two or three weeks, but if the span went for three months, it wasn't a surprise.

Rian loved Kurt's visits because he told her tales of faraway places, from Halifax to New Orleans. And every once in a while, he brought her a gift.

Kurt's seabag was strapped over his shoulder, and he carried something Rian didn't recognize. She ran to greet her uncle.

When Kurt saw Rian, he dropped his seabag and carefully placed the other package on the brick sidewalk. Rian leaped into his arms and—despite Kurt's bulk—knocked him back half a step.

"My goodness, *Liebling*! You're growing up so much. Soon you'll be too big to jump on me like that." Rian was pleased that she wasn't getting so big that he let her go right away but eventually unwrapped her arms from around his neck.

"Where did you sail to this time, Uncle?" She stepped back to look at him. Kurt was the tallest and beefiest of the three brothers. His hair was long and tied in a ponytail, and during these summer months, he was clean shaven. His skin was tanned dark from hours in the sun.

"It was an easy trip this time. My first visit to the island of Cuba. And I brought you a present." He reached down and picked up a wicker bird cage that held a bright yellow bird. "The city of Havana is a spectacular place, filled with white houses and cobblestone streets. The residents all have birds like this. They're called canaries. They keep them inside at night, but during the daytime, they hang the cages outside on the street. The streets are filled with their songs as you walk along. It's quite magical."

As if on cue, the canary emitted a chirp that Rian instantly fell in love with. "Does he have a name?"

"Nope, I thought you would want to name him."

"Then I'll call him Havana." *And now I'll have something to tell my troubles to.* Rian picked up Kurt's seabag and started walking toward her house. "Father wants to send me to some stupid school in Switzerland."

"He does, does he?"

"Yes, but I'm not going."

"And just how are you going to manage that?"

"I don't know yet." *But it might involve stowing away on your ship the next time you're in port.*

"How are your father and Jules doing?

"They're still not talking. I haven't seen Jules in a long time. I guess he's just concentrating full time on getting Freeman Hydraulics going."

"Why aren't you at the shop?"

"*Vater* let everyone out early. He said it was so that they could watch the launch of the *Pennsylvania* tomorrow, but no one was fooled. Everyone knows business is bad, and this is just an excuse to not pay them for the day."

"Ouch. Are you going to watch the launch?"

"Mm-hmm. Conor, Olivia, and I are gonna go down to the Navy Yard and find a place to watch."

"What about your father? Is he going to the launch?"

"Mr. Biddle invited *Vater* to be on the ship when they launch it."

"My brother's getting to be quite the bigwig. Being part of a ship's christening is pretty special. How did he wrangle that?"

"Mr. Biddle's brother is the captain of the ship. I think Mr. Biddle wants *Vater* to do business with his bank. But *Vater* is pretty loyal to Mr. Shippen. He likes the Bank of Industry."

"Yes, I remember. I don't like that Shippen fellow."

"He's my friend Trey's father. I don't know if I like him or not. Do you want to watch the launch with us? The Tuckers would probably like it if they thought Olivia would be with an adult."

"Hmm, the only time I met Randolph Tucker, his daughter laid into him for taking a prostitute to see Joice Heth. I'm not sure he'll appreciate seeing me."

"If you don't say anything, he won't either."

"What about Conor? Won't he be with us?"

"Uh, we're not telling the Tuckers about Conor because he's Irish. They wouldn't like her consorting with the poorer elements."

"So, Tucker and I won't mention our only awkward meeting. You're not telling them at all about Conor because he's Irish. That, dear Rian, sounds like a foolproof plan. How much trouble could we possibly get into?"

TUESDAY, JULY 18

· MADDIE ·

Maddie hooked her arm into her husband's and pulled him close as they walked east on Lombard Street. "You are in a pensive mood this morning, Mr. Freeman."

"Oh, I'm just a bit agog at this day's events. Seventeen years ago, I was a runaway yokel who had heard that Philadelphia was a place I could call myself free. And now? Now I'm walking with my beautiful wife to go sailing with the richest Black man in Philadelphia—one of the richest men in Philadelphia, period."

"I think you underestimate your worth. You came to Philadelphia with carpentry skills. You could read and write. You demonstrated your character by immediately volunteering at the Aid Society to help better the lot of your fellow Negroes . . ."

"Where I met you."

"You applied your skills and ably served as Otto Krieger's foreman as his business grew . . ."

"A stroke of fortune afforded few Black men. It was only because I saved Otto from getting a thrashing the day he got off the boat from Germany."

"And you were his first employee when he started making wheelbarrows and stuck with him as he grew his business . . ."

"Before he fired me."

Maddie laughed and drew him even closer. "But in the meantime, you built your home and started your own business. Your children go to work with you every day. They watch you and they learn from you. They adore you. You now employ five other Negroes. You have been active in the Underground Railroad for more than a decade. I think that qualifies you to get on James Forten's boat."[13]

---

13. The grandson of four ex-slaves, James Forten had been born free in Philadelphia. After the Revolutionary War, he apprenticed to a white sailmaker. Forten learned his trade well, and eventually became the foreman of the sailmaker's shop. When his employer retired, Forten purchased the business. He invented machinery that made the business even more profitable. He took risks, expanded the operation, and bought

"Thank you for your confidence in me. Speaking of our children, have you had the birds and bees conversation with Martha yet?"

Maddie smiled and looked at the cobblestones as they continued to walk. "I don't know who was more embarrassed, her or me. She claims that she has no interest in boys at the moment, and there certainly is no one special. While we're on the subject, what would you think of Thomas Forten as a match?"

"James's son? How old is he, twenty? Three minutes ago, you said I underestimated my worth. I have to marvel at you, dear wife. Now I see what is happening. You have ambitions far loftier than watching the launch of a ship from a sailboat in the Delaware."

* * * * *

· MARTHA ·

Before Martha's parents had left for their sailing excursion, her father had pressed three quarter-dollars into her hand. "Your mother and I will be out on the boat with the Fortens and the Purvises," Jules had said, "so you're in charge. There will be street vendors all up and down the waterfront. This should be enough to buy you and your brothers and sisters something to eat. The battleship launches at three."

Hoping to find a good vantage point to watch the launch of the *U.S.S. Pennsylvania*, Martha hustled her five younger siblings out of the house with plenty of time to get to the docks near the Navy Yard. As the current of people grew heavier on Christian Street, she held tight to ten-year-old Gladys's hand. Farther on, the crowd became so dense that walkers spilled off the sidewalks and into the street. She led her group around a landau and pair at a standstill. For once, out of sheer numbers, the walkers ruled the streets and were loath to cede space to the carriage, despite the driver's cursing.

The crowd's numbers could have been overwhelming, but everyone except for the carriage's occupants was in a joyous mood.

---

real estate in and out of Philadelphia. He loaned money to other people, both Black and white. He bought shares of ships sailing as far away as China.

Forten's wealth allowed him to advocate for the rights of his fellow free Blacks and campaign for an end to slavery. He stalwartly campaigned against the movement to deport freed slaves to Africa, and was instrumental in convincing William Lloyd Garrison to oppose the colonization movement. He became a major contributor—monetarily and through letters and articles—to Garrison's newspaper, *The Liberator*. In the early 1820s, he attempted to form a Black fire company in Moyamensing, but the venture failed due to the antipathy of the white press. In 1833, he and James Mott joined a dedicated cadre of whites and Blacks to found the American Anti-Slavery Society.

Closer to the wharves, vendors sold popped corn, meat pies, firecrackers, and hard candies. Martha stopped to examine some little American flags. The vendor pointed out that it carried 26 stars in honor of Michigan, the state most recently admitted to the Union. Owners of warehouses along the wharf used the occasion to make some quick money. They stationed themselves outside the buildings to hook passersby into viewing the launch from their rooftops.

"Best view in Philadelphia! Rooftop viewing! Only a half-dime!" called a man with an Irish accent. He stood atop an upside-down apple box in front of a large sliding door. A sign behind him said *Building 3*. His shirt and pants were quite ratty, noteworthy in that most of the people along the wharf had dressed up to celebrate the launch of the *Pennsylvania*.

Martha peered into the cavernous darkness of the three-story warehouse. She couldn't see anything but heard the footsteps of someone descending a staircase. She did some quick math. *I can pay a nickel for each of us and still have money left over for food.* However, her mother had taught her well. She fished one of the quarter-dollars out of her purse and showed the man. "This is all I've got, Mister. How about letting all six of us in for twenty-five cents? My little sister here won't take up much space anyway."

Martha was being doubly bold. Under normal circumstances, Blacks and whites would not mix, or a different section would be set aside for Blacks to sit, but Martha figured that this was a wildcat operation and the man probably wouldn't care as long as she flashed real silver in front of him.

"Well, Little Pretty, I think we can come to some sort of accommodation. Six for the price of five seems fair to me."

Martha saw through the hawker's smarmy solicitousness. *He's being nice because he wants my money, but I want to see the launch. This is a fair deal. I don't have to like the man.* "Then we have a deal," she agreed, silently complimenting herself for her negotiating skills.

"In that case, my associate will be happy to help you." The man turned to a figure emerging from the warehouse's shadows. "Logan, please accompany these fine young people to the third floor. Give them rooftop seating if they want it."

Martha felt her heart skip a beat. *This is the young man who delivered the message from Krieger Locomotive yesterday.* But then she remembered his comment. She replaced her smile with a stony visage.

"Logan, please take these fine young people to the third floor," the man repeated.

Logan looked at Martha, then addressed the hawker. "Can't do it. It's full up there."

The man looked at Martha with an oily smile. "Oh, I'm sure there's still plenty of room on the roof yet."

Logan eyed Martha, then shifted his attention to the hawker. "No, the roof wouldn't be safe for these little kids."

Martha didn't believe the safety of her brothers and sisters was even remotely Logan's motivation for declining her business. *He doesn't want to take us to the roof because we're Black. Father has taught me to swallow my pride when I have no other options, but this time I've got a choice. I can just walk away.*

Logan turned to the hawker. "Andy, can we talk over there for a moment?"

The hawker wasn't interested in having a private conversation. "Logan, just take them to the third floor and hand them off to Eddie."

"I can't. I know this girl."

"What do you care? They're Africans."

Confused but knowing that this was not a good situation, Martha said, "I think we will take our money elsewhere. Good day."

* * * * *

· OTTO ·

Otto tamped down his nervousness as he and Nicholas Biddle stood at the right side of the entrance of the giant shiphouse in the Philadelphia Navy Yard. *Just put aside your apprehensions for the moment and admire this*, he said to himself. Before them towered the stern of the mammoth ship-of-the-line *U.S.S. Pennsylvania*. He craned his neck to gaze up at the rail that surrounded the main deck, sixty feet above. To their right, the wall of the shiphouse sloped gently inward. Directly ahead, Otto eyed an array of perhaps forty rough-cut 5x5s that angled into the side of the ship to hold it upright.

Biddle followed Otto's gaze. "Those timbers have supported the ship's hull for more than a dozen years, and in less than an hour, they'll be gone."

Otto studied the curved behemoth with the eye of an experienced designer and craftsman. "The lines are so graceful. It is truly awe-inspiring. Thank you for inviting me to this event, Nicholas. My experience is solely with vehicles that maintain contact with *terra firma*. This is the artistry of a totally different realm."

As they entered the shiphouse, they passed a worker who stood in the middle of the slipway—two parallel wooden tracks about twelve feet apart and five feet above the ground—that descended gently five hundred feet from past midship all the way into the Delaware. The worker was slathering generous gobs of tallow onto the slipway.

"I was here last week," Biddle commented as he eyed the workman. "They were building this slipway. The slope seems shallow, but James assures me it will be more than enough for the ship to slide down into the water."

And that spoke to the first thing that Otto was nervous about. *This ship weighs three thousand tons. It's more than fifty feet wide. Those skids have to keep it upright until it hits the water. Who here has the skills to determine that the skids will do their job? No one has ever launched a ship this large before.* He shoved that thought down. He had never met Biddle's brother James, a commodore in the U.S. Navy and in charge of today's launch, at least ceremonially. "Where is your brother?"

"Up on deck, I assume, greeting dignitaries."

Otto and Biddle walked into the cavernous darkness of the shiphouse. Otto touched the massive ship supports as he walked by them.

"Look," said Biddle, "they've even pre-positioned the mallets." Each mallet looked like a pickaxe handle inserted into the side of a six-inch-diameter billet of wood. "The workers will have to pound all these supports away to free the ship. Otto, this is so exciting."

Otto had to admit, it was exciting, but not in the way Biddle thought about it. *And here comes the second of my apprehensions.* They were about to ascend a set of rickety stairs that climbed sixty feet to the deck of the *Pennsylvania. Heights*, Otto said to himself, *not my favorite thing.*

* * * * *

· RIAN ·

Launch day! Rian's plan started perfectly. Conor, Kurt, and Rian walked to the Tucker summer house on Spruce Street, but Conor hung back so Rian and Kurt could pick up Olivia. In contrast to Rian's shop clothes, Olivia was dressed in a festive red, white, and blue pinafore.

They walked to the Navy Yard amid an ever-growing river of people and a party-like atmosphere.

Then things went awry. Amid all the movement and jostling, Rian and Olivia lost track of Conor and Kurt. Rian climbed a lamppost to try to spot them, or at least be spotted, but had no luck. *Hard to believe I can't see Uncle Kurt. He's gotta be one of the tallest people in this crowd.* As the three o'clock launch drew near, Rian and Olivia gave up on the other two. Amid all these people, they couldn't see the giant shiphouse that would soon disgorge the *Pennsylvania.*

Belatedly, they decided that watching from someone's rooftop might be their best option, but it was getting close to three o'clock. Although there had been hawkers in front of all the warehouses when they walked by the first time, the entrepreneurs had gone up to watch the launch themselves and shut their doors behind them.

"Best view in Philadelphia! Rooftop viewing! Only a half-dime!"

Rian heard the call from a distance. She and Olivia walked in the direction of the voice, eventually encountering a man standing at a huge sliding door in front of a three-story warehouse. A sign on the side of the warehouse tersely stated *Building 3*. Another smaller sign said *U.S. Navy Personnel Only*.

Rian approached the man, who stood atop an overturned apple crate. "How good is the view?"

The hawker looked down at her. "Depends upon how brave you are." He pivoted and pointed up to the third-floor windows. "There's probably some space left up there. But if you're not scared of heights, there's plenty of room on the roof. That's the best view anyone will have from the shore. You gotta make your decision right away, though. The ship's going to launch in a few minutes. I'm about to close up."

The man scanned the crowd, looking for other potential customers. "Best view in Philadelphia! Rooftop viewing! Only a half-dime!"

Rian was not intimidated by the idea of standing on the roof. "How do I get onto the roof?"

"It's easy." He hooked his thumb back toward the interior of the warehouse. "My associate will escort you up the stairs to the third floor. Then there's a hatch that opens to the roof. You better decide quick. Do you have five cents?"

"How many people are already up on the roof?

"I dunno, kid. A lot. You gonna go up or not? I'll let the last remaining window go for two cents. Roof's a half-dime."

Rian turned to Olivia. "Want to try the roof?"

Olivia smiled and nodded. Rian fished a dime out of her pocket. "We'll take the roof."

"A good decision. You'll never forget this day." The man grabbed Rian by the elbow, a little more roughly than she thought appropriate, and turned her toward the gaping warehouse door. "You'll have to wait a moment; we're a little shorthanded. One of our associates just quit. Apparently, he didn't want to miss the launch of the century."

* * * * *

· MARTHA ·

Martha and her siblings walked along with so many people that she despaired of ever finding a good vantage point to see the launch. Her rhythm was more *step-stop-step-stop* than a walk. She held Gladys's hand and instructed Grace and Rufus to hang onto Jeremiah and Missy in the same manner. Then Logan Gallagher somehow appeared at her side.

"Go away," she said to him.

"It's not what you think."

"How do you know what I think?"

"Because you had the same look on your face that you had yesterday."

Martha searched for a way out of the dense current of people but couldn't figure out how to maneuver her five siblings along with her. "Please just go away," she said a second time.

"Look, if I had taken you to the third floor, two men at the top of the stairs would have hit you on the head, stolen your money, and thrown you and your brothers and sisters into a storage room."

Martha scowled at Logan. "How do you know that?"

He hesitated for about three steps. "Because I was working for them."

Martha kept walking. "Was?"

"Yeah, was. I just quit."

"Why did you quit?"

"Because I didn't want to see you get hurt."

Martha looked around her to see if anyone in the stream of people could overhear their conversation. "But it was okay to hurt other people?"

"Well, I guess it was okay until it got personal."

"What do you mean?"

"Until it was somebody I knew."

"Even if that somebody's Black?"

Logan bent over, picked up a tiny 26-starred American flag that had dropped onto the wharf, and handed it to Gladys. "Yes, even that."

* * * * *

· JULES ·

Jules and Maddie arrived at James Forten's sailmaking loft just south of Pine Street and found their host preparing his thirty-foot pleasure schooner *Isabella* for an afternoon sail on the Delaware. Forten and his wife Charlotte greeted them warmly, and Forten, happy to have crewmembers to order around, put them to work. Jules read the schooner's name, written in flowery script on the transom. "James, who was Isabella?"

Forten straightened from his task on the boat and smiled. "Not who. What. The *Isabella* was the slave ship that brought my great-grandfather here in the late 1600s. I named her as an homage to him. To him, the name meant a life of servitude. It took a few generations, but to me, it means freedom."

Shortly thereafter, the Fortens' daughter, Harriet Purvis, arrived with her husband Robert, and the six mariners departed from the Willing & Francis Pier.

In no hurry to head directly to the launch site, Forten steered the *Isabella* back and forth across the Delaware between Philadelphia and Camden, allowing his passengers to admire the two cityscapes from near and far. He occasionally engaged in impromptu races with other boats, and the *Isabella*'s sleek lines and generous sails assured that it acquitted itself admirably. Eventually, Forten set a deliberate course to the ideal spot to witness the launch of the *U.S.S. Pennsylvania*. Satisfied, he threw out the *Isabella*'s anchor and settled back into his captain's chair at the stern. "That's the shiphouse that holds the battleship," he said, pointing at a huge white barn-like building in the Navy Yard. "It was built 16 years ago to house the ship."

Jules counted four stories of thirty windows each across the length of the building. "Sixteen years. That's a long time to build a ship even of this size."

"Not the shipbuilders' fault. Congress cut the budget numerous times."

Jules took in his surroundings. He acknowledged that predictions of a hundred thousand people descending on the waterfront were probably accurate. Spectators lined the wharves, hung out windows, and sat on rooftops. In addition, watercraft of every description—from rowboats to barges to steamships—were anchored in the Delaware River.

Forten pulled a towel off a wicker basket and started distributing fried egg and cheese sandwiches. "Robert and Jules, what do you hear from our friend Phineas Jenks? Any progress on derailing the "white men only" amendment to the new Pennsylvania constitution?"

"Good news," said Jules. "The Constitutional Convention has defeated the Sterigere amendment. The 'white only' clause is history."

"And now," chimed in Purvis, "the Convention has adjourned and won't reconvene until October."

"Then it's settled," said Forten. "The right of the Black man to vote is secure. Time well spent, gentlemen. My compliments to you both."

Jules still felt guarded. "It was Robert who did the hard politicking. All I did was write a few letters. However, I suppose we shouldn't crow about this until the new constitution is ratified. That's probably over a year away."

"Absolutely," said Purvis. "Take nothing for granted. But the provision was defeated 61 to 49. I think that is a pretty comfortable margin."

Forten handed out cigars to the two men. "Which is why I brought these. Ladies, please indulge us men as we celebrate our small victories."

Still enjoying his sandwich, Jules accepted the cigar but put it in his breast pocket.

The wake of a passing steam ferry rocked their boat, making all the occupants grab for anything that might tip over.

"Bastard," muttered Forten.

"Isn't there a speed limit for this part of the river?" asked Harriet Purvis as she watched the ferry steam away from them.

"Of course there is, but Frank Jessum's piloting that boat. He knows the *Isabella* is owned by a Negro, and he was getting his jollies. At least, that's part of it. But truth be told, steamboat crews look down upon us men of sail, whether we be Black or white. They plan on dominating the high seas the same way they're muscling sail craft out from along the coast."

Jules reached into the basket for another half sandwich. "Have they hurt your business?"

As the rocking ceased, Forten set a wine bottle back down on the table. "My business is down because of the depression, just like everyone's. There are not many orders for new keels, whether for sail or steam. But old ships still need new sails, so I'm doing all right."

"How long before steamships put sailing ships completely out of business?" Jules asked.

"Completely? It will never happen. Sailing's too much fun. But I look at how the steamship builders are innovating. It won't be long before they're so efficient that they can cross the Atlantic."

"When do you think that's going to happen?"

"I know the exact answer to that question. Sometime this week in Bristol, England, a shipyard is launching a steamship that will be the largest passenger ship ever built—forty feet longer than the *Pennsylvania*—and it's been built specifically for transatlantic voyages."

"So the days of sail are already numbered," Jules speculated.

Forten shook his head. "First of all, they haven't installed the steam engines in the *Great Western* yet. They're sailing her from Bristol to London so Maudslay & Sons can install two side-lever steam engines. That'll take almost a year."

"Sailing? So it's a steamship, but it still has sails?"

Forten nodded. "Even with engines that can get her across the Atlantic, she will also be equipped with four masts and a complement of sails, not just for added propulsion, but also to help stabilize her and keep both her paddlewheels in the water. So even with these innovations, I'll still have a market."

Purvis used a telescope to peer into the shiphouse that would soon give up the *Pennsylvania*. "Strikes me that the Navy's a bit slow adapting to steam. I'd say they're about to launch a dinosaur. Think how much havoc a properly armed steamship could wreak amidst sailing ships on a calm day."

Forten shrugged. "Well, they laid the keel for the *Pennsylvania* sixteen years ago. Back then, who but the visionaries would have thought that steamships would become such a force?"

"What time is it?" Charlotte Forten asked in a transparent attempt to change the topic.

James Forten looked at his pocket watch. "Three fifteen. They're already late. No one's ever launched a ship this size before. It's got to be pretty tricky. I'm sure they're in no hurry."

Jules scanned the crowd on the waterfront with Purvis's telescope. He fleetingly focused on two people who could easily have been Rian Krieger and Olivia Tucker as they disappeared into the gaping door of a warehouse.

＊ ＊ ＊ ＊ ＊

· RIAN ·

Rian heard footsteps descending the staircase, and a young man appeared out of the darkness.

"Egan," said the hawker, "these two young people want a rooftop view. Would you please make sure they get good seats?"

"Right this way, good sir and madam," said Egan with exaggerated politeness. He walked toward a set of wooden stairs. "Looking for a good view, are ye?"

Something about the man's words took Rian aback. *That was what the man said when my father arrived in America. 'Looking for a job, are ye?' He led Vater down an alley and tried to steal his tools, but Jules rescued him.*

Egan led them into the warehouse's darkness to a set of wooden stairs, then stepped aside for Rian and Olivia to precede him. "After you."

Rian climbed the first set of stairs to the second story with Olivia behind her. The second floor was cavernous and strewn with barrels and giant reels of rope. The thick oaken floorboards were well-worn and stained. The air was pungent with the smell of hemp and whale oil. There were no people at the windows. She expected to hear voices from the third floor but could hear none. "Where are all the people?"

"I guess they moved up to the roof," Egan said from behind them.

Rian walked to the next flight of stairs with growing unease. As she started up the steps to the third floor, Egan spoke in a raised voice. "Looks like our last two customers, Eddie. They want to go up to the roof!"

* * * * *

· LOGAN ·

Logan continued walking with Martha even though she hadn't spoken to him after their initial exchange. She still held her sister's hand, and her four other siblings trailed behind. The wharf was so crowded with pedestrians that it was impossible to tell that Logan was purposefully walking at her side. That fact provided him with some comfort, for a single Irish kid his age walking in public with a Black person—male or female—was likely inviting a thrashing for both of them.

"Thank you," Martha said in a voice so soft that Logan wasn't sure she had uttered anything.

"For what?"

"For saving us from getting mugged. I assume it wasn't an easy decision to make."

Logan was about to say, *It wasn't much of a decision at all. I knew you were going to get hurt, and I didn't want that to happen,* but before he could do so, the crowd parted like a river around a large rock. Directly in front of them stood a well-dressed Black man in his early twenties, about six feet tall, almost a head taller than most everyone else in the crowd.

The man looked at Martha and gave her a big, warm smile. "Good afternoon, Martha. What a pleasure to see you here. It looks like you have the entire Freeman brood today."

Martha stopped walking and offered her hand to the man. "Good afternoon, Thomas. Yes, Mother and Father left me in charge. I think they're out on the *Isabella* with your father."

If Martha hadn't thanked Logan just moments before, he would have cut his losses and kept walking. That would have been the smart thing to do.

Instead, he stopped. Just stopped. He didn't look at Thomas, whoever he was. Didn't look at Martha. Didn't look at her little brothers or sisters. Just stood there like a stick caught in the mud of the river. Revelers walked around them. *And now, here I am, obviously talking with a couple of coloreds.*

"And who might you be?" asked Thomas as he held out his hand to Logan, friendly as could be.

Logan, who until he met Martha yesterday had rarely spoken to a Black person, looked around. No one in the slow stream of passersby was paying attention to them. He shook Thomas's hand. "My name is Logan Gallagher." Thomas's grip was firm and friendly.

"Gallagher," said Thomas.

"Gallagher?" said Martha at the same time.

Thomas drew Logan slightly closer. "My name is Thomas Forten. Are you related to Seamus Gallagher?"

"Yes, he's me brother."

"Are you here to watch the launch, Logan?"

Ten minutes ago, I was here to lead as many people as I could up two flights of stairs where they would get smashed on the head and robbed of their valuables. "Yup. Er, yes, that's why I'm here. To see the launch."

"Logan just saved the six of us from getting a thrashing by some ruffians just north of here," interjected Martha. "He may have saved our lives."

Thomas looked down at Logan with his big smile. "It appears that gallantry runs in your family, Mr. Gallagher. I thank you for coming to our dear Martha's rescue." Thomas hooked his thumb toward the building behind him. "Elmer Brookes owns this warehouse. He left for Europe last week. Since he had no designs on his building today, he suggested that my father use it to watch the launch of the *Pennsylvania*, but Father chose to watch from the water instead. I was about to go up and join the others. Any brother of Seamus Gallagher is welcome to join us."

Until this moment, Logan had always been a bit ashamed of his brother's involvement with the Black community. Now, he somewhat enjoyed the good will showered on him by virtue of his brother. And he wanted to stay near Martha, but not in such a public place.

This is a bad idea, Boyo, he said to himself. "I would love to join you," he said to Thomas Forten.

* * * * *

· RIAN ·

Rian led the way up the stairs with increasing misgivings. With Egan right behind them, they had no way to go but up. When Olivia grabbed hold of her shirttail from behind, Rian took it as an indication that Olivia shared her apprehension. Rian unobtrusively fished out her pocketknife and opened the blade.

With five steps to go, Rian saw two men waiting for them at the top. One wore a beaver hat, and the other sported a bright green vest. They were smiling.

Four steps to go, railings flanked the stairs on both sides. Hat-guy leaned over the railing on the right. He held a truncheon unobtrusively in his right hand. Vest-man hung back a bit on the left.

Three steps to go, vest-man smiled and said, "Welcome to the third floor. We still have space on the roof."

This is bad. This is really bad.

With two steps to go, Rian could see that there were no people looking out the third-story windows. She silently prayed that her suspicions were wrong but knew they weren't. Olivia twisted Rian's shirttail, a silent signal that Rian interpreted as *do what you must.*

* * * * *

· OTTO ·

Otto Krieger climbed the fifth flight of rickety steps toward the deck of the *U.S.S. Pennsylvania* with growing unease. With two flights to go, he felt himself becoming increasingly closed in. His shoulders were inches away from simultaneously touching the inward-sloping wall of the shiphouse and the side of the ship.

The sense of confinement and the slight swaying of the stairs, given the number of people climbing all at once, made him more than a little uncomfortable. *Dummkopf [Idiot]*, he said to himself. *The thought of thrashing another man causes you no apprehension whatsoever, yet heights and confined spaces make your heart speed up. Just don't look down.*

Behind him, oblivious to Otto's discomfort, Nicholas Biddle provided a running commentary. "Less than a week ago, this was all scaffolding. The only way to get to the deck was to climb several ladders. They built this staircase just for today's festivities. Wait 'til you see the expanse of the top deck, Otto. You could play a game of tennis on it."

Otto had never seen a tennis court. He reached a landing, which was merely one stout board about a foot wide. Despite his previous decision not to do so, he looked down toward the floor of the shiphouse fifty feet below. The queue of people waiting to ascend the stairs had become even longer than it had been when they started their climb ten minutes ago.

Otto focused on the man on the steps in front of him. *Was mache ich hier [What am I doing here]?* he asked himself. He felt his stomach do another flip-flop.

"It's going to be the largest ship-of-the-line the world has ever seen," Biddle continued. "It'll carry 120 guns on three gundecks. It will soon be the pride of the U.S. Navy, big enough to go toe-to-toe with anything Great Britain has to offer."

Otto arrived at the top of the stairs and gratefully stepped onto the battle-ship's expansive main deck. For no reason save gauging the height, he reached up and could almost touch the horizontal tie beam of one of the shiphouse's trusses above him. "There is no room for masts."

"Of course not," said Biddle, slightly out of breath from the climb. "They will be erected after the ship is launched. I'm so happy you could come with me today, Otto. Given all the difficult economic news, it is good for the country to have something to celebrate." Biddle looked around the deck of the ship. "Otto, I want to check in with my brother. I'll be gone for a few minutes, but I won't desert you."

Otto suddenly found himself alone on the crowded deck of the battleship with scores of men and women who seemed to have no doubt about their right to be there. It was noisy. *Dummkopf,* he said to himself for the second time that afternoon. *What am I doing here? These are not my people. No one will be able to understand me because of my accent.*

People clustered around tables at various locations on the deck. At second glance, Otto realized the "tables" were heavy planks set atop barrels. Uniformed sailors poured champagne into flutes. *I guess the teetotalers have not found the U.S. Navy yet.*[14]

"Krieger, I hoped you would be here today."

Otto turned to see his friend George Shippen holding two champagne flutes, one of which he held out to Otto. Otto gratefully took the proffered glass. "Yes, I was just despairing of finding anyone to talk to."

---

14. In 1830, consumption of alcohol peaked in America at 7.1 gallons of pure alcohol per person (compared to 2 gallons today). In response, the temperance movement gathered momentum on a nationwide scale. Drunkenness, which ruined thousands of lives and families, was becoming part of the American conversation. Teetotalers, those individuals who had taken the pledge of total abstinence from alcohol, held a hard, judgmental line. This era also witnessed soaring church membership. Churches and teetotalers frequently found common cause based in a rigid Protestant sense of moral righteousness.

"No need for apprehension. I'm happy to stick with you a bit." Shippen hooked his elbow into Otto's arm. "Let me give you a bit of a tour."

Otto looked over at Biddle, who had joined a cluster of men, some in uniform. "Who is Nicholas talking with?"

"The Biddle brothers are quite the powerhouse, although Nicholas's influence is thankfully waning. James is the *Pennsylvania*'s captain. They're chatting with the naval architect Samuel Humphries. He designed this ship. Interesting character. He turned down an offer from the Tsar of Russia to modernize the Russian navy. I marvel that a powerful despot half a world away finds himself more closely aligned with our young republic than the British."

Otto was still a bit peeved at Biddle for inviting him to this ceremony, then immediately deserting him. "Those men over there. Who are they?"

Shippen sniffed. "A bit of an odd couple. The man on the left is our senator, James Buchanan of Lancaster. His companion is William Rufus King, senator from Alabama."

"What is a senator from Alabama doing here?"

"They are both bachelors—roommates in Washington. Andy Jackson used to call them Miss Nancy and Aunt Fancy. Rumor has it that they are paramours."

"Really? Do you approve of that sort of thing?"

Shippen shrugged. "Buchanan has his uses. Despite Old Hickory's disdain, Miss Nancy calls himself a Jacksonian Democrat. He hated Biddle's National Bank, which suited me just fine. I wish he looked more favorably on internal improvements."

"Given their predilections, I'm a bit astounded that those two have risen this far in politics."

"I'm sure that's about as far as they will go. From what I hear, neither one is particularly adept. There's John Swift, mayor of Philadelphia, talking with Secretary of the Navy Mahlon Dickerson."

"A mixed group."

"Yes, as I look around, I see Jacksonian Democrats, Whigs, Anti-Masons. I guess everyone loves a good party. And the opportunity to be seen, of course."

Otto grew tired of Shippen's tour. "George, I have some business to discuss. If you don't mind, we could do it here and save me a trip to your office."

"Schiffler told me you asked for an extension on this month's payment on your mortgage."

"Yes, as you know, business is down considerably. I was counting on payment for a carriage we built for a German prince, but he has since canceled the order. I am unable to make a payment at this moment. I intend to sell some railroad stock soon. I can use that to make this month's payment."

Shippen put his champagne flute down on a barrel, took his eyes off the crowd, and bored into Otto. "I hope it doesn't come to that, Krieger. The value of *PW&B* stock has plummeted since the crisis began. I think it's time to fire some of those Irish workers you hired last year."

"Only two Irish are left, and they are doing little more than sweeping floors."

"Then I suspect your concessions will have to come elsewhere. I assume you haven't started building on that land you bought across the street from the factory."

"No, I suspect that is now years away."

"Well, that land should be the first thing to go, but I'm telling you, you bought that property at the peak of the market. No one will buy it for what you paid for it. And if you can't sell it, the bank will foreclose on it, and you will still owe us more money to make up the difference. That is why Schiffler demanded your house as collateral. I will stall the bank board off as long as possible, but sooner or later, they will demand a reconciliation. The process is quite heartless."

Shippen's dire explanation made Otto's heart pound. *My God, my recklessness has ruined me. Not just the factory, but the house, too. What am I going to do?* The blood thumped rhythmically in his ears, so hard that he felt like the ship's deck was shaking beneath his feet. Then Otto realized the thumping in his ears coincided with the *thonk* of wooden mallets striking the 5x5 supports fifty feet below. The workers were hammering the timbers away from the sides of the ship. The deck of the *U.S.S. Pennsylvania* truly was shaking. The largest ship-of-the-line the world had ever seen was moments away from its launch.

* * * * *

· LOGAN ·

Logan sat on the sloped warehouse roof next to Martha. Now the acknowledged knight in shining armor who had rescued Martha and her siblings from dastardly ruffians, he continued to play the role.

He had climbed a ladder through a hatch in the roof, emerged into the sunlight, and become overwhelmed by too many things to think about at once. The roof sloped gently toward the Delaware. The view of the wharves, the river, and New Jersey was spectacular. There was no guardrail, and the drop to the wharf below was easily forty feet. The *Pennsylvania*'s shiphouse was a mere thousand feet to the south. Twenty Black people—men, women, and children—sat near the peak, some looking at him with curiosity, some with disinterest, none with hostility.

As Martha's siblings emerged through the hatch, Logan helped them step onto the roof and cautioned them to stay away from the edge. He helped Martha, the last in line, with dutiful courtesy. Jeremiah and Missy wanted to play gotcha-last, but he quickly put an end to that. Martha waved polite hellos to various people but made no attempt to talk to any of them.

Logan didn't relax until everyone was seated. "I think this is the best view in the city. We got real lucky."

"You didn't tell me you were Seamus Gallagher's brother."

"I don't believe you ever asked me name yesterday."

"And you didn't introduce yourself. Are you going to join the United No Name Fire Brigade?"

"Until an hour ago, I expected I would join Moya. Now I don't know. Who is Thomas Forten?"

"He's the son of a friend of my father's. He's twenty. Mother thinks we would be a good match."

"What do you think?"

"I think I'm only seventeen, and I don't need to decide yet. Besides, I like working at Freeman Hydraulics. If I got married, I would have to quit. What about you? Are you going to continue your life of crime?"

Logan had no idea how his decision to desert the muggers would affect his future, but he didn't think now was the time to be wishy-washy. "No, I think me life of crime is behind me. I think I can make something of meself at Krieger Coach."

A small cannon fired near the entrance to the shiphouse. Then a roar built up from a hundred thousand people who had massed at the waterfront and on the Delaware. Bells rang. Steam whistles blew. A band started playing "Yankee Doodle."

Ever so slowly, the *U.S.S. Pennsylvania*, the largest warship yet to grace the seas, emerged from the shiphouse and slid down the slipway toward the Delaware River.

* * * * *

· RIAN ·

Olivia's silent signal cemented Rian's decision. *Attack where your enemies are not prepared. Go to where they do not expect.* Rian thanked Sun Tzu for his two-thousand-year-old wisdom. Before she reached the top step, she plunged the blade of her pocket knife as hard as she could into hat-guy's thigh.

"Shit!" he yelled as he dropped the truncheon. "The little fook stuck me!"

Rian stole a quick look behind her. Olivia faced downstairs. Egan, who had been following them, was nowhere to be seen.

She heard Uncle Kurt call her name from down below just as Egan yelled, "Someone's coming, Eddie!"

"Uncle!" Rian yelled.

Vest-man tried to strike Rian in the head from the other side of the railing, but she ducked out of the way. With no contact to break his momentum, he lost his balance and almost flipped over the railing. Rian swiped at him with her knife but nicked only his shirt near the shoulder. He recovered and backed up to give Rian room to climb the last step. She picked up hat-guy's truncheon.

"Rian, are you up there?" Kurt called from the bottom of the stairs. She heard Conor yell something unintelligible.

Outside, the crowd started to roar.

"Uncle, help us!" Rian yelled.

"Conor, come quick!" yelled Olivia.

The roar from the crowd increased. Olivia reached the top of the stairs. She spotted a discarded 2x4 and picked it up.

Vest-man smiled malevolently at Rian. "So, yer a ferocious one. Come to Eddie. I'll show ya how to properly use that toad-sticker."

Cannons boomed, boomed again, and boomed again.

Rian glanced behind her to see Olivia blocking hat-guy with her board. He was holding his bloody thigh and not particularly interested in fighting. Egan had disappeared. *Olivia could have run away, but she didn't.*

Rian assessed their situation. Vest-man was an inch taller than Rian and forty pounds heavier. He had assumed a fighting stance with his truncheon in his right hand. Rian had her knife in her right hand and hat-guy's truncheon in her left.

"We're coming, Rian!" Kurt yelled from below.

With reinforcements arriving momentarily, Rian didn't feel a need to push vest-man too hard.

"Come on, you little prick," vest-man muttered.

Then Uncle Kurt, six-foot-four and two hundred pounds, appeared with Conor, already five-foot-ten but skinny as a rail. Kurt wielded a large box-end wrench, and Conor had his pocketknife out and ready.

"Who are these guys?" asked Kurt.

"Not friends," Rian responded, relieved to have the numbers overwhelmingly in her favor.

Outside, a band played "Yankee Doodle."

To her right, hat-guy said, "Eddie, he stuck me pretty bad. I've gotta get out of here." With a glance, Rian saw a growing stain on the man's thigh and more blood on the floor.

That made it three against one with no likelihood of help coming from the long-gone Egan or the injured hat-guy. Eddie reassessed. "Tell you what, Buckoes. You let me help my friend down the stairs, and you'll never see us again."

No one relaxed, but they stepped aside to clear the way for the two muggers. Eddie grabbed hat-guy under the armpit and stooped to pick up a satchel near the top of the stairs.

"No," said Kurt. "Leave the satchel."

"Aw, come on!" Eddie complained.

In response, Kurt banged the wrench down hard on the stair railing.

Eddie reluctantly dropped the satchel. He assisted his bleeding friend as he hobbled down the stairs.

Kurt still held the wrench at the ready position. "Jaysus, Rian, I thought you said you would stay out of trouble."

Rian shut her eyes briefly and shook her head. She started shaking. "I just stabbed a man."

Conor reached over and pried the truncheon out of her hand. "Well, you've proved it once again."

Rian reached back to the stair railing for support. "What's that?"

"What your da always says. Krieger means warrior in German. You're a Warrior by name and a warrior by nature. You're thirteen years old, and you've stabbed a man."

Rian felt too overwhelmed by the confrontation to take much credit for anything. "Thanks for coming to get us."

"Not sure I want this to get back to me brothers," said Conor. "Hugh Callaghan ain't going to like it when he finds out it was us who screwed up his boys' little operation." Conor walked over to look inside the satchel. He found money, jewelry, a silver cigarette case, a wallet, and a few cigars. "Who does all this belong to?"

As if in answer to his question, they heard someone pounding on the door of a storage room built into the corner of the warehouse.

* * * * *

· OTTO ·

Otto stood at the portside main deck of the mastless ship, dejected about his finances, but relieved that the *U.S.S. Pennsylvania* had successfully launched. He watched crews in a dozen tugboats straining at their oars, some towing the ship toward its berth, others pushing directly into its side to move it toward the Navy Yard dock.

Nicholas Biddle, who had been socializing the entire time, finally circled back to Otto. "What did Shippen have to say?"

"We talked business. It wasn't good. I'm afraid I have overextended myself."

"Well, Shippen is not in a position to chastise you for overextending. Last month, so many people ran to the Bank of Industry to pull out their savings that he had to close for a week. He called in three loans that I know of that ruined men who I would describe as gold-plated members of Philadelphia's elite. I'm surprised he's held off on doing the same to you. Do not give him an excuse to call in your loans. He is drowning. He won't hesitate to bring down others to save himself."

Oh, Rian, I'm afraid I have ruined your chances of ever marrying well. I am so sorry. Now, the meager savings I have left will go to that school in Switzerland. That way, you will not have to watch my humiliation. I shall recalibrate my dreams. I don't have to be successful. I just have to make sure you marry well. And now that can happen only if you sail to Europe.

SUNDAY, JULY 30

· RIAN ·

Rian, Conor, and Jabez sat on the roof of the Sparks Shot Tower and watched the sun set to the west. It had been hot at the base of the tower, but here a cool breeze wafted by them. From this vantage point, the city seemed beautiful and serene. Long narrow shadows from church spires and factory chimneys lengthened incrementally. People emerged from their summer-baked houses for after-supper walks around their neighborhoods. A gaggle of kids played rounders in a vacant field, their voices wafting up to the watchers.

"Your da's ship is coming in tomorrow," said Conor.

"How do you know?" asked Jabez.

Conor hesitated, then said, "I heard two men talking about it at the Merchants' Exchange."

Smart lie, thought Rian. *I don't think letting Jabez know that Conor and I broke the businessmen's code would be a good idea.*

"I don't care. I hate him," responded Jabez.

Rian was still angry with her father, but she certainly didn't hate him. *Conor doesn't have a father to hate. Olivia hates her father because he's a slaveholder. Jaysus.* "Don't you want to see him? It's been almost five months since he dropped you off. He'll have some great stories to tell."

"Everybody thinks Captain is such a great man. He's not great at all. He sits in his cabin all day. That's why he got fired from his last ship."

Conor beat Rian to the obvious question. "He got fired from the *Albatross*?"

"Yes, he did. Ship captains on the China run are supposed to be the best in the world. Well, they might have thought Captain was for a while, but after our third trip, his partners took the *Albatross* away from him and gave him a choice: take over the *Bridger*, or they would buy him out. He took the *Bridger*."

Rian looked over at Jabez. "I saw the *Bridger*. It's a Baltimore Clipper. It's beautiful. I imagine it's fast, too."

"That's just it. It has to be fast. It's a slave ship. The faster they get from Africa to Cuba, the fewer slaves die. Plus, they can outrun any Navy ship that tries to stop them. Doesn't matter who it is, American or British, the *Bridger* is faster."

Rian looked to the south, as if the *Bridger* might be sailing up the Delaware at this very moment. "If it's a slave ship, what's it doing coming up here?"

Jabez spat off the side of the platform and watched his spit descend until it was out of sight. "The one time I made that trip, we sailed to Africa loaded with stuff to trade for slaves in West Africa: gunpowder, rifles, rum. Then we dropped the slaves off in Cuba and loaded up with stuff that is valuable up here, like sugar and coffee. That's when I jumped ship. I couldn't stand the thought of all the moaning and crying from down below. When somebody died, they just threw the body overboard. The stink was awful. I'll never do that again."

"You jumped ship because your father became a slaver?"

Jabez gazed at something on the western horizon. "First mate said that if Captain came north with all those platforms still in place, people would know the *Bridger* is a slave ship. Captain said no one would give a shit. Plus, he said he didn't give a shit, either. All he ever did anyway was sit in his cabin and drink."

"Jaysus," Rian and Conor said in unison.

TUESDAY, AUGUST 1

· ADRIAN ·

"What are you going to say to Levi?" Otto asked Adrian as they approached the Imlay & Potts Pier.

Adrian fleetingly thought of several questions. *Why didn't you tell us you were in town? Why did Jabez change so much in his five years at sea? Why aren't you captain of the Albatross anymore?* "I'm going to ask him why the *Bridger* has been docked in Philadelphia for a full day, and he has not yet come to see his son."

Otto stopped and looked up at the ship. He had been using his lumber rule as a walking stick. Now he rested it on his shoulder. "Rian is the one who called my attention to the Harbor List. She says Jabez doesn't want to see his father."

"I can't imagine that having him sail into port for the first time in five months and not bother to say hello helps any."

The Imlay & Potts Pier was busy. Two cranes serviced the ship. One crane's rope disappeared into the *Bridger*'s forehold. The other had lowered a pallet of burlap sacks onto the pier. Men were loading the sacks onto a wagon.

A guard stood at the bottom of the gangway that led to the ship. Adrian straightened himself and assumed his most commanding demeanor. "We are here to see Captain Howes."

The guard looked at Adrian, then Otto. "Captain's busy. Who might you two be?"

"We are his brothers-in-law," said Adrian.

"First mate's instructions are to let no one aboard. No exceptions."

Adrian looked at Otto. *How are we going to get by this gump?*

Then a voice from the deck above: "Higgins, who are those two men?"

The guard turned to a man standing at the top of the gangway. "They want to see the captain, sir. They claim to be kin."

"Let them board."

Adrian and Otto climbed the gangway and greeted the man, who didn't smile, didn't bow, didn't offer to shake their hands. "My name is Harris. I'm first mate of the *Bridger*. Follow me." Harris turned and headed for a door that led belowdecks. "Shouldn't be doing this, but something's gotta be done."

Adrian examined the interior as Harris escorted them down a ladder and along a hallway to the captain's quarters. To his untrained eye, everything looked shipshape.

"Captain hasn't been feeling well this trip," said Harris. "We've barely seen him. A visit from you two might do him good."

The first mate knocked on the captain's door. There was no answer, but he opened the door and walked through, leaving Adrian and Otto in the hallway. Otto started to say something, but Adrian put his hand on his brother's arm to shush him. Adrian listened as intently as he could. *Muted voices. Indistinct. The first mate insisting. Levi's response was more of a growl.*

Harris returned to the hallway. "Captain can't see you now."

"Is the captain ill?"

"No, Captain's fine. He just doesn't want to see you. I'm to escort you back dockside."

Adrian gave Otto a look: *We could just barge through the door.* Otto shook his head and turned to follow the first mate. When they arrived at the top of the gangway, Adrian hesitated and addressed the first mate. "Are you sure the captain's not sick?"

"Sick in the head, maybe. Not your affair. Begone now."

Otto started down the ramp. Adrian turned to follow him.

"Makes my job easier," the first mate said to Adrian, almost as an afterthought. "Been running the ship for lack of effort from your brother-in-law. Only wish I were getting the captain's share of the profits."

"If we could just speak with him . . ."

The first mate shook his head. "Captain don't give many orders these days, but this one was clear. He wanted you escorted off this ship. Sorry, gents. We just wasted your time and mine."

* * * * *

· OTTO ·

Otto and Adrian reached the bottom of the gangway, turned, and looked back up toward the main deck of the *Bridger*. The first mate was already nowhere to be seen.

"Uncles!"

Otto looked toward the voice and saw Seamus Gallagher and three other men aboard a pallet that one of the cranes had lifted out of the hold and was lowering to the pier. Seamus held onto a guy rope with one hand, seemingly unconcerned by the height.

It had been five months since Otto had fired Seamus for his role in Rian's Underground Railroad activities. Whatever ire he harbored from Seamus's transgression had cooled to a simmer. He chastised himself. *I have given little thought to my nephew's new circumstances. He's a stevedore—a day worker—not much different from the ditchdigger he was before I hired him two years ago.*

Adrian, who hadn't taken sides in the snit between Otto and Seamus, immediately started walking toward the descending pallet. "Seamus! How good to see you!"

Seamus stepped off the pallet before it seated on the pier. "It's noontime break. We've got an hour. Most of the men go home for dinner, but there's a grog shop on Water Street that serves a pretty good mutton stew. How about if me favorite uncles treat me to a meal?"

* * * * *

Otto, Adrian, and Seamus found an isolated table in the dark, low-ceilinged tavern and ordered the stew. Otto was relieved to find that their conversation, stilted at first, loosened up as they caught up on each other's lives. Seamus was scraping by working at the docks, firefighting, occasionally pilfering in the evening, and—an enterprise Otto had never envisioned—selling information about incoming ships to people who could profit by advance notice. *However, he doesn't tell us how he gets this information.*

Otto admitted that business at Krieger Coach was down dramatically, and what little savings he had left would be spent sending Rian to finishing school in Switzerland come September. He feared he was going to lose everything.

Adrian said that business was also down at Krieger Locomotive. Freeman Hydraulics was helping by ordering boilers for their fire pumps, but with a few more bad months, all the Krieger factories could go out of business. On a personal level, he was disappointed with Jabez Howes. Jabez wasn't the same boy who left him and Mila as an eight-year-old. This new Jabez was withdrawn, sullen, unmotivated, and even lazy.

Seamus smiled at the serving girl as she set the bowls on the table. "So, why were you two visiting the *Bridger*?"

"Jabez's father is the *Bridger*'s captain," Otto said. "The ship's been gone for almost five months. Levi Howes hasn't bothered to come ashore to visit his son. We tried to talk to him, but he wouldn't see us."

Seamus sampled his stew and added a pinch of salt. "I didn't know you were related to the captain, but I may have some scuttlebutt that fills in some holes for you. There's a few crew members doing repairs in the hold while we're unloading the sugar sacks. They talk. The captain barely came out of his cabin this entire trip. The only person who sees him is the first mate, and the story is he's getting a mite discontented with the situation."

"What's wrong with Levi?"

"Well, now the story becomes a matter of speculation. Perhaps it's because his son is no longer with him. Perhaps it's because he's been knocked down a peg because his partners took his China ship away from him. But the story that'll make the hair stand up on the back of your neck is that the *Bridger*'s a slave ship, and Captain Howes is ashamed of his current profession."

Otto's spoon clattered into his bowl. "A slave ship? That can't possibly be true."

"Uncle, I've been down in the hold the better part of two work days. I can tell you that it is true. There are platforms stacked one above the other down there, with little more than a foot of room to the one above. I did the calculating. There's room on that ship for more than two hundred people. The crew says that the poor wretches lie on them for weeks as they cross the Atlantic. The rings to hold the chains are bolted to the platforms. The hold still stinks of filth from those poor people, even though the holds have held nothing but sugar and coffee for the past two weeks. It's disgusting."

When the three men exited into the light and heat of the day, Otto said, "Something should be done. The transatlantic slave trade has been illegal for thirty years."

Seamus put his hands in his pockets. "Are you going to turn in your brother-in-law? He'll lose his ship. Probably go to jail. That'll probably affect Jabez even worse."

"Something should be done. When does the *Bridger* leave port?"

"We just finished unloading her. Strawboss says we've gotta have her loaded back up by quitting time tonight. She sails with the morning tide tomorrow."

"In that case," said Otto, "I'm going to talk to the harbormaster. Perhaps he can do something about this." He turned and headed south on Water Street. *The additional walk will do me good.*

* * * * *

· JULES ·

Is this a dream or a nightmare? Jules thought to himself. *How can I feel elated and discouraged at the same time?* He stood on the corner of Sixth and Haines Street with thirty adults, pretty evenly divided between Black and white, male and female. *A gathering in public like this may be almost unprecedented in Philadelphia history.*

Jules scanned the crowd. He knew most of the men from his work with the Pennsylvania Anti-Slavery Society or through Maddie's work with the Philadelphia Female Anti-Slavery Society. The Quakers Lucretia and James Mott were there, as were Robert and Harriet Purvis and James and Charlotte Forten.

The occasion was a tour of the recently cleared site for Pennsylvania Hall, the Pennsylvania Hall Association's future "Temple of Freedom." Twine that ran from stake to stake defined straight lines and a perfect sixty-two-foot by hundred-foot rectangle. A crew of ditchdiggers had already started shoveling the trench for the building's foundation along Haines Street.

Daniel Neall, president of the Association, faced the gathering with his back to the site. Next to him stood the Hall's architect, thirty-one-year-old Thomas Somerville Stewart. "We want to thank all of you shareholders for your generous financial support to make Pennsylvania Hall a reality," Neall announced. "To date, we have sold fifteen hundred shares at $20 apiece, which puts us more than halfway to our funding goal."

The crowd erupted in polite applause and a *huzzah!* The mood was light, optimistic.

"I now turn you over to Mr. Stewart," said Neall, "who will spark your imagination with a tour of what you will see on this site a mere nine months from now."

Stewart raised his arms as he walked backward across Sixth Street. "Ladies and gentlemen, please follow me."

Some people immediately followed Stewart. Others, cognizant of traffic coming from both directions, hesitated. Jules found himself crossing the street next to Lucretia Mott. A man driving a freight wagon could have reined his horses to allow the entire group to pass. Instead, he slapped the reins to encourage his horses forward.

Jules impulsively grabbed Lucretia's arm to hold her back from the oncoming wagon, then immediately released it. *What were you thinking?* he said to himself. A Black man touching a white woman in public was the sort of thing that could get him beaten.

The wagon driver looked down at Jules and Lucretia, leaned over, and spat a hocker of tobacco juice onto the street as he passed. His opinion of the mixed Black and white group was unmistakable.

Lucretia made no attempt to put distance between herself and Jules as they continued to cross the street. "I thank thee for thy care, Jules. I'm afraid I am not very good at looking both ways simultaneously. That wagon driver is someone whose mind must change before we can win this war."

Lucretia's choice of words was not lost on Jules. *A pacifist who speaks of our struggle as if it were a war.* Safely across the street, he looked at the men digging the Hall's foundation. They had stopped work to look at the crowd. Their stares weren't friendly. "I'm afraid we have many minds to change." He watched Architect Stewart walk the group through the anticipated layout of the Hall's ground floor. "We should get closer if you want to listen."

"Oh, I am fine, thank you," said Lucretia. "I know the layout by heart. James and I often walk over here after supper. Thanks to thee and Maddie for thy generous contribution to the Association. I know thee also gives generously to the Vigilant Committee."

Jules watched the group as they walked away from them down the scrubby lot. "Both worthy causes. I wish it could be more."

Architect Stewart continued with his tour. "You are walking on what will soon be the central corridor of Pennsylvania Hall's ground floor," he said before his words faded in the distance.

Lucretia followed his gaze. "Once Pennsylvania Hall is complete, it will become a beacon of hope for those of us who advocate for an end to slavery."

A wave of melancholy suddenly washed over Jules. "I don't know. I think we should get our own house in order first."

"What does thee mean?"

Some of the ditchdiggers continued to stare at him and Lucretia. *Don't let the bastards cow you.* "Let's ignore for the moment that most white people are indifferent to the plight of my enslaved brethren. Slavery doesn't affect them directly, and indirectly it makes their lives easier by making cheap goods possible." He looked at the group that was listening to Architect Stewart. "All the folks listening to Mr. Stewart right now want an end to slavery. However, I would wager that most of the whites would not be very enthusiastic about living amongst a significant population of free Blacks."

"That may be so."

Jules pointed to a man hanging on the periphery of the group. "That's Jonathan Wilbur. He wants to end slavery but then invoke mandatory transportation of freed slaves to Africa. The fact that their ancestors might have been living in America for hundreds of years is of no significance."

Lucretia looked up at Jules. "The colonization movement is waning. No leader of any note advocates for that anymore."

Jules shook his head. "For argument's sake, let's just say that we abolitionists comprise 5 percent of Philadelphia's population. The movement to colonize my freed brethren may be waning amongst us but in the other 95 percent? I doubt it." Jules pointed to another man. "Then, people like William Birch over there favor gradual abolition in the South; children born after a certain date would be born free. All slaves would become free at a certain age, perhaps 28."

"That is how we eliminated slavery in Pennsylvania."

"And it took fifty years for it to happen." Jules pointed to Edward Long. "Edward favors immediate abolition, but he wants to compensate the slaveholders for the loss of their property."

"But Jules, that is why we are building Pennsylvania Hall—to discuss these differences and to bring like-minded folks into agreement. To gradually bring them over to our way of thinking—an immediate end to slavery with no compensation for the slaveholders."

"And every time someone like you or William Lloyd Garrison says those words, they are seized upon by the pro-slavery press to whip up antipathy toward the entire anti-slavery movement. Lucretia, I look at the building we are about to erect, and I should be filled with hope. Instead, at this very moment, I feel like the change is too monumental to ever happen."

"Do not lose heart, dear Jules. We are chipping away at this curse a little bit at a time. The tide of opinion will eventually come over to our side. Then you will see more peoples' sentiments change, and that change will come more rapidly."

"And how long do you think it will take?"

"I have no idea. Fifty years, perhaps."

"The same fifty years it took to end slavery in Pennsylvania. I don't want to wait that long . . ."

"Hi, Lucretia. Hi Jules. You two almost got run over by that freight wagon."

Jules turned to see Rian and her friend Olivia. *My God, it's been five months since I saw her last. She's grown a couple of inches.*

"Well, good morning, Rian," said Lucretia. "Good morning, Olivia. I assumed thee would be working at the Krieger factories, Rian."

"Things are pretty slow at the shop. Ernst couldn't think of anything to keep me busy, so he sent me on an errand. When my father heard about it, he tacked on something else." With that last part, Rian made a face.

Olivia elbowed Rian. "Rian's getting fitted for two new dresses to wear in Switzerland. That's where I came in. I was her fashion advisor."

"A very impressive title, my dear," said Lucretia. "When does thee sail home to Charleston, Olivia?"

Olivia frowned. "The day after tomorrow. Mother could have delayed another two weeks, but I think she's had it with Philadelphia this year. She isn't happy with who I'm consorting with."

Jules's dark mood was still winning. "Then I guess you should hope they don't see you with us. Your parents don't like Rian?"

"Oh, Rian isn't her favorite, but it's Conor McGuire. Because he's Irish."

Lucretia folded her arms in front of her. "Oh, Otto told me about the incident on the day of the launch. It must have been frightful."

Olivia smiled. "Rian and I were too much for the bad guys. And we had a little help from Conor and Rian's uncle."

Lucretia looked down Sixth Street as if Olivia's parents might be walking north at any moment. "Apparently, thy parents don't know about the men at the warehouse."

Olivia shook her head. "Please don't tell them, Mrs. Mott. I would never be let out of the house if they knew everything. Even now, I don't know if we'll return to Philadelphia next summer."

"Your secret is safe with me, Olivia. It seems our secrets are mounting up. After all, just over a year ago, the four of us helped one of your father's slaves escape."

Jules looked at Rian. "And Otto is still intent on sending you to Switzerland? When do you leave?"

"My father plans to take me to New York on September 2, but I'm not going."

Jules smiled. "What do you mean you aren't going?"

"I'm going to figure out a way to stay here. It's good seeing the two of you. I've got to get back to the shop."

Jules watched Rian and Olivia dodge around a carriage as they dashed across the street. "Otto has his hands full with that one."

Lucretia nodded. "Thirteen years old. She's already been kicked out of three schools, engineered an enslaved woman's escape to freedom, been walloped by a slave catcher while rescuing a captured self-emancipator, and stabbed a man in the leg. I have to agree with thee. I was horrified when Otto told me about the altercation with the slave catcher. And now the stabbing? Those two incidents have awakened all my pacifist Quaker sentiments."

"Yet what should she have done? Allowed that poor woman to be returned to a life of slavery in Maryland? Allowed herself to be assaulted?"

"What she should have done was not allow herself to get into those situations in the first place."

"Agreed. But once she was in such a fix, I admire her ability to get herself out. And they did free all those people who had been mugged and returned their possessions."

"Hopefully, Switzerland will knock some sense into her."

Jules smiled at his Quaker friend. "That didn't sound very pacific of you, Lucretia."

"Hmm. It didn't, did it? I'm afraid that young woman's education will become a real wrestling match."

* * * * *

· RIAN ·

Rian slowed her pace after dashing across Sixth Street.

Olivia caught up and shouldered into her playfully. "So what are you going to do about Switzerland?"

"I'm going to stow away on Uncle Kurt's ship the next time he comes into port."

"I think that's a dumb idea. Your uncle will just return you to Philadelphia as soon as he can. That will only slow your father up by a couple of weeks. What good does that do you?"

"Well, the boat to Europe will have sailed."

"And your father will just put you on the next one. Who is going to chaperone you to Europe?"

"Father's hired my Aunt Lilly to go over with me. Seamus's ma. Now that's a real dumb idea. She can't read English, much less speak French. I'm going to be guiding her. It should be the other way around."

"I think the reason your father has hired her is to make sure you get to Switzerland."

"I'm not going to go to Switzerland."

"Well, you better cook up a better plan than what you've got so far. Rian, if you get sent away to Switzerland, will you come home for the summertime?"

"I don't know. Why?"

"Because I don't want to return to Philadelphia if you're not here. It wouldn't be any fun."

* * * * *

· ADRIAN ·

Adrian returned to Krieger Locomotive for a meeting with Heinrich Aldrich to review plans for a new engine that Heinrich had drawn up. Even though new orders had dried up, the two men prided themselves on improving each machine over anything previously built, both by Krieger as well as its many competitors.

In the design in front of them, the train engineer could operate hand levers to throw the locomotive into reverse. For every locomotive produced worldwide to date, the engineer had to stop the train, dismount, and wrestle pistons into a proper configuration before the engine could be backed up. If this design worked, it would be a much less laborious operation than on any current models. Rumors from their competitors' shops indicated that they were all working on the same problem. Adrian and Heinrich wanted to be the first.

"Any luck with the *Mohawk & Hudson*?" asked Heinrich.

Adrian idly pointed to the plans on the desk. "They commissioned this locomotive a year ago and we've added a slew of innovations since then. They got cold feet when the Panic set in. I tried to save the deal, but they officially backed out yesterday. Left their deposit on the table."

"Who's next in the queue?"

"There isn't anyone in the queue. I've written to everyone who's inquired in the past year. Told them we've lowered the price. In truth, I would sell this one at cost just to keep our doors open. No one's written back."

"So, are we going to go ahead with this on spec?"

Adrian shook his head. "I don't think we should start spec work until we get some inquiries. In a week, the only work we will have are three fire engines for Freeman Hydraulics. Now that's ironic. I took on that subcontract as a favor to Jules. Now it's the only thing that's keeping us afloat."

Rian Krieger knocked on the door and ushered in two gentlemen dressed in fashionable business attire. "Uncle Adrian, these two men came to the Coach offices looking for you."

Adrian turned his attention to the two visitors as Rian settled onto a stool in the corner of the office. That wasn't unusual, and after a few seconds, he forgot she was there.

"Good afternoon, Mr. Krieger," said the taller of the two men in an accent that Adrian didn't recognize. He carried a cane and displayed the ramrod-straight bearing of a military man. "My name is Colonel Alexander Malkovich. This is my associate Count Sheremetev. I know we don't have an appointment, and we apologize for this imposition. We wonder if we could meet with you sometime this afternoon."

Adrian stood up and somewhat protectively placed himself between the two visitors and the plans for the new locomotive. "Now would actually be a good time to meet. How can we help you?"

Colonel Malkovich handed a business card to Adrian. "We are traveling in America at the behest of Tsar Nicholas Romanov, Emperor of Russia. It was his wish that we purchase the most modern locomotives currently produced in America to bring back to Russia. Krieger Locomotive has been mentioned in every discussion we have had with railroad executives. It seemed appropriate to finally meet you."

Potential business, thought Adrian. *This is a godsend. Where is Otto? He usually handles our sales.* "I'm certain that we can accommodate you. I have to confess I'm a bit surprised. Some fine engines are being produced in England these days. Why aren't you shopping closer to home?"

"We started there. The English machines are well-crafted but not as rugged as your locomotives. You manufacturers here in America have been forced to grapple with long distances, harsh weather, minimal repair facilities, and rough terrain. Much like America, Russia is a vast country, and the Tsar would like to bring his people closer to one another by creating roads of steel between its major cities."

"How many locomotives are we talking about?"

"Many. But since we have been here, we have come to some realizations. New improvements in locomotive design seem to be made weekly. Norris creates a machine with longer-lasting wheels and axles. Baldwin's next machine incorporates those features, adding a more rigid engine assembly. Eastwick & Harrison steals those innovations and lengthens the locomotive to distribute the engine's weight over longer sections of track."

Adrian smiled. "Nobody's stealing anyone's designs. We study them, then improve what they and we have both done in the past. The drive to improve our machines is relentless."

With a twinkle in his eye, Malkovich bowed slightly. "I stand corrected. Forgive my terminology. Then Krieger Locomotive incorporates all those improvements into its new design and adds," Colonel Malkovich waved his hand at the plans for the newest Krieger locomotive, "your own innovations. Then Norris 'studies' all those ideas and the cycle starts all over again."

Adrian looked at his visitor's business card. "Colonel Malkovich, I am honored you chose to visit us. We pride ourselves on building locomotives that are durable and innovative."

"We have done our research." Malkovich gestured with a smile toward Rian. "Your associate over in the corner even gave us a brief orientation as he conducted us to this office. We are well aware that you produce fine machines. Regarding innovation, that is not how things are done in Russia. Change is not a respected attribute in our country. In a battle between innovation and tradition, tradition wins out."

"Well," said Adrian, belatedly moving away from the drawings of their latest, locomotive. "Mr. Aldrich and I stand ready to sell you our most advanced machinery."

"Ah," said Colonel Malkovich. "I have been unclear. That is no longer what we want."

"What do you want?"

"We want the Krieger factories to move to our country. We want you to change the culture of Russia."

* * * * *

· OTTO ·

The harbormaster's office occupied the entire third floor of a rather decrepit building at the end of the Pine Street Public Landing pier. Otto climbed two flights of rickety outside stairs and entered the office. An array of windows on three sides offered generous views of the entire Philadelphia waterfront. Other than a telescope and tripod in one corner, three desks and one chair were the only furnishings. One desk was covered by stacks of papers, one held a box of rolled maps, and the third was home to the harbor log and three links of a large chain that seemed to serve no purpose but to act as a paperweight.

Behind the desk, in the only chair in the room, sat harbormaster Dickie Pricker. He looked up from his log book and said, "Haven't seen you in a while," expressing no pleasure at Otto's entrance.

"Yes, I've just come from the Imlay & Potts wharf."

"The *Bridger*. Levi Howes," Dickie said, demonstrating his ability to keep track of all the doings along his waterfront.

"Yes, the *Bridger*. She's a slave ship. Something should be done."

Dickie shifted in his chair. "How do you know this?"

"The crew talks. The evidence is in the hold."

"Are there slaves down there?"

"I don't believe so."

"Listen, Herr Kreiger. I've heard the rumors about the *Bridger*. Ships have to make a buck, or they'll spend their lives in port. Unless the *Bridger* is caught with slaves aboard, the Navy can't do a thing, and I certainly can't even if I wanted to. You should quit sticking your nose into places it doesn't belong."

Arschloch [Asshole], Otto said to himself. "Well, thank you for your perspective. Good day."

Dickie returned his attention to his log book and never said another word as Otto left his office.

* * * * *

· RIAN ·

Rian had been listening to her father and Uncle Adrian's conversation from the kitchen. She entered the diningroom, placed a bowl of red raspberries and a pitcher of cream before her uncle, and quietly sat down at the table's head.

"Otto, I'm still reeling," said Adrian without acknowledging the berries. "This morning I was contemplating mortgaging my house and still having to lay off more workers. Now, it looks like I'll be moving Krieger Locomotive and my family to Russia. I could become wealthy overnight."

"What does Mila say?"

"She thinks it sounds exotic. The thought of living in St. Petersburg and attending balls amidst royalty put a twinkle in her eye."

"How do you know these men haven't concocted some sort of ruse to get your money?"

"What money? We're all just about broke. But to answer your question, they have offered to deposit earnest money in the Bank of Industry as soon as I say yes."

"How much money are we talking about?"

Adrian leaned back in his chair and smiled. "One hundred thousand dollars. The sum was astounding. More than I thought I would ever make in my lifetime."

"The Tsar of Russia is that rich?"

"Yesterday I couldn't have told you who the Tsar of Russia was. After Malkovich and Sheremetev left, I sent Rian to the library to do some research."

Both brothers turned their attention to Rian. She straightened in her chair. "The Tsar's name is Nicholas Romanov. The Romanovs have run Russia for more than two hundred years. Russia is the largest country in the world and it's got the world's biggest army. Russia isn't like the United States. If the Tsar wants something to happen, his subjects have to do it."

Adrian returned his attention to her father. "Otto, it's not just Krieger Locomotive. They want Coach and Rail, too."

"Did you talk to Aaron?"

"Yes, he's not interested. He says they're pretty hard on Jews over there. I think I should go. Take one other person. Get the lay of the land. Send for more people next spring. You, Aaron, and the rest stay here. Keep innovating. Keep scrapping. This Panic can't last forever. When the American economy gets back on its feet, I'll be happy to come home."

"We always said our strength is in our proximity. The three companies collaborate. Support one another. Are you willing to give that up?"

"These are extraordinary times. A dramatic change like this will breathe new capital into all three enterprises. Sheremetev wants locomotives, rolling stock, and track to be produced in Russian factories by Russian labor. He's willing to pay us up front to move the machinery in our shops to Russia."

"So we move everything?"

Adrian savored a spoonful of raspberries while he considered this. "No, we strip both factories down to half strength. Box them up and take them with us. That will satisfy him. They didn't say anything about design, though. Our design expertise will remain here in America. You produce what you can sell here and abroad with the machines that you have left. You and Heinrich will design for the Krieger companies in America and Russia. We can peel off some of the Tsar's money to pay for design work for both locomotives and coaches. Between the machinery and the design, it will take months of pressure off you."

"I still can't believe this. How can any person be that rich?"

"For the locomotives, rail, and rolling stock, Sheremetev is talking about a contract for three million dollars."

Otto whistled.

"It's not just the hardware Sheremetev is interested in," said Adrian. "He wants to build a railroad from St. Petersburg to Moscow. He says railroads will help to change the culture of Russian society. And he has some pretty interesting thoughts about how to get us started. I get the impression that unless we're being paid a king's ransom, no one will pay attention to us."

"So I guess you should go. I've got a suggestion, though. Talk Seamus into going with you. He can help you get your factories set up."

"I'll talk to him. I was also thinking about taking Jabez with me. He has seemed lost since he returned to us. Maybe Russia will shake him out of his lethargy."

Rian stirred in her chair. *Good-bye Switzerland,* she said to herself. A slight smile crept across her face.

SUNDAY, AUGUST 6

· SEAMUS ·

Twenty feet separated Seamus from Hugh Callaghan in the after-mass crowd that socialized outside St. Philip de Neri Catholic Church. Seamus stood with his ma and siblings while Hugh surveyed the group with his wife and daughters, the ever-present toothpick dangling from his lip. Siobhan smiled at Seamus, which made Seamus's heart leap. She and he had gone nowhere since Hugh had put the kibosh on Seamus's marriage proposal over a month ago.

Hugh waggled his hand back and forth in an *I-want-to-talk-to-you* gesture.

The two rivals walked toward each other and met in neutral territory.

"What's so important, Hugh?"

"I want to talk."

"So talk."

"No, not here. It'll take longer than we can do here."

"Clancy's?"

"No, this is nothing I want me boys to know is going on. Not even a whisper."

"Well, I have to say, you've piqued me interest." Seamus gave the thought of a meeting place some consideration. "How's the firefighting business these days?"

"There's always fires. The Panic can't affect that. The payments from the insurance companies come a little slower, that's all. Why do you ask?"

"How's the steam fire pump that we gave you doing?"

"Doing great. We're thinking about getting another one."

"Only one outfit in town makes steam fire pumps—Freeman Hydraulics."

Hugh sucked on his toothpick for a bit. "Not sure I want to buy a fire pump from your African friend."

"Jules only makes the chassis for the fire pumps. Adrian Krieger makes the boilers. Start with Jules. Talk to him about buying a new pump. Then head to Krieger Locomotive. Time your visit so that you arrive at 6:30 on Tuesday evening. No one who will recognize you will be in the shop much after 6:00.

I'll make sure someone meets you at the door and escorts you to a place where we can have a private conversation."

"I thought you and the Kriegers parted company."

"We did. Lately, we've mended a few fences."

TUESDAY, AUGUST 8

· SEAMUS ·

Seamus had brought two chairs from the Krieger Locomotive office into the factory's Finish Room. He was reading an article in the *Philadelphia Independent* by the afternoon sunlight that streamed in through the cupola when Rian opened the sliding door enough to let Hugh Callaghan in. Seamus gave Rian a wave, and she shut the door.

Hugh looked over his shoulder at the shut slider. "I hope that little brat can keep her trap shut. If me boys think anything's going on, there'll be a rebellion."

Seamus didn't bother to rise to greet Hugh but gestured toward the other chair. "Don't worry about Rian. How did you make out with Jules?"

Hugh sucked on his toothpick and smiled. "I'd say he was a bit surprised when me and two of me lads showed up at his shop. I told him we were thinking about buying another pump. He seemed a bit confused, but he showed me around the place. He's got a couple of pumps in production. Talked about improvements he's making. Told me on the side there'd be a discount if I extended the truce. I had no intention of buying a pump, but he's making it attractive."

"Then you took your lads to see Adrian? How about him? He'll be making the boiler."

"He said he could work with whatever deal Jules and I make."

Seamus started to tamp some tobacco into his pipe. "How'd you ditch your boys?"

"They were getting thirsty, so I sent them home. Told them that I don't often get this far north, and I wanted to take a stroll around the reservoir." Hugh looked around the Finish Room, which was devoid of projects. "I figured Adrian would be a little more eager to do business. Didn't look like much is going on in his shop."

"Things have changed just recently in that aspect. I think the Kriegers have a bright future." *Yeah, a bright future in Russia.*

Hugh shook his head. "You must know something I don't know, but I'm not here to talk about the Kriegers. I want to talk about the *Bridger*."

"The *Bridger* came and went just last week. Probably won't be back for another five months."

"Yeah, I know. The *Bridger*'s a slave ship. I want to put an end to her."

Seamus struck a loco-foco on a strip of sandpaper and lit his pipe. He drew a few times to get the tobacco going. "You're no friend of the Negro. What do you want to sink a slave ship for?"

"Well, I've done a lot of thinking in that regard. You're right. I don't like Africans. Don't want to live with them. Don't want to do business with them. But ships like the *Bridger* keep bringing more of them over. Some percentage manages to escape, and some of those like the environment here in the City of Brotherly Love."

"What are you proposing, Hugh?"

"I've broached the subject with me boys—you know, just joking—but they don't give a shyte what the *Bridger* is doing. They don't share me lofty perspective."

Hugh, you're crazy. "And you think I do?"

"You've read Sun Tzu, same as me. 'A wise commander is able to recognize changing circumstances and to act expediently.'"

"And what are the changing circumstances?"

"I told you. There's too many Africans flowing into Philadelphia."

"Then you'd be better off teaming up with someone like Austin T. Slatter."

"Slatter has his role to play. I have mine. Me boys aren't with me on this. When you're a leader, you can't be too far out in front of your troops because they won't follow you. I'm so far ahead of them on this, I might as well be standing on the shore of the Mississippi."

"Why me?"

"You helped that African woman escape last year, so I know you're not above such extralegal activity when it's warranted."

"So what are you thinking, Hugh? Become a pirate? Board the ship? Kill the crew?"

"Nothing quite that dramatic. But I still want to make a statement. Let's assume the *Bridger* sails into port in five months. I think a raid is in order—just you and me. We board the ship, go below, start a fire, and get out. The more cargo that's aboard, the better. If the *Bridger* burns to the waterline, so be it. Maybe the owners will think twice before they send a slave ship over to Africa again."

"Let me get this straight. You hate Black people. You're willing to destroy a Baltimore Clipper because it brings them to this side of the Atlantic."

"That's about the size of it."

"What would be in it for me if I said yes?"

"Besides the knowledge that there's one less slave ship to bring Africans over here?" A sly smile crept over Hugh's face. "How about if we divest the *Bridger* of some cargo before we burn it?"

The added larcenous dimension to Hugh's plans made Seamus smile. "Well, I'll tell you what, Hugh, you're just a little too late. Under normal circumstances, I'd be interested in your little caper, but I won't be around at the end of the year."

"Where are you going to be?"

"I'll be setting up a locomotive factory in Russia, and I'm going to ask your daughter to come with me."

Hugh straightened up in his chair. "Now you're starting to irritate me, Seamus. You realize that this will end the truce between Moya and No Name. The only reason it's lasted this long is because you feed me information from the telegraph towers."

"Calm down, Hugh. I've already thought of that. The day I leave, my guy at the Merchants' Exchange is going to start leaving the information at a place where Conor McGuire will pick it up every day. The only difference is that you'll have to pay a modest amount to Conor, and he'll pass it on to my guy."

"This plan better work, Seamus, or me lads go back to beating up No Name and your African friends. As far as Siobhan is concerned, Mikey McGuire doesn't impress her very much. Feel free to ask her, but I'll tell you, she's not going to go off to Russia without a ring on her finger."

* * * * *

· JULES ·

Jules Freeman and Robert Purvis took their seats in the back of the hearing room of Magistrate Hyram P. Stone in Kensington. Jules gazed around the room. Surprisingly, no one paid much attention to them—a Black man and a man whom the uninitiated would perceive as white. "I guess people in court are no longer surprised to see a white man and a Black man sitting together when the Vigilant Committee is involved."

"Let their eyes and their prejudices tell them I'm white. I have no need to educate them."

Jules chuckled. "As long as we don't get the stuffing kicked out of us for sitting together."

On the left, a self-emancipator named Pluto and his lawyer, Jonathan Simmons, faced the magistrate's table. On the right were Austin T. Slatter, who had captured Pluto on the Kensington Wharf north of Philadelphia, and a lawyer named Alton Davis.

Davis was questioning Jonah Arbuckle, the slaveholder who claimed that Pluto was his property.

Robert Purvis leaned toward Jules and whispered, "This is the third time the Vigilant Committee has gone up against Slatter in a magistrate's court. Have you noticed how well he's dressed when we're in court?"

Jules glanced at Slatter. "I didn't until you mentioned it."

"I know slave-catching is lucrative, but Slatter looks more like a banker than a slave catcher these days. It makes me sad that a devil like Slatter is prospering."

The two Vigilant Committee members returned their attention to Davis's examination of the slaveholder. Davis consulted notes on a sheet of paper. "And how long have you owned Pluto, Mr. Arbuckle?"

"Why, since the day he was born. At least twenty years."

Davis jerked his thumb over his shoulder at the defense table. "So you are sure the man sitting over there is Pluto?"

Arbuckle glanced at Pluto. "That's him. I've worked him every day of his life since he could hold a hoe."

"Personally?"

"Of course. I own only three slaves. I work right alongside each of them."

"Thank you, Mr. Arbuckle. Those are all my questions for the moment."

Magistrate Stone looked toward Pluto's lawyer. "Mr. Simmons, cross-examination?"

Simmons rose and buttoned his jacket. He had no notes. "Yes, sir. Mr. Arbuckle, where is your farm?"

"Near Georgetown, Sussex County."

"I'm sorry. I meant, in what state is your farm?"

"Delaware."

Simmons crossed his arms. "And why do you believe you have a right to reclaim your alleged property just because you live in Delaware?"

"Because slavery's legal in Delaware."

"Are you a constitutional scholar, Mr. Arbuckle?"

Arbuckle leaned back in his chair. "No, sir. I'm a farmer."

"So what qualifies you to declare whether or not Delaware is a slave state?"

Arbuckle scowled at Simmons. "Because everybody knows it. It's common knowledge."

Simmons turned to the magistrate. "Your Honor, I would like my client to be set free on the grounds that the plaintiff has not adequately established that Pluto ran away from a state in which slavery is legal."

Alton Davis sprung up from his chair. "Your Honor, this is absurd. Of course Delaware is a slave state. It has been since it was the first state to join the Union. We should not have to prove common knowledge in your court."

Magistrate Stone frowned at the plaintiff's attorney. "Mr. Davis, do not tell me what should or should not be proved in my courtroom. You have not laid a proper foundation for your case. Until you supply a witness versed in the constitutional law of Delaware, I will halt this proceeding. The man known as Pluto will be held in the jail around the corner until that time. If, by some chance, you and Mr. Arbuckle win this case, expenses for Pluto's room and board will be borne by Mr. Arbuckle." The magistrate banged his gavel. "Court is adjourned."

Jules sat stunned by the suddenness of the decision. "Did you know this was going to happen?" he whispered to Robert.

"I suspected something was afoot. Magistrate Stone's sympathies run with the abolitionists. He can't out-and-out defy the law, but he can make the plaintiff adhere to the minutest letter of the law."

Slatter rose. "Your honor, we all know that no guards stay in the jail overnight. What's to prevent this African's advocates from freeing him while no one is watching the henhouse? They are highly motivated and not constrained by the rule of law."

Magistrate Stone looked at Slatter from across his desk. "And you are, Mr. Slatter?"

Slatter straightened and pulled on the front of his coat with both hands. "Of course, your honor."

"If you fear your bounty is in jeopardy, I welcome you to sleep inside the jail until I reconvene this hearing. I warn you, you will not be compensated for this, and if Pluto is not sitting in that seat when we reconvene, the person under arrest will be you."

Stone again banged his gavel. All the people in the room rose to leave. Slatter stopped as he passed Jules and Robert, who were still sitting. He ignored Jules completely and focused on Robert, the Black man he obviously assumed was white.

"Well, congratulations. Your people won a round, but all you did was delay the inevitable. In two days, we'll supply some professor from Newark College who will tell the magistrate what we all know. Your side will fuss some more, but eventually, that African will be returned to his rightful owner, and I'll get paid a tidy sum."

Robert stood, put his hands in his pockets, and returned Slatter's glare. "But we will have kept a man free for a few weeks longer."

"Not so sure. The magistrate said he'll be kept in jail. That doesn't sound very free to me."

"But you'll be guarding the henhouse, making sure Pluto doesn't slip away again. That means you won't be out hunting for some other poor souls."

"Oh, balls, even I have to sleep. Might as well be here as at home. Sleep is sleep. And all these delaying tactics just encourage me to circumvent all this legal shit and take your Africans back to their owners directly."

"It's a pleasure making you work so hard, Mr. Slatter."

Slatter shrugged. "My work is doing a pretty good job of paying the bills so far." He turned to walk out of the courtroom, hesitated, and turned back and looked down at Jules. "I know it was you who beat me up by the river and took that slave girl away from me. You should have killed me when you had the chance. From now on, I want you to be looking over your shoulder every time you're outside that pretty little house of yours."

Jules rose, shoulder to shoulder with Robert. "That's nothing new for me, Slatter. That's how I spend my life anyway."

"Well, then, I've got a question for you. How are you going to be looking over your shoulder and watching out for your wife and six kids at the same time?"

TUESDAY, AUGUST 15

· SEAMUS ·

"Come to Russia with me."

As he said those words to Siobhan, it was the first time that Seamus believed that he was leaving everything he was familiar with and going to a land about which he knew almost nothing.

It was far past midnight. As he had done a few times previously, Seamus waited in the shadows outside Clancy's Saloon until Siobhan finished her shift as a barmaid. This time, she was with two of her sisters. When he made himself visible, one of them elbowed Siobhan and pointed to Seamus. The sisters giggled. One said something to Siobhan that irritated her. She flounced over to Seamus, leaving the girls to walk home without her.

Siobhan gave Seamus a look that he found inscrutable. "So let me get this straight. You used to have a good job working for your uncle, but he fired you because you helped Rian steal a slave and didn't tell him about it. Then some swell who claims he's from Russia asks your other uncle to move half his operation to someplace a world away. Then Adrian asks you to help him make the move. Then you decide to do it, leaving all your mates at No Name. And now you're asking me to end things with Mikey McGuire and come with you."

Although Siobhan's tone was harsh, she got all the facts right. Seamus chose not to split hairs. "Yes."

"Is there a marriage proposal anywhere in this grand scheme of yours?"

"Of course," Seamus said, putting a touch of indignation into his response as if marriage had always been implied.

"Well?"

Seamus finally got the hint. "So, will you marry me?"

"I don't know yet. I've got to think about it."

"What's to think about? Within a year, I'll be the richest man you know. You'll live in a big house. We'll be going to balls."

"In a year, the only balls you'll be thinking of are your own, and that's because they'll be freezing off. It's Russia, for Chrissakes. Look, here's the problem as I see it. If I marry Mikey McGuire, I get someone who knows who he is. He's a good Irish lad who sticks with his mates. You? You don't know who you are. Two years ago you were a ditchdigger. Then you started working for the *ispinis*. Then you turned your back on your own kind and started putting out fires for the coloreds."

"Hey, you told me I might be right on that one."

"That's not me point. Me point is that I don't know who I'd be marrying. Your latest scheme is to become a rich entrepreneur in Russia. You keep changing on me, Seamus."

"I'm not changing. I'm growing. I'm twenty-one years old. I think I'm worth the gamble. Besides, Russia might be the place."

"What place? What the fook are you talking about?"

"The place where nobody knows I speak with an Irish accent. All they'll know about me is that I'm an American. They won't look down on me because I was born in County Clare. I'll have money. Maybe I'll fit in with all the richies."

"Is that what you want? Becoming a member of the impatient class?"

"No, I don't want that at all. But I don't want to be excluded from some places just because of me mellifluous Irish brogue."

Siobhan shook her head, then looked him in the eye. "How much time do I have? To give you an answer?"

"We sail from Philadelphia on September 1. That's two weeks."

"Today's Tuesday. Meet me here after work on Thursday. I'll have me answer for you."

Seamus noted that Siobhan didn't ask him to walk her home.

* * * * *

· OTTO ·

George Shippen sat at his desk in his Bank of Industry office. He opened up his cigar box and offered one to Otto. "*Deus ex machina*, Krieger. Do you know what that means?"

In the chair opposite Shippen, Otto accepted the cigar. *Mein Gott [My God]. He is as elated as I am. With the infusion of the Tsar's funds and me getting current with my loan, I've also given him some breathing room.* "I am afraid my Latin is a little rusty, George."

"*God from the machine.* During their plays, the ancient Romans created elaborate machines to lower the gods—actors, of course—from above. The gods would magically straighten out whatever pickle the mortals had gotten themselves into. You, dear Krieger, have been saved by the gods, swooping down from the heavens with a solution to all your troubles. Your factories are moving to Russia. Who would have predicted that a month ago?"

"We are shipping only half the machinery from Krieger Coach and Locomotive to St. Petersburg. The rest will stay here. We will proceed at half-strength until the depression ends."

"But for now, your financial troubles are over. Congratulations."

My troubles, and apparently yours, thought Otto, *at least for the moment.*

* * * * *

· JULES ·

Jules sat at his desk and stared at Seamus Gallagher. "So, does Hugh intend to buy another fire pump or not?"

Seamus had taken a chair opposite Jules's desk. "I think so, but that's only an excuse for this meeting. None of his boys know I'm here. Hugh's got a bee in his bonnet. He wants to burn this slave ship the next time she's in port. His boys would disapprove, so he's looking for some aiding and abetting outside his gang. He came to me first. I told him I was going to be in Russia. He came back to me after mass the other day and asked if you'd be interested. I'm participating in this meeting only to make introductions."

"I don't like the man. He doesn't like my kind. I don't trust him."

Seamus held up his hands. "I don't trust him either, and he may be a little crazy, but just hear him out. I'll be gone in a couple of weeks, so whatever you two decide to do is up to you."

Maddie Freeman ushered Hugh Callaghan into the office, gave Jules an *I-hope-you-know-what-you-are-doing* look, and said, "Husband, I'm going home. Don't be late."

Jules didn't get up to greet Hugh. He gestured for him to sit in the chair next to Seamus. "Seamus tells me you want to burn a slave ship."

Hugh adjusted himself in his chair and briefly surveyed Jules's office. He returned his gaze to Jules. "Seamus should have let me make my own case."

Jules stared back at Hugh and thought, *Interesting. Hugh speaks the Queen's English when it suits him.* "Here we are. Make your case."

Hugh pulled his toothpick out of his mouth, put his elbows on the arms of his chair, and leaned forward. "I don't like what the *Bridger* is doing. Bringing your brethren over here. Shouldn't that be enough?"

"You don't care about my people. Until you and Seamus declared the truce a year ago, you harassed my people at every possible turn. You burned our homes to the ground. Your men beat up our men, women, and children with impunity. Even now, you refuse to put out fires in our houses."

"That's right. I didn't like your people before the truce. I still don't."

Jules said nothing. He let Callaghan's detestation wash over him.

"And that's why I want to do this," continued Hugh. "One less slave ship means that fewer Africans are forced to come over here . . . which, I assume, should be appealing to you."

I can't argue with that. "That part is appealing. But the Atlantic slave trade has been banned for almost thirty years, yet it flourishes because human beings are a valuable commodity. Burning one ship would not make a dent in the tide of people smuggled every year into the Caribbean. We know the smugglers also sail into Charleston, Savannah, and New Orleans."

Callaghan leaned back in his chair. "Jules, rumors around town are that you are involved in the Underground Railroad."

Jules froze.

"Don't worry. I'm not gonna do anything about it just as long as you keep your African passengers moving north. But let's do a little arithmetic here. Let's say you've been at your little hobby for fifteen years. Let's say one person a month comes through to wherever you hide them. That means that you have personally been responsible for helping to free 180 people over a decade and a half. According to Seamus, the *Bridger* carries 200 people every time it crosses from Africa. In one evening, you can outperform all the work you and your pretty wife have done in fifteen years."

Your math is off by quite a bit, you old shit. Maddie and I have protected twice that number. But you've made your point. Still . . . "I'm not going to help you."

"Why not?"

"A lot of reasons, but the one that should make the most sense to you is insurance. Ships and their cargo are insured, just like the buildings you and your Moya boys rush to save when they are on fire. As long as that ship is insured, no matter how badly it is damaged, it will be repaired or replaced and back on the high seas in a matter of months. The owners will suffer an inconvenience, not a financial disaster."

"You're telling me that your decision hinges on insurance?"

"Well, if you want to go down that road, insurance is only part of it. Mostly, I don't like you, and I don't trust you."

Hugh got up from his chair and walked to the door. "Well, I guess that pretty much ends our discussion. I don't much like you either, but I respect you and what you are doing." Hugh again surveyed Jules's office. "This business.

Your commitment to your family. Even your evening activities. All things I admire. Let me leave you with a parting thought. *Amicus meus, inimici inimici mei.*"

Jules stared at Hugh for a long moment. "I guess I would have expected you to quote Sun Tzu at this moment. I don't know Latin."

"It means the enemy of my enemy is my friend." Hugh opened the door and turned back toward Jules. "Think about it." He turned to leave, then pivoted a second time. "As far as my boys are concerned, our negotiations are progressing. I want to buy a pump. We're still haggling about the price." He closed the door softly behind him.

* * * * *

· ADRIAN ·

"Must you take Jabez with you?" asked Mila.

"I think it will be a good thing," Adrian responded. "He's been with us for five months, and he's shown little enthusiasm for anything. Not school work, not work-work. All he wants to do is gad about with his friends."

"But you will have even less time to keep track of him in Russia. Who knows what demands will be placed on you there?"

"I must admit, I don't know what I'm getting myself into," responded Adrian. "Even when I lived in Wurttemberg, Russia was a strange and far-off place. It seems even more so from here."

"Have you talked to Jabez about it?"

"Oh, yes. I think it came as quite a shock. His initial reaction wasn't very positive. It seems like he's finally settling into life in Philadelphia, which I interpreted as he's finally made a couple of friends, and he doesn't want to leave them."

"Then what if I go with you as well?

"Give me a year to establish myself. Maybe forcing Jabez to take some responsibility in Russia will break him out of his lethargy."

THURSDAY, AUGUST 17

· RIAN ·

Jabez Howes and Rian hung on the periphery of the group that gathered at the Walnut Street Wharf to bid the Tuckers *bon voyage* before they steamed back to Charleston.

Olivia broke off from her parents and strode over to Rian and her cousin. "I guess this is farewell for a while. I don't think we're coming back to Philadelphia next summer. Papa thinks I get into too much trouble."

Rian hugged Olivia. *Olivia. Another person I'm going to miss.*

Olivia looked at Rian for a long moment. "Good luck stowing away to wherever you stow away to. I still think it's a stupid plan."

"I've got some other ideas. But no matter what, we won't see each other for a while."

Olivia again hugged Rian. "We had adventures, didn't we?" She turned and walked toward her parents. Then she turned back toward Rian. "I love you," she said quietly.

Rian didn't respond. She watched as Olivia rejoined her party. Olivia, her mother, father, and two slaves walked up the gangway. The slaves went below. The Tuckers stayed on deck and chatted with the well-wishers on the pier until a tow boat with eight men straining at their oars pulled the *Carolina Princess* to the middle of the Delaware.

With final waves to the departing travelers, the group broke up. Jabez and Rian headed back north.

"Rian, what if your uncle doesn't sail back to Philadelphia before September 2? You'll have no boat to stow away on. What are you going to do then?"

"I've got a new idea. But I'm going to need your help."

When Rian finished describing her new plan, they had reached Washington Square. Jabez sat on a bench. "You're crazy. Your father will kill you when he finally gets his hands on you."

"Maybe. Maybe not. I don't think he wants me around anymore, so why would he be mad that I ran away?"

"Oh, he'll be mad, and he'll take it out on me and Conor."

"Conor hasn't been around the house since Otto kicked him out." Rian elbowed Jabez. "You might lose your place as the son he's always wanted."

Jabez didn't take the bait. "If you don't want to leave Philadelphia, how come you're willing to go so far away?"

"That's just it. I don't want to go. I'll be leaving you and Conor, not to mention all that's happening in the factories. But at the school in Switzerland, I wouldn't get any of that, plus I'd have to wear a dress all the time and learn about manners. If I go to Russia, I'm with Uncle Adrian, and he's in the railroad business."

"So girls don't wear dresses in Russia?"

"There's no place in my plan for a dress, but I'm gonna have to do some fast talking."

* * * * *

· SEAMUS ·

Seamus was waiting for Siobhan when she and her sisters closed up Clancy's Saloon past midnight. He noted there were no giggles when her sisters peeled away from Siobhan this time.

Sensing which way this was going, he threw all his chips into the pot. "So, will you marry me?"

"I'm sorry, Seamus, but no, I'm not going to marry you. I want you to know I've thought long and hard about it."

Seamus was crestfallen. Deep down, he assumed that with the thought of a new life, the chance of untold riches, an exotic locale, and his belief that Siobhan genuinely loved him, she would willingly join him. "I'm surprised," he said.

"It wasn't an easy decision. I do love you, you know, but you're a fooking moving target. I'm afraid I'll wake up some morning and the man I married will be somebody else."

"Did your da talk to you about this?"

"No. Me da stayed out of it. This was my decision. Seamus, you're a good man. You're even trying to make the world a better place. But you keep changing on me."

"You know what, Siobhan? You're missing out. In Russia, no one will know that I have an Irish accent. They aren't going to care. All they'll know is that I'm a rough-and-tumble American, there to break through tradition and get things done. We'll be welcome in the best hotels, the best dining rooms, the ballrooms. We'll be somebody in Russia. Wouldn't that mean something to you?"

Siobhan looked up at Seamus for a few heartbeats, then gave him a light kiss on the cheek. "Write me from Russia if you figure out who you are."

Then she turned and walked away.

SATURDAY, AUGUST 19

· ADRIAN ·

Adrian, Seamus, Colonel Malkovich, and Count Sheremetev were making decisions at dizzying speed. They had already purchased tickets to depart on the *Elizabeth* on September 1, and the clock was ticking.

The four toured the Krieger factories after holding one last meeting before the Russians left Philadelphia to visit Washington and Virginia. The plan was to meet Adrian and Seamus on the Walnut Street Wharf in ten days.

Travel plans had solidified. Jabez had stopped blurting out reasons why he shouldn't accompany Adrian to Russia. Mila was reconciled to joining them in St. Petersburg in the spring once Adrian got the lay of the land. Seamus was coming to terms with Siobhan's rejection and the reality that he would be traveling without his beloved.

"Just as well, for all of you," commented Count Sheremetev. "You will save money."

Saving money didn't seem to be a high priority to Adrian, knowing that this trip was backed by the Tsar's hundred-thousand-dollar down payment.

"The colonel and I have been thinking," Sheremetev said. "If you come to St. Petersburg just as you are, the courtiers at the Winter Palace will eat you alive. Your situation demands a certain degree of artifice. I would say more than an implication of wealth. And let's add some—how do you say it?—good old American showmanship?"

Adrian and Otto had already committed to stripping Krieger Coach and Krieger Locomotive of half their machinery. Sheremetev had more ambitious plans. He acted like a kid in a candy shop when they walked through the Krieger factories.

Sheremetev eyed a one-quarter-sized working model of Krieger's hopper locomotive that steam-engine genius Heinrich Aldrich had created years ago. "Crate that up. It will amuse the Tsar."

A whale oil lamp designed to light the way for a locomotive as it ran at night? "That too."

A thirty-inch cast-iron drive wheel that could drive a locomotive fifty miles per hour? "Yes. Definitely, yes."

The count noted workers assembling a boiler for one of Freeman Hydraulics' pumps. "What is this?"

Adrian straightened with a touch of pride. "That is a steam-powered fire pump. Nothing else like it in America."

"Can it be finished in time to get it on the ship?"

"Well, we only make the mechanical parts. Freeman Hydraulics made the chassis. It's not ours to sell."

"You have a hundred thousand dollars in the bank. Tell Freeman Hydraulics that you will pay them more for the machine than their current buyer."

Adrian looked at Seamus, who shook his head slightly. "Well, that's the thing. It's supposed to be delivered to Seamus's fire brigade next week."

"It must come to St. Petersburg. No one in Russia has even conceived of such a thing."

Seamus turned to Adrian with a look of near panic on his face. Adrian assumed the new pump had become something of a sop thrown to the No Names in light of Seamus's abrupt departure.

Adrian nodded. "I'll talk to Jules. I expect he'll be pleased to get paid more for this machine and get a new order to boot."

"What about hoses?" asked Sheremetev. "Demonstrating a fire pump without hoses would be quite difficult. The pump must come with hoses."

Seamus looked up at the shop ceiling. "Standard is for a pump to come with a thousand feet of hose."

"Better make it two thousand."

Seamus nodded. Adrian nodded. The fire pump and hoses would be packed and loaded onto the ship.

As they walked through the Krieger Coach factory, Sheremetev lifted a tarp that covered the lavishly appointed landau Prince Friedrich of Hohenzollern-Hechingen had commissioned but never paid for. "This will be your carriage in St. Petersburg. People will notice."

In Krieger Rail, he pointed to a dozen newly fabricated 16-foot rails cooling on the floor. "Bring eight of those and whatever tools you need to install them."

Then the Russians bid adieu. "We will be back in ten days to sail with you to Liverpool and on to London. That's where we will continue our preparations to help you rough-and-tumble Americans conquer the Winter Palace," said the count.

* * * * *

· RIAN ·

Harriet Purvis escorted Rian into her husband's study. "Robert, you have a visitor. It's good to see you again, dear."

Robert Purvis sat at his desk, working on a ledger. "Well, hello, Rian. What brings you here? Business or pleasure?"

"I guess you'd have to call it business, sir."

"So, what business can we attend to?"

"I'd like to use your embosser. Just for a minute."

Purvis sat back in his chair and crossed his arms. "The last time we used that embosser was to make Mammy-Rose's forged emancipation paper look official. That caused a huge ruckus in Moyamensing."

"It's nothing like that. I guess you'd have to call it personal business."

"Care to tell me what kind of personal business?"

Rian fidgeted. "When we were planning Rose's escape, Maddie Freeman taught me about Rule Number 1. That means if you don't need to know about something, you don't get to know about it. Can we make Rule Number 1 apply here?"

Purvis frowned at his visitor, but there was a warmth there. "How much trouble can I get into if this goes wrong?"

"I would never rat you out if I got caught."

"Who will be mad at me if you get caught?"

Rian tried to respond with her most winning smile. "Rule Number 1?"

Purvis sat and contemplated the situation. Then he pulled a key out of his vest pocket and unlocked a drawer in his desk. "I would never do this if we didn't have such a rich history. I hope you don't make me regret this." He held out the embosser to Rian.

Rian gratefully accepted the heavy instrument. "I don't think you will, Robert." She reached into her pocket and unfolded two sheets of paper. She fit the first paper between the two metal disks of the embosser, squeezed the handles hard hard hard, examined her work, repeated the process with the second sheet, and handed the embosser back to Purvis. "Thank you, sir. That's all I need."

Robert accepted the implement. "Then I guess our business is done."

"What do you hear about the Constitutional Convention? Is the 'white men only' clause still out?"

Purvis rose from his desk. "Why, thank you for asking. I'm still cautiously optimistic, although I do hear rumblings. I fear we still have a fight ahead of us."

"I'm sorry for that. I hope it works out for you."

"Thank you, Rian. I appreciate your concern. Good luck with your personal business."

THURSDAY, AUGUST 31

· RIAN ·

The bright sunlight of a midsummer afternoon briefly blinded Rian as she shinnied herself through the hatch in the roof of Sparks Shot Tower. It was cooler at this height than on Carpenter Street, 140 feet below. "Whoa," she said to herself as she stood up.

Conor and then Jabez followed Rian onto the roof, Jabez carrying a three-foot naval telescope that his father had given him when he had whisked him off to sea five years ago. Rian walked around the roof.

"Can I use your telescope?" Rian asked Jabez. Familiar landmarks viewed from this unfamiliar vantage point popped out at her. Directly to the west, five piers for a railroad bridge across the Schuylkill neared completion and rose out of the river like short soldiers at attention. Fairmount Reservoir to the northwest looked serene. Five degrees to the east: "I think I can see the Krieger factories from here."

"Let me look," said Conor as he tried to grab the telescope.

"Not yet. You'll have the rest of your life to look at this view. I don't know if I'm ever coming back."

"You sure you want to do this, Rian?" said Conor. "The *Elizabeth* leaves tomorrow."

"Somebody's gotta go. Jabez doesn't want to. I don't want to wear a dress for the next five years. This plan solves both our problems."

"Well, I think your plan creates some new problems. You're going to freeze your ass off."

Rian used the spyglass to follow Front Street, the straight-as-a-die thoroughfare that fed all the wharves along the Delaware as it extended north. Wagons laden with cargo plied their way to or from warehouses. Two men sat in chairs outside a barber shop. A woman showing quite a bit of cleavage chatted up a sailor. A man in an apron chased three kids out of a store.

"Otto doesn't want me here. He wants to get rid of me because I'm a girl. In Switzerland, I would have to learn how to serve tea. In Russia, I'll be able to help Uncle Adrian build factories."

Conor again tried and failed to grab the telescope. "Your father's going to kill Jabez when he finds out. And I lose my best friend."

Rian followed Front Street to Walnut, which ran east–west a little more than a half-mile away. Just north of Walnut, she found the Morris & Evans Pier. She focused on the outline of Captain Ellsworth's *Elizabeth*. *And tomorrow I'm going to be on her*, she told herself.

"Can I have the spyglass now?" asked Conor.

"One more minute," Rian replied. She followed Walnut back to Front and found Dock Street, one of the few diagonal thoroughfares in the city. Two men were operating the mechanical arms of a semaphore on the roof of the Merchants' Exchange Building. "Hey, they're sending signals from the Merchants' Exchange."

Conor looked toward the building a mile away. "It's only four o'clock. They'll be sending messages as long as it's light out."

"How come they're looking to the north? Messages come from Cape May."

Conor, who had been delivering messages from the Merchants' Exchange for six months, assumed an air of authority. "It's not just Cape May anymore. Last year they finished a series of towers all the way to New York City."

Rian handed the telescope to Conor but kept looking toward the north. "How far away is New York?"

"I don't know. A hundred miles, maybe."

"How long does it take to get a message to New York?"

Conor put the telescope to his eye. "Depends on how long the message is. Less than an hour."

"That's nothing," said Rian, "but why does anyone in New York need to know what's going on in Philadelphia that quick? You can get there by train in eight hours."

Conor scanned the waterfront with the telescope. "It's all about business. The same as messages coming from the mouth of the Delaware. If the merchants know something nobody else knows, they can make a profit out of it."

"Conor," said Jabez, "I know they can send messages from Cape May to Philadelphia. Can they send messages from Philadelphia down to Cape May?"

"Of course. They do it all the time. Why?"

"Because it will take a day for the *Elizabeth* to get to the mouth of the Delaware. When Uncle Otto finds out that Rian has stowed away, he can send a message to Cape May and get Captain Ellsworth to kick her off."

"Regular people can't send messages. Only merchants."

"Yeah, but Uncle Otto is friends with a bunch of business people. Is Mr. Shippen part of the consortium?"

"Sure. I deliver messages to him all the time."

"Then he can get George Shippen to send the message for him."

Oh shit, thought Rian.

FRIDAY, SEPTEMBER 1

· OTTO ·

It was embarkation day for Adrian, Jabez, Seamus, Colonel Malkovich, and Count Sheremetev. The farewell party of five—Otto, Rian, Conor, Mila, and Aaron Bassinger—had traveled to Morris & Evans Pier to bid *bon voyage* to the travelers. It was the first time Otto had spent significant time with Conor since he had fired him six months ago. *And if things had been different, Jules would have been here too.*

The group arrived at the pier in three carriages because Adrian and Seamus were traveling heavy, including the landau the German prince had ordered, then backed out on. Yesterday, stevedores had loaded machinery stripped from the two Krieger factories.

Rian was the first to hug Adrian goodbye. Then she gave Jabez a hug and a playful slug on the arm. For the hundredth time, Otto marveled at how similar the two cousins looked. *They have the same height, same hair color, same facial structure, same gap between their front teeth. Today the only difference between how the two are dressed is that Jabez is wearing a frock coat—a bit heavy for the warm September weather, but perfectly appropriate for a long voyage—and Rian is wearing a new set of shop clothes she bought the other day.*

Otto was sorry that Adrian had decided to take Jabez to Russia with him. He would have liked to take over Jabez's mentorship in his brother's absence.

Rian turned to Otto, gave him a brief hug, and whispered, "I love you, *Vater*." She and Conor walked to the pair of horses that had delivered the Hohenzollern-Hechingen landau to the pier and tied them to a carriage.

She called me Vater. She hasn't done that in months. "Can't you wait until the *Elizabeth* leaves, *Liebling?* I'm sure it won't be more than an hour."

"Conor and I are taking the horses back to the livery. Then I'm going to pick up the two dresses that I'm taking to Switzerland."

"Hey, Jabez!" called Conor. "You forgot one of your bags. Come and get it so we can leave."

Jabez turned to Adrian. "Uncle Adrian, I'm not feeling very well. I'm going to go aboard and find my cabin." He ran toward Conor and Rian and disappeared briefly behind the wagon. Moments later, bag in hand, he proceeded to the ship's gangway and disappeared from view.

Otto turned his attention back to Rian and Conor and got a fleeting view of them as the carriage turned the corner onto Swanson Street.

It is curious that Rian goes to pick up the dresses without prodding from me, Otto thought. *Just a few weeks ago, she kicked and screamed about those dresses. Now all that fussing seems to have passed. I shouldn't begrudge Rian spending her few remaining hours in Philadelphia with Conor.*

Tomorrow he, Rian, and his sister-in-law Lilly would be the departers, leaving on the ferry for Camden, and then New York City via the *Camden & Amboy Railroad.* Rian and Lilly would sail directly for Le Havre, take a steamer up the Seine to Paris, and then a sequence of coaches to Zurich.

Seamus seemed in a buoyant mood despite leaving without Siobhan. The count and the colonel bowed and boarded the *Elizabeth.*

Otto hugged his brother. "This venture to Russia is a good decision, Adrian. I sent a letter to George Dallas.[15] He is now the American Ambassador to Russia. I suggest you make an appointment to see him. I am sure that he will be happy to nudge Russian officials at the appropriate time. After all, America is now an important Russian ally."

Adrian grabbed his brother by the shoulders. "I marvel at the number of people you have become acquainted with by eating lunch at the hotel every day. Well, thank you for writing the letter, brother, but it seems that Sheremetev has things well in hand. Just make sure the operations in Philadelphia don't fall apart while we're making us all rich over in Russia."

Otto laughed, hugged Adrian again, and let him go to say his final goodbyes to Mila. He waved to his friend Captain Ellsworth, who was mingling with the onboarding passengers.

Aaron joined Otto. "Pretty cavalier of the captain to socialize just before they leave the dock."

"His duties won't kick in for a while yet. Even though Ellsworth knows the Delaware well, the harbor pilot still takes responsibility for getting the ship past the Navy Yard. However, once the pilot leaves the *Elizabeth,* the ship is Ellsworth's and he's all business."

"I guess I'm just surprised he doesn't have duties to attend to."

---

15. George Mifflin Dallas served briefly as mayor of Philadelphia in 1828–29.

"He loves to tell stories, and they start the moment you come on board. My brothers and I first met him when we sailed to America from Hamburg. He was a second mate then. A few years older than us, but he'd been at sea all his life."

"What do you mean all his life?"

"He ran away from home at age eight to become a cabin boy. He thinks life is one big adventure, and for him, it all started then. He claims that children today are coddled and overprotected . . . well, at least the children of the well-to-do. He is why Kurt took to the sea rather than become a landlubber like Adrian and me."

Otto turned his attention to the crane lifting the landau onto the ship. The stevedores made the task look easy.

An hour later, a tugboat with ten oarsmen towed the *Elizabeth* to the middle of the river. With her sails unfurled, she gracefully made her way down the Delaware.

* * * * *

Otto was surprised when the afternoon went by and Rian had not returned. *I haven't considered how difficult it must be for her to leave her best friend.*

He walked home and changed his clothes for dinner. Alice had the meal on the table when he came down from his bedroom. He noticed a folded sheet of paper next to his plate. In his daughter's precise hand, he noted one word: *Vater.* With growing apprehension, he unfolded the paper.

September 1, 1837

Vater,

 As you read this letter, I am heading out West. I would rather live and work on the Mississippi than wear a dress in Switzerland.

 I love you, and I know you will be angry with me. I hope you are able to forgive me sometime. I will write to you when my future becomes clearer.

 Please take care of Havana for me.

 Your daughter,
 Rian

* * * * *

· JULES ·

Jules stared at Hugh, who had entered Freeman Hydraulics and settled into the chair in front of his desk as if he were a frequent, welcome visitor.

"I take it you aren't here to haggle about the price of a new pump," Jules said.

"As far as my lads are concerned, we're still negotiating. But I've got some news that may interest you. I did a little research and found out who was insuring the *Bridger*. I paid a visit to the Insurance Company of North America. It seems the good captain and his partners neglected to inform the ICNA that the *Bridger* is involved in the slave trade. They had no idea he sailed to Africa. He told them he was sailing to London, then Amsterdam, then Havana."

"Very enterprising of you, Hugh. So what?"

"Insurance companies like to know those sorts of things. They informed his partners here in town that they have canceled the ship's insurance immediately. The partners sent a note to Havana that'll be waiting for Captain Howes when he arrives. If the Navy stops him while he has slaves aboard, they'll confiscate his ship, and the ICNA won't shell out a nickel. No matter what, he'll be sailing into Philadelphia naked."

"I've got to grant you one thing, Hugh, you are tenacious. However, I told you last time that there were two other reasons why I wouldn't get involved with you on this mission. I don't like you, and I don't trust you."

"You just don't listen, Jules. The enemy of my enemy is my friend. I'm handing you a golden opportunity to strike a blow for your people."

"My plate is full. This meeting is over."

"I'm sorry that's your answer. Get hold of me if you change your mind."

SATURDAY, SEPTEMBER 2

· ADRIAN ·

The *Elizabeth* had cleared the mouth of the Delaware Bay and was now sailing in open water. Adrian and Seamus leaned over the port rail on the deck. It had been an hour since they last sighted land. Adrian took in the seemingly limitless expanse, the sun still a few hours from setting. He hadn't seen another sail since this morning. "This is the farthest out to sea I've been since my siblings and I sailed to America in 1820. That's seventeen years."

Seamus seemed to be in an equally pensive mood. "My family and me came over in steerage. I was a mite. Don't remember spending any time on deck."

More silence as the two took in the horizon. The sea was calm. The wind was brisk.

Seamus put his elbows on the rail. "Did Jabez appear for breakfast? I missed him at dinner last night."

"I knocked on his door this morning. He grunted about still not feeling well."

"Hi, Uncle Adrian. Hi, Seamus."

Adrian turned, relieved that his nephew finally felt well enough to emerge from his cabin. For a moment, he couldn't make what he saw mesh with what he thought was true. He had expected to greet his nephew Jabez. Instead, his niece Rian stood before him on the deck of the *Elizabeth*. A day and a half ago, he had said goodbye to her on the wharf in Philadelphia. "Rian . . . for a moment I thought you were Jabez. How did you get aboard?"

"I switched places with Jabez. I want to go to Russia with you."

* * * * *

· OTTO ·

Otto sat at his office desk, his head in his hands. He had not slept the night before. He had walked to the station for the *Philadelphia & Columbia Railroad* and asked every worker he could find if they had seen his daughter. No one had seen Rian. The same for the *Philadelphia & Trenton*, two miles away. The same for the steamboat *Telegraph*. In desperation, he had walked to Jules's house and awakened him and Maddie. Jules knew nothing, but he awakened Rufus to see if he knew anything. *Nothing.*

"Otto," said Jules, "this transcends our problems. Let me know if you learn anything."

At noon, his sister-in-law Mila entered the office with Jabez Howes in tow. "Otto, we have a problem."

Otto looked at Jabez, who should have been aboard the *Elizabeth*. "Jabez, what is going on?" And then he thought, *Oh no.*

* * * * *

· RIAN ·

Rian didn't know what she expected of her Uncle Adrian, but what she got was anger.

Adrian grabbed Rian by the wrist and dragged her to the helm. He caught the eye of a seaman standing next to the helmsman and asked, "Is the captain about?"

"You'll most likely find him in his cabin."

Without releasing his grip on Rian, Adrian walked her to the captain's cabin and knocked on the door.

"Enter," said a booming voice from inside.

Adrian entered, still holding Rian by the wrist.

"Why hello, Adrian. And what have we here? I haven't met your nephew yet. Thanks for bringing him by. Good lord, you look remarkably like your cousin Rian."

"Captain, this *is* Rian. She's a stowaway. Well, not exactly a stowaway. She switched places with my nephew Jabez. Just came up from her berth a few minutes ago."

Captain Ellsworth placed his quill in an inkwell and looked sternly at Rian across his desk. "A stowaway. And what are your plans, Little Miss Stowaway?"

"I want to go to Russia with Uncle Adrian and Cousin Seamus."

"This ship is sailing to London. You would need papers even to get off the boat."

"I have papers."

Adrian stared down at Rian with incredulity.

The captain held out his hand. "Let me see them."

Rian fished two sheets of paper out of her pocket and handed them to Ellsworth. "I look so much like Jabez that I thought I could get by on his papers, but just in case Uncle Adrian didn't want to do that, I made a copy with my name on it."

August 22, 1837
To Whom It May Concern:
Re: Rian Krieger, male
Age: 13
Height: 5'6"
Weight: 125 pounds
Address: 134 North Ninth St., Philadelphia, Pennsylvania, U.S.A.
This document certifies that the above-named individual is a citizen of the
United States of America, of good health, and eligible to travel to various
foreign lands with Adrian Krieger and/or Seamus Gallagher.
Jeremiah P. Sloan
United States Customs
Philadelphia, U.S.A.

Embossed over the signature of Jeremiah P. Sloan, United States Customs, Philadelphia, U.S.A., was an image of an American eagle clearly defined by a series of bumps and surrounded by a circle of raised stars.

Captain Ellsworth ran his finger over the bumps. "Did Mr. uh . . . Sloan issue this document for you?"

Rian hesitated, but she decided the truth was the best course since her plan had already fallen apart. "No, sir. I wrote it myself."

"This seal. The embossed eagle. It's impressive. Where did you get that?"

"A friend. He keeps an embosser in his library. He embosses his books if he loans them out so that people will be sure to return them."

"And Mr. Sloan. What about him?"

"He's nobody. I made him up."

Ellsworth put the forged document down on his desk and unfolded the second document, which was the same except that it described the traveler as Jabez Howes. Ellsworth spread his hands over the creases. He again ran his finger over the embossed eagle. He looked across his desk at Rian. "Stowing away on a ship heading to a foreign land and forging official papers. These are severe transgressions, Rian. How old are you?"

"Thirteen and a half."

Captain Ellsworth stared at Rian for a very long moment. Then he started laughing—not a little tee-hee laugh, but a big belly laugh. He shook his head. "My God. A thirteen-year-old. Forging papers. With a fooking library stamp. And this document looks more official than half the papers that come across my desk. I daresay this will get you into any country you travel to, my dear Rian."

Uncle Adrian took a deep breath. "Uh, Captain Ellsworth. That's the thing. I was hoping you could take Rian back to Philadelphia when you return. You know, to look after her like you did with Conor McGuire two years ago."

The captain's mood changed abruptly. "Adrian, I'm afraid that this time I can't be the solution to your problems. I'm getting too old to cross the North Atlantic in the fall. The storms are too damn violent. When the Elizabeth leaves London, we're sailing to the Mediterranean. We won't return to Philadelphia until late March or early April."

"How about if you keep Rian through the winter? She can be your cabin boy . . . er, girl."

Ellsworth took off his glasses and placed them on his desk. "I granted your brother a big favor when he asked me to be responsible for Conor two years ago. And that was only for nine weeks, if I remember correctly. I am not inclined to do it again, especially with a youngster who is intent on running away and so highly creative. I'll hear no more on this subject. Dismissed."

Adrian tugged at Rian's shirt, a silent indication that further pleas to the captain would be useless.

Ellsworth scanned the document one last time. He held it out to her uncle. "One piece of advice, Adrian. I notice that these forged papers identify Rian as a male. Over the years, I transported hundreds of Irish. I've met both men and women named Rian. Assuming you choose to take Rian to Russia, I speculate you—and she—will have a much easier time if she continues this subterfuge as a male."

"Thank you, Captain," said Adrian. He turned to leave the cabin.

"And, if you decide that Rian will travel as Rian, not Jabez, make sure changes are made in the passenger manifest. Work it out with the purser during dinner."

Rian was reeling. As she followed Adrian out of the captain's cabin, she turned back to say *Thank you, sir. Sorry for the trouble, sir.*

Before she could utter the words, Ellsworth shook his head and gave her a wink that only she could see.

* * * * *

· ADRIAN ·

As Adrian and Rian walked toward midships to regroup with Seamus, Adrian no longer held her by the wrist and instead rested his hand on her shoulder. Seamus, still at the rail, turned to them when they returned.

"Seamus, I just asked Captain Ellsworth to take Rian home on his return to Philadelphia. He refused. We've got to solve this problem another way." He leaned over and put his hands on his knees to reach Rian's eye level. "Niece, you snuck aboard the ship hoping we would take you all the way to Russia."

"Yes."

"And in this grand scheme of yours, what would you be doing in Russia while we set up factories?"

Rian sheepishly shrugged. "Same things as Jabez would have, I guess."

"Jabez was going to have a tutor while I worked. All day. That's not a method of education that has worked for you in the past. Is that what you're angling for?"

"Not really. I was hoping I could help you set up the factory. I kind of already did that once two years ago when we moved from the old shops."

"Niece, thirteen-year-olds don't start factories."

Rian shifted her gaze to the sea, then back to Adrian. "I could also be your coachman. And your groom."

"Girls aren't coachmen. That's why they're called coach*men*. Girls aren't grooms either."

Rian's only response was a shrug of her shoulders and a shy smile, as if to say *And therefore* . . .

Adrian stood up straight and looked at Seamus.

Her cousin's smile indicated that the situation made him more amused than perturbed. He shrugged. "Dressing her up as a coachman isn't any more fantastical than any of the rest of this journey we're on. A month ago I was a stevedore, working sun-to-sun, and you were afraid Krieger Locomotive was headed for bankruptcy."

Adrian bent over again to get eye-to-eye with Rian. "You are saying that you want to pretend to be a boy as long as you stay in Russia. That no one will know you are a girl."

"Yes, I can do that."

"The count and the colonel, do they know you are a girl?"

"I don't think so. I only saw them that day I brought them to your office and then yesterday."

"We'll have to cut your hair."

Rian swallowed hard. "Yes."

"I don't know how long we will have to keep you in Russia. It will be next spring, at the very least. It could be years."

"I know," was all that his niece said, but Adrian detected the slightest of smiles.

SATURDAY, SEPTEMBER 9

· ADRIAN ·

Adrian knew that there would be long stretches in this Atlantic voyage that would be tedious. He hoped to learn at least the rudiments of Russian from Colonel Malkovich and Count Sheremetev. Planning for a four-week crossing, he had armed himself with numerous books, plus paper, pen, and ink to write letters to Mila.

Surprisingly, the two Russians were unfazed when Adrian told him about Rian-the-stowaway. "If he wants to be a coachman, then he shall be a coachman," Sheremetev had said. "Properly presented as a carriage driver, your nephew can be part of the American showmanship I am looking for."

Adrian's anger at Rian for switching places with Jabez slowly dissipated. Given recent experience, he conceded that Rian would be more of an asset in Russia than Jabez. However, Rian had never been to sea before. *What will she do to while away the hours?*

It turned out that his worries were unfounded. Rian practiced her violin at least once a day. Many evenings, Captain Ellsworth joined her with his own violin for duets.

Rian also read the serialized copies of *The Posthumous Papers of the Pickwick Club*,[16] which Captain Ellsworth had given her early on. "I'm sure that more pamphlets have been published since the *Elizabeth* was last in London," Ellsworth told her. "If you like the story, you will have to buy them at a book shop when we arrive in London."

---

16. During this era, British publishers did quite well by printing pamphlets of amusing illustrations that were supported by equally amusing short stories. In March 1836, the publishing house Chapman & Hall printed the first installment of *The Pickwick Papers*, which featured the illustrations of Robert Seymour. They had hired a relatively unknown author writing under the name of Boz to provide text explaining Seymour's illustrations. They sold five hundred copies of the first installment, which made it a modest success. A month later, Seymour died by suicide. Chapman & Hall considered ending the series, but the author made an intriguing proposal: *Let me drive the story with my words. You find a lesser-known illustrator to create scenes from my text.* Chapman & Hall went with Boz's suggestion. Subsequent installments were published monthly from April 1836 through October 1837. The October installment sold forty thousand copies, and Boz, whose real name was Charles Dickens, became one of the most famous authors of the nineteenth century.

But the Russians occupied an unexpectedly large amount of Rian's time. They had their own way of whiling away the hours—card games. It didn't matter what the game was, but card play usually started shortly after breakfast. In the morning, they played a Russian game called "durak" that Adrian never bothered to learn, but he noticed the colonel and the count were only too eager to teach it to others, including Rian.

Four people generally played durak with a 32-card deck, and the game involved some sort of attack and defense. It was very raucous, and the loser—the last player holding cards—had to pay a penalty, perhaps an act or confession that would become the object of good-natured derision. The mockery lasted only until the next hand was dealt.

Adrian wasn't sure how his brother would react to his daughter learning to play cards but figured when Rian eventually returned to Philadelphia, Otto would have much bigger fish to fry. He noticed that while Rian was playing these games, she was also learning to speak Russian.

The Russians always took a break for the midday meal, then reconvened for the afternoon. At these times, the games were more cerebral, like whist, or involved betting small amounts, like vingt-et-un or monte. Adrian sat in several times and realized he was not interested in cards because he wasn't good at the games. However, to learn some Russian, he participated whenever Sheremetev and Malkovich were playing.

On the other hand, Rian turned out to be a very competent player, so competent that she was a sought-after partner in whist. "Your nephew picks up these games very quickly, my friend," said Malkovich. "He has card sense. It all has a logic to it. The bidding. The play of the hand. I'm not sure I can say the same thing about you."

When the Russians suggested playing poker in the evening, Seamus showed interest in cards for the first time. While Adrian had never heard of poker before, Seamus had watched a few hands but never played.

"Come. Sit. Play with us. This game is new to us, as well," said Sheremetev. "When we sailed to America, we were accompanied by an American gambler. He says this game is popular on the riverboats that steam up and down your Mississippi."

For the first few evenings, Rian was allowed to watch the game but not to play. She sat between the two Russians, each showing her their hands. One or the other would ask which card she thought he should play. Sometimes they would take her advice, sometimes not.

Although Adrian enjoyed the camaraderie, he had no more affinity for poker than the other card games the Russians tried to teach him. As had occurred several times one evening, he lost a pot to Sheremetev. It wasn't a big pot at all. They were only playing for pennies, and Adrian took the loss good-naturedly.

"Rian," Sheremetev said with a chuckle, "I feel guilty taking all your uncle's money. Go sit next to him and help him out."

With Rian's help, Adrian won a few hands.

The following night, for lack of players, Sheremetev gave Rian a seat at the table and staked her to some pennies. He was amused when Rian won the first two pots. After that, thirteen-year-old Rian became a regular in the nightly poker games and financed her own games.

By the end of the voyage, no great wealth had been exchanged through the nightly card games, but the evenings had passed quickly. Adrian was grateful he would never have to earn a living as a gambler.

"Watch out for your nephew, though," Sheremetev said with a smile. "He is what that Mississippi gambler would have called a cardsharp."

WEDNESDAY, OCTOBER 4

· ADRIAN ·

Almost five weeks had passed since the *Elizabeth* had sailed down the Delaware. Although Adrian was anxious to get on with the remainder of their voyage to Russia, they had been stalled in London for a few days, with departure set for Friday.

Their stay in London was important for three reasons. First: Savile Row. Count Sheremetev declared Philadelphia fashions too parochial to elicit proper respect at the Court of Tsar Nicholas Romanov, Emperor of Russia, King of Poland, and Grand Duke of Finland. Only in the garment district of the largest city in the world's most powerful nation would the two men be able to purchase attire appropriate for the Tsar's court.

Their wardrobe requirements would be considerable—business coats; morning coats; frock coats; overcoats; waistcoats and vests, both single- and double-breasted; light trousers for day, dark for evening; additional evening attire; hunting outfits; cravats and suspenders; smoking jackets; opera capes. Also, top hats, beaver hats, hunting hats, and slouch hats. Gloves for the cold, and gloves for dancing. Then there were the accoutrements—walking sticks, tie pins, studs, hairbrushes, tobacco pouches, opera glasses, hunting rifles, and a telescope. In addition, of course, the many trunks in which to pack these items.

Seamus observed that his expenses for toiletries alone were more than he had made in his months as a stevedore.

Second: servants. The count had chosen not to broach this subject until their ship had left Philadelphia. Only a veteran and skilled English valet could provide the rough-hewn Americans with the polish they would need to survive the status consciousness and intrigue of the Winter Palace: table manners, proper attire for every occasion, topics of conversation, how deep to bow (or not to bow).

Sheremetev initially advocated for Adrian and Seamus to each have their own valet. However, Rian's presence changed his position a tad. "The illusion we are creating can be maintained just as well with one valet and a coachman."

Although the valet they hired came with his own livery, the count deemed his costume not up to snuff. Therefore, Adrian shelled out for additional clothing for their servant. And Rian needed her own coachman's getup. Adrian was amused to note how happy Rian seemed as the tailor measured her for her new clothing.

After their fourth day of shopping, Adrian realized the Tsar's hundred-thousand-dollar down payment might not have been exorbitant after all.

And there was the third reason, one that Adrian hadn't anticipated: ladies. Sheremetev entertained an unending parade of comely young English women who were enamored of his title but equally interested in Malkovich's military rank and the two Americans' rough-hewn demeanor. They even overlooked Seamus's Irish accent, taking their cues from his newly acquired wardrobe instead.

Although the two Americans often dined with the Russians and however many young women they had gathered to join them, Adrian never engaged in any post-dinner activities except for one evening. In this case, he had made his usual excuses to return to the hotel, but one of the young women had suggested that the group go back with him to their suite and play charades, a game unfamiliar to the rest of the party.

The raucous group of nine—the two Russians, two Americans, and five bubbly young women intent on enjoying the Russians' sumptuous hotel accommodations—arrived at the suite, only to find Rian in the sitting room, reading the latest installment of *The Pickwick Papers*. Sheremetev and Malkovich, both quite inebriated, enthusiastically greeted their card-playing companion and included Rian in the charades game before Adrian knew what was going on.

As it turned out, Rian was as adept at charades as she was at card games.

THURSDAY, OCTOBER 5

· RIAN ·

Rian stood on the clothier's stool and stared back at the coachman in the mirror—her first look at herself in her new duds. She placed her top hat on her head and adjusted it numerous ways until she established its most proper jaunty attitude. *I think I'm going to enjoy this.*

"Can I wear this suit right out of the shop?" she asked the attendant, who expressed satisfaction at her transformation from factory worker to coachman in an obviously prosperous household.

"You may do as you please," he said. "Count Sheremetev made it quite clear during your fitting that he wanted you to be happy with your new uniform. We will wrap up your second suit and your old clothes for you and have them delivered to your hotel. I hope your troupe has a successful mission in Russia."

Rather than return directly to the hotel, Rian walked a few blocks to Hatchards Booksellers on Piccadilly. A bell tinkled as she opened the door.

"May I help you?" asked a man behind a counter, his voice carefully modulated between solicitousness and disinterest.

"Yes, I would like to purchase the latest installments of the *Pickwick Club*. I need everything after March."

"Aha," replied the bookseller. "An American. That explains it."

"Explains what?"

"An Englishman, whether gentleman or servant, would know enough to take off his hat when entering an establishment such as Hatchards. You Americans are notorious for your ignorance of commonly agreed-upon deportment."

Rian snatched her hat off her head. "Sorry. Uh, *The Pickwick Papers*?"

The clerk left his post behind the counter, leading Rian to a bookshelf near the front window. "I daresay Mr. Dickens will be pleased to hear this news."

"Mr. Dickens?"

"Oh, yes, of course. You would have no way of knowing . . . Boz, the author of *The Pickwick Papers*, is the pen name of Charles Dickens. He was in here the other day. He will be pleased that his readership has now leapt across the Atlantic."

Rian idly ran her fingers around the rim of her top hat. "I don't know anyone who has read these pamphlets in America, and I'm heading to Russia."

A wry smile crept across the bookseller's face. "Russia will do."

"You know Mr. Dickens?"

The clerk sifted through numerous pamphlets and handed five of them to Rian. "Yes, he is an up-and-coming author. We are proud to carry his works. Here are the installments from April to September."

Rian examined the pamphlets. "Where's May?"

"There was no publication in May. Mr. Dickens's beloved niece died earlier, and he took some time away from his writing. Are these books for your master?"

"No, they are for me, although I'll probably share them with my uncle and cousin. I'm their coachman."

"And what are you three Americans going to do in Russia?"

Rian leafed to the last page of the September issue of *The Pickwick Papers*. "My uncle is going to build some railroad factories for the Tsar. We sail out tomorrow. Is there any way you can mail the next installments to me?"

"We do that sort of thing all the time. Where should I mail them to?"

"We are going to be staying at the Tsar's Winter Palace."

"Guests of the Tsar. Very impressive." The clerk paused. "You know, Mr. Dickens had a dispute with the publisher of *The Pickwick Papers*. He is already well into publishing his second novel in serial form, just as he has done with *The Pickwick Papers*."

"What is it called?"

"It's called *Oliver Twist*. It comes out every month in a literary magazine called *Bentley's Miscellany*. I think you will like it. It's about a young boy like yourself, although Oliver grows up in a life of poverty." The clerk pointed to a bookcase behind his counter. "I have all of Bentley's publications over there. I believe there are seven issues so far."

"Can you mail new editions of these to me as well?"

"I daresay Mr. Dickens will be pleased that his works are regularly mailed to the Tsar's residence. I do have a word of warning, however."

"What is that?"

"A man named Benckendorff runs the Third Section of the Imperial Chancellery. The Third Section is in charge of censorship of all literature and theater in Russia. They have confiscated some literature we have mailed to Russia in the past. I wouldn't leave these pamphlets lying around the Winter Palace."

Rian knew nothing about censorship, but she made a note.

MONDAY, OCTOBER 9

· OTTO ·

Otto arrived at Baltimore's Pratt Street Station in a dejected state. His meeting with Louis McLane, President of the *Baltimore & Ohio Railroad*, had not gone well. Four months ago, he had been on the verge of closing contracts with the *B&O* for twenty railroad cars, two locomotives, and miles of track. Then the Panic hit. McLane stopped responding to his letters. To save the deal, Otto traveled to Baltimore to speak with him directly.

"Frankly, Krieger," McLane said when Otto met him in his office, "this Panic is kicking my ass. Ridership is down. Freight is down. It's not just the *B&O*. My understanding is the same goes for the *Baltimore & Port Deposit*. You must have noticed on your way here yesterday. I heard the *B&PD*'s morning train from Havre de Grace arrived with two empty cars."

Otto confirmed McLane's statement with a nod. "I could cut back on some of the extras. The cars would not be as well appointed as we had originally quoted, but will be well crafted and last for years."

"I wouldn't take them even if you gave them to me. They would be in the way. Our plans for a new railroad yard have gone on hold, just like everything else. I'm sorry, Krieger, but we have to ride this depression out as best as we can. Talk to me when we get to the other side of this unpleasantness. I'm sure the economy will come back sooner or later."

With no hope of saving the deal, Otto chose to return to Philadelphia. Walking along the Pratt Street Station's platform, he noted the *B&PD*'s latest cost-cutting measure: There were two fewer passenger cars on this train than the one he had arrived on.

The first two passenger cars were completely occupied. Otto tossed his carpetbag up to the brakeman, who stood atop the third car. He waited for a man to climb into the first compartment ahead of him, but the guy got partway into the compartment, hesitated, then backed out. "Don't go in there unless you mean to ride with an African," the man said to Otto as he walked to the next compartment.

Otto couldn't have cared less whom he rode with. He had no intention of talking to anyone. He was not surprised to find the compartment occupied by a gentleman sitting beside his slave. One of the ironies of riding on trains both north and south of the Mason-Dixon Line was that some railroads allowed a slave owner to bring his property (the slave) with him in the passenger compartment. However, if the Black individual were free, they would have to ride in a separate coach. If such a coach were not available, then the top of the car or a freight car were the only options.

Otto settled himself into his seat and surveyed his compartment mates. The gentleman wore blind man's glasses. The opaque circular green lenses hid whatever damage had been done to his eyes. In addition, he had wrapped a scarf around his jaw that emitted a pungent, sweet smell, an indication of liniment to ease the pain of a toothache. The scarf obscured most of the man's face. The man's right arm was carried in a sling.

Observing the man's many maladies put Otto's recent troubles in perspective. *All I have to worry about is a runaway daughter and a failing business.* He shut his eyes, slouched in his seat, and hoped no one else would join them in the compartment. He didn't bother to open his eyes when two additional people considered riding in the compartment, saw the occupants, and went elsewhere.

"Board!" yelled the conductor.

The locomotive's whistle blew. The train started with a lurch. Otto lapsed into a fitful sleep, disturbed only when the train stopped at stations to take on passengers and water. The brakeman, walking atop the passenger cars, announced the stops in a stentorian voice loud enough to register through Otto's doze. Stemmer's Run . . . Magnolia . . . Perrymans . . . Aberdeen.

"Havre de Grace!" announced the brakeman from above. "End of the line!"

Moments later, the train started to slow. Otto sat up in his seat. He had a crick in his neck that he knew would plague him for a day or two before he worked it out.

"Excuse me, sir," the slave said to Otto. "Is this Philadelphia?"

"No," replied Otto. "We are only about a third of the way there. The *Baltimore & Port Deposit Railroad* ends here. We take a steam ferry across the Susquehanna River, then catch the *Delaware & Maryland* to Wilmington, then the *Telegraph* to Philadelphia."

Otto noted a look of panic on the slave's face, and his master stirred uneasily but said nothing.

"The man at the counter said our tickets were to Philadelphia," said the slave.

"I suspect they are. Let me see them."

The slave fished through his purse and produced two tickets, which he handed to Otto.

Otto looked at the printed tickets. "Yes, you have paid all the way to Philadelphia. I will happily stick with you to make sure you make all your connections."

"The *Telegraph*. What is that?"

"The *Telegraph* is a steamboat that runs from Wilmington directly to Philadelphia. You'll be fine. I'll make sure you get there." Otto noted that the slave relaxed only a bit. "Why doesn't your master talk?"

"My master's name is Simon Starr. My name is Jack. He is traveling to Philadelphia for medical treatment. As you can see, he is blind, and when we arrived in Baltimore, he developed a toothache."

Simon nodded slightly to verify Jack's rendition.

Otto addressed Simon. "I am sorry to hear about your troubles. I will make sure you get to your destination. Where are you staying in Philadelphia?"

Jack answered for his enslaver. "We intend to find a hotel in the city, then catch a train to New York tomorrow."

"You will have to cross the Delaware to Camden. From there you can take the *Camden & Amboy* to New York. I thought you said you were seeing a doctor in Philadelphia."

"Uh, no. I meant New York."

Otto escorted Simon and Jack onto the ferry that crossed the Susquehanna and then to the train to Wilmington. He made sure they boarded the steamboat *Telegraph*, which he had last been aboard when George Shippen paid for two hundred people to attend the fireworks in celebration of the joining of the western two-thirds of the *Philadelphia, Wilmington, & Baltimore*. In two hours, the *Telegraph* would tie up at Wharton Pier, just south of Walnut Street in Philadelphia.

It didn't take much insight to see the precariousness of the travelers' plight. Starr was blind. Jack, his "eyes," was illiterate. Otto did not attempt to remain with them once aboard the *Telegraph*.

Otto sympathized with the poor wretches who were enslaved like Jack. By favoring immediate emancipation for all slaves with no compensation to the enslavers, his thinking aligned with the most radical abolitionists of the day. However, unlike radicals such as William Lloyd Garrison or Lucretia Mott, he took no action. Whereas Garrison, who had dined at Otto's house two years ago, railed stridently against the evil institution, Otto chose to tend to his businesses.

Whereas his next-door neighbor Lucretia refused to buy any produce—food or manufactured goods—tainted by the hand of slavery, Otto chose to ignore his second- or third-hand complicity in the economic system that perpetuated human bondage.

However, a fleeting thought crept into Otto's consciousness as he leaned against the rail. *If I could ever catch Jack when he's away from Simon Starr, I could whisk him to freedom and there would be nothing Starr could do about it.* Although he felt sympathy for the blind man's plight, Starr was holding another human in bondage. Otto surprised himself at the thought. *Perhaps some of my daughter's instincts have rubbed off on me. Oh, Liebling, I miss you so. How could I have driven you to such desperate measures?*

Fifteen minutes after they steamed by Chester, Pennsylvania, Otto leaned on the railing of the portside deck, looking at the shore as it passed by. *Seven months ago, somewhere near that spot, my daughter almost got herself killed while trying to rescue a slave named Peach.*

A movement to his left caught his eye. Simon Starr and Jack walked purposefully toward the bow, the blind man clinging to the slave's arm. *Something is odd about those two—something about how Starr clings to his slave.*

A few minutes later, Otto was displeased to note that Hans Schmidt was also a passenger on the *Telegraph*. He had fired Hans for refusing to take orders from Jules because Jules was Black. Later, Hans joined Austin T. Slatter in the slave-catching business.

Otto recognized Schmidt's voice when he approached a passenger who was also leaning on the railing. "Excuse me, sir. Did you see an African and a white man pass by here a few minutes ago? I'm looking for a fugitive slave, and I thought I saw him heading this way."

Otto turned to face Schmidt. "You're wasting your time, Hans. That man is traveling with his master so his master can get medical treatment. Go crawl back into your hole and leave decent people to their privacy rather than spread your misery to others."

Hans turned his attention to Otto. "Well, if it isn't Mr. High and Mighty Otto Krieger. I hear you fired your African friend. I'd consider coming back to work for you if you'd get rid of the rest of the Irish."

Otto couldn't think of an appropriate retort. He turned back to watch the shore go by.

But Hans wasn't finished. "I'm returning from a trip to Virginia. Took a runaway back to Richmond. Reward was a big one. I bet I made more money this week than you did."

"Perhaps, but at least the money I made wasn't through the misery of another human being. Someday, Hans, you will pay for your sins."

"Do you eat meat, Otto?"

"Of course I do."

"Do you condemn the butcher for killing the cow?"

"No, of course not."

"Yet you are perfectly willing to wear clothing made of cotton produced by slaves. Same with sugar, rice molasses, rum. The only difference between me and you is that I'm not afraid to admit what I am: A person whose life is intertwined with slavery. So I guess that leads me to another difference: You are a hypocrite and I am not. Is there going to be a place in hell for me when my time comes? Perhaps. But I'll tell you what: If I get there first, I'll keep a seat nice and warm for you."

Otto continued to watch the shore go by. *Jules, Maddie, Seamus, even Rian and her friend Conor have all taken great risks because of their beliefs. Yet here I stand, watching the shore go by, risking nothing.* "Go bother someone else, Hans."

"I suppose you won't tell me where the African went then."

Otto thought quickly. *If I thought about stealing Jack from the blind man and escorting him to freedom, then Hans probably has thought of stealing him and selling him South.* He turned to Hans. "I have paid little attention. Try the bow."

"In that case," Hans said, "I guess I'll just go aft. Never know what I might find."

Otto smiled to himself. *A small victory.*

* * * * *

When the *Telegraph* arrived in Philadelphia, passengers gathered in a cluster on the main deck to disembark. Otto spotted Hans toward the front and purposefully remained back to avoid further interactions with the odious man. He hadn't spied Simon Starr or Jack for the rest of the voyage and was curious whether Hans had ever confronted them. When he finally descended the gangway onto Wharton Pier, he was surprised to see Conor McGuire standing in the shadow of the steamboat company's ticket office. He hadn't seen Conor since he abetted Rian as she stowed away aboard the *Elizabeth*.

Otto chose to shelve whatever ire he harbored toward Conor for assisting in his daughter's flight. "Conor, what are you doing here?"

In answer, Conor jerked his head in the direction of the warehouse that served the Fries Wharf just to the north. Austin T. Slatter stood in a gaping doorway and was talking with Hans Schmidt. "Following him."

"Slatter? Why?"

"I'm done delivering messages for the day. Slow day at Freeman Hydraulics. When that happens, Jules asks me to tail Slatter or Hans and see what they're up to."

"You work for Jules now?"

Conor shook his head. "The money I used to make at Krieger Coach helped to pay for the apartment for me brothers and me. We got kicked out after you fired me. Jules lets me sleep in the shop, so I do odd jobs for him when I get back from washing dishes at McSweeney's."

Otto was chagrined that when he fired Jules, Seamus, and Conor, he never considered how devastating that could be for the thirteen-year-old and his three brothers. "You should have talked to me. You could have come back with Rian and me."

"You kicked me out the same day you fired me. I didn't think I was welcome."

Otto nodded; Conor's point was well-made. "So what is Slatter up to?"

"He comes here a lot, just to see if there's any fugitives he can sweep up. Sometimes he goes to the Morton Pier to meet the boat coming from the Delaware & Chesapeake Canal. Sometimes he goes across the river to Camden to catch folks trying to board the *Camden & Amboy*."

"And what do you do if he captures someone?"

"I go back and tell Jules. He doesn't let me do anything beyond that. I think he learned his lesson about utilizing youngsters. He doesn't let Rufus do anything, either. Slatter generally takes the fugitives to jail. I think he learned his lesson, too. He tries to do it all legal-like. But then Jules and Mr. Forten hire lawyers to defend the fugitive. Some of the time, they're not fugitives at all. They're free Blacks that Slatter snaps up in the hopes he can sell them South and get away with it."

"Does Slatter know you tail him?"

"I don't think so. I'm pretty good at blending. A lot of kids in the street look like me."

Otto pointed with a jerk of his head toward Hans. "Did he know Hans was on the ship?"

"Doubt it. Kind of surprised they're still hanging around. Everyone's off the ferry. Slatter usually heads back to his house by this time. He lives pretty fancy these days. Hans goes to the brauhaus on Sansom Street."

"Hmm, maybe they're sticking around for a reason. There was a white man and his slave that I helped get aboard the *Telegraph*. Hans was looking to question them on the ship."

Just then, Simon Starr and Jack walked down the gangway and stopped so that Jack could get his bearings before proceeding. They were talking with one another, but they were too far away for Otto to hear what they were saying. They started walking toward Water Street. Then it dawned on Otto. *Oh my God. I've got it all wrong.*

Schmidt and Slatter stepped away from their position at the warehouse and walked into the path of Simon and Jack.

"You two looking for a place to stay for the evening?" asked Slatter, just as polite and solicitous as could be.

"Thank you, sir," replied Jack. "But I believe we will stay in a hotel this evening."

"I don't believe I was speaking to you, boy. I was asking your master."

"My master can't speak. He has a toothache."

Otto had heard that "place to stay" ploy before, a lure to lead him down an alley and steal his belongings. "Conor, run out to Water Street and hail a cab. Get it here as soon as you can."

Otto left Conor, shifted his lumber-measuring rule so that its stout end rested on his shoulder, and addressed Jack. "Excuse me, you have no reason to trust me, but I am telling you, do not go with these men. They are slave catchers, and they do not much care if you are a slave or free. If you end up in their clutches, you will quickly find yourself on a ship to Charleston, and the next day you will be picking cotton."

"Stay out of this, Krieger," growled Slatter. "It's none of your business."

Otto noted Jack and Simon holding one another, frozen in fear. He turned to Slatter, his lumber rule still at the ready. "I'm making it my business." Then he addressed Jack and Simon. "Navigating this city on your own is a mistake. Therefore, you have a decision to make. Go with these men, who I tell you are not to be trusted, or go with me, and you will not be harmed."

Just then, a landau with its top up came roaring down the alley between the Wharton and Fries warehouses, kicking up swirls of soot and dust behind it. The coachman wheeled the horses to the south and reined them to an abrupt stop. The soot and dust eddied behind the carriage, then settled at the feet of the antagonists.

"Your carriage, sir," said the coachman in a calm voice, as if his arrival had been expected.

Otto looked at Simon. "I suggest you make a decision quickly, Mr. Starr. If I leave without you, your fate will be sealed."

Simon and Jack came to a wordless decision. Jack nodded. "We will come with you."

Otto opened the carriage door for Simon, who climbed in. Jack followed, then Otto. Otto was not surprised to find Conor in the forward-facing seat. The carriage started. Otto looked out the window to see Hans and Slatter growing smaller behind them.

"How did you talk this man into coming to rescue us?"

"He's Mr. Forten's driver. I ran out to Water Street to find a cab, but nobody would stop for the likes of me. Then he just happened by. I flagged him down. It wasn't hard to talk him into it."

Otto looked over at Simon and Jack. He noticed that Simon was clinging tight to Jack. He was shaking. A tear trickled down his cheek from underneath his opaque glasses. The tear confirmed Otto's suspicions.

"Conor, what is Mr. Forten's driver's name?"

"Jerry. Why?"

Otto looked toward the roof of the landau's canopy and yelled, "Corner of Fitzwater and Twelfth, Jerry."

"That is Jules's house," Conor blurted out. "You can't take a slave owner to his place."

"I don't think that should be a concern in this instance."

"Why not?"

"Because Jack isn't your slave, is he, Simon? And you aren't a man. You are a Black woman so light-skinned you can pass as white. And you two are fugitive slaves escaping to freedom."

TUESDAY, OCTOBER 10

· JULES ·

Jules stood in a mixed group of Black and white men at a wide spot on a path in the middle of Washington Square. Without exception, they presented themselves as proud, well-dressed citizens about to exercise their right to vote as established by the 1790 Constitution of the Commonwealth of Pennsylvania. They were all members of the Pennsylvania Anti-Slavery Society, which they referred to as PASS.

"Are thee ready for this?" James Mott asked Jules.

"Ready as I'll ever be. What do I have to be afraid of? I'm over twenty-one. I'm a landowner. I pay my taxes. I've done this before."

"Yes, my friend, but not in this climate. Things have changed since the Panic. There will be men there who have been paid to prevent thee and thy brethren from voting. I fear it will be ugly."

"And for that, I thank you and the white members of PASS for joining us. It is gratifying to have your support."

Mott surveyed the group. "I am afraid that I add only my presence to this endeavor. Sadly, if the situation turns violent, I will not lift a hand to defend thee, or myself, for that matter."

Robert Purvis left a knot of PASS board members and joined James and Jules. "It looks like everyone who said they would show today is here. I wish there were more."

Jules surveyed the group and counted fifteen in all. "Still sure you want to do this? A torrent of shit is about to rain down on our heads."

Purvis squared his shoulders. "Jules, this is our right."

"And neither candidate for city council from our ward is a friend of the Negro. And no matter who gets elected, the council will vote thirty to nothing to return Mayor Swift to office. Our votes won't count."

"Feeling faint of heart, Jules?"

"Honestly, yes. And a bit disappointed that more white PASS members didn't show up to support us this morning."

Purvis shrugged. "We have known forever that this is our fight. It's time to go."

Jules nodded, knowing the next half hour was going to be excruciating.

A muted cheer rose from the group, and Jules turned to see Otto Krieger ambling down the path toward him. He gave every appearance of being out for a Sunday stroll.

"What are you doing here?" Jules asked.

"The farmer came early with the milk this morning. Lucretia and I were out with our pitchers at the same time. She told me what James was up to. I figured it might be fun to join you."

James Mott shook Otto's hand. "Neighbor, do thee know what thee is getting into?"

"I'm not sure I ever told you this, James. Krieger means warrior in German. My father was a cavalry officer during the Napoleonic Wars. He used to say he was a Warrior by name and a warrior by nature. Admittedly, I am getting a little old for this, but it feels good to dust off some old pugilistic skills."

"I'm pleased you came, Boss," said Jules.

"I am not currently your boss, but perhaps we should discuss that."

Energized by Otto's arrival, Jules turned to the group and said, "Gentlemen, it is time to do our civic duty."

Jules and Purvis led the way as the small band cut catty-corner across Walnut and Sixth Streets to enter the grounds of the State House.[17]

"Maybe by voting early, we'll avoid the worst of the crowd," he said to Purvis as they approached the building where the Declaration of Independence was ratified and the U.S. Constitution was drafted.

Then Jules saw the crowd.

---

17. All votes in Philadelphia during the 1830s were cast at the State House—what is now called Independence Hall. Voting was a chaotic process, with partisans of all candidates scrapping for voters' support. Citizens from each ward waited in separate lines to pass their ballots through a small window to a voting inspector. As no one outside the window was assigned to maintain order, the area near the window was often so crowded that the only way to get one's ballot to the window was to pass it to a friend up front. Fights frequently broke out. And all of this mayhem occurred between white factions. Special antipathy was expressed for the occasional Black voter who showed up to exercise his constitutional right.

THURSDAY, OCTOBER 12

· JULES ·

Jules limped into the kitchen, which smelled of pot roast and frying turnips. He kissed Maddie on the back of her head and gave her rear a friendly pinch.

Maddie swatted his hand away. "Behave yourself. We have company."

Jules turned around to see seventy-two-year-old James Forten sitting at the kitchen table. "Good evening, James. What brings you here?"

Forten chuckled at Jules's kitchen shenanigans. "Checking up on you. Making sure you are still alive after the ruckus you caused at the State House the other day."

Jules danced a semblance of a jig in the middle of the kitchen. "Barely limped on my way home from work today. As Otto Krieger says, 'Don't let the bastards see you bleed.'" Jules sat down heavily on a kitchen chair. "It's a shame that exercising your constitutional right can be called 'causing a ruckus,' though."

Forten, still sitting, leaned forward on his cane. "What did you hear out there today?"

"Oh, the whole town knows eight Negroes voted and seven white PASS members showed up to support us. Four of them were Quakers, so they weren't much help. Otto Krieger arrived just before we walked into the State House. We gave out worse than we got. Of course, we'll never know what the damned voting inspector did with our ballots on the other side of the window."

"Jules, mind your language," Maddie said over her shoulder.

Forten smiled at the interplay. "Who got the worst of it?"

"Me, I guess. Your son-in-law is quite a pugilist. Otto stuck with us in the Moyamensing line, took some licks, and gave out more. Then he had to get back into his district's line and vote at his window. It was quite a show." Then Jules broke out a big smile. "But we voted. Damn, they knew we voted."

"And what did dear Maddie say when she saw you?"

Jules shrugged and rolled his eyes.

Maddie turned around from the stove. "It frightens me, of course. He could have been killed, but I'm proud of him. I wish he weren't the one who was the most visible. I lose sleep, afraid of every noise in the night. I know he's doing the right thing, but I fear the hotheads will resort to far worse than fisticuffs . . ."

Jules raised his hands in supplication. "Any news about elections in other parts of Pennsylvania?"

Forten pulled a sheet of paper out of his coat pocket. "Bucks County, next door to the north, is a little interesting. The Democrats got beat. Our Whigs and the anti-Van Buren crowd took five of six local seats."

"Good. Maybe that will send a message to Washington, or at least to Harrisburg."

"Well, we may have won the battle and lost the war. The elections were close. One of them was decided by two votes. And apparently 39 of our fellow Negroes voted, and the Democrats are already contesting the election. The losers filed a petition with the Bucks County Court this morning."

"That was quick. What are the grounds for the petition?"

Forten folded the paper and put it back into his coat pocket. "They claim that Blacks do not have the right to vote in Pennsylvania. They want the results overturned."

Jules felt a chill course up and down his spine. "But that's nonsense. The current Pennsylvania constitution makes no mention of the color of a man's skin. The attempt to add a 'white only' clause to the new constitution failed."

"You know that, and I know that, but the facts don't seem to deter these people."

"So, what now?"

"Get back to work. Until the new Pennsylvania constitution is ratified without that heinous clause, we must not rest. I believe our problems with the 'white only' clause just came back to life."

FRIDAY, OCTOBER 13

· OTTO ·

Otto stared at the sheet of paper that Aaron had placed on his desk. The report was grim. Sales of carriages, rolling stock, locomotives, and rails continued to be weak. Despite the light demand, production delays in the coach and locomotive factories had pushed back deliveries and thus created a cash crisis that could have been avoided.

Ernst Winther isn't up to the job in the coach factory. It just doesn't run the way it did when Jules and Seamus were involved. I don't think Harry is able to fill Adrian's shoes at Krieger Locomotive either.

Otto had no more than finished that thought when Jules entered the office without knocking, limped to Otto's desk, and placed an envelope in front of him. "Here is last month's rent for my shop. Sorry it's late. Next month will be on time, assuming I get paid on time. I sold another pump."

"How is your knee?"

"Oh, I'll live. We certainly kicked up a fuss the other day. Sorry it had to come to that, but not sorry we did it."

"Nor am I, Jules. Please count on me for future election-day actions. I think it is important to remind our fellow citizens that the Black man has every right to perform his responsibility as a member of our republic."

"For a while, at least. Thank you for joining us the other day, Otto. What about my other activities? Any change of heart there?"

"Oh, helping that runaway couple was a one-time-only escapade for me." Despite the faint clatter coming from the shop, he lowered his voice. "I will leave the Underground Railroad activities to you, although you can assume I am supportive."

"I look at your response as progress. When you were at my place on Monday, I never asked how business is going."

Otto reflexively picked up Aaron's report, then placed it back on his desk. "We are struggling. How about you?"

"An order comes in every once in a while. My workers are learning their craft. We're paying our bills and saving a little bit. I took a cue from you and Adrian; we mount a plaque that says *Freeman Hydraulics, Philadelphia USA* on every fire engine we roll out the door. That makes me proud."

A knock occurred at the office door.

"*Betreten* [Enter]!" yelled Otto.

Ernst Winther walked deferentially through the door. "Otto, are you going to fire me?"

Otto stared at Ernst for a few seconds, "I have no plans to. Why do you ask me this?"

"It's just that I saw Jules walking through the shop for the first time in six months. I figured he was here to talk about getting his old job back. Hello, Jules."

"Good to see you, Ernst. I haven't any plans to return. Otto hasn't asked me, and that's not why I'm here."

"Well, I'm glad you're here because I want you to hear this. Otto, I wonder if I can have my old job back."

"What seems to be the problem?"

"A lot of things. I don't think I'm very good at being a foreman. I don't like giving directions to the men. They don't like taking orders from me. We keep running out of materials. The machines keep breaking down. Things ran more smoothly when Jules was here."

"And you take responsibility for these problems?"

"*Jawohl*, most of them. I'm not sleeping well."

"Thank you for your candor, Ernst. You can sleep easy tonight. I am not going to fire you, and we will figure something out together that solves our problems on the shop floor."

Ernst gave Otto a polite nod, said goodbye to Jules, and left the office.

"He who cannot dance will say the drum is bad," said Jules.

"What is that?"

"An old Ashanti proverb I heard from my mother before I was sold away from her. Ernst didn't complain about the drum. He took responsibility for most of the problems. He's a good man. You should keep him on."

At that moment, Aaron Bassinger entered the Krieger Coach office. "*Die Post ist da* [The mail is here]."

Otto looked up from his desk. "Anything interesting?"

Aaron plopped three folded sheets of paper sealed with wax on Otto's desk. "I believe so. Mail from the travelers."

Otto gestured for Jules to take a seat and picked up the letters. "Finally." He broke the seal on the one with Rian's handwriting and scanned the letter. He sighed and addressed both Aaron and Jules. "Rian says that Adrian tried to talk Captain Ellsworth into bringing her back to America but he refused. She has talked Adrian into taking her to Russia. She doesn't know when she'll be home. She likes the count and the colonel. They are teaching her to play cards."

"Could be worse, I suppose," said Jules.

Otto shook his head. "I was hoping Ellsworth would bring her home on his return trip." He opened the next letter. "Ah, interesting. Adrian has scribbled at the top of this letter. 'Captain Ellsworth has hailed the French ship *Esprit*, which is bound for Philadelphia from Le Havre. They are sending a longboat to us to exchange mail. I expected to finish this letter in London but figured you would breathe easier with at least a little bit of news about Rian.'" Otto continued to scan the letter. "Adrian says that she is a good traveling companion. Oh, good lord."

"What?" asked Jules and Aaron at the same time.

"She forged her own papers. The papers say she's a boy. They've cut her hair. They plan to make her their coachman and groom, so they intend to buy new clothes for her when they get to London."

Jules smiled and shook his head. "Well, I'm sure that part makes her happy."

Otto picked up the last letter. He scanned the letter and cracked a smile.

"Who's that one from?" asked Aaron.

"Captain Ellsworth. I should have expected this from him. 'I could have kept her with me this winter as we plied the Mediterranean, but that's not the adventure Rian is destined for. Your daughter is in good hands with Adrian. Or maybe I should say Adrian is in good hands with Rian. She is a pistol. The count and the colonel have taken a shine to her. She will be fine. She will be back to you soon enough. I dare say that you might have some problems getting her back into a dress, though. She is a smart cookie. She figured she could have become Jabez Howes because they look so much alike, but if Adrian didn't like that idea, she forged a second set of papers identifying her as a boy. So now she is Rian Krieger, age thirteen, male. Adrian and Seamus thought it would be easier all the way around if they maintained her subterfuge. Adrian assumes Jabez will join him in Russia next year, so it would ultimately be less confusing. Sheremetev and Malkovich either don't know or don't care. You have an amazing daughter, Otto. I assume she will tire of this coachman thing and be returned to you shortly. If she doesn't become your bookkeeper or get in line to run Krieger Coach, she has promising careers as a forger or a cardsharp. Good luck.'"

Otto rubbed his hand through his hair, then looked up at Jules. "Jesus, I have made so many mistakes. What am I going to do?"

"Not much you can do. Trust Adrian to make good decisions for her. Trust her to figure out she's made her statement and it's time to come back home."

"Her statement?"

"She didn't want to go to that school in Switzerland."

"That now seems very apparent. Everyone on the ship seems unworried by Rian's little disguise."

"She pulls it off half the time here in the factory. I think she's got a good shot."

"I can think of a dozen ways she can be exposed. I may have initiated one of them. The new ambassador to Russia was mayor of Philadelphia a dozen years ago. I've had lunch with him several times at the United States Hotel over the last couple of years, including just before he left for Russia this spring. I wrote to him before our folks sailed and asked him to stop in to see Adrian. Of course that was before Rian and Jabez colluded in the big—what do you call it?—the big switcheroo."

Aaron shuffled through some papers at his desk. "I wouldn't waste time worrying about all that. The likelihood of him encountering Rian is minuscule. Remember, Rian is a coachman. Ambassador Dallas will never notice her. Coachmen are invisible. Meanwhile, where is Jabez? He was supposed to be doing bookkeeping with me this morning."

"I do not know," said Otto. "I have not seen him all morning."

"So he may not have come in to work again?" Aaron shifted in his chair. "Otto, this isn't working out. Jabez is bright enough, but he is unmotivated. He's not putting any effort at all into the bookkeeping."

Otto looked at Jules. "My nephew Jabez has been a problem since he arrived. Mila reenrolled him in school, but he skipped out half the days and caroused around the wharves. Apparently, our second attempt to get him involved in the shop has also failed."

Jules shook his head. "I'm sorry, Otto. I imagine you had high hopes for him."

Otto tossed Captain Ellsworth's letter on the desk. "I used to get frustrated with Rian when she would come home with some of the bad habits she learned from the workers. You know, the swearing and so on. It seems that Jabez happily absorbs the bad habits but none of the skills."

"So does that change your mind about your daughter's capabilities?"

Otto shook his head. "My daughter will become a powerful helpmate to whatever husband chooses her. I guess I will have to be very discriminating about her suitors. I don't think she will be the right wife for your average young man."

"Thankfully, you are years away from that," said Jules. "I have to get to work. It's a short day for Maddie and me. Lucretia is speaking in North Philadelphia this evening, and we are going along to listen."

"In all these years, I have never heard Lucretia speak."

"Want to go along?"

"Yes, as a matter of fact, I do. How about if I drive my landau?"

"That would be perfect. There will be room for the Motts as well."

"Then we have a plan. We'll have more time to talk on our way there."

* * * * *

· JULES ·

Otto drove his landau north on Broad Street as Jules sat beside him. It was a perfect autumn day. The setting sun cast a golden glow on the road. Lucretia and James Mott and Maddie rode inside the carriage with the canopy up.

"You know, Jules," Otto said, "I agreed to do this more to continue our rapprochement than to further my anti-slavery education."

"I am aware, and I appreciate your sentiment, but pay attention to Lucretia's message. You might learn something."

"How many people do you think will show up tonight?"

Jules tried semi-successfully to shrug off the stare of a man on the street, which he interpreted as disapproval of a Black man and a white man riding together on the driver's seat of the landau. "Hard to say. Our party might outnumber the attendees, or there could be 75 to 100."

"Jules, I made a huge mistake."

"Coming with us this evening? Or sitting up here with me?"

Otto smiled. "Neither. I meant firing you. Firing Seamus. Firing Conor."

"That's an easy fix for two of us. Getting Seamus back from Russia might take longer."

"You would consider coming back?"

They passed a man burning a pile of leaves in his front yard. He broke from his chore to stare at Jules and Otto.

Jules tried to ignore the stare. He waved his hand casually in front of his face as they passed through the plume of smoke. "Two men in a burning house must not stop to argue."

"Is that another one of your mother's Ashanti proverbs?"

Jules smiled and nodded.

"And whose house is burning, yours or mine?"

"Both, as far as I can see. You need me to restore some order to the little business you have left. I need any extra income I can cobble together."

"But I acted so rashly."

"Otto, I placed Rian in danger. I lied to you. If you can forgive me for those transgressions, I can forgive you for tossing me off the job. It allowed me to get Freeman Hydraulics up and running. It would have been the best thing that could have happened to me if it hadn't been for this damned depression."

Maddie's disembodied voice came from inside the landau. "Watch your language, Husband. We can hear you in here."

"Duly noted, my dear. Sorry, Lucretia and James."

"We have all heard the word before, Jules," James said from inside the carriage. "Just make sure you two finish your reconciliation before we get to the meeting house. My wife has to prepare herself for her task ahead and cannot be distracted by the remains of a squabble between you and our next-door neighbor."

"So, will you come back?" asked Otto.

Jules spied a rider who looked like Robert Purvis cantering south on Broad Street. "I will if you hire Conor back, too. He's been sleeping in my shop because his brothers don't have room for him. He's a good kid, but I keep tripping over his bedding in the morning."

"With my newfound Russian riches, I believe I can afford both of you. Do we have a deal?"

"Yes, if I can have the same routine I had before you fired me. I'll come in to work after I know things are running smoothly at Freeman Hydraulics." *I was right. It is Robert,* Jules said to himself. *Something's wrong.*

Robert Purvis approached the landau and held up his hand, signaling Otto to rein in his horses. "Good afternoon, Herr Krieger, Jules. Do you have the Motts aboard? If so, I regret to inform you that the meeting has been canceled for the evening."

Lucretia Mott stuck her head out the window of the landau. "Good afternoon, Robert. Canceled? Why?"

"There have been threats to the church leaders. Threats to the speakers."

Lucretia descended from the carriage and stood in the street to address Robert. "But surely it would never come to violence. I understand that these people make a big show of their hatred, but they are merely misguided. They would not stoop to harming us. We should proceed."

Robert looked down at Lucretia from his horse. "The elders have already canceled the meeting. Shots have been fired through the windows of the church."

"Well, I disagree with that decision. We must not let the threat of violence deter us from our rightful path."

Jules nudged Otto. "Time to turn the rig around. You can take this as an indication that I have learned my lesson. Now is no time to place our loved ones in harm's way." *But the bastards won this round.*

FRIDAY, OCTOBER 20
(OCTOBER 8 O.S. [OLD STYLE] IN RUSSIA)

· ADRIAN ·

The travelers arrived in St. Petersburg after a fourteen-day voyage from London.

"So I don't get it," said Seamus. "Is today's date October 20 or October 8?"

"You are in Russia now, my friend," said Sheremetev. "It is October 8. I will teach you about our Russian calendar, and you will have a little insight into the mind of Tsar Nicholas. We operate here under the Julian calendar, not the Gregorian calendar that most of the world works on."

"Same months. Same number of days. Why are the two different?"

"Starting in the time of Julius Caesar, everyone used the Julian calendar. But the Romans didn't quite get the formula right for keeping the years on track, even when they built in leap years. By the 1500s, the equinoxes and solstices fell far from the dates they were supposed to."

"How far off did the old calendar get?"

Sheremetev shrugged. "Over the course of fifteen hundred years, eleven days. A newly proposed calendar corrected the leap year error, but even so, Pope Gregory had to decree that some days would have to disappear to get the calendar back on track."

"I'm glad America never had to deal with that."

"You did, but before you were born. When you were still British colonies, September of 1752 was only nineteen days long. Since that time, we here in Russia have lost another day."

"Why didn't you guys make the change?"

Sheremetev stiffened. "Russia does not take orders from your western pope. We are a country dominated by the Orthodox Catholic Church."

"So how does this relate to Tsar Nicholas?"

"In our international dealings—diplomacy, commercial and naval fleets, astronomy, meteorology—we are already forced to use the Western calendar.

The Department of Public Instruction petitioned the Tsar eight years ago to make the change universal. Tsar Nicholas considered it but determined that the change would likely produce too many upheavals. In short, he does not like change."

"Yet here we are, bringing the railroad to Russia, and change will come with it, so I guess some change is okay as long as the Tsar is concerned."

Sheremetev hesitated for a moment, then uttered, "Welcome to St. Petersburg."

During their stopover in London, a guide had described London as the world's largest and most powerful city, which was easy to believe. At well over a million people, it was more than ten times larger than Philadelphia.

However, London struck Adrian as a medieval city that had matured, somewhat sadly, into the modern era. Its streets meandered as if they were merely paved-over cow paths of a thousand years ago. The Thames was an open sewer and smelled like it. The haze created by thousands of coal stoves blotted out the sun. Coal smoke gave Londoners a perpetual cough and London streets a patina of filth.

Although St. Petersburg was only half as large as London, Adrian was more impressed by its grandeur. Compared to London, St. Petersburg was a youngster—fresh, vibrant, rich, and full of vitality.

Adrian's first significant purchases in Russia were two jet-black matched geldings to pull the Krieger landau. "Make sure you overpay for the horses," the count had told him. "Word will travel."

Rian, who walked off the ship fully outfitted in coachman's livery, assumed her duties with solemnity. As the most knowledgeable judge of horseflesh, she inspected each animal, running her hands over the horse's withers and haunches, checking each leg to make sure it was clean, picking at his hooves, and looking at his teeth and gums. She hung on each horse's back to assure herself he had a good temperament. With Seamus's assistance, she climbed on each horse's unsaddled back and rode him around the block.

The horse trader became impatient. Rather than yield to his entreaties, and with Adrian's tacit approval, Rian harnessed the two horses, hitched them to the landau, and drove them around the block again. Finally, she hugged each of them as she deemed them worthy of pulling the carriage of two very important visitors from America.

Count Sheremetev conducted the group's first tour of St. Petersburg from the comfort of the landau while Colonel Malkovich sat on the driver's bench with Rian. The city's architecture was so monumental, so foreign, that Adrian soon tired of peering out the window of the landau. "My neck is getting stiff. Let's put the top down."

Sheremetev agreed but continued with his narration while Rian folded the landau's canopy. "One hundred thirty years ago, Peter the Great decreed that a new Russian capital would be built right here, on what was a vast marshland. He wanted this city to be Russia's Window to the West, a vast set to awe visiting dignitaries. The tsars who came after Peter embraced his vision and demanded even grander architecture. They constructed public buildings and cathedrals on a monumental scale."

"Well, it works," commented Adrian.

"If you Americans are going to impress the residents of the Winter Palace—really grab their attention—you will have to create some of that awe yourselves, just like these buildings do. The tsars recruited brilliant architects from France and Italy during their building sprees. They spared no expense. Also, please note the prevalence of waterways. Peter the Great wanted the city's most monumental structures to be admired from the water. St. Petersburg is called 'the Venice of the North.' Having visited that city, I believe the comparison is apt."

Adrian pointed to a massive rectangular building fronted by eight two-story columns. "What is that?"

"That is the Manege, our first destination. It is the riding hall and stables of the Imperial Horse Guards. A good example of Western architecture that I mentioned."

Adrian whistled. "This is a stable? It's bigger than the State House back home."

Malkovich ushered the group under the portico, past a guard, and into the Manege's Grand Foyer, which emptied into the cavernous riding hall. Despite the muffling effects of a generous layer of sawdust, their voices echoed off the ceiling. "This room is big enough to accommodate a hundred horsemen as they drill through our Russian winter," said Malkovich. "Next come the stables."

The stables housed hundreds of horses, each with its own stall. Stall after stall was arrayed on both sides of four long corridors. Seamus summed up the Americans' awe. "These horses are living better than me family did when I was growing up."

"I'm glad you like it," said Malkovich. "Rian is going to spend a lot of time here. I have arranged for these two stalls to house the horses that you just purchased. Some of the baubles we brought from Philadelphia to impress the Tsar will be housed across the corridor over there."

Adrian shook his head. "Gauging by the grandiosity of this place, we might not have brought nearly enough stuff."

* * * * *

Kaleidoscope. That word came to Adrian's mind as they rode through the city. The count pointed to one building after another, saying they were of the baroque style. Adrian had never heard of baroque architecture before, and it was much different from the relatively simple lines of even the most important buildings of Philadelphia. Many St. Petersburg buildings were tall, ornate, dramatic, and curvy, with lofty domes, vibrant colors, and gilded statuary. Inside the buildings, light danced through windows and accentuated the prevalent golds and rich blues.

Rian brought the team to a halt in the middle of a paved expanse that fronted the largest building yet.

"This is going to be your home until we can get you wild and woolly Americans established," said Sheremetev. "Welcome to the Winter Palace, the Tsar's residence."

Adrian was forced to recalibrate his sense of awe. The palace was huge. "This is the Tsar's home?"

Sheremetev nodded. "The Tsar and his family, various nobles, short-term residents like you, house staff, bureaucrats, the Imperial Guard. At any given time, three thousand people live and work here. It's essentially a rectangle. Each side of the rectangle is three stories tall. The facade you are looking at is seven hundred feet long."

"The colors. No one in Philadelphia would dare create a building that is mostly green and white. Haven't they ever heard of bricks?"

"All the white you see? That is marble quarried in Tuscany and shipped here. When you have a virtually unlimited budget, you choose the whitest Carrara marble you can find for your facades, not brick."

"How many rooms are there in this beast?"

"No one knows for sure—more than 1,500. There are 117 staircases if you count those set aside for servants."

Adrian looked to his left. In the middle of this plaza stood a tall spire twelve feet in diameter placed on an ornate pedestal. "What is this?"

"This is the Alexander Column. It was erected three years ago to commemorate Russia's victory over Napoleon in the Patriotic War. It is more than eighty feet tall and weighs six hundred tons."

"How the hell did they put it up? I can't imagine the machinery that it must have taken."

"Never underestimate the will and abilities of the Russian people. The granite was quarried in one piece in Finland." Sheremetev pointed toward a dock along the Neva River, which was mostly hidden behind the mass of the Winter Palace. "It was brought here on a barge that docked over there. When it was time to set it on the pedestal, it took three thousand men less than two hours. It is held in place by its weight alone."

Adrian looked to the right of the facade of the Winter Palace. "That building over there. Is that part of the palace or something separate?"

"That is the Hermitage. It was built by order of Catherine the Great when she decided she needed an occasional refuge from the affairs of state. It runs parallel to the east side of the palace all the way to the river. Now it is mostly a museum that holds some of the most precious artwork in the world. It is a separate building, but it is connected to the Winter Palace in three places."

"Can we go in there?"

"I will be sure to arrange a tour."

The count directed Rian to drive the carriage through the archway to the Grand Courtyard, a paved open space within the four sides of the Winter Palace that was almost as big as Washington Square in Philadelphia.

Adrian and Seamus were granted an apartment in what seemed to be a remote section of the Winter Palace. The suite was spacious and far more opulently furnished than Adrian's home in Philadelphia. There were even small rooms set aside for servants. Thus Rian and the valet had their own accommodations. A well-banked fire warmed the central parlor.

"Count Sheremetev, I'm lost," said Adrian. "Where are we in the building?"

Sheremetev smiled. "Consider the Winter Palace a rectangle with the Grand Courtyard in the middle." He went to the window. "We are in the northeast corner of the rectangle. You have a spectacular view of the Neva River from here. Across the river is the Peter and Paul Fortress, burial place of the tsars, as well as a prison you never want to call home. If you walked just a little bit farther down your corridor, you would arrive at the Flying Gallery, one of the three bridges that lead to the Hermitage.

Adrian turned, taking in delicate chairs, gilded tables, and rich wallpaper. "It was good of the Tsar to put us up here."

Sheremetev chuckled. "I doubt the Tsar knows you are here."

In London, when Sheremetev told the Americans they would be the guests of the Tsar, Adrian envisioned that he and Seamus would be invited to tea or, if they were lucky, dinner. Adrian's fantasies of dinner with the Tsar faded.

"Don't get used to these accommodations, my friend," cautioned Shereme-tev. "The former occupant of this suite made the mistake of having an affair with the Tsarina's favorite lady-in-waiting. Her Royal Highness Alexandra Fe-odorovna banished him from the Winter Palace."

"Sounds harsh," joked Seamus. "But good for us."

"Not entirely," responded Sheremetev. "As this is prime real estate, I suspect you will soon be evicted with little notice."

Adrian ran his hand over a gilded clock on the mantel above the fireplace. "This apartment is magnificent, but why do you call it prime real estate? Every-thing I've seen in this building looks pretty good to me."

"The value of everything and every person in this building is measured by their proximity to the Tsar. We are six hundred feet from the Tsar's concert hall. Beyond that are the royal family's apartments."

Seamus whistled.

"This gives me an opportunity to make three points. First, fortunes can change here in a heartbeat. We are one misstep from disaster or one fortunate encounter from success. Second, the walls in this building have ears. Everything you say and do will likely find its way to Prince Volkonsky, the Minister of the Imperial Court. If the prince becomes aware of our true mission here, changing the character of Russia, he will not be pleased, and we will be in danger."

Adrian reflexively looked over his shoulder. "Are you part of the *we*?"

"Without a doubt. Colonel Malkovich as well. Third, your time here in the Winter Palace is limited. Others are already coveting this space. They will soon make their wishes known to the majordomo. If enough money crosses his palm, despite the exorbitant sum I have already paid him, he will find it expedient to evict you."

"How much time do you think we have?"

Sheremetev shrugged. "It won't happen right away. I'm sure the majordomo is testing the market right now. Maybe two months. I suggest you make every day count while you are here."

SATURDAY, OCTOBER 21
(OCTOBER 9 O.S.)

· ADRIAN ·

The day after they moved into their apartment, Sheremetev arranged for the visitors to take a tour of the public rooms of the Winter Palace.

"Prepare yourselves," said the count. "Are you familiar with the Stendahl effect?"

"No, what is that?" said Adrian.

"A French author named Stendahl was touring Florence two decades ago. You should go there sometime. Stendahl was so awed by the beauty that inhabits every nook and cranny in that city that he became overwhelmed. The same may happen to you on your tour today."

Their guide was an attractive lady-in-waiting to Countess Orlov who spoke German. Adrian translated for Seamus, with Rian tagging discreetly behind, wearing her coachman's livery. Despite the language barrier, the young woman seemed eager to flirt with Seamus. Adrian marveled at how easily they engaged in the game despite their lack of common language.

Some items stuck out in the blur of room after room of paintings, statues, gilded furniture, and history. Priceless oils by Raphael, Michelangelo, da Vinci, and Rembrandt. Artwork that Napoleon had looted from the German Confederation in 1806 and that Tsar Alexander I had removed to Russia after Napoleon's defeat. Solid silver this and solid gold that. *Maybe that man Stendahl was onto something*, Adrian said to himself. *After a while, all this beauty loses its effect.*

In Field Marshals' Hall, massive gilded chandeliers drew Adrian's eyes upward and competed for attention with the ornate white woodwork. A narrow balcony ran around the perimeter of the second floor. Portraits of various field marshals from Russia's glorious military past lined the walls.

Next door was the Small Throne Room. Adrian got the impression that they weren't supposed to be there but guessed the young woman was trying to impress Seamus.

"How many thrones does a king need?" Seamus muttered to no one in particular.

"This room is used only one day a year," said the lady-in-waiting.

Adrian didn't think their comely little guide spoke English, so she probably wasn't responding to Seamus's comment, but still . . .

The lady-in-waiting pointed to a chair placed in a raised alcove. "That is Peter the Great's throne. On New Year's Day, the Tsar greets nobles and diplomats who come to the palace to pay him homage."

They walked through a long, narrow vaulted hallway lined with huge paintings of military figures. "This is the War Gallery of 1812. All these paintings are of prominent leaders and generals from the war. That one over there is of Tsar Alexander, our current Tsar's brother and victor of the Patriotic War. There is King Frederick William III of Prussia. Over there is Emperor Francis I of Austria." Adrian knew very little about any of them.

The lady-in-waiting led the group through a set of massive double doors and waited for Adrian and Seamus to stop muttering quiet exclamations to one another. "This is one of the largest rooms in the palace. It is called St. George's Hall. It is the Tsar's principal throne room."

Adrian's sense of awe had stalled three rooms ago because each room was more staggering than the last. *Yup, I've been Stendahled.* The ceiling of this hall was painted with fanciful scenes that Adrian assumed were drawn from Russian mythology.

"That throne is the Tsar's most prized possession," said the young woman. "It symbolizes his power and dominion over all the Russias."

Adrian pointed to two doors at the far end of the hall. "What is beyond those doors?"

"That? That is one of the three connecting passageways to the Hermitage."

"And what is the Hermitage?" asked Seamus, who hadn't paid attention when they first arrived.

The lady-in-waiting didn't need to wait for a translation. She looked at Seamus as though he was a country bumpkin. "It was built by Catherine the Great," she said in German, "as her refuge from the hurly-burly of state affairs. Now it is a museum. It houses more of the Tsar's most important artworks. More art than you have seen here today in the Winter Palace."

Count Sheremetev had once described Tsar Nicholas as the richest, most powerful person in the world. After the tour, which encompassed a small fraction of the Winter Palace, Adrian was inclined to agree.

THURSDAY, OCTOBER 26
(OCTOBER 12 O.S.)

· ADRIAN ·

"It seems like there is something you aren't telling us," Adrian said to Colonel Malkovich as they walked toward the Winter Palace along Nevsky Prospekt, the central boulevard of St. Petersburg. They had just held another fruitless meeting with an imperial bureaucrat who expressed sympathy for their endeavor but was powerless to help them.

Malkovich tipped his top hat to a man and woman walking toward them and waited until they passed. "We told you before we left Philadelphia that Russia is hidebound in tradition."

"No, this goes beyond tradition. Four days ago, we met with the owner of a plot of land suitable for building our factory. He was happy to build a factory to our specifications but unwilling to sign a lease until we had a loan commitment from a local bank. The banker was happy to talk with us but unwilling to consider a loan until we had a signed lease."

"Yes, that was a bit frustrating."

"So we thought instead of renting, we should buy a parcel of land a little bit farther out. You set up a meeting with an owner who was eager to sell. We even agreed on a price, but we couldn't proceed until we got a certificate from the little man at the St. Petersburg Bureau of Land Transfer that stated that we were going to build a factory on the site. The little man tells us we can't get the certificate until we have the financing. So this time, we talked to a different banker. He can't consider a loan until we have a letter from the little man saying that a land purchase is okay. This time the little man can't help us until we have a note from the Minister of the Interior confirming that I, as a foreigner, am allowed to purchase any property in the city. The Ministry of the Interior is happy to help us, but the investigation will take weeks."

"What we have here, my friend, is a clash of cultures," Malkovich said. "You Americans are used to charging forth into the face of whatever problems lie before you. You assume that planning, hard work, and a little luck will bring you success."

Adrian didn't bother to take in the view of the Fontanka River as they crossed the Anichkov Bridge. "Doesn't it?"

"Maybe in America. Not in Russia."

"Then what are we doing here?"

Malkovich held up his walking stick as if it were a pointer. "What we are doing here, my friend, is getting the Tsar's attention. Once the Tsar endorses this project, every certificate magically gets signed, every investigation gets completed overnight, every restriction gets waived."

"The Tsar threw a hundred thousand dollars at us to get us over here. I thought we already had his attention."

"I'm afraid Count Sheremetev and I were not entirely truthful with you about that. We were tasked by the Tsar to purchase locomotives. We took it upon ourselves to change the mission. Rather than purchase locomotives, the count and I decided it would be better for Mother Russia if the locomotives were built here."

Are you telling me the Tsar hasn't endorsed the idea yet?"

"Not yet, but he will."

"Then where did the hundred thousand dollars come from?"

Malkovich marched on, placing his walking stick ahead of him for a few strides. "From the count."

"Sheremetev? All that money we spent in London was his?"

"Yes. And he still considers it a wise investment. When we land the contract to build the Tsar's railroad from here to Moscow, we will all become very rich *and* we will change the nature of Mother Russia."

What the hell am I doing here? thought Adrian. "Count Sheremetev is already rich."

"This will be a different kind of rich. While you and I are noisily rattling around St. Petersburg trying to get our nuts and bolts in order, Sheremetev is whispering in the ears of the appropriate people in the Winter Palace. Patience, my friend. You will see. Once the Tsar makes his wishes known, all doors will open before us."

"So what do we do now?"

"Same as we have been doing. Make an appointment, then doggedly go on to the next one. So far, you have only learned about the difficulties surrounding the procurement of land and capital. It will be to your advantage to gauge the scope of other problems we will undoubtedly encounter: lack of skilled labor, quality—or lack thereof—of machine tools, the weather, and shipment of raw materials to St. Petersburg."

"I guess I just thought we would be making more progress by now."

"We are making progress, my friend, but change doesn't come to Russia overnight. Even when we get the Tsar's blessing, this project will take years. Please be patient."

THURSDAY, NOVEMBER 2
(OCTOBER 21 O.S.)

· RIAN ·

As usual, Rian rose long before Seamus and Adrian to feed the horses. According to the clock on the mantel above the fireplace, it was 5:00. She looked out the frost-covered window. Although she couldn't see the moon, she knew it had risen because it was casting shadows. Across the Neva River, she could see the Peter and Paul Fortress to the right, and to the left was the pontoon bridge crossing the river to Vasilyevsky Island.

The Winter Palace never slept. Nobles kept their own hours. Some stayed up late drinking and playing cards. It wasn't unusual for one group or another within the palace to stage a play or concert that extended late into the night. Many men and women seemed to be involved in trysts in each other's bedrooms. She knew that because, even in the short time she had been here, she had seen both men and women leaving suites in the early morning, wearing what looked to be last night's finery.

Rhythms were quite different for the many civil servants who lived in the Winter Palace. They were more likely to go to bed early and get up early, although not as early as Rian.

And then there were the many drudges and employees who kept the Winter Palace running: cooks, bakers, scullery maids, linen keepers, chambermaids, woodsmen, doctors, wine stewards, table decorators, butlers, footmen, fireplace stokers, clock winders, candle lighters, barbers, hairdressers, pharmacists, bodymen, plumbers, guards, firemen. These people arose as early as Rian and often went to bed later than she did. The workers, the cogs that made the palace run, scurried about the massive building at all hours of the day and night.

And that is why it was so much fun to live in the Winter Palace. Dressed in the London-purchased livery, she found she could come and go as she pleased. Walking with an attitude of purpose, for instance, she strode through many parts of the vast building far from her apartment. If she carried something, a stack of books or a neatly folded garment, people who should have known better assumed she was on an errand for the Duchess of who-knows-what and let her pass. However, if she walked too slowly to admire a painting, she was sure to be shooed along.

By this time, the guards were used to her. She always smiled at them and gave them a friendly "*Privet* [Hello]." Some even smiled back.

Rian enjoyed her early morning walk to the Manege. It was only a half mile away, and the Russian weather hadn't been as cold as she expected.

This morning, she walked out of the apartment, down a grand staircase (which she knew servants weren't supposed to use, but at this time in the morning, no one would be there to chastise her) and out a servants' entrance (saying "*Privet*" as she passed the guard outside the door) to a small courtyard. *Well, I guess it's only small if you compare it to the Grand Courtyard.* This one was a hundred feet square.

She exited the courtyard through an archway, passed another guard ("*Privet.*"), turned left, and walked underneath the Flying Gallery that connected the second story of the Winter Palace to the Hermitage, saying her final "*Privet*" to the guard standing in the shelter of the Gallery.

Rian turned left, with the long facade of the Winter Palace on her left and the river on her right. The occasional rotten, fishy smell wafted up from the river. *Just like the Delaware.* She walked past her apartments two stories above on the left, past the hut that guarded an entryway to the vast building's basement, past the remaining length of the Winter Palace, and past the Palace Gardens. She crossed Nevsky Prospekt, which ended at the river. She walked past the Admiralty Building, the administrative center of the Russian Navy, a long, ornate structure almost as imposing as the Winter Palace. Beyond the Admiralty Building, she stopped to admire The Bronze Horseman in the moonlight.[18]

Rian assessed her situation as she looked at Peter the Great astride his steed. *It's mostly good. I'm learning my way around St. Petersburg. I practice my Russian every day. The Winter Palace is the best house in the world. I'm an excellent coachman. I've got my very own pocket watch. And best of all, everyone except Adrian and Seamus thinks I'm a boy. But I figured we'd be building a factory by now.*

---

18. Catherine the Great, grandmother of Tsar Nicholas I, was originally a Prussian princess who came to Russia as the bride of the German-born Tsar Peter III. She assumed the throne after a palace coup that resulted in the death of her husband. Eager to establish herself as a legitimate Russian empress, she commissioned a statue of Peter the Great, the very popular Tsar who started Russia lurching toward modernization and brought St. Petersburg into existence through force of will. The statue sits atop the Thunder Stone, reputed to be the largest stone ever moved by humans. Peter's horse tramples a serpent, the symbol of those reactionary forces who resisted Peter's reforms.

Two hours later, the moon had set. Sunrise was still an hour away. The temperature had dropped, and a squall had kicked up from the Neva River. Having finished her chores at the Manege, Rian half-ran to the Winter Palace to keep a biting wind from sucking all the warmth out of her. She was gratified to finally spot the lantern next to the hut that guarded the basement entrance to the palace.

Someone had parked a wagon filled with firewood nearby, which wasn't unusual, even for this early in the morning. Although some of the fifteen hundred rooms in the Winter Palace were heated by furnaces in the basement below, many others had fireplaces—so many fireplaces that there were men whose sole duty was to assure that the fires were always well banked.

Rian slowed her pace long enough to spy a serf gathering an armload of wood from the wagon. Even though he wore many layers of clothing, Rian could tell he was tall and beefy. His clothing was well-worn but not raggedy. Without giving it much thought, Rian walked to his side and said, "*Ya mogu pomoch' vam* [I can help you]," one of the many sentences Colonel Malkovich had taught her during their card games on the *Elizabeth*.

The man initially looked at her with suspicion, appraised her coachman's coat, and then relaxed. "*Blagodaryu vas* [Thank you]."

Rian and the serf each muscled together an armload of firewood. The guard left his station and held the door for them. The serf led Rian down a stairway she had never explored and into a room partially filled with firewood. He deposited his armload onto a neatly ordered stack, and Rian did the same. Rian noted how warm the room was.

She unbuttoned her coat. "It's warm," she said in Russian. "My name is Rian. I don't speak much Russian."

The serf, in his early twenties, pointed to himself and said, "Lev." He put his hand on the stone wall and signaled her to do the same. The wall was hot to the touch. He then led her down the hall. An oversized furnace in the room next door produced a prodigious amount of heat. A man in shirtsleeves dozed in a chair near the furnace. *Smart*, said Rian to herself. *The firewood gets to dry out a bit before they use it.*

Grateful to feel warm again, Rian offered to continue helping her new friend. After making two trips with armloads of wood, instead of heading back to the wagon, Lev led her farther down the hallway. They passed a second room filled to the ceiling with firewood. He signaled her to follow around a corner to a third room and a fourth room, all filled with firewood.

Lev pointed to himself and said something Rian interpreted as, "I did this."

232 · ROGER A. SMITH

"*Otlichno* [Very good]," she said. She gestured that they should go back outside so she could continue to help him.

Lev nodded but signaled her to follow him farther down the hall instead. They passed numerous doors: A laundry room with sheets drying on lines. Another laundry room with women scrubbing clothing. An apothecary with bottles in strange shapes and the acrid smell of astringents. Storage rooms. A repair shop filled with hand tools. Farther down the hall, the aroma of baking bread drew them forward.

When Lev led Rian into the bakery, he was greeted by a chorus of hellos from the female staff. He affectionately grabbed one of the women by the arm and pulled her to Rian. "*Moya tetushka* [My aunt]. Her name is Yana."

Rian extended her hand to Yana. "*Menya zovut Rian* [My name is Rian]."

Yana graciously took Rian's hand, but then quickly pulled back as if she had grabbed a hot poker. She looked at Rian intensely and again grasped her right hand, this time not to touch it but to examine it. "*Pozhar*," she said, but it was a word Rian was unfamiliar with. "*Pozhar*."

Rian raised her hands in a questioning gesture. *I don't know what you mean.*

Yana grabbed Rian by the wrist and pulled her to a huge brick oven. She opened a cast-iron door and pointed to a small pile of sticks blazing merrily, providing enough heat to bake the ten loaves of bread within. "*Pozhar*," she said. She pointed to the burning sticks again. "*Pozhar*." She placed her index finger lightly on the center of Rian's chest. "*Ty pozhar*."

Rian nodded and smiled at Yana but was confused. *She's telling me I am fire.* She turned to Lev, who was eating a slice of black bread slathered with a generous slab of butter. Lev shrugged, smiled, handed Rian a slice of her own, and indicated with a wave of his arm that it was time to leave.

Rian finished the bread before they left the palace. It had a delicious, slightly sweet-and-sour taste. *Definitely worth hauling a couple of armloads of firewood.*

Rian and Lev made two more trips to the wood storage room. Then Rian said goodbye to Lev and continued to the apartment.

* * * * *

Count Sheremetev and Colonel Malkovich joined the Americans in their palace apartment every Thursday to play poker. "Hopefully I'll be able to win some of my money back from Rian," the count would always joke. "Besides, your coachman is learning Russian much faster than you gentlemen. I wish we conducted our card games entirely in Russian. It would help you to learn."

Adrian dealt a new hand. "We are surrounded by Russian all day, every day. This is our time to relax."

Too bad, Rian thought. *They will miss out on a lot if they don't try to learn.*

Sheremetev was a good poker player, but after half a dozen evenings, Rian noticed that he nervously and repeatedly fanned and closed his cards if he had a strong hand. Conversely, if he held unpromising cards, he became quiet and kept his cards closed. That bit of knowledge alone meant that Rian didn't lose big hands to Sheremetev very often. She began to scrutinize others at the table to see if their behaviors changed depending on the nature of their hands.

As one new hand was being dealt, Rian told the poker players about her interaction with Yana. "What do you think she meant when she called me 'fire?'"

Sheremetev fanned and closed, fanned and closed his hand. "Russia is an incredibly superstitious country. And not just amongst the peasantry, but from top to bottom, urban and rural. Look at me. I knock on wood three times when I hear someone express certainty about the future."

"The Irish have been doing that for centuries," said Seamus.

"Well," Sheremetev said to Rian, "it sounds like this woman considers herself quite the seer. I wouldn't completely discount it. Fortune tellers are very influential in our society. They sense things that most of us do not. On the other hand, she could be a charlatan. Did she ask you for money to tell your fortune? If so, I suggest you stay away."

"No, she just pointed to me and said 'fire.'"

"And her reaction was immediate? As soon as she touched your hand?"

"Yes, like she'd touched something burning hot."

Sheremetev threw his two kopeks into the pot. "My guess is that she really is a soothsayer. But keep your guard up. It could be that your new friend Lev pegged you as someone who might have a few kopeks in his pocket, and he brought you to his aunt to hatch a scheme that they've pulled off many times before. If you run into Lev again, I don't see anything to fear. Just keep your money in your pocket."

Adrian shrugged. "I think this Yana woman got it right. Rian is one of the fieriest people I know."

MONDAY, NOVEMBER 13
(NOVEMBER 1 O.S.)

· RIAN ·

It was a Monday. In the short time she had been living in Russia, Rian had learned that Russians considered Mondays unlucky. Yet today, Rian felt about as lucky as she could be. And happy, she acknowledged, given that she was a million miles from home.

As usual, Rian had risen early to feed and exercise the horses. As usual, it was long before sunrise on a cold morning when she arrived at the Manege. She said "*Privet*" to the guard who stood in the portico, entered the building, and walked through the cavernous riding hall to the stables. Although the Manege was unheated, it was tightly enclosed and much warmer than the pre-sunrise riverfront.

Her ritual was now becoming a habit. She fed a scoop of oats to Washington and Franklin, the two horses named after squares in Philadelphia. Then she saddled Wash and led him down the corridor lined with scores of stalls to the gigantic riding hall. A few other grooms were already working their charges.

Sometimes she encountered members of the Imperial Horse Guards exercising their horses before they assumed their daily duties. During these early morning hours, the guardsmen often relaxed the pecking order that seemed so rigid during the day. Love of horses was a bond that drew everyone in the building together. Grooms and cavalrymen traded stories, lore, jokes, and supplies in equal measure.

Rian worked Washington for half an hour, returned to the stall, and was brushing him down when an officer appeared at the stall door and asked for something in Russian that Rian didn't understand. Although she suspected he was not yet fifty, his close-cropped hair was already infused with flecks of gray. He had a full mustache that extended far beyond his cheeks. He was lean and sinewy, with the weathered look of a man who had spent years in the saddle.

Rian turned to the officer and said, "*Ya ne ochen' khorosho govoryu po russki* [I don't speak Russian very well]," another one of the phrases that Colonel Malkovich had taught her on the *Elizabeth*. As an afterthought, she added, "*Angliyskiy* [English]?"

The officer shook his head and was about to turn and leave.

"*Nemetskiy* [German]?" Rian threw out tentatively.

The officer smiled and said in Prussian-accented German, "*Hast du ein liniment* [Do you have any liniment]?"

Having found a common language, they spoke for half an hour.

The officer told her that he had been a cavalryman since he was in his teens. He had fought against Napoleon and harassed his retreating army during the French invasion of Russia in 1812. Rian acknowledged that her grandfather had been an officer in the army of Wurttemberg, fighting on the side of the French, and had retreated from Moscow that same winter.

The officer stiffened momentarily. Sensing that the officer might still harbor hostility toward the invaders, even though it was more than two decades ago, Rian added, "I never knew my grandfather. He died before I was born. I was born in America."

"Born in America. You speak two languages. Have at least a rudimentary knowledge of the Patriotic War. You are not a typical groom. What are you doing in St. Petersburg?"

"I'm with my uncle and cousin. I'm also their coachman. They are trying to do business with Tsar Nicholas."

"Trying?"

Rian searched her cabinet for horse liniment. "I don't think they've had any luck yet."

The officer hooked his thumb over his shoulder. "That bay across the hall. All that stuff arrived a couple of weeks ago. Is that yours?"

Rian knew the officer didn't really think the locomotive and the fire engine were hers. "My uncle and cousin brought them to show the Tsar as an example of our American craftsmanship."

The officer walked across the hall and partially lifted a tarp that covered the hopper. "What are they?"

"That one is a working model of a locomotive. The real one would be much bigger."

The officer lifted the other tarp. "And this one?"

"That's a steam-powered fire pump. The hoses for it are stored over there."

"Why a fire pump?"

"Count Sheremetev thought it might catch the Tsar's attention. My cousin runs a fire company in Philadelphia. He designed it."

"Sheremetev. He is responsible for this expedition?"

"I guess so. He convinced my uncle to move to Russia to build a railroad."

"And your cousin, the firefighter, why is he here in St. Petersburg?"

"He helped my father start his factory in Philadelphia. Since he's already done it once, my uncle asked him to come here to help out."

"Very impressive. And what are your uncle and cousin trying to accomplish here in St. Petersburg?"

"They want to build locomotives and rolling stock for the Tsar, but they haven't been able to get an appointment yet."

"Ah, I have heard whispers about your uncle."

"Good whispers or bad whispers?"

"Let's just say that the Tsar is of two minds. On the one hand, he considers himself to be the father of his people. Like all fathers, he wants his children to be happy. On the other hand, he is an advocate of all things Russian, and in Russia, tradition is a very powerful force."

"So you know the Tsar pretty well?"

The officer smiled. "No, I don't. I have been in the Tsar's presence much of my adult life, but I am not in his inner circle. My name is Captain Mikhail Sergeyovich Stepanov."

Rian handed a can of liniment to the captain. "My name is Rian Krieger. I am pleased to meet you."

"Thank you for this."

"I have to exercise Franklin. Just put it back in the cabinet when you're done with it."

"Good luck with the Tsar."

"Do you mean that? Do you favor progress over tradition?"

Stepanov shook his head. "You are referring to a matter of state. In such instances, I cannot afford to have an opinion. My job is to do what the Tsar orders me to do."

Rian saddled Frank, worked him for half an hour, brushed him down, checked the horses' water, stroked them both on the neck, and walked back to the Winter Palace. It was still dark.

* * * * *

Rian and Henry Sommes, the manservant, were polishing boots in the anteroom when Count Sheremetev and Colonel Malkovich arrived at the apartment. Usually relaxed despite the frustrations of continued delays, this morning Sheremetev was agitated. "Rian, please summon your uncle and cousin."

When Henry rose to leave the visitors, Sheremetev said. "Come with us, Sommes. I want you to hear this as well."

With everyone seated in the parlor, Sheremetev took a deep breath. "I fear I have been remiss. I have not grounded you all to what you must know to survive here."

Rian stirred uneasily, fearing that her jaunts around the Winter Palace may now be causing problems.

"This is not America," stated Sheremetev, "where you can say anything about President Van Buren and not suffer consequences." He turned to the manservant. "This is not England, where criticism of your new Queen Victoria seems to be a national sport."

"What's happened?" asked Seamus.

"You are being evicted from the Winter Palace. Something one of you said made its way to Prince Volkonsky. He has ordered that you be moved to the Anichkov Palace."

"Where is the Anichkov Palace?"

"Two versts—more than a mile. But farther away from the Tsar than I would like. The chances of us encountering him are now much more remote."

"That was quick," said Adrian." You said we had two months. We lasted one."

"Look, when Colonel Malkovich and I came to the United States, our original intention was to purchase locomotives to bring back to Russia to power the Tsar's railroad. After we had been in America for a few weeks, we saw how rapidly your country was changing, and railroads were at the center of this change. We decided to bring not merely your locomotives but your entire operation to Russia. We want similar changes to come to this country. We and our closest associates are the ones who are advocating for this change, not the Tsar. We have stuck our necks out to bring you here."

"The Tsar doesn't want to transform Russia?"

Sheremetev snorted. "There are three pillars of Russian ideology under Nicholas I." He started counting, using his thumb. "Orthodoxy. That means the dogma of the Russian Orthodox Church." He extended his index finger. "Autocracy. That means the supremacy of the Tsar in all matters. Think of him as the father of all of Russia, and he can be very stern." He extended his middle finger. "Nationality. That means that all things Russian are good, and conversely, ideas imported from the West are suspect. Freedom to think for yourself. Liberty. Tolerance. Individualism. Rationalism. All the *-isms* of the Enlightenment. These are not ideas to be bandied about in the parlors of the Winter Palace over cards and vodka. These are threats to the fabric of Russia."

Adrian straightened in his chair. "I might have said something. I was at a gathering in Count Solovyov's apartment three nights ago. I wasn't playing cards, like you implied, or drinking, for that matter. But I did have a conversation with a man about how my life changed after I moved to America."

Sheremetev shook his head. "That could have been all it took. Gentlemen, it is dangerous to be a tsar. Nicholas's father and grandfather were both assassinated here in St. Petersburg. Furthermore, on the day Nicholas took the throne, a group called the Decembrists—officers and nobles—revolted and tried to replace him. They wanted more reform than Nicholas was prepared to offer. He crushed the Decembrists brutally. Now he trusts only his inner circle. He has secret police everywhere, both in and out of the palace."

Rian didn't know anything about Russian history. She didn't know why Sheremetev wanted her to hear all this.

Sheremetev continued. "Someone here criticized the Tsar. Who here called the Tsar an idiot?"

Seamus raised his hand. "That might have been me. I was in the bedroom of an attendant to Countess Orlov. The one who gave us the tour on the first day we were here. She doesn't even speak very good English. I was just talking."

"What did you say exactly?"

"I was saying that it was to Russia's advantage and ours that we build a railroad from St. Petersburg to Moscow. 'Why doesn't the Tsar support us? He must be an idiot.' Count Sheremetev, I was just talking big to impress the girl."

"Well, Seamus, I'm afraid you impressed her more than you bargained for. I want you all to assume that every bit of information you naively entrusted to others has reached the Tsar. The secret police have thousands of informants throughout the capital. Does anyone else have anything to tell me? I can only try to undo all this damage if I know what I'm dealing with."

It finally dawned on Rian that perhaps she had played a role in their problems. She raised her hand. "This morning I was talking with a member of the Imperial Horse Guard. He was very nice. He was interested in the locomotive and the fire pump."

"And what is this nice guardsman's name?"

"Mikhail Stepanov."

Sheremetev again shook his head. "Mikhail Sergeyovich Stepanov is Captain of the Tsar's Imperial Horse Guards. He has been a member of Nicholas's staff since the Napoleonic Wars. Long before Nicholas became the tsar."

"He seems like such a nice man."

"Captain Stepanov may be a nice man, as you call him. But I dare say his visit was not happenstance. He is a pipeline to the Tsar. He may be sympathetic to the reforms the Decembrists rebelled to implement. Or, he may sympathize with the Tsar's reactionary impulses. Until proven otherwise, you cannot trust him."

Maybe the Russians are right. Mondays are unlucky, Rian said to herself.

TUESDAY, NOVEMBER 14
(NOVEMBER 2 O.S.)

· ADRIAN ·

During the move to their new quarters in the Anichkov Palace, Count Sheremetev encouraged Adrian and Seamus to act like aristocrats. That meant leaving all the work to Rian and Henry, the manservant. However, after those two struggled as they lugged the fourth of twelve trunks into the apartment, Adrian decided it would be more efficient to dispense with protocol. "If we leave this up to you two, it'll be May before we're settled in," he told them lightheartedly as he helped Rian with a trunk.

Adrian and Seamus left the apartment with Rian and Henry, descended two flights of stairs, and returned to the baggage wagon in the courtyard.

"Excuse me, might you be Adrian Krieger?"

Adrian turned, gratified to hear someone speaking English. Looking out from the window of a landau was a man in his forties with a prominent equine nose and hair that flowed over his ears.

"Yes, I am. May I help you?"

The man descended from the carriage. He was dressed in a heavy overcoat but wore no hat. He extended his hand to Adrian. "It is my job to help *you*. My name is George Mifflin Dallas. I am the American Ambassador to Russia."

Adrian shook the ambassador's hand. "Ah, Mr. Dallas, we finally meet. When I stopped by your office last week, your secretary said you were stacked up. Thank you for coming by."

"Actually, you have been on my task list for a month, long before you stopped in. Your brother and I have been lunch companions at the United States Hotel in Philadelphia a few times. He wrote to me that you and your nephew were moving to St. Petersburg with a colleague. Helping the Tsar build his railroad, I understand."

Adrian immediately became guarded. Otto's letter said *nephew*, not *niece*, which meant he was referring to Jabez Howes, not Rian Krieger. Otto had written the letter before Rian and Jabez switched places. "Yes, that is true." Adrian tried to steer the subject away from nephews. "I'm so sorry your visit wasn't yesterday. We could have met in the Winter Palace."

"So I understand. The majordomo informed me you had moved here." Dallas sized up the Anichkov Palace. "Not exactly a hardship, but much farther from the Tsar than I'm sure you wanted to be. Have you had any luck with your business pursuits?"

"None yet, but we're still learning the lay of the land here."

A few feet away, Henry and Rian exited the building to pull the next trunk from the wagon. Rian climbed aboard the wagon and, with a grunt, started shoving a large trunk toward the back. Dallas glanced at Rian. "That trunk looks rather formidable for your coachman. My driver will be happy to help you out."

"Uh, we're fine," Adrian responded. "We don't have any other obligations today, so it doesn't matter how long it takes. I've been helping them on and off all morning."

"No, I insist," said Dallas, who seemed to be in a jocular mood. "Consider it part of the service the United States Department of State can offer our entrepreneurs abroad."

Dallas showed no inclination to do any physical work but was happy to yammer on as the others labored. "Honestly, I've been here only a few months myself. I'm afraid there aren't many Americans in St. Petersburg. Our relations with Russia are more cordial than with France or Great Britain, but this post is a bit of a backwater. My only task is ensuring the Tsar continues supporting America's Monroe Doctrine. I guess that's what I get for defending the Second National Bank. Jackson isn't in office anymore, but he doesn't forget those who disagreed with him and still pulls Mr. Van Buren's strings. I hoped to be sent to the Court of St. James, but wiser minds determined otherwise."

Adrian, preoccupied with hauling a trunk up two flights of stairs with Dallas's coachman, would have preferred that Dallas either shut up, help, or leave. But he kept silent.

They arrived in the new apartment, now clogged with a growing number of trunks.

Dallas surveyed the drawing room. "Yes, I think you will do very nicely here." He cocked his ear when the manservant said, "Rian, help me get this into Mr. Krieger's bedroom before we go down to get the small steamer."

"And your nephew Jabez, where is he? It must be exciting for him to be in such an exotic land."

"Uh, Jabez didn't come with us."

"And who is that? The young man helping your manservant?"

Adrian signaled with a jerk of his head that he wanted to speak with Dallas privately. The two walked to a window that overlooked Nevsky Prospekt. "Uh, that young man is, uh, my niece Rian."

"Otto's daughter?"

Adrian nodded. "My nephew Jabez Howes was supposed to make this trip with us. He didn't want to come, and she did. They look alike. They switched places. We didn't learn about it until we were on the high seas. We couldn't send her back from London, so we brought her here, but we were counseled to have her pose as a boy. We figured it would be easier this way."

Dallas stiffened. "I am not sure that I approve. This does not reflect well on the United States government."

"This has nothing to do with the U.S. government. We are private individuals conducting business in Russia."

"Nonetheless, if this subterfuge is ever revealed, it will jeopardize your endeavor. The penalties for flaunting accepted norms in this society are harsh. Now I think it is fortunate that you were evicted from the Winter Palace. The farther away your niece stays from the prying eyes of those who protect the Tsar, the better."

"I have no intention of revealing Rian's secret to anyone. Even our sponsors don't know, nor our manservant. We have no desire to become the objects of curiosity in St. Petersburg."

"Objects of curiosity? Apparently I haven't made myself clear." Dallas looked out the window for a few seconds. "Ivan VI. Have you ever heard of him?"

"Uh, no."

"No reason why you should have. He was Tsar of All the Russias for a year almost a hundred years ago. He was an infant. Despite his tender age, his aunt had him thrown in prison so she could become the Tsar. He was held in solitary confinement for 22 years, all through his aunt's reign and the Tsar who followed her. He was finally strangled in his cell during the reign of Catherine the Great."

Adrian was quite disgusted at the thought of a child growing up in a prison cell. "Why are you telling me this?"

"Because in this country, if a royal infant Tsar can be locked up for no reason but a powerful person's whim, so can you. So can your niece. This little masquerade of yours puts you in danger. If your niece's true nature is revealed, you won't become objects of curiosity. You will be thrown into prison, and so will she."

Adrian took a deep breath. "Then we will be doubly careful. I assume that given your sentiments, I can rely on your discretion?"

Dallas nodded. "Except that I am obligated to make a report to Secretary of State Forsyth. I do not want him to be caught unprepared if this blows up in your face and becomes an international incident. Good day."

Adrian wistfully watched Ambassador Dallas gather his driver and exit the apartment. *I guess it's time for a family meeting. All I want to do is build a railroad. Now I have to worry about becoming an international incident.*

FRIDAY, NOVEMBER 17
(NOVEMBER 5 O.S.)

· ADRIAN ·

Now that they had moved lock, stock, and opera capes out of the Winter Palace, Adrian felt almost invisible in the comings and goings of St. Petersburg. Count Sheremetev had arranged for invitations to various social functions and had accompanied Adrian and Seamus to act as interpreter. Sheremetev would introduce them both as railroad men from America. The sentiments of most people could be summed up by the reaction of one bejeweled matron at a ball— a protracted look up and down through her lorgnette, a sniff, and the response "*Kak stranno,*" which Malkovich interpreted as "How quaint."

Adrian had the growing sense that the mission was failing. There had been swirls of activity, but almost nothing had happened. Meetings with no results. Encounters that bore no fruit. Leads that led to dead ends.

Then Sheremetev's note arrived. "*Prince Volkonsky, the Minister of the Imperial Court, has finally relented! The Tsar will be passing through the Palace Garden at 2:00 tomorrow afternoon. Volkonsky wants us to set up the hopper there for the Tsar to see. He will make sure the Tsar stops to observe the hopper in action. Volkonsky has even arranged for five serfs to join you at 6:00 a.m.*"

So, here they were—two American entrepreneurs and their purported coachman—in the Winter Palace Garden three hours before sunrise, attempting to set up a demonstration of Heinrich Aldrich's one-quarter-size hopper prototype in one morning.

The work crew, five willing but uneducated peasants who didn't speak English, arrived before there was even a hint of light.

Temperature? Probably close to twenty degrees. At least there's no wind coming off the river, thought Adrian. "Seamus, we'll be lucky to have the prototype up and running by 2:00 this afternoon. We're already pinched for time. How are we going to communicate with these gumps?"

Seamus was setting the peasants to work with hand gestures when Count Sheremetev appeared out of the darkness. "Good morning, Adrian. Good news. Prince Volkonsky has asked to meet with you."

"Now that's a sign of progress. When?"

"Right now."

"Now? At six o'clock in the morning?"

"The Tsar is an early riser; therefore, so is Volkonsky."

Adrian turned to Seamus. "Do you think you can handle this by yourself?"

Before Seamus could answer, Sheremetev interrupted. "No, Volkonsky wants to meet with both of you."

"Then we'll have to cancel our demonstration."

Sheremetev kicked at a clump of snow. "This is unfortunate. I don't know when the Tsar will be out here again. This may be our only opportunity for weeks."

Rian spoke up. "I can start the men shoveling until you get back from your meeting. I know one of them. His name is Lev. He's the one I told you about. His aunt is the soothsayer.'"

"Rian, you're thirteen years old," Adrian countered, irritated by the bad timing of the appointment with Volkonsky. "You don't speak Russian."

"No offense, Uncle Adrian, but you don't speak Russian. I've been learning. I think I can do it." Rian smiled. "Count Sheremetev, sir? If you tell these men I'm in charge, will they follow my orders?"

"They are serfs. They will do what I tell them to do, although they may be somewhat reluctant in your case. I'm afraid they won't be able to understand you."

"If I get stuck, I'll just play charades with them."

Sheremetev smiled. "I doubt these gentlemen have ever played charades."

Adrian brightened. "Well, I guess this morning they're going to learn. Please tell them they're going to be shoveling snow."

* * * * *

Adrian, Seamus, and Sheremetev walked through the archway to the Winter Palace's massive courtyard. Seamus eyed the main entrance to the palace, still three hundred feet away. "This Volkonsky guy. You said he's a prince."

"Yes. He is the Minister of the Imperial Court and the Tsar's gatekeeper. Every piece of information that the Tsar sees passes through the prince's hands."

"If he's a prince, why does he have to work?"

"A prince isn't a prince like in England. He is a noble, but not a member of the royal family. Not all nobles in Russia are wealthy, although Volkonsky does quite well. As a prince, he outranks me, a count, although I am far wealthier than he is."

"Okay, let me ask my question again. If Volkonsky is rich, how come he chooses to work?"

"Because, dear Seamus, some men believe that wielding power is more important than being rich. Prince Volkonsky is one of them. In that sense, I could make the case that Prince Pyotr Volkonsky is the second most powerful man in the world."

"Wait'll I tell me ma about this. She's not going to believe it," Seamus commented dryly.

* * * * *

· RIAN ·

One step at a time, Rian said to herself. She whistled to grab the peasants' attention and was greeted by five blank faces in the lantern light. "*Wam nuzhno* [We need] . . ." She didn't know the word for *shovel* but put the lantern down and acted like she was shoveling snow with an invisible one.

Lev understood what she was doing. "*Lopaty.*"

Rian smiled in the darkness, grateful that Lev had acknowledged her effort. "*Da, pyat' lopaty dlya snega* [Yes, five snow shovels]."

Lev said something to the other men that Rian didn't understand, and they all started to saunter off. She headed them off. Using a combination of rudimentary Russian and her best charades gestures, she told them that one man could get the snow shovels. *You four follow me.* She directed the men to a pile of railroad ties.

Well, they aren't real railroad ties; they're logs that Uncle had some woodsman hand-hew into something that looks like railroad ties when we first got here.

Rian started clearing the snow off the stack of ties by hand and signaled the men to do the same. The men willingly set to work, but the ties were frozen together. It had rained earlier that week, and ice now held them together in a steely grip.

"*Nam nuzhen* [We need] . . . a digging iron," Rian said as she slammed an imaginary digging iron into an imaginary hole. She had no idea what the word for digging iron was in Russian but figured it didn't matter. *Digging holes has to be the same in Russia as it is in Philadelphia.* Lev seemed to get the gist of what she was looking for. He talked to one of the other men, who sauntered off.

Thus, Rian set the pattern for the morning. She spoke fractured Russian to the serfs until she needed a word she didn't know. Then she reverted to pantomime. Lev became her most adept interpreter. When he helped her, she rewarded him with a big smile and an enthusiastic "*blagodaryu vas* [thank you]."

When the man finally returned to the group, he had a digging iron.

This time, rather than pantomime, Rian took the digging iron from the peasant and started chopping away at the ice. It was hard work. Lev relieved her when she began to slow down. Then another man relieved Lev. Rian counted 24 ties. *It will take the men forever to get all these ties to the Winter Palace Garden,* she said to herself.

Half an hour later, the four peasants were lugging the first two ties to the Winter Palace Garden. When they arrived, the man who had been sent for the shovels was waiting for them. He had brought five shovels but had not yet cleared anything.

The temperature was still well below freezing. The sun had risen ten minutes ago, so the lantern was no longer necessary. Early morning rays lit the tall Rostral Columns that flanked the St. Petersburg Stock Exchange across the Neva, and as soon as it peeked around the southwest corner of the Winter Palace, it would start to warm them. Rian looked at her pocket watch. It was almost nine o'clock.

Still no Adrian or Seamus. The Tsar is supposed to pass by around 2:00. Five hours to go, she said to herself. *At this rate, we won't even have all the ties at the site by then.*

Rian scuffed markers in the snow with her boot to delineate boundaries. "You two, start shoveling. You two go back for another railroad tie. Lev, you come with me."

Rian and Lev walked the half mile to the Manege to get Wash and Frank. The guard recognized her but barred Lev from entering the riding hall. Rian didn't speak Russian well enough to plead her case. She was about to leave Lev at the entrance to harness the horses by herself.

"*Kapral, chto zdes' proiskhodit?*" which Rian took to mean, "Corporal, what is going on here?"

Rian turned to see Captain Stepanov. "Oh, Captain, I want to bring this man in to help me . . ."

"*Tishina* [Silence]!"

Captain Stepanov and the corporal spoke back and forth for a minute before the captain turned to her. "*Sag mir, was du tust, mein sohn* [Tell me what you are doing, son]."

"*Vielen dank, Kapitän* [Thank you, Captain]. I am trying to set up a track in the Winter Garden to demonstrate the locomotive to the Tsar. I need the horses to haul the ties and rails." She hooked her thumb at Lev, who was now standing behind her. "This man is going to help me."

"Setting up a demonstration for the Tsar. This is not a task for a youngster. Where are your uncle and your cousin?"

"They were supposed to be here, but they were both called away for an appointment."

"An appointment? With whom?"

"A man named Volkonsky. I think he's important."

"Prince Volkonsky." The captain paused momentarily, then spoke extensively to the corporal in Russian. He turned to Rian. "I have told the corporal to let your man in and out as many times as necessary this morning. Don't make me regret it."

"There are four more serfs back in the Winter Garden. I may need to bring them here to get the locomotive."

Stepanov again addressed the guard. The guard nodded. He held the door for Stepanov. Rian and Lev followed.

Stepanov walked briskly through the great riding hall. "I will also speak to the guard at the stable door."

"Thank you, sir," said Rian as she hurried to keep pace with the captain. "Last week you told me that you don't have an opinion about tradition versus progress . . ."

"I said I can't afford to have an opinion about them."

"But you just helped me out."

Stepanov abruptly stopped walking. "How old are you, son?"

"Thirteen."

"American children are different from Russian children. You are very impertinent. Get on with your day."

* * * * *

· ADRIAN ·

Adrian, Seamus, and Sheremetev had been sitting in the anteroom of Volkonsky's office for four hours.

"I smell a rat," said Count Sheremetev.

Adrian looked at his pocket watch for what felt like the hundredth time. The morning had slipped away. "What do you think is going on?"

"I think Volkonsky wanted today's little demonstration to be a failure."

Fifteen minutes later, an aide emerged from the double doors of Volkonsky's office and ushered them in.

The count said something to Volkonsky in Russian that Adrian assumed was, "Thank you for seeing us, Your Excellency."

More exchanges occurred between Volkonsky and the count. None of the three was offered a seat. The prince shook his head numerous times, which required no translation for Adrian. Four minutes later, Sheremetev turned to Adrian. "It is time to go."

They exited Volkonsky's office. Sheremetev stormed toward the exit with Adrian and Seamus hurrying to keep up.

"Are we going to meet with the Tsar?" asked Adrian.

"No, he says the Tsar's schedule is filled for the next three weeks."

"Do you believe him?"

"Of course not. When the Tsar passes by today, he will have nothing to see but a disorganized demonstration. A failure. His opinion of your American know-how will harden against us."

Anticipating a blast of cold air as soon as they left the palace, Adrian pulled his hat tight on his head. "That son of a bitch."

"Gentlemen," said Sheremetev. "We have been thwarted for today."

Seamus tugged at Adrian's arm. "We should go rescue Rian. Knowing her, the poor peasants have shoveled half the Palace Garden by now."

* * * * *

· RIAN ·

By the time Rian and Lev returned to the Winter Palace Garden, the peasants had carried three more ties to the demonstration site, and the area was about halfway cleared of snow. "You four, keep shoveling. Lev, come with me."

With the horses dragging six ties at a time, the task proceeded much more quickly. After the first trip, she sent Lev and the horses to get the next six ties. She remained with the men and grabbed a shovel.

There was a foot of snow on the ground. Layers of light snow were sandwiched between coats of ice. The shoveling was difficult, and the larger the shoveled area became, the farther she had to carry each shovelful.

Still no Adrian and Seamus. Uncle, I need you. Lev delivered the rest of the ties in three round trips. The men shoveled snow down to the grass and created a perimeter of piled snow about 16 feet by 72 feet. *I've already done more than I said I was going to do. Think! Think! The railroad ties are all here. Now get the rails.*

Rian led the peasants and horses to a pier on the Neva River, where the eight 16-foot rails had been left when the travelers arrived in St. Petersburg. This time, they had the digging iron to free the rails from the ice.

Each rail weighed four hundred pounds. Lev led the horses as they dragged four rails to the demonstration site. With one more roundtrip, they had delivered all the rails.

Adrian and Seamus, where are you? I really need you. In Pennsylvania, I watched plenty of crews laying track. I should have paid closer attention. Think! Think! We need more tools. Dang it. I could have got them when we harnessed the horses.

"All of you, come with me. Bring the horses." The peasants dutifully followed her to the Manege, past the guard, through the riding hall, and down the stable hallway to the area where the coach, hopper prototype, and carriage were stored.

Think. Think. Every step. Determined to avoid any more extra trips, Rian planned all the remaining tasks as if Adrian and Seamus weren't returning anytime soon. It took a few minutes for her to find everything she needed.

"Take this tarpaulin off the locomotive and fold it up." The men went about the task, exposing the hopper, which sat upon a short pair of rails that were, in turn, anchored to a pallet. Lev whistled, a long, low, admiring whistle that meant the same thing in Russia as it did in America.

The hopper had been wrapped in the tarpaulin since it was packed for shipment in the Krieger Locomotive factory. *This locomotive may be a quarter of the size of the real deal, but it still weighs a ton. There's no way we could lift it onto the rails even if Adrian and Seamus and the count ever get here.*

Rian was gratified to note that the hopper sat on a pair of rails, shorter versions of the ones the horses had just dragged to the Winter Palace Garden. *And the pallet? Just the thickness of a standard railroad tie. God bless Adrian. He knew we would run into this problem three months ago."*

One of the men lifted the tarp that covered the steam-powered fire pump, which was stored between the hopper and Krieger Coach's carriage. *What is this?* he motioned to Rian.

"It is a fire pump driven by a steam engine. I helped to build it," she said in fractured Russian. By their responses, Rian thought the men were impressed.

With Rian's direction, the group picked up track tongs, sledgehammers, and two sacks of railroad spikes and laid them on the hopper. They hooked Wash and Frank up to the pallet. Horses and men struggled mightily to drag the hopper and tools to the Winter Palace Garden.

Rian directed two men to pick up a railroad tie and place it next to the pallet. *Just as I suspected, they're the same height. If we construct this thing right, we can roll the prototype right onto the rails.*

The men spaced out the rest of the railroad ties so they extended 64 feet.

Rian grabbed a railroad tong and demonstrated how it clamped onto a rail. She handed a tong to each of the men. She positioned the men equidistantly down the 16-foot length of the rail. More gestures: *Pick up the rail and place it right there, so that it meets the rail on the pallet.*

With Rian orchestrating, the men clamped their tongs onto the rail and lifted in unison. They walked the rail into place and set it so it butted right against the rail on the pallet.

Their activity was starting to attract attention. Strollers briefly hesitated as they walked by, but no one stayed for long. *Too cold,* Rian imagined. *But maybe it isn't wise to be too curious in Russia.*

Rian didn't trust that she could make the rails run parallel just by eye, and she hadn't thought to bring a measuring stick from the stable. (*Idiot!*) Worse, she didn't remember one being packed from America. *And we sure didn't bring that two-wheeled wheelbarrow that assured the rails were the proper distance apart.*

Come on, Eena, think. Think! You can figure this out. She grabbed a snow shovel. She positioned the handle of the shovel between the wheels of the hopper, took out her pocket knife, and made a notch in the fork handle. Using the snow shovel handle as her template, she directed the men to jimmy the rails into perfect position using the breaker bar. Then they pounded spikes into the ties to secure the rails the proper distance apart. *Not bad for never having done the job before,* she congratulated herself.

The sun finally hit the demonstration site. *No Adrian. No Seamus. No Sheremetev. No food. We've got to keep working.*

Rian and the men untied the ropes that held the hopper into place. Rian jumped aboard the machine and released the brake. The men pushed the hopper from the pallet . . .

Slowly . . .

. . . slowly . . .

. . . onto the first pair of rails, which were the perfect distance apart.

Triumphant, Rian sent Lev and the other four peasants to the palace to get water and firewood.

For the first time that day, she paused to admire their work. She heard a wild Irish whoop from a distance behind her. *Finally!*

Adrian and Seamus ran the last hundred yards through a foot of unshoveled snow. Count Sheremetev walked behind at a more dignified pace.

Adrian beamed. "Honestly, with all of us here at six this morning, I thought we would be lucky if we finished our task by the time the Tsar rode by. You have accomplished this without our help and without speaking much Russian."

Sheremetev arrived and took in the scene. "Rian, I believe your talents are being wasted as a coachman."

The five men arrived with buckets of water and armloads of firewood. Rian turned to Sheremetev. "We're using the Tsar's firewood. I hope he won't mind. I didn't know what else to do."

"A minor transgression," said Sheremetev. "I will settle up with the majordomo."

Rian led the horses into a patch of sun and leaned into Wash for warmth. "The men worked real hard today. Any chance we can get them something to eat?"

"We all deserve some food. We'll figure something out after the Tsar passes by."

With twenty minutes to spare, Adrian had a fire roaring in the machine's firebox. When the water started boiling, they ran the hopper up and down the 64 feet of track numerous times. It worked perfectly.

The sound of horses on the bridle path attracted the work party's attention. Rian spotted Captain Stepanov in the lead of a column of the Tsar's Imperial Horse Guards. Stepanov raised his arm to signal the column to a halt next to the hopper. "Who is in charge here?" he asked in German. He showed no sign of recognizing Rian.

Adrian and Sheremetev looked at one another. The count nodded to Adrian. Rian's uncle stepped forward. "*Ich bin* [I am]. My name is Adrian Krieger. This is my associate Seamus Gallagher. That is Count Vladimir Antonovich Sheremetev."

Stepanov bowed slightly to the count from his horse. "Good to see you again, Lord Sheremetev. It has been a while." He nodded to Seamus. "*Der Feuerwehrmann, nehme ich an* [The firefighter, I presume]." He returned his attention to Adrian. "What is the purpose of this?"

"We hope to demonstrate to the Tsar the efficiency of our locomotive."

"Rather small, isn't it?"

"It is a prototype. One-quarter the size of a locomotive we would like to build here in Russia using Russian labor."

"I would like to see it operate."

"Gladly," said Adrian. He bowed and walked to the locomotive. Then he hesitated and turned to the captain. "This machine is so easy to operate, even a coachman can handle it." Adrian looked at Rian and indicated with a jerk of his head for her to mount the engine.

Rian leaped on the back of the machine, engaged the clutch, and the locomotive eased forward with no evident strain on the engine. It gathered speed for a short distance before Rian hit the brake and brought it to a halt inches from the end of the track.

"Very impressive," said Stepanov. "The Tsar will not see this demonstration today."

"Why not?" asked Adrian.

"He returned to the palace via another route. I expect you went to a great deal of trouble to assemble this display today."

"Yes, sir, we did."

"Make sure it is disassembled by this time tomorrow." With that, Stepanov urged his horse forward and left, followed by cavalrymen.

On the off chance that Stepanov was wrong about the Tsar, Adrian, Seamus, and Rian waited for another hour.

The Tsar never passed by.

MONDAY, NOVEMBER 20

Anti-Slavery Newspaperman
Killed by Mob in Alton, Illinois

Exclusive Report to the *Philadelphia Independent*
By Harold Foote

Washington, District of Columbia

On Tuesday, November 7, 1837, former Philadelphia resident Elijah Parish Lovejoy was shot to death in Alton, Illinois, as he defended his printing press from a pro-slavery mob.

Lovejoy, a Presbyterian minister, was the editor of the abolitionist newspaper *St. Louis Observer* in 1836 when vandals destroyed his first printing press. He moved across the Mississippi River to the nearby town of Alton, Illinois, to continue his anti-slavery publishing in a free state. Sadly, anti-abolitionist sentiment knows no state boundaries.

On three more occasions, the *Observer*'s printing presses were destroyed by vandals. Each time, with the help of abolitionist supporters, a new press was purchased. The final printing press was set up in a warehouse outside of Alton. On November 7, an altercation occurred between a pro-slavery mob and a militia of anti-slavery compatriots sworn to protect the new printing press.

The pro-slavery thugs drove off the militia and set fire to the warehouse. Elijah Lovejoy was shot and killed as he attempted to extinguish the fire.

Word of Mr. Lovejoy's martyrdom reached Washington yesterday, and politicians lined up in predictable fashion. Former President and current Massachusetts Representative John Quincy Adams called Elijah Lovejoy "the first American martyr to the freedom of the press and the freedom of the slave." Various pro-slavery advocates declared that Mr. Lovejoy was fomenting unrest, and the mob's actions were a predictable response when lawful and constitutionally sanctioned activities were injudiciously attacked.

* * * * *

· JULES ·

As had been his habit since Otto rehired him, Jules arrived at his own business long before dawn, intending to assure himself that things were running smoothly here before walking to the Krieger factories. However, Jules hadn't accomplished a thing in three hours. He sat at his office desk, not thinking about work. *I feel like I've been trying to shingle a roof in a hurricane for months.*

Four months ago, Austin T. Slatter threatened him and his family as Slatter left the hearing room of Magistrate Hyram Stone.

Six weeks ago, Lucretia's speaking engagement was canceled because of the threat of violence. *Lucretia put on a brave face when she heard the news of the cancellation, but we were right to turn around.*

Two weeks ago, the self-emancipator Pluto was returned to Delaware because Jonathan Simmons, the lawyer the Vigilant Committee hired, ran out of legal tricks. *The poor man wept. That could just as easily be me someday.*

This morning two gusts of the "hurricane" almost blew him off the roof. Harold Foote's article appeared in the morning edition of the *Philadelphia Independent*. He had never met Elijah Lovejoy, but he knew people who had, and they all had regarded him highly. *The threats of violence are real. It can happen any place, any time.*

And in this morning's mail came news that another order for a fire pump had been canceled. Although the fire company's secretary could have offered no reason for the cancellation, he did so anyway: "We found out you are an African outfit, and we don't buy anything from Africans." *Thanks for the clarification, you bastard.*

Jules tried for the tenth time to put aside his troubles and get to work when Maddie entered the office with Robert Purvis behind her. "Jules, we have a guest."

Jules rose to greet his friend. "Robert, what brings you here?"

"Bad news, I'm afraid. The Pennsylvania Constitutional Convention has started its fall session here in Philadelphia, and our old foe Sterigere is at it again. He is beating the drums of racial hatred."

"What has he done this time?"

"Yesterday he submitted petitions from the good citizens of Bucks County. Hundreds of signatures. They want the 'white only' clause added to the new constitution." Purvis pulled a piece of paper from his pocket. "I have a Sterigere quote from the convention yesterday. 'Africans should not be placed on an equality in political and social rights with white citizens.' The convention voted. It went 84 to 29 against us."

Jules pushed his *Philadelphia Independent* to the side of his desk. "That means we lost over thirty votes since the summer. Any other news?"

"The judge in Bucks County should rule soon about the petition to nullify the October elections there. The judge could help us by reaffirming that Negroes have always had the right to vote, but I doubt that he will."

"Why?"

"He was appointed by Andrew Jackson."

* * * * *

· OTTO ·

Otto held his pencil over a design for a new passenger car when he realized that, for the tenth time, he hadn't been working on his task at all. *Quit allowing your troubles to affect your work. Concentrate!*

Then Jules arrived from his morning at Freeman Hydraulics and barely spoke a word. He sat at his desk, looking for something that eluded him, opening and closing drawers with more vehemence than Otto thought was necessary.

Otto put his pencil down and looked at Jules. "How are you doing?"

Jules hesitated, then started spewing. He talked nonstop for five minutes. Nothing was breaking in his favor, except the occasional self-emancipator who sheltered in his home. He wrapped up with, "I'm sick of it, Otto. Legal maneuvers only delay the return of self-emancipators to their enslavers. I had to suffer the smirking superiority of Slatter when we lost Pluto to them. Violence lurks around every corner. My business suffers, not because I am a bad businessman, but because I am Black."

Jules looked chagrined that he had taken up so much of Otto's time. "Now that I've unloaded my burdens, tell me. How are you doing?"

Otto leaned back in his chair. "I'm not getting any work done. I have had no more letters from Europe. I expected I would receive something from Russia by now. The lack of information is driving me crazy. My daughter is masquerading as a coachman. My brother and nephew are building factories that will ensure our family's financial stability for years to come. Has Rian been exposed as a girl? Have Adrian and Seamus installed the machinery yet? Do people even make steam engines in Russia capable of driving the machines? Without news, my fears run rampant."

Jules smiled at Otto. "Is that it?"

"Well, no, now that you ask. Things with Jabez are not going well. He blatantly disobeys Mila. He no longer goes to school. He sneaks off with a rough crowd of boys and prowls the waterfront. I am worried that Mila is losing him. I promised Adrian I would look after him until he and Mila join him in Russia. I am failing completely."

"Anything else?"

"Logan Gallagher didn't come into work today. That's not like him. He has been a steady worker since we hired him."

Before Jules could respond, Conor McGuire entered the office without knocking. "Oh good, you're both here."

Maybe I should be aware of my blessings as I list my troubles, thought Otto. *Conor has been a godsend since he moved back in with me.* "Conor," Otto said, "I figured you would have left by now. You should be delivering messages for the Merchants' Exchange by this time of day."

"I've already been doing that for two hours today. I'm delivering one to a guy near here, so I thought I would stop by and tell you a couple of things that probably shouldn't wait."

"Good news or bad news?"

"I would say bad news and interesting news. I ran into Logan Gallagher's ma this morning. This is the bad news. Logan got beat up by some Ratters last night."

Otto rose from his desk. "Is he badly hurt?" *I am failing to look out for one nephew. Now I find out I am not protecting another.*

"He's in pretty rough shape. That's why he didn't come to work today. I suspect he'll be mobile in a couple of days. No broken bones."

"The Ratters. Most of those men belong to the Moyamensing Hose Company. That's Hugh Callaghan's outfit. Seamus told me Hugh hoped Logan would join that gang someday. Why did they beat him up?"

"Dunno. He wouldn't tell his ma." Conor sat heavily in the wooden chair in front of Jules's desk. "That brings me to the messages I'm delivering for the Merchants' Exchange. One of the owners of the *Bridger* is all in a lather because they canceled the *Bridger*'s insurance."

Jules straightened in his chair. "Hugh Callaghan told me about that three months ago." Then he looked at Otto. "Hugh is thinking about buying a pump from me. We talked."

Conor wasn't finished. "The owner tried to get some other outfits to insure the ship. They've all turned him down. There's four partners who own the *Bridger*. I delivered this guy's notes to all of them."

"And why should this interest us?" asked Otto.

"One of them is a relatively new partner. He bought in a couple of years ago. He's got a real nice office on Water Street with big windows that look out onto the wharves."

"And?"

"It's Austin T. Slatter. That's why he's so rich. Slatter is part owner of a slave ship."

Otto straightened in his chair. *The man who smashed my daughter's face with his gun butt doesn't just recapture those poor wretches when they escape. Now he is getting rich by trafficking in human chattel.* Then Otto slumped back. *But that is the way the world works. Perhaps someday, that will change.* "It is difficult to hear the news that people we don't like are prospering. Doubly so when it is through a repulsive business. This news about Slatter is unsettling, Conor, but we have always known that such illegal activities occur. There is nothing to be done about it."

Otto looked over at Jules. He wasn't nodding in agreement. He wasn't shaking his head. Otto couldn't interpret his expression. *What is it? Anger? Hurt? Disappointment?* "Jules, are you okay?"

"I'm fine," said Jules. "Just thinking."

THURSDAY, NOVEMBER 23

· JULES ·

Jules looked up from his desk when Hugh Callaghan entered the Freeman Hydraulics office without knocking. Jules didn't say a word, leaned back into his chair, and indicated with his hand that Hugh could take a seat.

Hugh waved him off and paced the office instead. "Conor McGuire said you wanted to see me. This better be what I hope it is because I don't like being summoned by an African. You people are supposed to come to me."

I really don't like this man, Jules thought. "It might be what you hope it is, Hugh. We've got to haggle first. You want me to help you destroy the *Bridger* when it returns to port. If I were to be involved, I don't want anyone killed."

"What do you care? They're slavers. I figure the less of them there are, the better."

"Perhaps my perspective is a bit loftier than yours is. There will be some who suspect that the ship was destroyed by people who disapprove of the slave trade."

"Which is true, although you and I are coming at it from different directions."

Jules gave Hugh a nod, validating his statement. *You hate Negroes and don't want more of them in America. I hate the slave trade and want it to end.* "But if someone dies, he will become a martyr to the pro-slavery faction, just like Elijah Lovejoy has become to the anti-slavery movement. Those sitting on the fence in the pro-slavery/anti-slavery discussion will move away from my position."

"It's your position, not mine. But I'll go along with this. No one dies."

"This little operation is just you and me. No one else needs to know about it."

"I think I have more to lose in that respect than you do. If any of my boys find out I'm involved in this, there'll be hell to pay."

Am I a fool for working with this man? The fact that we have a temporary common interest says yes. But he hates me, and I dislike him and everything he stands for. Jules rose to escort Callaghan out the door. "Speaking of your boys, I heard they beat up Logan Gallagher the other day. I thought you wanted Logan to join Moya someday."

"Still might, if he'd get his head straight. That order came down from me. I figured you, of all people, would approve. I was doing you a favor."

Jules stopped, his hand on the doorknob. "What do you mean?"

"You don't even know, do you? Logan Gallagher was seen a little too often in the company of an African girl."

Jules felt a spasm of apprehension course up and down his back. *Oh, no, please don't tell me this.*

"That African girl is your daughter. I believe her name is Martha."

FRIDAY, NOVEMBER 24

· JULES ·

Jules and Maddie stood before Logan Gallagher and Martha as they sat together on the settee in the Freeman parlor. Logan's face was still puffy from the thrashing that Hugh's men had given him two days before.

"Logan," Jules said, "you are a fine young man. You have been doing good work at Krieger Coach for seven months. But we forbid you to see our daughter anymore." *White boys like you have had their way with Black girls like Martha for centuries. I'll be damned if that will happen to my daughter, even if it was of her own free will.*

Logan sat up straight. "Jules, I respect you. I had no idea this was going to happen to us. We didn't plan to fall in love. It just happened." He put his arm protectively around Martha. "I won't make a decision by meself. Martha and I will make it together."

Jules shook his head. "Martha is eighteen years old. You are seventeen. You got beat up two days ago by men who claimed to be your friends. Friend or foe, it doesn't matter. They will hate you for what you two are doing. Logan, it was you who got beat up this time. What are you going to do if the next time it's Martha?"

"I would find that person, and I would kill him."

If we found that person, you would have to get in line behind me. "These things rarely happen by the light of day. Then you would be saddled with the knowledge that the woman you love was harmed solely because of her relationship with you. Are you prepared to live with that?"

Logan hung his head. "No, I couldn't."

Martha looked up at Jules and Maddie. "Don't I have anything to say about this? Logan, you said we would make this decision together."

Logan looked at Martha. "Your father is right. This can't work."

Jules nodded. "I'm glad you see it our way." He looked at Maddie, who nodded, adding her assent to Jules's words. "Take five minutes to say your good-byes. Then I expect that you will never try to contact Martha again. I want you

262 · ROGER A. SMITH

to know I bear you no ill will. I hope you understand that our demands come from a place of love for Martha, not because you are an unsuitable suitor. I believe you have a bright future ahead of you. It's just that you are the wrong color."

Five minutes later, Jules heard the front door close, and Martha started to wail.

MONDAY, DECEMBER 4

· LOGAN ·

It was ten o'clock, long past when most people had gone to bed. A smoky haze from the chimneys of Moyamensing obliterated the stars. Logan leaned into the rock in the vacant lot near the Freeman house, and his ass immediately started to freeze. He draped a blanket over his shoulders and shifted to ensure it provided a layer between himself and the rock. He heard the footsteps and started to shake but he couldn't tell if the shaking was from the cold or nervousness. "Ssst."

"Logan?" said Martha.

Logan rose from the rock, the blanket still around his shoulders. "Over here."

Martha found Logan and hugged him. "Pop-Pop is going to kill us."

Logan wrapped the blanket around Martha's shoulders and guided her back to the rock. "No, we agreed. Whatever romance we thought we had is over. Now we're friends. I just couldn't stand not spending time with you. I tell you things that I can't tell anyone else."

"Like what?"

Logan sighed. "I quit Krieger Coach. Your da was treating me different, and I wasn't exactly friendly with him."

"Oh, no, Logan. This is terrible. What are you going to do?"

She's not going to like this. "Hugh Callaghan found me the other day. He said all is forgiven. He still wants me to join the Ratters."

Martha stood up from the rock. The blanket fell away. "Logan, are you crazy? They're the ones who beat you up. They beat you up because of me."

"That's why no one can find out about us. That we're still friends."

"What about United No Name Fire Brigade? Why don't you join them? At least they put out fires in the Black houses."

"They're a lot smaller than Moya—fewer opportunities. Besides, Dylan's been running No Name since Seamus left. He's never tried to find me and ask me to sign up like Hugh did."

"Oh, Logan, I wish your brother was here. He'd tell you this is a bad idea."

"Yeah, well Seamus isn't here, is he? He left me and Ma and me brothers and sisters and a wad of cash that's running out. He's in Russia, and we're here. I'm the man of the house now, and I've gotta do what I can for my family. Right now, the Ratters is the best deal I've got."

THURSDAY, DECEMBER 21
(DECEMBER 9 O.S.)

· ADRIAN ·

Thursday night was the group's regular night for cards. A long, tedious, frustrating month had passed since the failed hopper demonstration. The Americans had since met with scores of people: bureaucrats, property owners, metallurgists, mining engineers, lumber suppliers, surveyors, and officials with fancy titles but little interest in sticking their necks out. To a man, they were unwilling to proceed until the Tsar issued an *ukase*—a proclamation—that anointed the Americans with his blessing. The railroad project was no further along than the day they arrived in St. Petersburg.

Count Sheremetev and Colonel Malkovich arrived at the Americans' apartment in the Anichkov Palace promptly at 8:00. Adrian immediately noticed that the two Russians weren't in their usual light-hearted card-night mood.

"How did your appointments go today?" asked Sheremetev.

"Well, we had two," said Seamus. "One was with the Minister of Delay. The other was with the Director of I Can't Help You. They were a waste of time."

Sheremetev doffed his overcoat, draped it over the back of a settee, and wearily sat down. "It is time to throw in our cards, my friend."

"I assume we aren't talking about poker."

"I believe Malkovich and I overstepped when we were in America. We were supposed to come back with locomotives. Instead, we hoped to change the face of Russia with you two. We were foolish. The Tsar has not been receptive to our project. Members of the court have been whispering in his ear. Some want no railroad at all. Others don't like the idea of the four of us—you two Americans, Malkovich, and me—running the railroad factories in Russia."

Adrian had been dreading this moment for weeks.

"Adrian, the Tsar is about to issue an *ukase* naming Count Golitsyn as his designee to build the *St. Petersburg to Moscow Railway*."

"Who the hell is Count Golitsyn?" asked Seamus. "Have we ever heard of him?"

"Golitsyn is Prince Volkonsky's brother-in-law. The gatekeeper never had any intention of letting us speak to the Tsar."

Adrian leaned into the settee for support. "All your money. All those purchases in London for things I never wanted and will never need. All this time away from my family."

"Yes, I understand. I estimate you probably have ten thousand dollars left from the original hundred thousand. It's time to cut your losses. The machinery from your factories will stay here, of course. You may be able to sell some of the items that you bought in London. Not for the price you paid, of course, but you can recoup some of your expenses. I am sorry, my friend."

"So we never had a chance."

Sheremetev shook his head. "Apparently not, because we will never get past Volkonsky. As long as he is the gatekeeper, we could hold a hundred meetings with lesser officials, but they would be all for naught."

"So, what do we do now?" asked Adrian. "Just pack up and go home?"

Sheremetev nodded. "The Gulf of Finland is already frozen shut. If you choose to leave immediately, you will have to travel by sleigh and coach. The trip will be arduous. You could stop at inns for the evening, but that will lengthen the time of your trip, and the accommodations are paltry, especially in Poland. Most people choose to travel all night. If Riga remains unfrozen, you can sail out of there. Otherwise, you will have to continue by coach as far as Hamburg."

"How far is Hamburg from here?"

"Well over twelve hundred miles. And then, of course, you will have to brave the North Atlantic in the middle of the winter. Not a pleasant thought. I suggest that you not rush home. Wait until the ice breaks in March. In the meantime, see some sights. Travel to Moscow. Enjoy a Russian Christmas with us. In fact, you can enjoy two Christmases and two New Years."

* * * * *

· JULES ·

Jules and Otto toured the Krieger Coach factory together to plan for the coming year. With half the shop's machinery stripped away and shipped to Russia, the production floor was about as busy as a juggler keeping one ball in the air. Still, there was enough racket to make talking difficult. Rather than return to the office, they entered the Finish Room, shut the large sliding door, climbed into a passenger car that had been sitting there for a week, and took seats facing one another.

The paint factory that was supposed to supply the paint had gone out of business, and paint from their new source had not yet arrived. "The delay is unfortunate but probably won't change our finances much," said Otto. "This car is supposed to go to the *Philadelphia & Columbia.* Their business is down as well. They are short of cash—probably sorry they ordered the car in the first place. It will be months before we receive our final payment, no matter when we deliver it."

Jules noticed the sliding Finish Room door open slightly. Ernst Winther entered the room, strode toward them, and stepped up into the passenger car. "Jules, there's a man named Purvis here to see you. I told him you and Otto were in a meeting, but he said it was important."

Jules started to gather up his notes. "Please send him in. We can talk here."

"I should leave," said Otto.

"Oh, stick around." Jules smiled at Otto conspiratorially. "Robert will tell us if his information is sensitive."

Purvis entered the passenger car, made his greetings, and sat next to Jules. "Slatter has been at it again. He found a family named Tarbell in Bucks County that had been working a farm for eight years—husband, wife, four kids, and the husband's brother. He claims they are fugitive slaves, and he intends to take them back to Delaware. The Vigilant Committee sprang into action. Got a constable to force Slatter to take them to a magistrate even though he was fixing to spirit them out of the Commonwealth without all the legalities. The magistrate ordered the Tarbell family all be housed in his jail until trial."

"Which magistrate?"

"Hyram Stone in Kensington, which Slatter fussed about because Stone favors our cause."

"Can we get an attorney in time?"

"One of the Vigilant Committee members is going to ask Jonathan Simmons. You and I saw him in court before. He's good."

"Does Slatter have a case?"

"There are no emancipation documents for any member of the Tarbell family. Their enslaver's name is Joseph Bride. He lives outside Wilmington, pretty close by. Slatter claims he can have him on the steamboat and in court on Friday. Jules, this is tragic. The family has been living in freedom for eight years. Their children were all born here in Pennsylvania, but an individual's slave status passes down through the mother. If the court determines that Mrs. Tarbell is an escaped slave, her children will become slaves."

Otto surprised Jules by speaking up. "This should not be allowed to happen. I would like to help this family."

Jules was gratified by Otto's interest. "Paying their legal fees would be very helpful. Simmons gives us a break, but the cost will still be significant."

"I was thinking of something beyond legal fees," said Otto.

Before Jules could ask Otto what he had in mind, the sliding door opened again. This time the interloper was Conor McGuire. Conor waved toward the passenger car as he strode forward, then hopped up the three steps into the car. "Good morning, gentlemen. I'm sorry to intrude on your meeting, but I have news."

Jules waved Conor in. "Apparently, whatever privacy Otto and I thought we had here is gone, Conor. Come and join us."

Conor looked at Robert Purvis, then back to Jules. "Well, actually, I'm the one who needs the privacy. I can really only say this to you and Otto."

"I can vouch for Robert. Whatever secret you have is safe with him."

"Well, then, I'm going to have to take your word for it. The Merchants' Exchange just got word through the optical telegraph towers. The *Bridger* entered Delaware Bay at seven o'clock this morning. She ran into a big blow on her way from Cuba, and one mast busted completely. It'll take a couple of days for her to get to Philadelphia."

Hugh Callaghan is going to want to hear this news, Jules thought. *I still can't believe I'm involving myself with that man.*

"But there's more news," said Conor. "The *Bridger*'s captain is dead. The first mate's in charge of the ship. I'm afraid someone's gonna have to tell Jabez that he's an orphan."

FRIDAY, DECEMBER 22

· ROBERT PURVIS ·

All day, Robert Purvis had allowed people to come to whatever conclusions they came to about his race. He had ridden the steamboat *Telegraph* from Philadelphia to its berth in Wilmington, Delaware, on a first-class ticket. *I conduct my daily life aligned with my Black brethren. No Black passenger would be allowed to walk the promenade deck of this ship, so I allow people to assume I am white today to serve a higher purpose.*

He never disembarked in Wilmington. Instead, he remained on the promenade deck and watched passengers climb the gangway below him, wondering which of them was Joseph Bride.

He started prowling the public spaces of the *Telegraph* as soon as it left for its return trip to Philadelphia. The steamboat would pull into its berth at Penrose Pier in four hours, but he was taking no chances. There were hundreds of passengers aboard, some strolling despite the cold, some enjoying a meal in the warmth of the saloon, and some playing cards. Intruding on a meal or a card game would be rude . . . *but I'll do it if I have to. Seven people's lives depend upon the success of my mission.*

He approached another stroller. "Excuse me, I'm looking for a man named Joseph Bride." The man shook his head and kept on walking. After an hour, he had accosted every sitter and stroller on the deck and resolved to enter the saloon to search there for Joseph Bride.

Two men exited the saloon. "Joseph Bride?" Robert asked before the men passed out of earshot.

The taller of the two men turned. "Yes, that's me."

"Oh good," said Purvis. "My name is Allison Brougham. I didn't want to miss you, so I came down from Philadelphia to make sure we found one another before you arrived in Philadelphia."

"What is this about?"

"I am helping Austin T. Slatter with some lost property he has recovered."

Joseph Bride brightened, then consulted a letter he pulled from his pocket. "Yes, he was supposed to meet me at Penrose Pier."

"That's why I'm here. There has been a change of venue for the hearing. Mr. Slatter felt that the original magistrate was inclined to adhere to the letter of Pennsylvania law, which would have delayed the return of your property and lengthened your visit. The new magistrate will likely return the entire slave family—including four children born in Pennsylvania—this afternoon. You can be on this same steamboat first thing tomorrow morning."

"Well, that was very smart of Mr. Slatter."

"These people are being aided by a local vigilant committee that has been paying their legal expenses."

"I have heard that vigilant committees have started to spring up in the area. You people shouldn't allow your Africans to think they can manipulate the legal system by delaying the return of a person's rightful property. They will start to assume all sorts of privileges. Where would that lead?" Bride took a cigar out of his breast pocket. "Before you know it, we would be forced to socialize with them on this promenade deck."

"Perish the thought," said Purvis. *You stupid bastard, you have no idea you are speaking to a Black man right now. I have no desire to socialize with you, but I'm about to take you on a wild goose chase.*

* * * * *

· JULES ·

Jules sat in the back row of the hearing room, leaning his chair into the wall so it rested on its two rear legs. Twenty-five minutes ago, Alton Davis, who represented the enslaver Joseph Bride, had approached Magistrate Stone and said that neither Austin T. Slatter nor Joseph Bride was present. Davis requested that the usual sequence of testimony could proceed, as that had now become an expected call and response in Magistrate Stone's fugitive slave hearings.

"Your honor," concluded Davis, "I have at great expense brought in an authority on Delaware constitutional law, as well as the prothonotary of New Castle County, both of whom are present and prepared to testify. Could we at least hear their testimony right now?"

Magistrate Stone stared at Davis from behind his desk. "This hearing will not proceed until all parties are present. I am inclined to dismiss this case out of hand, but I will declare a half-hour recess. If your client is not here at that time, I'll do you a big fat favor. Rather than freeing these individuals, I will continue to hold all seven members of the Tarbell family in jail through the weekend. If your client is not in this courtroom by the beginning of business Monday, they will be freed, and your client will bear the expense for their additional board. Are my sentiments clear?"

Alton Davis looked back at the magistrate and nodded. "Yes, your honor."

With his chair still propped against the rear wall, Jules smiled just a bit. *I can imagine Robert Purvis walking down the gangway of the steamboat with Joseph Bride right behind him. They pass by Slatter, who has never met Bride. Purvis takes Bride in his buggy to the wrong magistrate's office somewhere up in Spring Garden, and when Bride enters the building, Purvis leaves. Slatter wastes time thinking Bride wasn't on the ship. Soon he'll give up and come here to find the proceedings over for the day.*

It would have been wonderful if Magistrate Stone had released the family today. I was prepared to hustle them out of town if he had. I suppose that was too much to ask. Now the rest of our plan has to be put into motion.

Austin T. Slatter tumbled into the courtroom five minutes before Stone's deadline. His jacket, shirt, and cravat, which Jules had come to expect would be immaculate, were in disarray. "Your honor, I am present. I apologize for my lateness."

Magistrate Stone appeared to be slightly amused by Slatter's discombobulation. "And your client, Mr. Slatter. The property owner? Is he with you?"

"No, sir, he was not on the steamship from Wilmington. I hope we can proceed without him."

Stone grabbed his gavel and leaned back in his chair. "You know how this works, Mr. Slatter. I ask to hear proof of certain things; you supply the proof. As you have experienced in previous cases like this, the first thing I want to establish is proof of ownership. I want someone to testify that this group of Negroes is, in fact, who you claim they are. Is there anyone else besides the missing owner who can attest to that contention?"

Slatter looked around the room, spied Jules, and his visage darkened. He turned back to Magistrate Stone. "No, sir."

"In that case, I declare a recess until Monday. Mr. Slatter, your penchant for trying to circumvent Pennsylvania law is well known. I remind you that, just as in previous cases, if the Tarbell family somehow magically disappears over the weekend, a warrant will go out for your arrest. I adhere to the letter of the law, and I expect you to do so as well. As this family will occupy both cells in the jail, if you choose to sleep inside the jail, you will do so on the floor." Magistrate Stone then banged his gavel to signify that the hearing was officially over for the day.

* * * * *

· LOGAN ·

"I shouldn't have quit Krieger Coach," Logan whispered.

He and Martha had again rendezvoused in the dark at the rock. They huddled with Logan's blanket wrapped around them, as much for warmth as affection, but the affection was definitely part of it. As usual, the stars were obscured by a layer of smoke from thousands of Philadelphia chimneys.

"I bet Pop-Pop would take you back. He said they haven't hired anyone yet."

"I don't know. Maybe. I've gone back to Moya."

"They beat you up because of me."

"I know. But I know all the lads. They want me."

"If my house were burning, they wouldn't lift a finger to put it out. United No Name would. If you're going to join a fire brigade, it should be No Name. Your brother started it."

"Dylan came and talked to me about it the other day. Maybe. I don't know what to do. Hugh's got us all lined up to do something on the wharf tomorrow night."

"Mother and Pop-Pop had a big argument. I could hear them arguing in their bedroom. I don't think they knew I was in the house."

"What was the argument about?"

"I couldn't hear everything. Pop-Pop is going to do something with a man named Bridger. Mother doesn't want him to do it. She said it is too dangerous."

SATURDAY, DECEMBER 23

· OTTO ·

Otto and his nephew Jabez sat in the captain's cabin of the Baltimore Clipper *Bridger*.

Behind a small desk, Ship's First Mate Harris sat facing them. "I'm sorry to be the one to tell you this, lad. This ain't the type of news that anyone wants to talk about."

Jabez didn't say a word. *I must say,* Otto said to himself, *my nephew's demeanor hasn't changed very much from before he knew his father had died.*

"I heard the shot," continued the first mate for lack of response from Jabez. "Came in here and found your dad slumped on this desk, a pistol in his hand. Have to admit, it didn't surprise me much. He wasn't a happy man. Rarely even came out of this cabin. I know you and I didn't get along much on the one trip you sailed with us, Jabez. Believe me when I say I'm sorry for your loss."

"I hated my father," Jabez said in a low voice.

The first mate shuffled some papers on the desk. "Hopefully, he's in a better place now."

"I hate all of you, too, for what you do to those poor people."

Otto put his hand on Jabez's arm. "We need not go into that now, Jabez." *Even though I agree with you.* He turned to the first mate. "My brother is Jabez's guardian, but he is in Russia, so I am acting in his stead. Are there personal effects we should take with us, or any documents to sign?"

"A few items we've boxed up and put on the main deck. His sextant, quadrant, compass, and telescope. His top hat. Some books. We buried him at sea in the clothes he was wearing when he died."

"I don't want any of it," said Jabez.

The first mate leaned back in his chair and knit his fingers together over his stomach. "Before he came to the *Bridger*, your father earned a captain's share of the profits from three trips to China, and he took two trips to Africa and back with us, although his partners may dispute his share for this last trip since he didn't complete it. In any case, your father was a rich man. Most of his holdings are in New York City. I suspect that you will inherit a sizable fortune when you become an adult."

"I don't want any of it," Jabez repeated.

"If it means anything to you, Jabez, I'm leaving the *Bridger*. The partners and I are in somewhat of a disagreement."

Otto turned his attention from Jabez to the first mate. "Would you care to share the nature of the dispute with the ship's remaining partners?"

"It's no secret. The whole crew knows about it, so no reason you shouldn't. Captain's share of the profit for this trip was eight percent. As first mate, mine is three percent. Captain barely came out of his cabin the second time we sailed to Africa. I'm the one who gave the orders and kept everyone aboard in line. I deserve the eight percent. In fact, I deserve eleven percent since I did both our jobs. The partners don't see it that way."

"What are you going to do?"

"What I was about to do when you and Jabez came aboard. Claim my share and walk away. On my way out, I'll tell the crew I'm no longer in charge, and they can do whatever they damn well please, for all I care. We arrived too late for any off-loading to occur today. If they want to get into some of the rum that we brought from Cuba, that would no longer be any of my affair. The crew don't get much shore leave. I expect there won't be a man on this ship in three hours. Amongst them, they'll have patronized every grog shop, tavern, and whorehouse on Water Street."

"Then we have taken up enough of your time," said Otto. *And I am not going to wish you good luck. You transported kidnapped human beings to a lifetime of slavery in Cuba. May you burn in hell.*

Jabez led Otto down the gangway. "Do you really think there won't be anyone on the ship tonight?"

"Like Harris said, the men don't get much time ashore. With no one to demand that some of them remain on guard, I doubt there will be a man on the *Bridger* this evening."

"Good," said Jabez.

Otto didn't bother to ask him what that was supposed to mean.

* * * * *

· OTTO ·

Otto found Ernst Winther talking to one of the men on the Krieger Coach shop floor. He waited until Ernst finished his conversation, then said, "I'm doing a favor for a neighbor this afternoon. I'm going to need the junk wagon, but it's half-filled with scrap. Could you please get someone to take it to the junkyard?"

Ernst shook his head. "We only make junkyard trips when the wagon's filled."

"I would like you to have it done this afternoon."

"Otto, the junk wagon is almost as big as the railcar transport wagon. It'll take an hour to rent four horses from Jimmy Kent and harness them, an hour to the junkyard, an hour to unload, an hour back, and another hour to take the horses back. Two men. That's ten man-hours."

"Get two men to harness the horses, then one man to make the trip. One man should be able to unload half a wagon in an hour. No need to unharness the horses when he returns. I'll drive the wagon to my place when I leave. That cuts it down to five man-hours."

"I'll have to take someone off the freight car. You said to rush that because those folks are paying cash on delivery."

Otto looked at his pocket watch. "Yes, do that for me, please. If you do it right now, the task will be done by quitting time."

"Pretty expensive favor you're doing for your neighbor," Ernst said as he turned on his heel to find someone to do the junkyard run.

Pretty expensive, Otto thought to himself. *Pretty dangerous. Perhaps something that will become a more common part of my life. And most likely something that my daughter will be proud of if she ever comes home from Russia.*

* * * * *

· LOGAN ·

A cold wind whipped off the Delaware. Logan buttoned his coat and looked down the length of Blight's Pier. Only one lantern was visible—at the top of the ship's gangway. "It's dark," he said, unaware that he'd spoken loud enough for Hugh Callaghan to hear.

Hugh chuckled. "You've got a lot to learn, kid. The first rule of burgling is to keep track of the moon. Our activities is best done in the dark. Tonight the moon doesn't rise for another hour and a half, and when it does, it's going to be as full as full can be, so we've all gotta be outta here in two hours maximum."

"Where are the guards?"

"There aren't any. Tonight, the Ratters are the beneficiaries of a financial dispute. The entire crew of this ship left this afternoon to enjoy the pleasures of

Water Street. All we've got to worry about is the occasional watchman, and he's got five or six wharves to worry about."

"What do you want me to do?"

"You? You'll be hauling sacks of coffee out of the hold, same as everybody else."

* * * * *

Logan climbed down the ladder into the hold of the ship. A few candles and oil lamps lit shelf after shelf of coffee sacks. "Jaysus," he said to no one. "I didn't expect this."

"What *did* you expect?" said one of the Ratters.

"I don't know. More open space, maybe. Doesn't seem like a very smart way to haul cargo."

"Depends upon the cargo," the man said as he fingered an iron ring bolted to one of the shelves. "I'd wager that you're in the hold of a slave ship. They force the Africans onto those shelves when they transport them to the Caribbean. They bring the coffee up north just to fill the ship. Doesn't matter what the cargo is on this leg. The real money's in the slaves."

A spasm of horror gripped Logan. *This hold makes my skin crawl.*

* * * * *

Climbing a ladder with a sixty-pound burlap bag draped over his shoulder was arduous work, but Logan was grateful every time he escaped the pall of misery that permeated the hold.

Fifteen trips up the ladder and down the gangway wore him out, so he volunteered to wheelbarrow the coffee to the Moyamensing Hose Company's warehouse.

Meanwhile, a few of the more industrious Ratters had rigged up a block and tackle and hauled a barrel of rum out of the forehold. Logan, pushing a wheelbarrow with two sacks of coffee, kept pace with them as they rolled the barrel along the pier.

Hugh, visible only in the faint light from the lantern at the top of the gangway, growled at the men when they reached him. "Jaysus, you boys have no sense. Rolling that barrel all the way to our place will attract too much attention."

"Whataya want us to do with it, Hugh? We've gone to a lot of trouble to get it this far."

Hugh looked to the east. "Point taken. We've got enough time. Go find the ship's carpenter's cabin. Grab his bit and brace. We'll drill a hole in this barrel and drink as much rum as we can right here." A muted cheer arose from the men nearby.

By the time Logan returned with the wheelbarrow, someone had tipped the barrel upright, bored a hole in its side, and caught the outflowing rum in three wooden buckets. Men were drinking rum from mugs purloined from the ship's galley.

At the end of two hours, a hundred sacks of coffee had been spirited off the ship. Hugh gathered the last Ratters to come out of the hold around the rum barrel. The full moon had just risen, illuminating Windmill Island half a mile away and making the Delaware shimmer. The cold wind still whipped. "Good job, lads. Be sure to dip a mug to fortify yourselves. If you're not going straight home, say hello to Clancy for me. I won't be sharing a drink with you this evening."

"Aw, come on with us, Hugh. What's more important than celebrating a successful mission with your lads?" one of the men said.

Hugh shrugged. "I heard a rumor that some abolitionists are going to burn the ship tonight. Figure she deserves a better fate than that. One of the owners is a man named Slatter, a kindred spirit of sorts. He's currently up in Kensington. Now that we've relieved him of all his coffee, I figure I'll go tell him that if he hurries, he can save his ship."

Hugh started walking away from the group, then turned back. "Oh, by the way, if somehow the anti-slavery folks are successful and light the *Bridger* afire, don't bother answering the fire bell. The ship is uninsured. There'd be no money in it for us."

Logan watched Hugh as he turned and walked toward Water Street and faded into the shadows. Well into his second mug of rum, Logan hadn't been paying much attention to the conversation. He was tired and looking forward to joining the men at Clancy's before he crawled home. Then Hugh's words started to sink in. *Last night Martha mentioned something about a man named Bridger.*

"Wait," said Logan, "who's Bridger?"

The man who tried to talk Hugh into coming with them said, "Not *who*, you idiot, *what*. The *Bridger's* the ship you just burgled of all its coffee."

The man grabbed one of the buckets and started walking toward Clancy's Saloon. Everyone but Logan followed.

* * * * *

· JULES ·

The rising full moon illuminated the length of Blight's Pier as Jules approached the *Bridger*. It was well below freezing, and the wind off the Delaware whipped at him. *Not ideal conditions to commit arson,* thought Jules.

"Ssst."

Jules looked toward the warehouse across the alley. *A thin shadow, just enough to hide in.* A figure moved into the moonlight. *Logan Gallagher.*

Jules walked across the alley and pushed Logan back into the shadow. "Logan, what the hell are you doing here?"

"Hugh Callaghan knows folks are going to burn the *Bridger* tonight. Guess I shouldn't be very surprised it's you. Hugh's gone to get one of the owners."

Jules looked toward the ship. In the growing moonlight, he could make out the name *Bridger* on the portside bow. "I guess I better get to work."

Logan grabbed Jules by the arm. "I want to help. It's a slave ship."

"This isn't your fight, Logan. I'm done getting young people into trouble."

"There's two stumble-drunk sailors aboard. They came back about half an hour ago."

This operation was supposed to be just Hugh and me. Hugh's not here, but Logan is. And now two drunk sailors.

Jules looked toward the ship, then back down the alley toward Water Street. "Okay, I do need you after all. It's going to take me a couple of minutes to find the drunks and get them out. Stay right here. When you see us come back on the deck, raise your arms straight out from your sides like this if the coast is clear, straight up if it's not." Jules leaned down and picked up a ballast stone the size of his fist. "If Hugh gets here with the owner while I'm below, chuck this stone toward midships. I'll be able to hear it no matter where I am. Then hightail it out of here."

Navigating by candlelight, Jules found the two sailors passed out in their hammocks in the crew quarters. They were too drunk to wake up. *These men work on a slave ship. I should let them burn to death, but if I did, it would be murder, and that would become the story.* He tipped the candle so that wax dripped onto a nearby table and stuck the candle upright into the melted wax. He then went down on one knee, laboriously rolled the smaller of the two sailors out of his hammock and onto his shoulder, rose, and grunted his way up the steep steps to the main deck.

He looked toward Logan's lookout spot. Logan stepped out of the shadows, held one arm out from his side, and raised the other straight up. *What the hell is that supposed to mean?*

Jules carried the drunk down the gangway to the middle of the pier and laid him on the freezing bricks next to a barrel. *One down, one to go.*

He scurried to Logan, who had returned to the shadows. "What was your signal supposed to mean?"

"Someone else boarded the ship."

"Oh, Christ! I can't keep rescuing drunk sailors. I'm running out of time."

"It wasn't a sailor. It was Jabez Howes."

Rian Krieger's twin. "What the hell is he doing here?"

"I don't know." Logan pointed toward the barrel in the middle of the pier. "He grabbed a bucket off the top of that barrel over there and walked up the gangway."

Jules knew he was running out of time and couldn't worry for the moment about Jabez Howes. *The second sailor is heavier. No way I can carry that much dead weight.*

As he passed the barrel and the passed-out sailor, he noticed a bucket on top of the barrel. He bent and sniffed at the bucket's contents. *No smell.* He dipped his fingers into about two inches of liquid and tasted . . . *freezing cold rum. And that gives me an idea. Rum burns.*

Jules grabbed the bucket, carried it down to the crew quarters, and threw the icy rum on the second sailor. The man gasped and sputtered at the rude intrusion into his slumber. Before he could lapse back into unconsciousness, Jules flipped the sailor's hammock, and he fell heavily onto the floor.

From a distant part of the ship, Jules could hear a *thunk! thunk! thunk!* He helped the man stand, then badgered and punched him until he climbed the stairs. Once on deck, Jules looked for Logan, who stepped out of the shadow again and raised both arms out from his side. The *thunk! thunk!* was louder now, more distinct, and coming from the ship's interior, but farther forward. Jules pushed the second sailor down the gangway. The sailor sat down with his back to the barrel and promptly joined his shipmate in slumber.

Well, I've done what I could. Hopefully, these boys won't freeze to death because they'll soon be warmed by the heat of the ship's fire.

Logan came out of the shadows. "I saw Jabez while you were getting the second sailor. He's the one making that noise. He has an axe."

Jules started running for the gangway, then stopped and turned toward Logan. "Are you going to stick around?"

"Yes, if you need me."

"Same signals. Throw the rock if Slatter shows up, then get the hell out of here."

A lot of the rum I dumped onto that sailor splashed onto the floor. If it weren't for Jabez, I could light it on fire and leave the ship. Now Jabez has complicated things. He returned to the crew quarters, grabbed the candle, wistfully looked at the puddle of rum, and climbed the steep stairs. He immediately descended another set of stairs, opening doors as he walked down a narrow corridor. At the end of the corridor, a sign on the door said *CAPTAIN*. He opened the door. The desk and cabinets, which had been smoldering until he opened the door, burst into flames. *Jesus,* he said to himself.

Jules ran back up the stairs to the main deck. Logan stepped out of the shadows, held both his arms out from his side, then pointed toward the rear of the ship. Jules walked aft, stepped around debris and rigging that hadn't been cleared up after the big blow, and found a hatch cover shoved aside. He peered down into the hold. *Can't see a goddamn thing, but something's going on down there.* Holding the candle in one hand, he descended the ladder and found himself in his worst nightmare: the hold of a ship designed to transport kidnapped human beings to a life of slavery.

At the other end of the hold, lit by a single candle, Jabez Howes splashed rum around the hold from a wooden bucket.

Jules walked toward Jabez. "Jabez, it's Jules Freeman."

Jabez turned, saw Jules, then turned back to his work. "You're not going to stop me."

"I don't intend to. It looks like you and I had the same idea. I think this should be enough rum to get a fire started. You've done enough, son. I'll take it from here."

"No."

"Let me handle it. All we have to do is light this rum, and we can leave."

"No, we need to do more. I've already lit one fire. I need to light more."

"Why?"

"We had a fire one time when I was aboard. They put it out real easy using the bilge pump. The bilge pump can put out one fire. It can't be in three places at once."

"I found the fire in the captain's cabin. I left the door open."

Jabez bent down and touched his candle to a puddle of rum. The liquid started to burn and traced a meandering path to the side of the ship. "Then we've got to hurry."

Jabez strode past Jules and started climbing the ladder. "I've been dreaming about this night for six months. Figured that's what it would be forever: just a dream. Then the first mate told Uncle Otto and me that there likely wouldn't be any guards tonight. I walked up and down Water Street until I found one of the men. He told me the whole crew was out on the town and the *Bridger* was deserted. The forward hold is filled with rum and molasses. I've already broken open one of the rum barrels with an axe. All I've got to do now is go down, light the rum, and get out. You should leave now."

"Seems like you've got a better plan than I had. How about if I stick with you, and we leave together."

Jabez headed for the ladder. "Suit yourself. Only wish Captain were here to see his ship burning up."

Then Jules heard a clatter up on the deck. *Logan tossed the ballast stone.* "That's my lookout," he whispered to Jabez. "Someone's coming."

* * * * *

· OTTO ·

Otto drove the junk wagon through Northern Liberties by the dark of night with Robert Purvis to his right. It was cold, and the wind whipped at his coat. "Have you ever seen the jail in Kensington?"

"Not the inside," replied Robert. "It's right around the corner from the magistrate's office. Probably built in the last century. An alley in the back. Surrounded by businesses, not houses where people will be sleeping. Quite ideal for our mission this evening. Otto, I hope you've brought proper tools to break these people out. I know very little about such things."

Otto chuckled. "I probably threw more tools into the wagon than we will need, but with my gear and the strength of four horses, I think we'll get the best of a barred window."

Robert adjusted his scarf over his mouth in reaction to a particularly bitter gust. "Magistrate Stone said the family was to be housed in two cells. The noise caused by the destruction of the first window might attract attention. I don't want to stick around very long after that, so we'll have to be quick with the second one."

Otto parked the junk wagon two blocks from the Kensington jail just as the full moon was rising. He and Robert found a place to observe the front of the jail from the shadows. They waited twenty bitterly-cold minutes before Hugh Callaghan banged on the jail door. Slatter let Hugh in. Three minutes later, Hugh and Slatter exited. Slatter locked the door and they started walking south toward Philadelphia. *Two miles. Fifteen minutes per mile. Half an hour. An hour for Slatter to rustle up some guards. Half an hour back. Plenty of time.*

Otto and Robert returned to the junk wagon. Otto reined the four-horse team down the alley and stopped beneath the first of two barred windows. He engaged the brake, hopped into the back of the wagon, and looked in the window. It was pitch dark inside. "Ssst."

A voice came from the other window. "Who's there?"

"A friend come to get you out of here."

"Thank you, friend. We're all over here, in one cell. The devil put us here so's he could sleep on the cot in the other cell."

Otto knew who *the devil* was. *This makes it easier. One window, and we're gone.*

Otto pulled the wagon forward fifteen feet. He handed a ten-foot length of one-inch hemp rope up to the window. "Do you know how to tie a good knot?"

"Worked on a farm all my life. 'Course I know how to tie a good knot."

"What's your name?"

"Daniel."

"Well, Daniel, we're going to get you and your family out of the lion's den now."

Otto looped another length of rope around a massive rock across the alley. He manhandled two double pulleys from the wagon—the same block and tackle rigging the men used to raise a railcar onto the transport wagon. Each pulley had a hook on its end. He hooked one pulley to the jail-bars-loop and the other to the rock-loop and tied the end of the rope onto a clevis at the rear of the wagon.

Rather than climb back into the wagon, Otto released the brake and walked to the lead horse. *Four horses rigged up to a double block and tackle . . . this should be easy.* He pulled on the lead horse's halter. She obediently stepped forward, and the other three horses followed. *They aren't even straining.*

The ropes tightened. The horses strolled ahead, now leaning into their harness. The rope tightened further. After Otto led the horses ahead fifteen feet, a six-foot section of the jail cell wall crashed down into the alley. Seven people stepped onto the wreckage and out to freedom.

Otto started gathering up the block and tackle. "Climb into the junk wagon, Daniel. Quickly now. All of you. There's food and plenty of blankets for everyone. In half an hour, my friend here will have you on a ship that's carrying hides to Boston."

"Where are you going?" asked Robert.

"I'm going to walk back to the Blight's Pier. Somebody might need my help. Good luck."

* * * * *

· LOGAN ·

Logan kept watch from a warehouse doorway at the base of Blight's Pier. He divided his attention between the deck of the ship and the alley toward Water Street. The cold wind whipped from the river. Occasionally he smelled smoke, but then a new gust would come from a different direction and chase away the smell.

When he spied Hugh Callaghan and Austin T. Slatter rushing up the pier, he stepped far back into the deepening shadows. As they passed, he heard Slatter say, "Where are your boys, Callaghan? They should have caught up to us by now."

Logan couldn't hear Hugh's response. After they passed him, he tossed the ballast stone onto the ship's deck, just like Jules told him to. His aim was off, and it landed toward the aft hatch, near where Logan had last seen Jules.

Slatter and Hugh heard the rock hit the ship. Slatter pointed. Hugh said something that Logan couldn't make out. Then, something odd happened. Slatter pulled his pistol on Hugh and used it to prod him up the gangway.

Jules had told Logan to leave after he threw the rock. *Not yet. This is getting too interesting.* In the distance, he heard the State House bell ringing. *The fire bell.* Two rings. *That's south.* Then three rings. *That's east. Southeast. That's here. Somebody alerted the steeplekeeper. Fire companies will be out looking for the fire, and they'll follow the smoke right here.*

* * * * *

· JULES ·

Jules followed Jabez up the ladder and out of the hold. As they reached the top, a blanket of thick, oily smoke enveloped them and then was whipped away by the wind. Jules peered down onto the pier and spied Callaghan and Slatter heading for the gangway. Slatter held a pistol.

Jabez blew out his candle and started running toward the bow. Jules followed him until the boy climbed down the forehold hatch. Jules stepped into a shadow, looked aft, and watched Callaghan and Slatter arrive at the top of the gangway. They turned toward the aft hold. Smoke coming from the hold was thicker now. First Hugh then Slatter disappeared into the ship's bowels.

Jabez reappeared. "I lit the fire. There's a lot of rum down there."

"Okay, the coast is clear. You've done what you came to do. Let's get off the ship."

Jules kept his eyes on the rear hatch as he and Jabez ran to the gangway. They descended to the pier, only to hear the strains of an Irish fighting song sung by dozens of voices, then scores of boots tromping on the gravelly pier, then steel-rimmed wheels traveling at a rapid clip. "It's a fire brigade. Hurry."

Jules and Jabez joined Logan in the shadows.

"Which fire company is it?" asked Jules after they had passed by.

"They're Moya boys," Logan said. "The fire bell's been ringing. I expect there'll be others soon."

Jules folded his arms and leaned back into the wall. "Won't do any good. There's no insurance on this ship. They won't get paid. We've done our job. We should leave."

"Not yet," said Logan. "Hugh and Slatter haven't come out yet."

"So what?" said Jules. "They'll either put the fire out or not. Either way, there's a bigger one going in the forehold. It's time to go."

"No, we should wait." Logan jutted his chin toward the aft hold. "Look there."

Austin T. Slatter emerged from the hold carrying some object that Jules didn't recognize.

"That's the bilge pump," said Jabez. "That means he put out the fire in the aft hold."

Slatter dropped the pump, dragged the hatch cover over the hatch, and latched it down.

"Hugh's not with him," said Jules. "This isn't good."

"Hugh didn't go down into the hold willingly," whispered Logan. "Slatter had a pistol on him."

Jesus, thought Jules. *Hugh is no friend of the Black man. If he died on the ship, the world would be a better place, but then he would become a hero, and this anti-slavery protest would create a pro-slavery martyr for the penny papers. I can't go rescue him. The Moya boys would beat the shit out of me.*

Just then, a new thump of boots and clatter of steel-rimmed wheels reverberated down the alley. Jules recognized members of the United No Name Fire Brigade, some of whom worked at Krieger Coach.

The Moya boys recognized No Names, too, as they set up their hoses.

Austin Slatter emerged from the forehold and ran down the gangway gesturing wildly. "Hurry! Hurry! The fire's raging down there. I'll pay! I'll pay whatever you want! Just get your hoses down that hold."

Then Slatter ran to Dylan, who held the No Name Fire Brigade's captain's trumpet. "I'll pay everything to the first hose company to train their hoses on the fire in that hold! Hurry now!"

Dylan yelled at his men through the trumpet. "C'mon, lads. Quickly, now!"

The two rival fire brigades formed near one another, each trying to get a stream of water onto the fire in the forehold first.

Jules watched their practiced efficiency from the shadows. "Have you signed up with either of these fire companies yet Logan?"

"Yeah, Moya . . . sort of."

"Well, it's time to make your decision final," said Jules.

"What do you mean?"

"I've got to get on that ship to get Hugh out of the hold. There's only one way to do it. You have to choose which fire brigade you want to join, then start a fight with the other one. They'll be so busy beating on each other that I'll be able to slip aboard and get the hatch cover off."

"Jaysus," said Logan. Both teams had their steam-powered pumps ready to go, the intake hose for each pump already draped off the pier into the harbor. Two men from each hose company were frantically trying to screw the outflow hose onto their machines. The Moya boys had a head start and were about to get their stream going. Logan left the shadows, walked between the two groups, and strode to the Moya hose that would start sucking water from the harbor in a few seconds. He pulled the hose out of the water.

A man from Moya ran up and punched Logan so hard that he almost fell off the pier.

A man from No Name ran to Logan's rescue and punched the Moya man. The melee was on.

* * * * *

Jules waited until both fire brigades were fully engaged in the brawl. Slatter was desperately trying to pull men off one another, but to no avail. Then the slave catcher tried to get the Moya pump operating by himself. *Good. Keep your attention on the pump, you son of a bitch.*

Jules got as close to the gangway as possible while still hidden in the shadows. Then he sprinted up the ramp and boarded the ship. Fire and smoke flowed out of the forehold. As he approached the aft hold hatch, he heard Hugh Callaghan yelling and pounding from within the hold. He unlatched the hatch cover, threw it off, knelt, and extended his hand to the man who made it his mission to drive Black families from Moyamensing.

Coughing and sputtering, Hugh took Jules's hand and climbed out onto the deck. Both men surveyed the situation on the pier below. The Moya lads, who far outnumbered the No Name boys, were winning. "Looks like the truce is over," said Hugh, ignoring the growing conflagration around him.

Jules shrugged. "For the moment. I saved you. Now you've got to get me off this ship."

"Where's Slatter?"

"Down on the pier, trying to put out the fire by himself."

The two men again peered over the deck rail. Slatter had slumped to his knees and watched the blaze at the front of the ship as it grew far beyond anyone's control.

"Gotta tell you, Jules," said Hugh, "this is a strange evening. Stay here. You'll have to figure out for yourself when the time is right."

Hugh sauntered halfway down the gangway, then stopped to admire the melee and the burning ship.

My God, Jules said to himself, *he's relishing all this. The man is crazy.*

Then Hugh descended to the pier, picked up the pace to a purposeful stride, hauled Slatter up by the scruff of his neck, punched and shoved him to the edge of the pier, and threw him off the pier and into the harbor.

Jules strode down the gangway and faded into the shadows.

* * * * *

Ten minutes later, Hugh had pulled enough men off one another to end the brawl. The *Bridger* was as good as lost, but the fire would rage for hours. At Hugh's direction, the Moya boys were dousing the nearby warehouse. With no hope of a bounty, the No Name men were packing their gear and preparing to leave. A No Name man clapped a Moya lad on the back, as if the evening's activity had been good entertainment.

Hugh sauntered to the shadows where Jules, Logan, and Jabez were getting ready to follow the No Name boys off the pier. "I think me lads'll be here for a couple of hours, but I've had enough."

"I've got a place to watch from a distance if you're interested," Jabez said.

The group agreed.

"Where are you all going?" came a familiar voice from half a block away.

Jules smiled to himself. "Glad you're here, Otto. We're going to watch the fire from a new location."

* * * * *

Jules stood at the railing on the roof of Sparks Shot Tower and took in the length of the Philadelphia waterfront, now illuminated by the light of the risen full moon. Half a mile to the north, the *Bridger* burned, the flames rising spectacularly then bending toward the warehouses because of the wind coming off the Delaware. To Jules's left stood Logan Gallagher. To his right, Hugh Callaghan, Otto Krieger, and Jabez Howes all contemplated the fire. *Never in the history of the world has a more unlikely assemblage of individuals been gathered together to commit such a righteous act of arson.*

He raised his voice so that everyone atop the tower could hear. "Thank you, Jabez. You found us the best seat in the house."

Hugh Callaghan pulled two cigars out of the inside breast pocket of his coat. "I want to state that just because we successfully torched that ship, I'm not suddenly going to be all buddy-buddy with you folks. I instituted this action because the *Bridger* was a slave ship that brought Africans to this side of the Atlantic. Some of those Africans somehow manage to end up in Philadelphia. The fewer of your people competing with us Irish in this town, the better."

To Jules's surprise, Hugh handed one of the cigars to him. Also to his surprise, he accepted it.

Hugh leaned down to use Jules's bulk as a windbreak, lit his cigar with a loco-foco, then stood up and handed the matchbox to Jules. After Jules lit his cigar, using Hugh in the same manner, Hugh said, "Jules, when the sun comes up, you and I will be right back to where we've always been. I don't like your people. I'll do whatever I can to drive your African brethren out of Philadelphia."

The man is so hateful, thought Jules. *Yet he offers me a cigar.* "Hugh, we have momentarily found common cause. We have burned a ship that brought misery to hundreds of people. We probably bankrupted the ship's owners . . ."

Otto leaned back from the railing to regard Jules and Hugh. "Hugh, Jules saved your life this evening."

Jules paused to let Otto's words sink in. "Could you at least look down at what we have done together and savor the moment?"

Hugh puffed on his cigar and waved it in the air. "Let's get some things straight. Jules did not save my life. I could have gotten myself out of that hold—"

Everyone else on the platform hooted.

"—but having Jules risk his neck to get me out of a jam might have changed my thinking a bit."

Otto pulled out a cigar of his own. "In what way?"

"I don't want to be seen in public with you, Jules, but I could see that working with you behind the scenes might work to our mutual advantage."

"For instance?"

"Well, let's assume for the moment that my suspicions are correct—that you're involved with the Underground Railroad."

Jules looked momentarily at the others on the roof. If they were surprised by Hugh's words, they didn't show it. "You can assume whatever you want."

"I don't want your runaway Black brethren settling in this town. As long as you keep them running north, I won't bother you."

Careful. Don't admit anything. "That's what the Underground Railroad does—keeps people moving to safety. The farther north they are, the safer they are."

"Then it sounds like we have a deal. But I tell you now, as far as the rest of the world is concerned, you and I are not friends."

"But, when it's just us?"

Hugh puffed on his cigar for a long moment, then smirked. "Maybe I'd tolerate you."

* * * * *

· LOGAN ·

Logan couldn't take his eyes off the ship fire half a mile away. Hugh moved over to Logan and nudged him in the side. "So, I guess you've made your decision. You're going with No Name."

"I'm still not sure. Probably. I just knew I had to start a fight to give Jules a way to rescue you. How come Slatter pulled his gun on you?"

"When I told Slatter that there was a plot to burn the ship, he said that the ship's insurance had been pulled but he and his partners would pay to have my men show up. I was trapped. We stopped by Clancy's on the way here and mustered the men. When we got to the pier, we saw smoke coming from the aft hold. I told Slatter he could probably put out the fire with the ship's bilge pump, but I wasn't going to go down until he showed me some money. He told me he didn't have the money on him and he didn't know what a bilge pump looked like. That's when he pulled his pistol. He wasn't happy when he saw the hold was empty and assumed I was the one who stole all his coffee and that I was playing both sides. He forced me to start working on the bilge pump. He let me go at it for a while. I was getting the best of the fire when he bashed me in the head. When I came to, the fire was out, and he was climbing the ladder with the pump."

Jules, who had been leaning on the railing, moved over to join Logan and Hugh. "Logan, how did you know I was going to show up at the pier?"

Because your daughter overheard you and your wife arguing about the Bridger. Your daughter, who I've been secretly meeting even though I promised you I would never see her again. "Uh, I didn't. Hugh told us someone was going to burn the ship. I wanted to see who showed up. I was surprised when it was you."

Jules started chuckling.

"What?" asked Hugh.

"It just dawned on me. I wonder what Magistrate Stone is going to do to Slatter when he finds out that the Tarbell family has been busted out of jail."

* * * * *

· OTTO ·

Otto put his arm around Jabez as they eyed the burning slave ship.

"I hated that ship," said Jabez. "I'm glad it's gone."

My daughter's twin. Just like her, a thirteen-year-old who insinuated himself into the adult world and got away with it. "Do you feel better having done it?"

"A little. Not much. I wish Captain were here to see this."

"Your father? Why?"

"He loved Baltimore Clippers because they are such fast ships. The *Bridger* was one of the fastest afloat. Now it's gone."

"You hated him that much?"

"He did bad things. He allowed bad things to happen on his ship. Yes, I hated him."

Otto removed his arm from around Jabez and leaned into the rail. *Rian has been gone for four months. She is five thousand miles away. I did not trust her when she made moral decisions that I was not yet prepared to make. Well, Liebling, I am following your footsteps, taking on a fight you led me to. I thank you for that. I hope you are keeping yourself safe. I miss you so much. Please come home to me. I am angry with you, but you and I know I will get over my anger. Keep yourself out of danger. Your Aunt Lilly says you have a hero's heart. And that is what I fear the most. You put yourself in harm's way as if you are invulnerable. I know how fragile life is. Come home to me, Liebling. Come home safe.*

Otto pulled his gaze away from the fire and found Hugh Callaghan. "When you went to the jail to get Slatter, you pulled him off his guard detail. You gave me the opportunity to free a Black family. How does that fit into your view of the world?"

Hugh continued to regard the fire and waved his cigar in the air. "Jules promised me that you would keep that family running faster than the broadsides could catch up with them. I just told Jules, as long as they don't stay in Philadelphia, I don't care what happens to them."

"You know what, Hugh?" said Otto. "You say all these hateful words, yet when your sensibilities did not align with your lads, you came to Jules. You may go back to your Moya friends, but the fact is you have kept a truce between Moya and the Black community for a year and a half. I think you have come to appreciate the advantages of that peace."

"Seamus Gallagher caught me in a moment of weakness. Then we extended the truce because we made a new deal."

"But the truce has held through terrible economic times. We are all suffering. Black, white, German, business owner, laborer . . . this depression has hurt us all."

"Some more than others."

"But the truce has at least alleviated that suffering a little bit. I think you want to keep it going."

"What makes you say that?"

Jules joined Hugh and Otto's conversation. "Well, for one thing, you could have told Slatter that it was me who was going to burn his ship."

"How do you know I didn't?"

"You threw him in the drink so he wouldn't see me when I got off the boat. I trusted you, Hugh. You could have betrayed me. You would have gotten away with it. If Slatter thinks I was involved in this, I'll be dead in two weeks."

Hugh chuckled. "Ah, hogwash, Jules. You're right. I didn't rat you out to Slatter. But I didn't rat you out because Seamus is in Russia. I just like having someone around to torment, that's all."

With the conversation finally restored to somewhat of a jovial level, Otto relaxed a bit. "Who's going to talk to Harold Foote?"

"The reporter?" asked Hugh. "Why is that important?"

"Jules didn't want anyone killed because this whole action was a protest against the illegal slave trade. In order for the protest to do any good, people have to know about it."

* * * * *

Slave Ship Burned at Blight's Pier
Act of Arson Allegedly a Protest by Abolitionists
No Loss of Life Reported

Exclusive to the *Philadelphia Independent* by Harold Foote

The Baltimore Clipper *Bridger* burned to its waterline at her berth at Blight's Pier on December 23, the alleged work of an anti-slavery group protesting its use as a slave ship. Austin T. Slatter, one of the owners of the

Bridger, claimed that the *Bridger* was not engaged in any illegal activities, including the transatlantic slave trade. It had sailed into Philadelphia from Cuba with a load of rum, molasses, and coffee, all perfectly legal. Slatter claimed that, rather than an anti-slavery protest, the ship had been looted of its cargo and set afire to hide the robbery.

No spokesperson for any abolitionist group has come forward to claim responsibility for this act of arson, so its roots as a protest against slavery remain speculation. However, a cloud of additional suspicion rests over the smoldering wreckage. Levi Howes, the ship's captain, died mysteriously on the trip from Cuba. The entire crew was on shore leave the night of the conflagration with no guards posted. The ship's first mate, who had been in a financial dispute with the owners, is missing.

Mr. Slatter was ordered to be held in a Kensington jail by Magistrate Hyram Stone for actions unrelated to the ship fire. Speaking from his jail cell, Mr. Slatter stated that the ship was uninsured for reasons that he does not understand. "This act of arson has ruined me," claimed Slatter. "It took years for me to save enough money to become an ownership partner in the *Bridger*. Now I am right back to where I was years ago."

FRIDAY, DECEMBER 29
(DECEMBER 17 O.S.)

· ADRIAN ·

Adrian and Seamus made their decision: remain in St. Petersburg through the Russian New Year, then make the arduous overland trip to Western Europe. Instead of sailing directly back to America, they intended to visit Amsterdam and Paris before sailing from London in March. Their departure now set, Adrian and Seamus suffered through a tedious string of social events at night that Adrian had no patience for.

The three Americans had each reacted differently to the decision to head home. Seamus pivoted without misgivings. "I came here thinking nobody in Russia would look down on me because I'm Irish. Well, that part is true, but it's because they look down on everyone who isn't Russian. So I'll go home with plenty of stories to tell and still have more money in me pocket than I would've made in a year of daywork on the docks."

Rian acknowledged that she was a tad homesick but enjoyed her role as coachman. *Yes, a coachman who almost everyone thinks is a boy*, Adrian thought to himself.

Adrian was the one who took the defeat the hardest. Since the decision to return home, he had spent much of the time brooding. The scores of meetings that he had participated in convinced him that he could build all the components for a railroad from St. Petersburg to Moscow if given a chance. Since the decision to throw in their cards, even though he had canceled all his business appointments, he found himself continually machinating about how to change their fate.

Now, Count Sheremetev and Adrian stood in the lobby of the Mikhailovsky Theatre, Adrian with irritation, the count with a show of good cheer. Mozart's opera *The Abduction from the Seraglio* would begin shortly. Yet, like everyone else who had box seats on the Belle Etage, they awaited the arrival of Tsar Nicholas. It was politically unwise for anyone to take their seat before the Tsar arrived.

"What do I care about politics?" Adrian groused. "I'm leaving in four days."

"Yes, my friend, but I am not. I thank you for playing out your hand with your head up."

Adrian harrumphed.

The crowd in the lobby hushed. Dukes and duchesses, counts and countesses, barons and baronesses parted as the Tsar and his wife approached.

For the first time, Adrian set eyes on Nicholas Pavlovich Romanov, Emperor of All the Russias, King of Poland, and Grand Duke of Finland. The Tsar wore full military regalia festooned with epaulets, gold, and medals. He was tall, lean, and ramrod-straight. His close-cropped hair, small mustache, and square chin all worked together to make him handsome. Though he nodded to numerous individuals as he passed through the lobby, not the faintest hint of a smile lit his face. When he passed Adrian, the Tsar looked him in the eye briefly but showed no sign of interest. The royal couple ascended the stairs and turned left toward their box.

The Tsar's entourage, both men and women, trailed in the royal couple's wake. Prince Volkonsky, sleek as a pampered housecat, nodded as he walked by. The cat gave Adrian the same regard as he would a mouse he had been torturing for the last half hour yet had let go out of sheer boredom.

Seamus, who had been practicing his Russian on the attractive lady-in-waiting who might or might not speak English, sidled up to Adrian and Sheremetev. "Well, that was quick. He seemed rather humorless, at least in the three seconds I had to see him."

"*Imperious* came to my mind," said Adrian.

"Use any adjectives you want in the privacy of your apartment," said Sheremetev. "But please, not here. The Tsar is not a man to cross and there are many unfriendly ears amongst us."

With Nicholas and his entourage now ensconced, the guests were free to take their seats on the Belle Etage. Sheremetev's box was situated directly across the theater from the Tsar's. Once seated, Sheremetev leaned over to Adrian. "Please note that Volkonsky sits right next to the Tsar. The gatekeeper never rests."

The orchestra members finished tuning their instruments. A legion of liveried attendants with long-handled candle snuffers doused the tapers on a score of candelabras arrayed along the aisles. The buzz amongst the patrons died down as the hall darkened. The curtain rose. Even though Mozart's opera was sung in German, rather than settling in and enjoying himself, Adrian found himself distracted by his unobstructed view of the Tsar.

On stage, Belmonte's true love Konstanze and his servant Pedrillo had been captured by pirates and sold to Pasha Selim. Across the hall, Nicholas and his empress seemed to be happily following along.

Ten minutes into the first act, as Belmonte resolved to break into the pasha's palace, Adrian spotted the curtain behind the Tsar's box drawn aside. He nudged Sheremetev and nodded in the direction of the emperor. Captain Stepanov bent to whisper in Volkonsky's ear. Volkonsky listened, then dismissed him with a wave of his hand.

Act I continued. Belmonte reunited with his servant Pedrillo. They resolved to rescue the beautiful Konstanze. Their way was blocked by Osmin, the pasha's ill-tempered servant.

There was more activity in the Tsar's box. Adrian again nudged Sheremetev. Stepanov whispered to Volkonsky. This time Volkonsky spoke to the Tsar, rose, and left with Captain Stepanov.

"Come on," Adrian said to Sheremetev as he stood up. "This is my chance."

"I know what you are thinking, my friend. This sort of thing only works in operas."

"I've nothing to lose."

"I assure you, you have much to lose. We are not in America, and the rule of law does not constrain powerful men."

Adrian squeezed past Seamus's chair. "Stay here. I'm going to talk to the Tsar."

"Now?" asked Seamus.

"It's now or never."

Adrian and Sheremetev walked purposefully around the carpeted, circular concourse behind the boxes of the Belle Etage.

"What will you say to the Tsar?" asked Sheremetev.

"I'm going to tell him he's giving the project to the wrong man."

"That is a bad idea, my friend. No one tells the Tsar he has made a mistake. Not even Volkonsky would do that."

"Big risk, big reward." As they walked past the curtains to the box seats, Adrian could hear Osmin block Belmonte's progress on stage. *Of course he was blocked. It's only Act I. There's two acts to go.*

As they approached the Tsar's box, an Imperial Guard held up his hand. Sheremetev and the guard exchanged hushed words.

Sheremetev returned to Adrian. "I told him we would like to speak with the Tsar. He says the Tsar isn't in his box."

"How could the Tsar have gotten past us?"

As if to answer the question, Captain Stepanov appeared at the top of a staircase farther down the corridor. He shouldered past the guard and confronted Adrian and Sheremetev in German. "*Was sind deine absichten* [What are your intentions]?"

Adrian balled his fists as if he were ready to fight. "We were hoping to speak with the Tsar."

"The Tsar is no longer in the theater. Please return to your seat."

Adrian looked at Sheremetev, who nodded. *We have no choice.*

Adrian felt his rekindled hope of saving the mission die. *I guess it's Act III for us, and no happy ending.*

Captain Stepanov turned to speak to the guard. Then he stopped, hesitated, and turned again to address Adrian. "Perhaps there is a better use of your time than watching Mozart tonight. Your firefighter nephew, is he with you?"

"Yes, he is in the count's box on the other side of the theater."

"Do you think he would want to see how we fight fires here in Russia?"

"What do you mean?"

"Before I leave the theater, I must ensure that the detail protecting Empress Alexandra Feodorovna understands their assignment. Then I ride to the Winter Palace to oversee the Tsar's safety. Please go to your carriage. I will meet you outside in five minutes."

"What is happening?"

"Field Marshals' Hall in the Winter Palace is filled with smoke. The fire marshal has not yet found its source. The Tsar has gone to personally supervise the operation so that no artwork is damaged." He turned, thrust the curtain to the Tsar's box aside, and disappeared from view.

Maybe we're only in Act II, Adrian told himself as he and Sheremetev walked back to the count's box to get Seamus.

"Grab your cape, Nephew. It's time to go."

"Great, I'm kind of lost here. Where are we going?"

"The Winter Palace is on fire. Stepanov wants us to come with him. You're our ticket in."

"Jaysus," Seamus said as he struggled with his cape. "Where did Rian park the rig?"

* * * * *

· RIAN ·

Rian had thrown heavy horse blankets over Frank and Wash, climbed inside the carriage, wrapped herself in a horse blanket of her own, and tried to sleep. As it was well below freezing, she wasn't successful. The cold seeped into her bones.

She had to admit that she didn't like this part of being a coachman. Now that they no longer lived in the Winter Palace, nothing was as convenient as it used to be. To deliver Adrian and Seamus to the theater, she had to walk more than a mile and a half from the Anichkov Palace to the Manege. She harnessed Frank and Wash, hitched them to the landau, threw horse blankets in the boot, and drove back to the Anichkov Palace. When they arrived at Mikhailovsky Square, she entered a long queue of carriages, each carrying people of importance to the theater. Finally, after twenty minutes of starts and stops, when they arrived at the theater's entrance, Rian set the brake, hopped down to the ground, and opened the door for Adrian and Seamus.

And that wasn't even the part she didn't like. What she didn't like was freezing her rear end off for two hours while Adrian and Seamus listened to Mozart.

Without warning, the door to the carriage opened. "Wake up, Sleeping Beauty. We've got work to do."

Rian realized that perhaps she had been dozing after all. "What's happening?"

"We're not sure. Your buddy Stepanov told us there's a fire at the Winter Palace. He asked us to come along."

"Why?"

Seamus looked back toward the theater. "Dunno, but we're about to find out."

Fire in the Winter Palace on December 29, 1837, Courtesy of Alamy.

Rian drove Wash and Frank hard behind a galloping Captain Stepanov. She was almost disappointed when they reached the plaza in front of the Winter Palace. Nothing was happening. The palace certainly didn't appear to be on fire. There was no activity beyond what she would expect at nine o'clock on a Friday night.

Stepanov rode through the archway that led to the palace's massive court-yard and dismounted at the main entrance, a door that Rian had never used even in the early morning hours. She brought the horses to a halt, donned her top hat, and hopped down to open the door for her passengers, but they were already descending from the carriage.

"Gentlemen," said Stepanov in German, "I cannot offer you any closer access to the Tsar than during this occasion. He is currently taking personal charge of whatever is going on in the palace. As far as the Tsar and his staff are concerned, I invited you to observe the palace firefighters in action. In the unlikely event that you have the opportunity to speak to the Tsar about your railroad, so be it. But I caution you: step very carefully. You are walking on a knife's edge, one misstep from disaster. Disaster for you and disaster for me."

Rian started to follow the group as Stepanov led them through a phalanx of palace guards.

The captain stopped, turned to Adrian, and said, "This is no occasion for a coachman."

"Sorry, Rian," said Adrian. "We have no idea how long this is going to take. I think you should take the horses back to the Manege and go back to our apartment." He turned to catch up with the others.

Rian heard Stepanov speaking to Adrian as they walked toward the palace entrance. "Let us see how severe the situation is. Perhaps you will have an op-portunity to demonstrate your steam-powered fire pump this evening."

Disappointed, Rian mounted the carriage and urged Frank and Wash forward with a kissing sound. As she exited the courtyard through the arch-way, there was more activity in Alexander Plaza than when she had driven the carriage through it ten minutes earlier. Someone had lit fires in numerous torchères, providing islands of light around the plaza. A detail of sailors lined up and awaited orders. Strollers stopped to gawk but were kept at a distance by a growing cordon of soldiers.

Rian noticed a familiar wagon inside the cordon and reined the team in that direction. Lev sat on his driver's bench, observing the activity, his wagon half-loaded with firewood.

Rian asked in Russian, "Were you delivering wood?"

Lev nodded. "They kicked me out before I could finish."

"What's happening?"

"A lot of smoke. Especially downstairs near the apothecary. I think it's bad."

"How bad?"

"Very bad, but no one listens to a serf. We should get your fire pump. I think they are going to need it."

"That's too much for just you and me. The traces are too narrow to hitch up to a horse. It takes at least three men to haul it here. Plus, we would need all the hoses we brought from America to pump water from the river."

"We can use my wagon for the hoses. My friends can haul the pump—the same ones who helped assemble the track. Do you think your master will mind if they ride in your fine coach?"

Rian smiled. "Hop up."

Before he did so, Lev grabbed a torch from his wagon, lit it by touching it to a torchère, and climbed aboard.

With Lev giving directions, Rian led the horses about a mile to a district of St. Petersburg that she had never visited before. The streets became narrower. The dwellings became humbler, then downright shabby. There were no streetlamps, and Rian was grateful for the torchlight. They stopped in front of a lachuga—a shack that looked little more than a one-room hovel with a chimney. Lev hopped down from the driver's bench. He banged on the door and yelled. A woman opened the door. Conversation. A call over her shoulder.

Lev gestured to Rian: *stay here.* He walked down the street, and the scene was repeated three more times. One of the men who had helped with the hopper came out of the first lachuga. Rian held the carriage door open and gestured for him to get in. The man hesitated, Rian repeated the gesture, and he hopped in.

With four passengers in the landau and Lev beside her on the driver's seat, Rian returned to Alexander Plaza to pick up Lev's wagon. The scene had changed dramatically.

"We have to hurry," she told him when they arrived.

Count Sheremetev had once described the Winter Palace as a gigantic rectangle. Fire was shooting from the roof of the side nearest the Neva River. *Our old apartment is already gone*, Rian said to herself.

* * * * *

· SEAMUS ·

Seamus, Adrian, and Count Sheremetev followed Stepanov through the palace's Grand Foyer, up a massive staircase, through a gallery, and into Field Marshals' Hall. The cavernous room was filled with smoke, and it was getting thicker by the moment, seeping up through the parquet floor and filtering down from the ceiling.

Seamus's eyes stung, and he did his best not to cough. He knelt and felt the floor. It was hot to the touch. "Adrian, this is bad. There's fire both below and above. This whole room is as good as gone; they just don't know it yet. They should start taking these paintings out right now."

Captain Stepanov checked in with one of his lieutenants, then returned to the group. "The Tsar has overseen the evacuation of his children from his quarters and is now conducting a personal tour of the building with the palace fire chief. He should be returning here soon. I am told that the smoke is contained to this room."

Seamus spoke, and Adrian translated to German. "Captain Stepanov, sir. In the past few years, I've fought scores of fires in Philadelphia. I'm telling you, this room is going to be in flames soon. All this smoke isn't a sign of a fire someplace else. It's right here, above us and below us right now. You should start pulling all these paintings off the walls immediately."

"I do not have the power to make that order."

"Who is in charge here?"

"Why Tsar Nicholas, of course."

"Is the Tsar a firefighter?"

"Of course not."

"Well, that's a problem. Please, if you have any influence with the Tsar, tell him to start emptying this room and the rooms on either side."

Stepanov stiffened. "I will do my best to convey your apprehensions."

His Royal Highness Nicholas Romanov appeared through the smoke, trailed by Prince Volkonsky and an entourage. He gave every appearance of calm. Captain Stepanov left Adrian and Seamus, walked to the Tsar, and waited to be recognized. After speaking with the Tsar, he returned to the Americans. "The Tsar said thank you for your advice. The firemen believe they have found the source of the fire in the basement, and they have given it a heavy dousing of water from the water pipes built for exactly this sort of situation."

"So he isn't going to remove all this beautiful artwork? It will be destroyed."

"The Tsar has instructed his men to break the windows to clear out the smoke in this room. That should prevent the artwork from receiving further damage."

"Captain, I'm telling you this room is already lost, but you still have time to clear the paintings. Right now the fires above us and below us are smoldering for lack of oxygen. That's what is producing all this smoke. If you break open these windows, that will give the fires just what they need to spring to life. You will have an inferno on your hands in minutes."

Seamus's vehemence took Stepanov back a bit. "Come with me."

With Seamus in tow, Stepanov returned to the Tsar's circle, but this time was prevented from speaking with him by Volkonsky. Stepanov and the gatekeeper exchanged words. From the gestures, Seamus thought Stepanov was doing a pretty good job explaining Seamus's apprehensions to the Tsar's advisor. The captain pointed to Seamus a couple of times.

Volkonsky relented and allowed Stepanov to approach the Tsar. Stepanov again made his case to the Tsar of All the Russias. Again, Stepanov pointed to Seamus. The Tsar looked at Volkonsky, a look that needed no translation. *What do you think?*

Volkonsky scowled and responded with a dismissive shake of his head.

The Tsar pointed to the windows that faced the courtyard—a broad, sweeping gesture that meant *break them all.* Volkonsky left the group and spoke to an army officer who, in turn, gave orders to his men to start breaking windows, which they did with great enthusiasm.

Stepanov returned to the Americans. "I am sorry, gentlemen. The Tsar has chosen to ignore your advice. And now we have all made a powerful enemy. Volkonsky is not happy with my actions. However, if this fire is as severe as you say it is, perhaps now would be a good time to demonstrate that fire pump of yours."

Prince Volkonsky broke off from his place at the Tsar's side and strode to their group. Count Sheremetev translated for the Americans. "Captain, these adventurers do not belong here. The Winter Palace has a fire brigade of more than two hundred men whose sole assignment is to deal with fires such as this. Please have your men escort them out of the building."

Sheremetev finished his translation and gestured toward the door that led to the staircase and the Grand Foyer. "Gentlemen, we have played our hand to the best of our ability. The cards were not with us tonight.

Seamus reluctantly allowed himself to be herded. "They are making a big mistake."

"I believe you," replied Sheremetev. "In a hundred years, the palace fire brigade has never had to cope with a fire in the Winter Palace. They have no experience. In all the time that I have spent in this building, I have never even seen them practice their profession. Or maintain their equipment, for that matter."

Before they reached the staircase, angry flames started licking at the ceiling twenty feet above them, fed by increasingly stiff gusts sucked through the shattered windows.

Sheremetev put his hand out, halting Adrian and Seamus. "Perhaps we should tarry just a bit, my friends." They kept their positions for five minutes. A cold wind whipped through the windows. The flames grew to the point that Adrian could hear them crackle above him.

Captain Stepanov left his position near the Tsar, strode to Adrian, and addressed him in German. "Breaking the windows appears to have been a mistake. The palace fire crew will soon be running fire hoses into the building. The Tsar now fears the water from the hoses will damage the paintings and has given the order to start pulling artwork off the wall."

"Right decision for the wrong reasons," Seamus said above the din. "Captain, this fire is moments away from becoming a monster. I recommend taking everything out that can burn. Not just the artwork. Our job now is to slow this fire down by taking away its fuel."

Adrian grabbed Seamus by the elbow. "Come on, Nephew. There's not much we can do here."

Seamus watched as the first embers descended from the ceiling to the parquet floor, charring the heavily oiled wood. "Do you think it's a good time to say 'I told you so' to the Tsar of All the Russias?"

* * * * *

Seamus, Adrian, and the count walked into the bitter cold of the palace courtyard and faced two phalanxes of sailors and soldiers awaiting orders. "Sheremetev," said Seamus. "Those men are just standing around. Someone should tell them to go into the palace and strip out everything of value."

"Only their commanders can do that."

"Then you must convince their commanders."

"I have no idea who is in charge out here."

"I think that is a problem all the way around." With that, Seamus grabbed Adrian by the arm and said, "I'm going back in."

"Nephew, Volkonsky made it quite clear. Our help isn't wanted. We finally caught the Tsar's attention, and he wasn't pleased with us. We should just go back home."

"Adrian, I know we're not gonna stay in Russia. But this entire palace is going to burn down. There are treasures here—masterpieces that will be lost forever if we don't do something."

Adrian looked back at the facade of the Winter Palace. He could see flames coming from the roof above Field Marshals' Hall. "Okay, I'll go in with you. So, where do we start?"

"I don't know. Grab whatever's nearest the door." The two Americans dashed back into the building. Seamus turned to urge the soldiers and sailors to follow them. None did. Just inside the main entrance, the walls of the immense anteroom were lined with artwork, statues, mirrors, and chairs.

Seamus pulled at the first painting he came to, a portrait of a young woman in an ornate gilded frame. It resisted. It had been hung by a single wire on a hook, but it freed from the hook only after he lifted the painting high with both hands. He felt the frame bend and realized how fragile it was. "Each painting is going to be a chore, Uncle!"

Seamus turned to exit the building with perhaps the most precious object he had ever held. Adrian did the same with another painting. At an awkward run, they carried the paintings past the soldiers. *Interesting: No one's helping, but no one's trying to stop us, either.* They carted the paintings across the hundred yards of the courtyard, through the archway, to the Alexander Column in the middle of the plaza, and leaned them against the giant column's pedestal.

Seamus turned and started running back to the palace. He passed Sheremetev arguing with a military officer. He and Adrian reentered the building. Still, no one followed them.

Out again with two more paintings. This time a soldier met him in the middle of the courtyard and grabbed the painting, saying something in Russian that Seamus interpreted as *I'll take it from here* but could just as easily have been *You're a damn fool for doing this.*

Seamus and Adrian ran back in to grab more artwork—in this instance, a painting of a Napoleonic era battle that barely fit through the enormous front door of the palace and took both of them working together to maneuver. Two sailors grabbed the painting from them on the steps to the palace entrance. Seamus and Adrian returned to the anteroom. When they arrived at the door a third time with more artwork, a handful of men were waiting for them. An officer in the courtyard was giving orders and pointing to Seamus. Soldiers and sailors started to enter the building.

Seamus positioned himself in the middle of the anteroom, pointed at a painting on the wall, and yelled to a young sailor to grab the painting off the wall and take it to the column. *That kid has no idea what you're saying, Bucko. But I guess he's figuring it out.*

A navy officer joined Seamus and started yelling orders to whomever entered the anteroom. Smoke from Field Marshals' Hall found its way down to them, forcing Seamus to cough. *The fire will pass through this room like buckshot through a rotten apple.* At Seamus's direction, army and navy personnel rescued artifacts and returned for more.

Rian appeared at Seamus's side, her coachman's livery burned, face smudged, determined. "Seamus, we're having problems getting the pump going!" she yelled over the cries of the sailors. "We need your help!"

"Rian, you shouldn't be here. Otto will kill me if you get hurt. You're wasting your time. Our little pump will be useless against this fire. My time is better spent here!" he hollered back.

Rian spun around one entire revolution in frustration. "My men have connected fifteen hundred feet of hose all the way to the river. We need your help!"

Seamus was about to refuse a second time when he thought, *well, we brought our little pump to demonstrate it to the Tsar. If this isn't the proper occasion, I don't know what is.* "Okay, come on!" He made eye contact with the navy officer, silently ceding control to him, and ran out the door. When he arrived at the fire pump, he realized Rian had not followed him out of the burning palace.

* * * * *

· RIAN ·

Rian joined the growing stream of soldiers and sailors who were pulling paintings off the walls and taking them outside. But it wasn't only artwork. Men grabbed chairs, side tables, and busts of men looking heroically into the distance. When they cleared out the anteroom, they moved up the sumptuous grand staircase to another hall where the smoke was even thicker. Rian pulled a painting off the wall and started to descend the staircase but was met by a soldier who grabbed the painting from her and, in turn, handed it to another soldier partway down the stairs.

She became part of a "bucket brigade" that passed artwork down the stairs. Smoke made her cough and burned her eyes. Someone passed by, handing out torn strips from a curtain to tie over her mouth. When artwork stopped flowing down the bucket brigade, she again ascended the stairs to find another painting.

The upper floor was hotter than the anteroom had been. When everything that could burn was cleared out, they moved to the next hall. Then the next. Officers shouted orders. More soldiers and sailors joined the effort.

She occasionally spotted Adrian hustling out a painting or a statue, some-times giving orders to men who probably couldn't understand him.

Seamus appeared and grabbed her arm. "Come with me!" he yelled over the mayhem of men yelling. Rian thought he was going to pull her out of the building, but instead, he led her to the Small Throne Room. The hall's floor sagged slightly in the middle, and Rian saw fire in the ceiling at the far corner. With the help of two seamen, they lifted the jewel-encrusted throne of Peter the Great, which was much heavier than she thought it would be. They worked their way through smoke-filled halls, now denuded of anything that could be removed, down the grand staircase, through the anteroom, and into the courtyard.

Seamus wiped sweat from his eyes but only succeeded in smearing soot around his face. "Have you seen your uncle?"

"Yeah. He's around someplace."

"You stay here. I'm making one more trip in."

"I'm going with you."

Seamus picked up a banner that some army private had probably dropped as he carried an armload of items to Alexander Square. "I'm not going to waste time arguing. Just keep up with me."

They ascended the staircase, picking their way around a burning section of ceiling that had fallen. Coughing, Rian tightened the cloth around her face.

"Stay low! Grab onto this banner! Stay with me!"

Rian did as she was told. The smoke stung her eyes. She coughed violently but gripped the banner tightly and kept up with Seamus. A window shattered outward. The smoke gushed into the courtyard and threatened to pull her with it.

A burning chandelier fell to the floor, driving two sailors to their knees. Men ran to their rescue.

"Hang onto the banner!" yelled Seamus. "Don't slow down!"

They entered St. George's Hall. The only other time Rian had been in this room, the flirty lady-in-waiting had told Seamus and Adrian that the throne in this room was the Tsar's most prized possession. Now the hall's ceiling was ablaze. They picked their way to the alcove that held the throne and tried to lift it. It was far too heavy for two people, especially when one of them was thirteen.

Two men joined them, and together they carried the throne toward the staircase. That was when Rian realized that one of the men with her was Tsar Nicholas I, the most powerful man in the world. The other man was Cap-tain Stepanov, whom she hadn't seen since he had prevented her from entering the building three hours ago. They passed the throne off to four sailors, who muscled the Tsar's most precious possession out of the building.

* * * * *

· SEAMUS ·

"Okay, that's it for you and me, Cousin," Seamus said to Rian when they reached the courtyard. "We've done our bit."

He was gratified to take a breath untainted by acrid smoke, but the winter cold immediately braced him. Seamus and Rian walked across the courtyard and stopped at the archway. Count Sheremetev was yelling and gesturing over the din at Prince Volkonsky, who was at the Tsar's side. Sheremetev saw Seamus and pointed at him.

Seamus turned and looked at the fire. A strong wind from the east freshened the fire, which had now engulfed the palace's northeast corner. Seamus could predict its path right down the north side of the palace toward the concert hall and the royal family's quarters. He knew it was merely a matter of time before the other three sides suffered the same fate.

The Tsar had apparently come to the same conclusion. Soldiers and sailors, now more than a thousand in number, were running into every entry to the building, gathering anything combustible, carrying it to Alexander Plaza, and returning to the conflagration.

Sheremetev left his conversation with Volkonsky and approached Seamus. "Thank you for your help. The Tsar is very appreciative."

"How's your fire expert doing?"

Sheremetev reflexively looked over his shoulder and pulled Seamus farther away from Volkonsky. "Now is not the time to make sarcastic remarks about His Majesty. He has abandoned hope of saving any of the Winter Palace. The task now is to remove precious objects from the building."

Seamus counted ten hand-pumped fire engines in the courtyard. Some were showering water on the blaze in the northwest corner of the building. "Those pumps are like pissing on a bonfire. They're not doing a lick of good. What happened to the in-house fire department that Volkonsky was bragging about?"

"Their machinery broke in the first hour, as did many of the palace's mobile pumps. The pumps brought by the city's fire brigades have done better. But now, even some of them are breaking. It is so cold that the water freezes in the hoses as soon as they stop pumping."

"What about the Hermitage? Is the Tsar going to try to save that?"

"That is what he and Volkonsky are discussing now."

"Count, tell the Tsar that the only way to save the Hermitage is to destroy the connecting passageways between the palace and the Hermitage. He needs to interrupt the path of the fire."

"I'm afraid the Tsar is not prone to listen to me."

Seamus kicked a kitchen pot that a soldier had rescued, a rescue that was a doubly wasted effort because the pot had little value and certainly wasn't going to fuel the fire. He watched a handful of fire brigades valiantly trying to douse the flames. *No number of fire pumps could put this fire out.*

He spotted the Freeman Hydraulics fire pump a hundred feet away. Adrian was aiming a fire hose at flames licking out a first-floor window. Serfs and a few soldiers hauled hoses heavily laden with water behind him. Rian had left Seamus's side to chuck firewood from a wagon into the pump's firebox.

Seamus strode toward the fire pump and shouldered into Adrian. "Time to pull the machine out of the courtyard, Uncle," he screamed above the chaos all about them. "This whole side of the building is as good as lost."

"There are soldiers in there!" yelled Adrian.

You said you were done for the night, Boyo. Now's not the time to do anything stupid, Seamus said to himself. He surveyed the courtyard, now littered with items rescued from the burning palace but dropped along the way to the plaza beyond the archway. He spotted a heavy woolen greatcoat, much thicker than the cape he had worn to the opera. He donned the coat, noting that it was a bit small but would serve its purpose. *This and me leather gloves'll protect me a bit from the heat.*

He again shouldered into Adrian, this time offering to take charge of the nozzle. His uncle seemed grateful for the relief.

Seamus directed the stream at a first-floor window, momentarily setting back the flames licking through. "I'm going to need help! Find me someone who can watch me back!"

Adrian gave Seamus a boost through the window. Peasants and soldiers muscled the hose in after him, then hiked Adrian in after the hose. He landed on all fours on the floor of a large room.

Seamus helped Adrian up. "Sure you want to do this, Uncle?"

"It had to be me. You don't speak Russian, and they don't speak English."

Seamus surveyed the large hall that had been stripped of its artwork. Both the ceiling and the floor were on fire. "Okay, your job is pretty simple. You're me extra eyes and hands. Watch me back. Make sure nothing's going on behind me that's going to kill me. Muscle the hose after me so I can concentrate on training the water where it's supposed to go."

Adrian nodded and Seamus directed a generous stream at a doomed staircase still in use by soldiers carrying artifacts of all sizes.

Our little fire pump is the gem I hoped it would be, he thought to himself. *Doing just what I designed it to do. What a workhorse.*

The peasants fed the hose farther into the hall. Seamus advanced. Adrian followed. A gilded wooden chandelier, already in flames, crashed to the floor. Seamus hosed it down and returned the stream to the staircase. A soldier ran down the stairs, his clothing on fire. Seamus doused him with water.

Soldiers and sailors descended the staircase and passed the chattel through broken windows into the eager hands of more soldiers and sailors. Seamus continued directing water onto the staircase until it was too ablaze for the soldiers to ascend and no one was coming down.

Fifteen minutes later, with the fire winning, Adrian grabbed at his coat and yelled, "You're wanted outside!"

Seamus looked around the hall. He had slowed the fire down a bit, and the effort had probably saved some lives. *Time to get out, Boyo.* When he left the hall through the window, Sheremetev was waiting for him. "The Tsar wants to talk to you!"

* * * * *

Tsar Nicholas and his entourage had moved to the southeast corner of the massive building, one of the places where the palace connected to the Hermitage. An officer of the Imperial Guard allowed Seamus and Sheremetev through a perimeter of soldiers surrounding the Tsar. However, Volkonsky put up his hand to stop them and physically put himself between them and the Tsar.

"Sheremetev," said Seamus, "tell Volkonsky that the only way to stop the fire is to create a firebreak. We have to destroy the connections between the Winter Palace and the Hermitage, top to bottom, and clear away all the debris!"

Sheremetev translated his words to Volkonsky. The prince turned to speak to the Tsar, but Nicholas held up his hand, impatiently signaling that he had heard Sheremetev's words. The Tsar pointed to the passageway that connected the Winter Palace to the Hermitage. A group of soldiers started attacking it with axes and crowbars.

Sheremetev nodded and turned to Seamus. "You have permission to work your destruction."

"Count, how many connections are there between the palace and the Hermitage?"

"Three. This one, the one in the middle at the Large Throne Room, and the one at the northeast corner of the building, near where you used to live."

"The Throne Room was on fire an hour ago. Our old apartments near the Flying Gallery are gone. The wind is coming from the east, so the fire is roaring toward the rest of the palace but creeping toward the Hermitage. We've still got time,"

Sheremetev nodded. "Go all the way around the Hermitage to get to the Flying Gallery. You will have to take care of that before you can get to the fire in the Large Throne Room. It will be very hot between the buildings. You would need a fire pump to lead the way."

"Well, we just happen to have one of those. I'll need some men to move the fire pump and the hoses."

"Of course," was the count's only reply. He beckoned to an army officer, and in short order, Seamus had fifteen soldiers and sailors.

Rian and her serfs were still in the courtyard, training a stream of water on the west side of the palace, when Seamus and his men commandeered the Freeman Hydraulics fire pump. Moving the engine and hose in fifteen-degree weather was no small task. Fortunately, as their work would occur closer to the Neva, they didn't need all fifteen hundred feet of hoses. They piled what they needed onto Lev's wagon, which was still partially laden with firewood.

Seamus grabbed an axe from an abandoned fire pump and signaled some soldiers to throw a wooden extension ladder onto the wagon. As he again passed the Tsar's entourage, he buttonholed Sheremetev. "Count, I wish we had some grappling hooks."

"Warehouses for the Baltic Fleet are a few miles from here. How many do you want?"

"All of them."

Sheremetev spoke to a naval officer who nodded and hurried away. Rotating teams of three hauled the fire pump around the Hermitage to the northeast corner of the Winter Palace.

* * * * *

How come you never volunteer for the easy jobs, Boyo? Seamus muttered to himself as he stared up at the Flying Gallery from the courtyard. At the northeast corner of the palace, the Flying Gallery was an ornate enclosed passageway, a bridge between the second stories of the palace and the Hermitage. To his right, flames had engulfed the entire length of the northern side of the palace. To his left stood the Hermitage with all its precious artwork.

Straight ahead, a good three hundred feet away, was the two-story connection between the Large Throne Room and the Hermitage. His work this evening wouldn't be done until all three connections were destroyed or the fire had beat them and leaped to the Hermitage. *One step at a time, Boyo.*

Rian's serfs arrived with the fire pump, a wagonload of hoses, and two more ladders that were immediately commandeered by a crew of sailors. Despite the cold, Rian's men primed the hoses, and the engine pumped a stream of water from the Neva onto anything that burned.

Seamus leaned into Rian so he could be heard above the roar of the fire. "Here's what we are going to do. I'm going to get up on the roof and start chopping holes. You're my translator. Direct two crews to cut through whatever beams connect this gallery wall to the palace and the Hermitage. If they question the orders of a thirteen-year-old, tell them the orders came from me. Have them work from both inside and out. Once we do that, we'll pull the son of a bitch down with grappling hooks."

Rian nodded her understanding and turned to start giving orders.

Seamus extended the wooden ladder to its full thirty-foot height and leaned it against the roof of the Flying Gallery. Axe in hand, he climbed to the roof and chopped away at wooden shingles. Soldiers with axes and crowbars joined him. Seamus could see Rian gesturing at the men down below.

Seamus and the soldiers chopped and pried two holes in the roof. Other crews attacked the walls at each end of the Flying Gallery from the inside and the outside. Captain Stepanov arrived with a dozen soldiers and teams of three horses. A crew of sailors ran up with armloads of grappling hooks and ropes. A sailor threw two of them to Seamus.

Seamus inserted a grappling hook into the first hole and pulled hard until it bit securely into the wall. A soldier did the same at the other hole. Soldiers hitched the ropes to two teams of horses and led their teams forward until there was no slack left in the ropes. Seamus stuck his head down through the hole and yelled to the men who were attacking the gallery wall. It took some wild gesturing, but they retreated to the safety of the Hermitage. Seamus and his men walked to the roof of the Hermitage. Seamus signaled to Stepanov below, yelling, "Pull, you bastards, pull!"

The soldiers whipped the frightened horses into action. The wall came crashing down to the ground, the horses continued pulling, and miraculously much of the wall remained in one piece as the horses dragged it toward the Neva. The roof of the Flying Gallery, now unsupported along one entire side, sagged dramatically but showed no inclination to depart without a fight.

You knew this wouldn't be easy, Boyo, Seamus said to himself.

* * * * *

The crew attacked the once ornate connecting walkway between the two buildings for the better part of an hour. They succeeded in pulling off half the roof and feverishly worked to weaken its remaining wall. The flames in the Winter Palace were becoming more intense, making it impossible to spend more than seconds at the western end of the gallery. One rope that Seamus had risked his life to attach to a beam had burned through before the horses could pull the beam off. The fire crew occasionally doused his wooden ladder because it caught fire.

The floor of the well-mauled Flying Gallery didn't sag the least bit. Seamus latched hooks to the last beam supporting the remaining roof so that the teams of horses below could work their destruction. He checked to ensure no one remained on the connector and stepped to the safety of the doorway to the Hermitage, one floor above the ground. He signaled the guardsmen to start pulling. Only then did he realize the people standing next to him were Rian and Captain Stepanov.

"You shouldn't be here, Cousin. I've already seen men die tonight."

"So have I," responded Rian. "The captain asked me to come up with him to translate. He says the joists that support the floor of the Flying Gallery are made of iron. You won't be able to chop through them."

The guardsmen urged their horses forward. The beam, roof, and the last wall of the gallery crashed to the ground. The horses hauled much of the wall away in one piece, and a company of soldiers shoved it down the embankment to the river. Soldiers attacked the remaining debris with crowbars, axes, and sledgehammers.

"You've got to leave. It's too dangerous," said Seamus.

Rian didn't acknowledge Seamus's order. "The captain also says that you should leave this to the soldiers. The Tsar has pulled everyone out of the Winter Palace. He's given it up to the fire."

"What time is it?"

Rian pulled out her pocket watch. "Almost three."

We've been fighting this fire for five hours, Seamus said to himself. "How much did they save?"

"Of the building? By the time it'll be over, almost nothing. Of the artwork? Almost everything."

"What's the story on the connection at the southeast corner of the palace?"

"It's demolished. All the debris has been moved away. They're moving operations to the connection at the Large Throne Room. They want you to do the same thing from the other side."

"Okay, I'm going. But this is it for you. You may not follow me. It's too dangerous."

"I won't follow you."

Seamus nodded and descended the ladder, which was now charred in many places.

* * * * *

· RIAN ·

I told Seamus I wouldn't follow him, but I didn't tell him I would leave here, Rian thought to herself as she grabbed an axe. *There's still flooring connected to the iron supports that can be cleared off.*

As if he had read her thoughts, Captain Stepanov grabbed the axe out of her hand and cautioned her with a wave of his index finger.

Rian relented. From her vantage point in the now denuded second-floor doorway to the Hermitage, she watched Seamus pass under the iron beams, gesturing to soldiers and her peasants to follow him with the Freeman Hydraulics fire pump.

Another pump appeared, and a crew of sailors climbed the charred wooden ladder to the gallery floor. Other sailors hauled the hose up to them. The additional height of the second floor allowed them to direct a flow of water into the burning palace as well as onto the walls of the Hermitage.

Stepanov walked out onto the gallery, dodged the flow of water, and attacked the floor with his axe. Rian heard his axe clang and clang again. *I guess he was right about the iron.*

Stepanov grabbed a crowbar from a soldier and pried at the wood flooring. Another soldier braved fire that had been momentarily checked by the stream of water. He attached a grappling hook to the exposed iron beam. A soldier did the same at Rian's end. Rian looked down toward the palace embankment. Illuminated by the fire, she spotted Prince Volkonsky. The prince stooped to pick up a shattered shard of board.

Her danger sense kicked in just as things happened at once.

"Captain! Get off the bridge!" she yelled.

Stepanov looked at Rian and took in the activity on the ground. Volkonsky smacked one of the horses on the hindquarters with the board, then walked to the other team and hit another horse. Stepanov grabbed a young soldier and shoved him toward Rian, who was standing in the safety of the exposed doorway to the Hermitage.

Horses neighed. Both teams shouldered their young handlers aside and bolted away from the fire. The ropes to the grappling hooks tightened. Stepanov could have followed the soldier and arrived at the doorway safely. Instead, he turned to save three more soldiers who were directing a stream of water toward the palace.

The iron beam rotated, throwing Stepanov and the three soldiers off the bridge and to the ground fifteen feet below.

"No!" yelled Rian.

Then one end of the beam fell, bringing burning debris along with it. Much of the debris landed directly on Stepanov.

Rian turned and ran into the Hermitage, down a hallway, down a stairway, out a door, and to the pile of debris that moments ago had been part of the Flying Gallery. Sailors pulled Stepanov and the three soldiers out of the rubble. Four Imperial Guardsmen appeared with an ornately carved door and lifted their captain onto it.

Rian walked next to him as the four guardsmen carted him away. She swept away the little remaining firewood from Lev's wagon to make room for the severely injured captain. The guardsmen lifted him into the wagon and took the door back to the site of the accident to retrieve the injured soldiers.

Stepanov grabbed Rian by the collar and pulled her close. "Child, listen to me," he said with a raspy voice. "I have been in enough battles to know I am dying."

"No," pled Rian, although she knew Stepanov was right.

"I have a message for your Count Sheremetev. I know he is trying to change the face of Russia. But Nicholas will never change. He is a lost cause. Tell the count he still has a chance with the children. The boys, Alexander and Konstantin, they will come to power someday. They may be motivated to make the changes that their father cannot. But he must get to them soon." With that, Captain Stepanov released his grip on Rian's collar, closed his eyes, and took his last breath.

Rian looked up to see the malevolent figure of Prince Volkonsky silhouetted by the inferno. The Minister of the Imperial Court, gatekeeper to the Tsar, guardian of Russian tradition, and murderer of Captain Stepanov watched her for a moment, then turned and walked away.

SUNDAY, DECEMBER 31
(DECEMBER 19 O.S.)

· ADRIAN ·

The fire had raged for thirty hours—all through the long Russian night, the five daylight hours, and well past midnight the second evening. It had consumed all four sides of the Winter Palace and was finally burning itself out. The Hermitage had been saved.

Adrian and Seamus leaned into the back of Lev's wagon, where Rian was sleeping, wrapped in a bearskin rug salvaged from the fire.

They stared ahead at nothing, merely nodding when a member of the Tsar's kitchen staff handed them black coffee, incongruously in cups of fine imperial-crested china that moments before had been in a heap somewhere on the plaza. They didn't even bother to stand when they were joined at the wagon by Tsar Nicholas I and his two wolfhounds.

Now the older of the Tsar's two large dogs sat at attention in the wagon, observing with distrust everyone who came within the Imperial Guards' perimeter. The younger one lay curled up next to the sleeping Rian. The two Americans and the Russian Tsar were bone-tired and covered with soot. Their exhaustion was evident on their faces and the slack of their shoulders. Their clothing was torn and burned, and they all had severe burns on their hands and faces.

The plaza still pulsed with activity, but not with the urgency of a day ago, and none of the three paid much attention. Fire hoses snaked from the Neva River to the pumps, but of the twenty hand-pumped engines that had arrived on the scene from all over St. Petersburg, only ten were still serviceable. The rest had broken down and long ago been scavenged for parts. Ambulances, bucket brigades, spectators, Imperial Guards, soldiers and seamen, displaced staff—all were ignored by the exhausted trio.

Soldiers surrounded mountains of chattel salvaged from the palace. Priceless paintings were thrown together with more mundane items: tables, chairs, pots and pans, a chandelier, tapestries, a globe on its stand, and clothing. Statues and grandfather clocks stabilized stacks of china. There were bureaus filled with items, bureaus without their drawers, and drawers without their bureaus. A butcher block table, desks, and the records of state were thrown together with boots, shoes, slippers, and a box of toys. Books, ledgers, maps, diaries, files, and portfolios had been piled so high that the stacks had long ago fallen over.

Captain Stepanov's replacement attempted to drape a blanket over the Tsar, but Nicholas waved him away. Although a ring of Imperial Guards surrounded the wagon, the occupants were in far less jeopardy than they had been during many of the past thirty hours.

"*Du sprichst Deutsch* [You speak German]," the Tsar said to Adrian.

"*Da*, I was born in Wurttemberg, but I sailed to America when I was twenty."

The Tsar cradled his coffee cup in his hands. "What did you say your name was?"

"I am Adrian Krieger. This is Seamus Gallagher."

"Why are you here?"

"We came to put out the fire. Seamus is a fireman back home."

"No, why are you here in Russia?"

"Count Sheremetev invited us to move here from America. To help you build your railroad. From St. Petersburg to Moscow."

The Tsar shook his head and snorted. "So, you are the ones. They told me you were fortune hunters."

Adrian nodded without speaking. He didn't think the Tsar was referring to Sheremetev.

"Are you and your companion as good at building locomotives as you are at fighting fires?"

Adrian lifted his tired and injured arm to point at the Freeman Hydraulics steam-powered fire pump, one of the few pumps still operating. "Do you see that fire pump over there? Notice that none of the men are pumping, yet the stream of water is stronger than any others. It is powered by steam. We built it. We brought it with us as an example of our craftsmanship. I never dreamed it would ever be demonstrated in this manner."

"A more complex machine than the pumps that we have. You should have brought more of them."

Seamus gave a slight shake of his head. "This was the biggest fire I have ever seen," he said while Adrian translated for the Tsar. "We had no chance of putting this fire out, even if we had twenty more fire pumps. Our only hope was to prevent it from spreading farther. I am sorry we couldn't do more."

"Had you not been here, Mother Russia would have lost many more treasures. I want to thank you for your valiant efforts. Your coachman, as well. I believe he was with us when we rescued the throne."

* * * * *

Before they parted from the Tsar, Adrian told him that his firemen could keep the Freeman Hydraulics fire pump, thinking that if nothing else came of this trip, Jules could use that fact in his advertising. Adrian and Seamus woke Rian. They trudged back to their accommodations in the Anichkov Palace, thankful to have been evicted from the Tsar's home a month ago. They did, however, find that they now had roommates. The fire displaced three thousand occupants of the Winter Palace—staff, bureaucrats, palace guards, and guests. Someone took the liberty of opening the Americans' suite and allowing a dozen or so staff to encamp there.

"This place is reminding me more and more like home," said Seamus. "The Gallagher family's always squeezing into some apartment that used to be somebody's bedroom." He was so tired that he didn't even mind. He stepped over the forms of six people sleeping on the floor, pushed an additional sleeper over to the far side of his bed, and flopped down beside him. He didn't bother to take off his shoes.

* * * * *

· ADRIAN ·

It was noon before the exhausted Americans rose from their beds. An hour later, they had worked their way to a temporary dining area in the Anichkov Palace that, until yesterday, had been a reception hall. Adrian, Seamus, and Rian were downing porridge at a makeshift table—two planks on sawhorses. They sat in delicate Louis XIV chairs that house staff had carried from other rooms in the palace.

Adrian was pleased that no one else was sitting with them. "One thing I have to say about the Tsar: He showed no lack of bravery the other night."

Seamus, still on guard, looked around to ensure that there were no eavesdroppers. "No braver than anyone sitting at this table."

"Still, we have to give him credit when credit is due."

"I'll tell you, Uncle," said Seamus. "I think it's a good thing we're leaving. The Tsar didn't know what he was doing the other night. He made a passel of bad decisions, or he made the right decision half an hour later than he should have."

"I'll grant you that."

"Plus, I can already sense that his people are trying to make this seem like less of a disaster than it is. We know that men died last night because we saw it happen, yet they're already telling stories about what a miracle it was that no one was killed."

Rian, who had been silent all morning, stirred her porridge. "Prince Volkonsky meant to pull the iron beam down while Captain Stepanov was on it. I think he meant to kill him, and he was willing to kill three other men to do it."

Seamus turned to Rian. "Why would he do that?"

"I don't know. Because of us? We wouldn't have been there if the captain hadn't brought us over from the theater. We know he doesn't want us to build the Tsar's railroad."

Seamus considered Rian's statement and looked at Adrian. "Do you think he's that ruthless?"

Adrian ate his last spoonful of porridge and brusquely pushed the bowl away. "For the past two months, we've been living in a world we don't understand. I have no way to tell how far people are willing to go to get what they want. I have no idea what people in power can do and get away with here."

"I tell you, Adrian, I believe Rian. The rules are as harsh here as they are for the Irish and the Negroes in America. Prince Volkonsky doesn't like us. I think it's long past time to go."

Count Sheremetev appeared with a bowl of porridge and sat down with them. "Good morning, gentlemen. I was hoping I would find you here. Did you get any sleep?"

Seamus half rose and shook the count's hand. "A bit crowded in our quarters last night, but we did okay."

"It's going to remain crowded for some time. The Tsar has moved his entire family here."

Seamus looked heavenward, as if a miracle had happened. "Well, you wanted us to get close to the Tsar. It looks like we're closer now than we've ever been. Too bad, because it's nigh time to leave."

"Yes, I want to talk to you about that."

"We were just talking," said Seamus. "We ought to pack up and get out of these people's way. They've got a lot of work to do."

"Well, you're right about that. It seems that getting noticed by the Tsar is no longer as important as it used to be. I think you should move over to my house."

Adrian had visited the count in his "house." Although nowhere near the size of the Winter Palace, his Italianate palazzo was much larger than any building in Philadelphia—by a lot. "You mean until we can take a sleigh out of here?"

"Oh no, not at all. I mean until you can find suitable long-term accommodations. It seems you three rough-hewn Americans made a favorable impression on His Majesty. A lot has happened in the last two days. The Tsar is not happy with the advice Prince Volkonsky gave him during the fire. Nor is the fact that the palace fire brigade was woefully unprepared lost on His Majesty. That also ends up at Volkonsky's doorstep."

"Good," said Seamus. "I don't like that bastard."

"Well, he is at least temporarily—how do you say this?—in the doghouse. His Royal Highness has chosen to listen to others, at least for the moment, on many issues. As this pertains to you, the Tsar has changed his mind. He wants you to build his railroad."

Adrian was stunned. *A moment ago, I was set to make an arduous journey home with my tail between my legs. Now, I have the blessing of the most powerful man in the world to engage in a momentous construction project.*

Seamus's spoon clanged into his porridge dish. "Yeah, well, we've got some information for you. Rian thinks Volkonsky killed Captain Stepanov on purpose. Rian was with Stepanov when he died."

Sheremetev turned to Rian. "I'm sorry about your friend, Rian. I know you thought highly of him."

"The captain told me something to pass on to you before he died. He said that the Tsar will never change. But his sons will come to power sometime, and you should put your efforts into educating them about changing Russia."

Sheremetev's face turned somber. "It seems I misjudged your friend Captain Stepanov, Rian. I wish we had revealed our true sentiments to one another. He would have made a valuable ally. All of us who want to bring fundamental change to Russia have had to be so careful since the Decembrist Revolt. The secret police are everywhere, and we don't know if anyone amongst us is an informant."

"Can anything be done to punish Volkonsky?" asked Rian.

Sheremetev shook his head. "He may be out of favor at the moment, but he is also a competent administrator and slavishly devoted to the Tsar. Ultimately, that loyalty will put him back in the Emperor's good graces."

The Tsar wants me to build his railroad. If I say yes to this, I'll be in Russia for years, thought Adrian. *The plotting, the intrigue—I'll become a part of it. And people will plot against us. Do I want this kind of life for my family and me?* He turned to Sheremetev. "Do you think you can get to the Tsar's sons?"

Sheremetev leaned back in his chair. "Until an hour ago, I would have been at a loss. Now it seems we have some possibilities. Tsarevich Alexander is only nineteen."

"Where was he the other night?" asked Seamus. "I don't believe I saw him when his da kept running back into the palace."

"There is no cause to judge him, Seamus. That same night there was a huge fire at the naval barracks on Vasilyevsky Island. The Tsar sent him there to supervise the firefighters. It was the first opportunity for the Tsarevich to show some leadership."

"How did he do?"

Sheremetev looked around the hall and leaned in conspiratorially. "Better than his father. Your information, Rian, couldn't come at a better time. We will forever be in Captain Stepanov's debt."

"The fire has changed so much," said Adrian.

"It gets even more interesting," said Sheremetev with a smile. "The Tsar has asked Alexander to take a special interest in the railroad. Adrian and Seamus, you will meet regularly with the Tsarevich."

Adrian grinned. "Now isn't that convenient. Alexander will someday be Tsar, and you hope to influence him while he is young and impressionable. Maybe 1838 is looking up for us after all." *I will be at a pivot point in history. If Seamus and I say the right words at the right time, we can change the fate of millions of people.*

"So I guess we don't get to see Paris," said Seamus.

Sheremetev shrugged. "The news gets better. I told you His Majesty was impressed with all three of you Americans. I included Rian in that. He saw Rian dash many times into the burning building to rescue artwork, capped off when you, Seamus, and you, Rian, were with him when he rescued his throne. He believes you are a very courageous thirteen-year-old."

Rian continued to stir her porridge but showed little interest in eating it. "Captain Stepanov was there as well."

Sheremetev nodded in agreement. "Yes, he was, and I am sorry about his death. But that is not my point. Rian, your days as a coachman are behind you. You are going to need a new set of clothes. Tsar Nicholas hopes that your bravery is contagious. He wants you to become the companion of Konstantin, the Tsarevich Alexander's little brother."

Adrian stared at Sheremetev, then at Rian. *This is not good. Ambassador Dallas knows Rian is a girl. He told us that if she is discovered, there will be hell to pay. Now the Tsar wants Rian to rub elbows with his son. Seamus and I may be sticking around here, but one way or another, Rian has to leave as soon as the ice breaks in the Baltic Sea.*

* * * * *

· RIAN ·

Rian folded her arms in front of her. She stared right into Uncle Adrian's eyes. "No, I'm not going home. You can't make me."

Sheremetev had sent a small army of servants to the Anichkov Palace to pack up the Americans' possessions and move them to his home.

During the packing, Adrian pulled Rian into her former bedroom, which was stripped down to its furnishings. "Rian, I was okay with you pretending to be a boy when you were our coachman. But I told you what Ambassador Dallas said. If you get caught, it will go badly for all of us. Volkonsky hates us. He is a powerful enemy. He'll look for any excuse to disgrace us. If you are exposed, and we're lucky, he'll drive us out of St. Petersburg. If we're less than lucky, we'll all be thrown into prison."

No, no, no. He can't send me home. I can do this. "Uncle Adrian, no one is going to find out about me. Everyone here thinks I am a boy. I liked being a coachman, but I'll also like being Konstantin's companion. Maybe I can talk about all the changes that are happening in America. That change can be a good thing."

"Konstantin is tutored all day long. He's only ten years old. You hated sitting at a school desk back in Philadelphia. You rebelled when your teacher tried to get you to work with kids who were slower than you."

He doesn't understand. "I'm not going back to America. *Vater* will send me to finishing school."

"You don't know that. He may have changed his mind by now."

"But I like it when everyone thinks I'm a boy!" Rian blurted the words so loudly that she looked toward the closed door for fear that people in the other rooms might have heard her. Her vehemence surprised her, and then she saw the expression on Adrian's face.

Adrian stared back at Rian for a long moment. Then he sat down on one of the two single beds. "That's what this is about, isn't it? You like being a boy."

Rian sat on the bed opposite him. She nodded. She had never put those words together but knew they were true. *I like being a boy. I wish I were a boy.*

Adrian stared at Rian for a long moment. "We don't have time to argue about this now, but I want you to think about a few things. This project will take Seamus, me, and a bunch of others a long time. I bet ten years. How long do you intend to stay with us?"

"I don't know. Ten years sounds good."

"Rian, you'll be fourteen in three months. When do girls start to become womanly?"

"I don't know. I don't pay attention to those things. When they're sixteen?"

"So, sooner or later, you're going to get titties. Your whole body is going to change. What are you going to do then?"

Rian looked away. "I don't want to think about it."

"Well, we all need to start thinking about it. And right now, my solution to that is getting you on the first ship out of St. Petersburg." Then Rian's uncle rose from the bed, pulled her into his arms, and hugged her. "It's all going to be okay," he whispered.

* * * * *

· SEAMUS ·

That evening, in honor of his new guests and the new year in most Western countries but Russia, Sheremetev hosted the Americans for a dinner of fried pork chops, potatoes, and cake.

After the meal, the party moved to a parlor for cigars and cognac.

Seamus sat next to Adrian on a settee. A blaze danced in the fireplace, making the room overly warm. *Two years ago, I was a ditchdigger*, thought Seamus. *Now I'm celebrating New Year's Eve with a count. Maybe an Irishman can be accepted in this country after all.*

Sheremetev stared into the fire. Rian, still exhausted and mourning the loss of Stepanov, was curled up on a settee behind them and not part of the after-dinner discussion.

"It's sad," said Sheremetev. "I was hoping to engage you Americans in some poker. I had thoughts of winning some of my money back from Rian."

The count's sarcasm made Seamus smile. "I'm amazed I'm still awake." He turned to say something to Adrian, but Adrian had fallen asleep, still holding his snifter. "I think we're all still pretty whipped. I doubt me fellow Americans are going to make it to midnight."

Sheremetev raised his glass. "May the new year continue Krieger Locomotive's arc toward prosperity."

Seamus gently pried Adrian's snifter from his hand and raised both his glass and Adrian's in salute. "Hear, hear," he said softly. "We wouldn't be here without you."

Sheremetev sipped his cognac, then swirled his snifter absentmindedly. "I think the Tsar is in trouble."

"I'd say," said Seamus. "His house burned down. Does he have insurance for that?"

Sheremetev shrugged. "His trouble is much more profound. His leadership has been called into question. He has declared that he will rebuild the Winter Palace in a year. Most knowledgeable people are saying ten years is more likely."

"Why the hurry?"

"The Winter Palace was built on a monumental scale to awe Russians and visitors alike. It was a symbol of the Tsar's power."

"So?"

"So, it had been the home of four tsars before Nicholas. It burned down on his watch. Russia is a superstitious country from top to bottom. Russians see omens in every event. Having the symbol of your power burn down as the year draws to a close can only be interpreted as an evil omen. To the peasants, the Tsar is a frightening half-man, half-god come down from the heavens. Now their god has been proven to be fallible. To the educated class, it is well known that the Tsar made decisions that exacerbated this disaster. The fire has diminished the confidence of his people—those he needs to maintain his power and those he expects to revere him on a visceral level."

Adrian leaned toward Sheremetev, who was outlined by the firelight. "Are you saying that there's a revolution brewing?"

Sheremetev shrugged. "A revolution? Not likely. Change? Perhaps, if we're lucky. Despite its size, its army, and its symbols of power, Russia is a backward country. I travel to Britain or America, and what do I see? Gas lanterns lighting your streets at night. Railroads spreading across your countryside like ivy."

"Russia just opened the railroad to Tsarskoye Selo."

"Pfft. A fifteen-mile vanity project so the Tsar can travel to a summer home he rarely visits. In America, you have vast systems of pipes that bring fresh water to your neighborhoods. Sewer systems that take your waste away. These should be the symbols of the power of a nation, not the size of the Tsar's residence."

Seamus took a sip of cognac, as if the liquor would give him the courage to ask the next question. "Count Sheremetev, are you a revolutionary?"

Sheremetev stared into the fire for a long moment. "When the Decembrists revolted 12 years ago, I was visiting my estate in Saxony. By the time I returned, the revolt had been crushed. Many Decembrists were inspired by your own Declaration of Independence, though they abhorred your system of slavery. They wanted to end serfdom in Russia. They wanted Russia to modernize. All that ended abruptly when Nicholas put down the revolt."

"But Decembrist sentiments still exist?"

"Certainly, but those of us who desire change must couch it in ways that appeal to the Tsar and make him appear stronger. I would describe myself as guarded when I talk about my true beliefs. You and I have known each other for four months. This moment is the first I have spoken of my true feelings. This discussion alone could create problems, and you would likely be tossed out of the country."

"Thank you for trusting me and for trying to modernize Russia."

"I trust both you and Adrian, although perhaps my tongue was loosened somewhat by this fine cognac. I would prefer you not reveal any of this discussion to outsiders."

* * * * *

· RIAN ·

An hour later, Seamus rousted Rian from the settee. "C'mon, darlin'. It's time you crawled into a proper bed."

As they wended their way back to their quarters, Rian placed her hand in her cousin's. "Did you notice that when you asked Count Sheremetev if he was a revolutionary, he didn't really answer the question?"

"You were awake then?"

"Mm-hmm. I think he really is a revolutionary but doesn't want to admit it. It's like Maddie Freeman says when you're in the Underground Railroad business. It's Rule Number 1. If someone doesn't need to know something, you don't tell them."

"I imagine you've about got the size of it."

"Is the Tsar being in trouble a good thing or a bad thing?"

"I don't know yet. I haven't figured out if he's a good guy or a bad guy. Maybe it doesn't matter for us. We're here to build a railroad."

* * * * *

Rian snuggled down into her new bed. *We're going to build a railroad. That's what we came here to do. But Uncle Adrian says he's going to put me on a ship as soon as the ice breaks. My almanac says that should happen in about nine weeks. I've got nine weeks to change his mind. I have to become so important as the Grand Duke's companion that no one will want to send me back to America. I don't want to go home. I like it when everyone thinks I'm a boy.*

Author's Notes

I include the notes below to help readers separate fact from fiction.

In Pennsylvania:

- Slave catchers openly roamed the streets of Philadelphia during this era. Their prey was both self-emancipated fugitives and vulnerable free Blacks who could be smuggled to a slave state. Pennsylvania law demanded that any individual captured and suspected of being a fugitive slave be brought before a magistrate and given due process. The slave catchers frequently tried to circumvent the legalities. Vigilant committees were formed in Philadelphia to provide legal assistance to both self-emancipated individuals and free Blacks who had been kidnapped.

- The rivalries among Philadelphia fire brigades were well documented. Equal parts social club, gang, and fire company, the groups formed along ethnic lines and battled each other for insurance bounties as well as control of the crime in their districts.

- Locomotives known as "hoppers" had a brief but notable run as steam engines evolved. They were soon supplanted by other innovations and are now considered a bit of an oddity.

- Robert Purvis, age 27 in the beginning of this book, was born in Charleston, South Carolina. His father was an English immigrant who had prospered in America. His mother was considered mixed-race because her father was Jewish and her mother was a Moor from North Africa who had been enslaved in the New World for ten years. In the eyes of South Carolina law, Robert Purvis was Black. Purvis's father moved the family to Philadelphia, where they could lead a better life. After attending Amherst Academy in Massachusetts, Robert returned to Philadelphia. Light-skinned and able to pass as white, he chose to identify with the Black part of his heritage. When his father died, he became one of the largest property owners in Philadelphia. His properties were frequently used as stations on the Underground Railroad.

- In all likelihood, James Forten, Purvis's father-in-law, was the wealthiest Black man in America and one of the richest men in Philadelphia. A POW as a fifteen-year-old during the American Revolution, he could have abandoned his comrades and gained his freedom but chose instead to join them on a prison ship in New York Harbor. He made his fortune as the owner of a sailmaking loft just off the Willing and Francis piers on the Delaware waterfront. He frequently contributed both financial support and written articles to William Lloyd Garrison's *The Liberator*.

- The Panic of 1837, belatedly precipitated by Andrew Jackson's Specie Circular, occurred as described. The resulting economic depression was long and hard, lasting more than seven years and, at times, putting a huge percentage of America's workforce out of work.

- Nicholas Biddle, President of the National Bank of Pennsylvania, possessed one of the finest financial minds of the era. However, he was also politically ham-handed and had the misfortune to run afoul of the juggernaut known as Andrew Jackson.

- The launch of the *U.S.S. Pennsylvania* on July 18, 1837, was witnessed by an estimated hundred thousand people. It never fired its guns in anger and spent most of its life berthed in Norfolk Navy Yard, Virginia. On April 21, 1861, shortly after Virginia seceded from the Union, the Navy Yard was besieged by newly formed Confederate militias. To prevent the *Pennsylvania* from falling into the hands of Confederate forces, Union troops burned it to the waterline at its berth.

I now delve into historical trivia that I find fascinating, but less geeky readers should feel free to skip to the next bullet. Numerous ships were destroyed when the Norfolk Navy Yard was burned, among them the *U.S.S. Merrimack*, a steam-powered frigate driven by a screw propeller. The *Merrimack* was raised by the Confederates, rebuilt into an ironclad ship, and rechristened as the *C.S.S. Virginia*. It participated in the first-ever clash between ironclads in its famous encounter with the *Monitor* at Hampton Roads on March 9, 1862.

The only other battleship named *Pennsylvania* was launched in 1915, a state-of-the-art super-dreadnought powered by fuel oil engines. Ironically, it never saw action during World War I because only coal was available in England, where it would have had to resupply. The *Pennsylvania* was in drydock at Pearl Harbor on December 7, 1941, and thus escaped the fate of its sister ship *Arizona*, moored not far away. The *Pennsylvania* was repaired and saw significant action from Alaska to the Philippines throughout the rest of World War II. Sadly, during the Cold War, it was twice used as an atomic bomb target off Bikini Atoll, studied for over a year, and finally scuttled in 1948.

- Philadelphia was termed "Workshop of the World" during the 1830s, and prominent among the corporations were locomotive manufacturers. Baldwin, Norris, and Eastwick & Harrison were all vibrant, innovative outfits. Lest you think that Krieger Locomotive's move to Russia seems a bit far-fetched, google "Eastwick & Harrison Russia," and you will find my inspiration for the story arc of Adrian, Seamus, and Rian in St. Petersburg. Joseph Harrison sailed to Russia in 1843. He accomplished his mission, completing the *St. Petersburg to Moscow Railway* in twelve years, and returned to the United States a rich man.

- The process of revising the Pennsylvania Constitution in 1837 proceeded as described. In numerous sessions, delegates to the Pennsylvania Constitutional Convention debated the "white only" wording, which denied the Black man the right to vote. The delegates named in this book played their roles as portrayed.

- The Sparks Shot Tower on Carpenter Street was built in 1808 and produced lead shot until 1913. It still stands, surrounded by a playground, but is not open to the public.

- Lest you think that the story of Simon Starr and Jack's creative escape from slavery is a bit fantastical, google William and Ellen Craft. You will find my inspiration for this scene.

- Pennsylvania Hall, the Pennsylvania Anti-Slavery Society's Temple of Freedom, was conceived as described. Its fiery death three days after its dedication will play out in Book 3 of Rian Krieger's Journey.

- Semaphore towers, also known as optical telegraphs, existed in this era. The string of towers between Cape May, New Jersey, and the Merchants' Exchange Building (MEB) in Philadelphia opened in 1809. Another chain of towers built in 1834 extended from the MEB to a building on Wall Street in New York City. Although a string of semaphore towers from New York City to New Orleans was contemplated and endorsed by the U.S. Postmaster, the project was never started. Samuel F. B. Morse's electric telegraph made semaphore towers obsolete in the 1840s.

I now indulge in another of those bits of historical trivia that is irrelevant to this story. Napoleon had semaphore towers built all over France in the early 1800s for two reasons. The first is easily guessed: The emperor wanted up-to-the-moment information about hostile armies that surrounded France. The second reason? To transmit the latest numbers from France's state-run lottery throughout the country.

- A pro-slavery mob in St. Louis murdered Elijah Lovejoy on November 7, 1837. News of his death spread throughout the republic and helped to polarize both sides of the slavery issue.

- The slave ship *Bridger* is a product of my imagination. The triangle trade—rum and guns to Africa; kidnapped humans destined for a life of slavery to the Caribbean; sugar, molasses, and coffee to the North—was real. Even after the transatlantic slave trade was declared illegal in 1807, the smuggling of kidnapped Africans into the United States continued. The last known ship to illegally bring enslaved people into America arrived in Mobile, Alabama, in 1860. I found no record of a ship burning on the Philadelphia waterfront in December 1837.

In Russia:

- The Manege—the stable and riding hall for the Tsar's Imperial Horse Guards—still exists, reconfigured as St. Petersburg's premier exhibition hall.

- Tsar Nicholas and Prince Volkonsky were watching Mozart's *The Abduction from the Seraglio* at the Mikhailovsky Theatre when smoke was discovered in Field Marshals' Hall. They left the theater to oversee the safety of the artwork, not knowing that disaster was about to strike.

- The Winter Palace burned on December 17, 1837 O.S. (December 29 by the Western/Gregorian calendar), as described. Having the Tsar of All the Russias, the most powerful man in the world, physically involved in the evacuation of artifacts from the palace might seem like a "Hollywoodization." Researchers who have delved into the event much more than I have concluded that he was present until the fire became too intense, and he ordered everyone to leave the building. I have tried to adhere as much as possible to contemporary accounts. The Tsar ordered the windows of Field Marshals' Hall to be broken, thus supplying the oxygen-starved fires with all the fresh air they needed to explode.

Considerable effort was made to destroy the connecting arcades to the Hermitage to deprive the advancing fire of fuel and save that building. Thirty men lost their lives in the fire, some of them when the Flying Gallery to the Hermitage crashed to the ground. Early sanitized accounts of the fire failed to mention any deaths. Nicholas remained on the scene without rest for thirty hours.

- After the fire destroyed the Winter Palace, the Tsar moved his family to the Anichkov Palace.

- Lest you think it was a bit of a stretch for Tsar Nicholas to bring Rian into his home as a companion to his son, that is exactly what he did when his older son Alexander was in his early teens.

- Most historians consider the reign of Nicholas I a failure. The Decembrist Revolt during Nicholas I's first days as Tsar shaped the rest of his reign. He became a strict authoritarian, trusting only a small circle of advisors. He brutally put down a rebellion in Poland and was a noted anti-Semite. However, he was a devoted family man, demonstrably loving to his wife and children.

  When the Winter Palace burned, Nicholas decreed that the symbol of his power would be rebuilt within a year. Although many experts believed ten years was more likely, the Imperial Family moved back into the rebuilt palace by Easter of 1839, just over a year after the fire. Contemporary accounts claimed that six thousand workmen died during the reconstruction. If true, that translates to fifteen men per day.

  Always fascinated by his army, Nicholas equated its million-man size with power. The Crimean War, which started in 1853, demonstrated otherwise. Modern militaries had become increasingly reliant on logistics, technology, and training, none of which were prevalent in the Russian army. The Russians were beaten in a savage, tragically brutal war that exposed all these weaknesses. Nicholas died in the Winter Palace in 1855, before the war was concluded.

- Ambassador George M. Dallas will make more appearances in Rian Krieger's Journey. After resigning his post in Russia, he returned to Philadelphia in 1839 and set up a law practice. He became Vice President of the United States under James K. Polk. During America's war with Mexico, he was an outspoken advocate of annexing all of that country into the United States.

- Prince Pyotr Volkonsky, Minister of the Imperial Court, loyally served Tsar Nicholas I until he died in 1852. Although his reputation was diminished after the Winter Palace fire, Nicholas returned his minister's loyalty. They remained steadfast allies until Volkonsky's death.

- In our era, when young women often reach puberty in their early teens, it is hard to believe that it has not always been so. Rian speculates that girls "become womanly" at age 16. My research indicates that she got it right. The average age at the onset of puberty in Germany in the 1830s, for instance, was 16.6.

I apologize in advance for any historical inaccuracies put forth in this book and would appreciate hearing your feedback. Please contact me through my website at rogerasmith.com.

Bonus Material

To receive a transcript of a 1915 recording
of ninety-one-year-old Rian Krieger
reminiscing about this era,
contact me through my website
rogerasmith.com
and ask for Book 2 Bonus Material.
I promise: no spoilers (but I might tease you a bit).

Bonus Materials are available
for each book of Rian Krieger's Journey.

Acknowledgments

I want to thank the many people and organizations who have supported me during this journey.

- The Brewster Writers Group, for sandwiching criticism between praise and helping me tinker, improve, and appreciate nuance.

- My readers/critiquers—Jim Lieb, Liz McDermott, Bailey Spencer, Bob Spencer, and Joan Talmadge—for their time, perspective, insight, praise, and criticism.

- Piper, Tempest, and Nisi, whose course *Writing the Other* taught me to craft my characters with respect, empathy, and humility and gives me ongoing inspiration.

- Author Ray Shepard, who assured me that I got Peach's voice "right."

- Sid and Margaret of Two Step Approach, developmental editors who made the macro-comments I needed to hear.

- Katherine Talmadge Sallé, copy editor extraordinaire, who was the last person to polish *The Coachman* before I sent it off to Sunbury Press.

- Michael Townsend, who escorted me through accessible parts of the Sparks Shot Tower and showed me historic architectural drawings and photographs. Jen Cox and the rest of the staff of the Shot Tower Recreation Center who were very gracious to me during their busy workday.

- Jake Wanamaker, Alex Meyers, Hayden Berg, Maureen Osborne, and Rikki Bates for assistance and perspective on transgender issues.

- The staff at Sunbury Press, who believed in me and the importance of Rian Krieger's Journey.

- A treasured community of friends, fellow members of the First Parish Brewster UU Church, former students and colleagues, and fellow authors who gave encouragement, helped me make connections, and sent me books, articles, and factoids of interest.

- My family—Susan, Matt, Alecia, Alex, and Courtney—for their constant support and encouragement.

ABOUT THE AUTHOR

Always fascinated by railroads, canals, the antebellum era, and social justice issues, Rog naturally gravitated to his first career as a high school history teacher. After ten years of inspiring young people, he yielded to passions for which he had no formal training: co-owning a summer camp, farming, founding a participatory science museum, co-owning a wilderness expedition program for teenagers, teaching entrepreneurship at the college level, woodworking, and leading a rural arts organization.

As an author, he draws lore and wisdom from all those professions, and joy from the thought that he is once again making history come alive to his constituents.

Rog and his wife lived and worked on a farm in Central Pennsylvania for 41 years. They currently reside in Massachusetts with their Great Dane and cat. They have three adult children and two grandchildren.

www.ingramcontent.com/pod-product-compliance
Lightning Source LLC
Chambersburg PA
CBHW011757010726
47497CB00013B/3248